OXFORD WORLD'S CLASSICS

THE MARQUISE DE GANGE

DONATIEN ALPHONSE FRANÇOIS, MARQUIS DE SADE, was born in Paris in 1740 into old Provençal nobility. After spending some of his early years with relatives in Provence, he attended the Louis-le-Grand Jesuit school and a military academy in Versailles, before embarking on a military career that ended with the conclusion of the Seven Years War (1756–63). A few months after marrying Renée-Pélagie de Montreuil in 1763, Sade was briefly imprisoned for committing sacrilegious acts with a prostitute, Jeanne Testard; five years later he was arrested again after an assault on a woman named Rose Keller. In 1772 an orgy in Marseille with his manservant and four prostitutes led to Sade being sentenced to death for poisoning and sodomy; to escape the sentence, he fled to Italy with his sister-in-law, Anne-Prospère de Launay, with whom he was having an affair. Two years later, Sade and his wife spent the winter in Lacoste with several young female servants, giving rise to the so-called 'little girls affair'. At the behest of his mother-in-law, Madame de Montreuil, Sade was arrested in 1777, and, aside from thirty-nine days on the run, spent the next thirteen years in prison, where he wrote several plays, short stories, and novels, including *The 120 Days of Sodom* and *The Misfortunes of Virtue*. He divorced his wife, at her request, upon his release from prison in 1790, and began a relationship with a former actress, Marie-Constance Quesnet, that would last until his death. Actively immersed in Revolutionary politics, Sade narrowly escaped the guillotine, and published most of his major works in the 1790s, including *Justine*, *Philosophy in the Boudoir*, *Aline and Valcour*, and *The History of Juliette*. Wrongly suspected by Napoleon of writing *Zoloé*, an anti-Joséphine pamphlet, Sade was arrested again in 1801 and transferred two years later to Charenton, a mental asylum, where he spent the rest of his life. He directed the asylum's popular theatrical performances and wrote several plays and three historical novels: *Adélaïde de Brunswick*, *The Secret History of Isabelle de Bavière*, and his last published work, *The Marquise de Gange*. He died in 1814 and was buried in an unmarked grave in accordance with his will.

WILL MCMORRAN is Reader in French & Comparative Literature at Queen Mary University of London. He has written widely on Sade and eighteenth-century fiction, and his translation with Thomas Wynn of *The 120 Days of Sodom* was awarded the Scott-Moncrieff prize in 2017.

T0058811

OXFORD WORLD'S CLASSICS

*For over 100 years Oxford World's Classics have brought
readers closer to the world's great literature. Now with over 700
titles—from the 4,000-year-old myths of Mesopotamia to the
twentieth century's greatest novels—the series makes available
lesser-known as well as celebrated writing.*

*The pocket-sized hardbacks of the early years contained
introductions by Virginia Woolf, T. S. Eliot, Graham Greene,
and other literary figures which enriched the experience of reading.
Today the series is recognized for its fine scholarship and
reliability in texts that span world literature, drama and poetry,
religion, philosophy and politics. Each edition includes perceptive
commentary and essential background information to meet the
changing needs of readers.*

OXFORD WORLD'S CLASSICS

THE MARQUIS DE SADE

The Marquise de Gange

Translated with an Introduction and Notes by
WILL McMORRAN

OXFORD
UNIVERSITY PRESS

OXFORD

UNIVERSITY PRESS

Great Clarendon Street, Oxford, OX2 6DP,
United Kingdom

Oxford University Press is a department of the University of Oxford.
It furthers the University's objective of excellence in research, scholarship,
and education by publishing worldwide. Oxford is a registered trade mark of
Oxford University Press in the UK and in certain other countries

© Will McMorran 2021

The moral rights of the author have been asserted

First published as an Oxford World's Classics paperback 2021

Impression: 1

Published in the United States of America by Oxford University Press
198 Madison Avenue, New York, NY 10016, United States of America

British Library Cataloguing in Publication Data

Data available

Library of Congress Control Number: 2021946059

ISBN 978-0-19-884828-8

Printed and bound in Great Britain by
Clays Ltd, Elcograf S.p.A.

ACKNOWLEDGEMENTS

I AM grateful to Adrian Armstrong and Eddie Hughes for their wise counsel when reading a draft of the introduction, and to Tom Wynn for his eagle eye when reading a draft of the translation. I would also like to thank Kiera Vaclavik for all her good words.

CONTENTS

INTRODUCTION

The Origins of The Marquise de Gange

ON the afternoon of 17 May 1667, Dianne de Joannis, Marquise de Ganges, known in her time at Louis XIV's court as *la Belle Provençale*, is faced with a terrible choice. Standing before her as she lies in bed are her two brothers-in-law: the Abbé and Chevalier de Ganges. The Abbé is holding a pistol in one hand and a glass filled with poison in the other; the Chevalier's sword is drawn. 'Madame,' the Abbé tells her, 'you must die: you may choose fire, steel, or poison.' The next few hours pass in a blur: poison swallowed, then furtively disgorged; escape through a first-floor window; flowerpots hurled down after her, narrowly missing her head; brief sanctuary amongst the women of the village; frenzied blows from the Chevalier's sword, its blade snapping in her shoulder; and finally, the Abbé's pistol, pressed against her bosom . . . misfiring. This is not the end of the Marquise's ordeal, but there is some respite at least. The women of the village come to her aid once more, driving back the Abbé and the Chevalier, who take flight, never to return. Her wounds are dressed, and she is taken back to the Château de Ganges. But despite her extraordinary courage and fortitude, the damage has already been done. She dies nineteen days later, and the autopsy confirms poisoning as the cause of death.

It was one of the crimes of the century, and word soon spread throughout France and beyond. With the national press in its infancy, news of shocking crimes—or 'faits divers'—were typically published in cheap bulletins of a few pages. A pamphlet entitled *The Veritable and Principal Circumstances of the Deplorable Death of Madame la Marquise de Ganges*, written by an anonymous 'officer from Languedoc', duly appeared in July, and was republished with additional material in August following the trial of the Marquis de Ganges, charged with conspiring with his brothers in the murder of his wife. It was a bloody tale—or *récit sanglant*—at a time when the reading public had an insatiable thirst for gruesome stories, particularly those based on current or recent events. The same vogue for tales of violence had already inspired several collections of *histoires tragiques*, a genre that blossomed in France when Matteo Bandello's *Novelle* (1554–73) were translated by François de Belleforest and Pierre Boaistuau.[1] By far the most popular and enduring of these collections was François de Rosset's *Histoires tragiques*, which included stories of murder, suicide, rape, sodomy, adultery and incest, all drawn from recent history. First published in 1614, with six new editions appearing within four years, Rosset's collection continued to thrive long after the death of its author in 1619, with over thirty further editions published posthumously over the next century and a half. In 1675, an expanded edition of the *Histoires tragiques* incorporated *The Veritable and Principal Circumstances of the Deplorable Death of Madame la Marquise de Ganges* for the first time. The murder remained fresh in the public imagination throughout the eighteenth century, with further accounts featuring in two of the most popular works of the time: Madame Dunoyer's *Lettres historiques et galantes* (1707–17), a fictional (or part-fictional) correspondence between a lady living in the provinces and her friend in Paris, and Gayot de Pitaval's famous *Causes célèbres et intéressantes* (1734–43),[2] a collection of case histories that also included the trial of Martin Guerre.

Sade had read both Dunoyer's *Lettres* and Gayot de Pitaval's *Causes célèbres* while imprisoned in the Bastille in the 1780s, decades before he would write his own version of this tragic tale, but he was certainly familiar with the story long before that, as a young man if not as a child. He may moreover have seen as well as heard of the Marquise de Ganges, in the form of a painting by Nicolas Mignard hanging in a church in the Provençal village of Villeneuve-lè-Avignon—a painting of Saint Roseline, for which the Marquise served as model. One cannot help but wonder if Sade's response to the painting resembled that of the Président de Brosses, a judge and writer from Dijon, who described the church in 1739:

---

[1] Some of the tales from these French translations of Bandello were in turn translated into English, inspiring a number of plays by Shakespeare (including *Romeo and Juliet*, *Cymbeline*, *Much Ado about Nothing*, and *Twelfth Night*) and by Shakespeare's contemporaries, John Webster and John Fletcher.

[2] Anne-Marguerite Petit Dunoyer, *Lettres historiques et galantes, de deux dames de condition, dont l'une étoit à Paris, et l'autre en Province*, 7 vols (Cologne [The Hague]: Pierre Marteau [Pierre Husson], 1707–17); François Gayot de Pitaval, *Histoire de la Marquise de Gange*, in *Causes célèbres et intéressantes, avec les jugements qui les ont décidées*, 10 vols (Paris: Guillaume Cavelier, 1734–43).

Along the aisles, several stories of Carthusian martyrs, by different hands; among others, a Saint Roseline, Carthusian nun, ravishingly pretty. Hmm! Blancey, how I would martyr her! I am sure she has damned more of these good Fathers than the Rule of Saint Bruno has saved.[3]

Like the Marquise de Ganges, Sade was born into distinguished Provençal nobility. Although he spent the first few years of his life in Paris, he was dispatched to Provence at the age of 4, and lived there, initially with his aunts in Avignon then with his uncle in the nearby village of Saumane, until the age of 10. As a young man, Sade often stayed in the family château in nearby Lacoste, organizing theatrical performances both there and at another château he owned in Mazan. Lacoste would later provide him with the seclusion he required to indulge his desires, and refuge when he was on the run from the law.

No doubt part of the lure of the murder of the Marquise de Ganges for Sade was its setting in a world and milieu he knew so well. Provençal locations such as Avignon, Aix, and Beaucaire come to the fore in the fictional episodes Sade adds to the Marquise's torments, while one of the most dramatic scenes in the novel sees his heroine escape the debauched Duc de Caderousse's château in Cadenet, a village just a few miles from Lacoste. But the greatest appeal of this macabre story for Sade may have been the manner of the murder itself. Something about the scenario of a beautiful woman offered a choice of death evidently struck a chord with Sade, an author with a habit for recycling the same characters, plots, and situations to different ends in different works. The third part of *The 120 Days of Sodom*, written in the Bastille in 1785, includes the following among its list of 'criminal passions':

67. She enters a chamber in a tower: in the middle of the room she sees a large brazier, some poison on a table, and a dagger—she is given the choice of three kinds of death. Usually she chooses the poison: it is a specially prepared opiate that plunges her into a deep stupor during which the libertine buggers her.[4]

In a darkly comic short story entitled 'The Successful Ruse', also written in the Bastille, a jealous husband forces his wife to choose

---

[3] Yves Florence, *Le président de Brosses* (Paris: Mercure de France, 1964), 14. Blancey, Brosses's interlocutor, was a dignitary of the Estates of Burgundy.

[4] Sade, *The 120 Days of Sodom*, trans. Will McMorran and Thomas Wynn (London: Penguin, 2016), 346.

between a pistol and some apparently poisoned lemonade, though this proves to be only a trick to force a confession of adultery.[5] A decade later, the eponymous heroine of *The History of Juliette* (1797–1801?) furnishes a torture chamber with a small round table, on top of which 'a pistol, a cup of poison and a dagger'[6] have been left. Like the fortresses and subterranean spaces which loom so large in the Sadean fictional landscape, these variations on a theme place their victims in a situation from which there is simply no escape—a fantasy of imprisonment, born of the Bastille.

Reading The Marquise de Gange

Though Sade had left the Bastille far behind by the time he came to write *The Marquise de Gange* (1813) (he followed Gayot de Pitaval in mistakenly omitting the 's'), he was once again a prisoner. He continued to write throughout the last years of his life in Charenton, with the permission of the asylum's director, the Abbé de Coulmier. In 1807, however, police seized the manuscript of *The Days of Florbelle or Nature Revealed*, a work of libertinage that apparently rivalled *The 120 Days of Sodom* in its ambition, and Sade made no subsequent attempts to write the kind of pornographic fiction that had made him so notorious. Until recently, the three novels he wrote thereafter (*The Marquise de Gange*, *Adélaïde de Brunswick* (written 1812), and *The Secret History of Isabelle de Bavière, Queen of France* (written 1813)[7] were largely regarded as evidence of a retreat into respectability—of Sade 'selling out to conventional morality and religion'.[8] For the pioneering Sade scholar, Gilbert Lely, the novel is the work of an older, mellower Marquis: 'It seems that, this time, the Marquis,

[5] This story is based closely on another episode from Dunoyer's *Lettres historiques et galantes*, with Dunoyer herself noting the manner in which it echoes the murder of the Marquise de Ganges.

[6] *Histoire de Juliette, ou les prospérités du vice*, in *Œuvres*, ed. Michel Delon, 3 vols (Paris: Gallimard, 1990–8), 3.476.

[7] *Adélaïde de Brunswick* and *Isabelle de Bavière* were not published until the twentieth century. The former was first published in English (Sade, *Adelaide of Brunswick*, trans. Hobart Ryland, Washington, DC: Scarecrow Press, 1954), with a version in French appearing a decade later (Sade, *Adélaïde de Brunswick, princesse de Saxe*, ed. Gilbert Lely, Paris: Cercle du livre précieux, 1964); the latter was published in 1953 (*Histoire secrète d'Isabelle de Bavière*, ed. Gilbert Lely, Paris: Gallimard, 1953).

[8] Mary Trouille, 'The Conflict between Good and Evil, Faith and Irreligion in Sade's *Marquise de Gange*', *Eighteenth-Century Fiction*, 17.1 (2004), 55.

himself tested by the cruelty of his story, succumbed more to sensibility and tears than to his habitual indulgence for the exploits of villains.'[9] Jean-Jacques Pauvert, a devoted biographer and editor, can find no trace of the Sade he knows and loves in these late works: 'For me *The Marquise de Gange* is of no interest other than for indubitably being by Sade, and for the success with which he almost entirely erased himself from it.'[10] Two other recent biographers of Sade are equally unimpressed: Francine du Plessix Gray describes his last three books as 'terribly proper little historical novels'[11] while Neil Schaeffer is similarly dismissive of *The Marquise de Gange*: 'The details of this moral and conventional story do not bear close examination.'[12]

A sign that *The Marquise de Gange* bears closer examination than these biographers suspect is that it has produced readings diametrically opposed to their own. More sceptical critics have detected 'a sardonic irony, a constant mockery of traditional values'[13] lurking beneath its respectable surface, leading them to see it as a 'Tartuffian novel dipped in holy water'.[14] From this perspective, the novel is nothing but a pastiche of self-righteous sensibility and Sade himself very much the same author he had always been. But what kind of an author was that exactly? It is always a mistake to confuse the narrator for the author, and this is as true of Sade's most extreme works as it is of his ostensibly respectable ones. He is as elusive an author as Flaubert intended himself to be in *Madame Bovary*, 'present everywhere but visible nowhere',[15] always hiding behind a carefully crafted authorial persona. From the imperious historian who opens *The 120 Days of Sodom* to the free-spirited libertine who introduces *Philosophy in the Boudoir* (1795), Sade's narrators are always characters playing a part. Although some of these may seem closer to the author that looms large in the public imagination, they tell us no more about him than the piously sentimental narrator we find in *The Marquise de*

[9] Gilbert Lely, *Vie du marquis de Sade* (Paris: Mercure de France, 1989), 586.

[10] Jean-Jacques Pauvert, *Sade Vivant*, 3 vols (Paris: Laffont, 1989), 3.438.

[11] Francine du Plessix Gray, *At Home with the Marquis de Sade: A Life* (New York: Simon and Schuster, 1998), 401.

[12] Neil Schaeffer, *Sade: A Life* (New York: Knopf, 1999), 504.

[13] Raymond Trousson, 'Histoire d'un fait divers, du Marquis de Sade à Charles Hugo', http://www.bon-a-tirer.com/volume9/rt.html.

[14] Jean Goldzink, 'Postface', in Sade, *La Marquise de Gange*, ed. Jean Goldzink (Paris: Autrement, 1994), 241.

[15] Gustave Flaubert, Letter of 9 December 1852, in *Correspondance*, ed. Jean Bruneau, 2 vols (Paris: Gallimard, 1973–80), 2.204.

Gange. Indeed they may tell us less: it is, perhaps counterintuitively, in those works where Sade hides behind the mask of a moralistic persona—in novels such as *Justine, or the Misfortunes of Virtue* (1791), or in the short stories of *The Crimes of Love* (1800)—that our sense of the author seems to be at its clearest.

The Marquise de Gange is a far more complex and subversive novel than may at first appear. As Mary Trouille recently suggested, to label it a work of '*mere* parody'[16] is as reductive as dismissing it as a work of *mere* sensibility, but it is certainly Sade's most self-conscious novel, and Pauvert's claim that Sade erased himself from it could not be further from the truth. This is evident from the very first line of the preface, in which the author announces, 'This is no novel we are offering here' (p. 3), echoing the narrator of Diderot's comic anti-novel, *Jacques the Fatalist* (1796), who repeatedly insists, 'This is not a novel'.[17] The preface also contains a subtle allusion to Sade's own oeuvre when the author defends the liberties he has taken with the facts: 'it is so painful to present crime triumphant that if we have not shown it in this light—if we have, so to speak, thwarted or corrected fate—it is to please the virtuous, who will be quite grateful to us for not having dared *say everything*' (p. 4). Aside from the obvious irony of a Sadean narrator expressing his pain at seeing crime rewarded (*The History of Juliette* was subtitled 'the prosperities of crime'), Sade explicitly alludes here to the dictum of his earlier, pornographic works—*tout dire*—and even italicizes it for good measure. For a novel he chose to publish anonymously, he seems curiously keen to leave clues to his identity for the reader to find. The most obvious of these is within the novel itself, when the Marquise de Gange (whom Sade rechristens Euphrasie) attends a ball in Avignon. As she enters the ballroom, 'A descendant of Laura, and a poet in vogue at the time' (p. 114) whispers into her ear some impromptu verse in praise of her beauty. Sade, proudly descended from Laure de Noves, Petrarch's muse, thus elects to give himself a cameo role in his own novel.

[16] Trouille, 'The Conflict between Good and Evil', 57. See also Chiara Gambacorti, *Sade: une esthétique de la duplicité* (Paris: Garnier, 2014).

[17] Denis Diderot, *Jacques le fataliste et son maître* (Paris: Flammarion, 1997), 76. Sade expresses his affection for 'our friend Jacques the fatalist' in some literary notes written *circa* 1803–4 (Sade, *Oeuvres complètes du Marquis de Sade*, ed. Gilbert Lely, 16 vols (Paris: Cercle du livre précieux, 1966–7), 15.28).

While it has long been unfashionable to discuss authors and their intentions in literary criticism, readers coming to Sade's works for the first time may soon find themselves asking questions that never occur to them in their encounters with more respectable writers. And perhaps the most persistent of these questions is—whose side is Sade on? As familiar as we are with unreliable narrators, unreliable authors pose a far more difficult challenge. Even when narrators are mad, bad, or dangerous to know, our faith that the authors behind them are sane, good, and safe to know typically remains unshaken. A novel like *The Marquise de Gange*, however, potentially presents the reader with the reverse: a morally reliable authorial persona serving as a foil to an amoral author. As if this were not disorientating enough, Sade seems intent on fuelling the reader's suspicions. There are moments, for example, when the narrator seems to forget whether his allegiances lie with his heroine or her persecutors: he observes at one point, 'Everything had been judiciously, or rather, maliciously calculated in the Abbé's plans' (p. 54); a little later, he seems rather disappointed to have to announce that—'unfortunately in one regard, though very fortunately in another' (p. 67)—these plans have gone awry. These self-conscious 'slips', on each occasion the initial sentiment implying a storyteller on the wrong side, suggest an author teasing his readers—including, no doubt, his censors. They also create an impression of complicity between this authorial persona and the Abbé (renamed Théodore) which is reinforced by the common language and strategies that they employ. A conversation between Théodore and his confidant, Perret, for example, echoes the anti-novelistic pronouncement of the preface:

'But do you think her virtue will abandon her . . .? Misfortune, far from diminishing strength, galvanizes it in a noble soul; and there are heroines of virtue who can never be made to succumb.'
'Yes, in novels, but this is not one of those . . .' (p. 41)

The parallels between storyteller and villain become increasingly evident as the novel unfolds: it is not just that they are both plotting the downfall of the doomed heroine, but that they are doing so according to the same principles. In the early stages of the novel, the narrator reminds himself of the need for a measured approach: 'let us not get ahead of ourselves, for softer shades may lighten those with which this fateful story begins' (p. 7). Eleven of the twelve chapters are indeed devoted to preparing the reader for the bloody climax of Euphrasie's assassination. *The Marquise de Gange*, like many of Sade's novels, is driven by a logic of escalation: as Roger Shattuck observes rather begrudgingly, 'The one stylistic effect that Sade has mastered is the crescendo. He knows how to turn the volume up slowly.'[18] Théodore, the orchestrator of the action within the novel, adopts the same incremental approach in his pursuit of Euphrasie: 'I must take it one step at a time: a torment today, an attempt tomorrow, and so on until she surrenders' (p. 64).

There is therefore more than one authorial presence in *The Marquise de Gange*, and like the novel's authorial persona—and indeed like Sade—Théodore is an author who hides behind a mask: as he tells Perret, 'No one is more skilled than I in the art of hiding behind circumstances, or of contriving new ones from a grain of truth' (p. 64). Moreover, like the authorial persona, his mask also slips on occasion. When he expresses the view that the truly devout do not need a church in order to pray, Madame de Châteaublanc, mother of the Marquise, observes, 'One should not, it seems to me, say such things robed in a habit such as yours' (p. 94). Théodore, a libertine in religious clothing, is a figure of perfect hypocrisy, an atheist who denies that atheists even exist: 'To preach the existence of God is to suppose there are people who do not believe in him; and I do not believe any such person exists' (p. 24). He is also an impersonator, at one point faking a letter from Euphrasie in order to accuse her of adultery. To add to this irony, Théodore has both Euphrasie and her mother imprisoned in the Château de Ganges ostensibly to prevent news of her scandalous behaviour from sullying the family name—a striking reversal of roles when set against Sade's own imprisonment at the behest of his mother-in-law, Madame de Montreuil.

As tempting as it may be in any Sadean work to identify the author with his libertine villains, it is of course never quite that simple. While *The Marquise de Gange* certainly teases the reader with the possibility that the narrator, and indeed the author, may be in cahoots with Théodore, there are also moments in the novel which suggest that the long-suffering heroine is not quite as alone as she may seem.

[18] Roger Shattuck, *Forbidden Knowledge: From Prometheus to Pornography* (San Diego: Harcourt Brace, 1997), 279.

As hollow as the narrator's gnashing and wailing may seem to many readers, not all of his sympathy for Euphrasie can be so easily dismissed, particularly when Théodore becomes her gaoler:

One has to have experienced the dreadful plight of a prisoner to be able to convey it [...] It is cruel indeed to see the days passing by in the same manner, to say to oneself, through tears, tomorrow I shall do exactly what I did today; there will be no variation for me; it is the darkness of the tomb that envelops me already; all that separates me from the dead is the awful despair of being alive; here I am, indifferent to all the events of my life; numb to all the sentiments of the soul; all its affections are now blunted, I remain a stranger to them all; this sweet gift of nature, this heart, the reason I exist, is already frozen in my chest, impassive to love, to hate, to hope. The beating of this automatic heart is but the swinging of the pendulum preparing me for oblivion; and as he no longer has the gift of love, the wretch in his cell who has also lost the gift of life is all but a cadaver ... To whom will he speak? To whom will he call in the terrible silence into which misfortune has plunged him? ... To God alone! ... Culpable authors, unbelieving barbarians, wallowing in those criminal pleasures your dangerous doctrines condone, take not from the unfortunate the only joy that can offer him some peace; leave him this God who reaches out to him (pp. 79–80)

The clear implication that the storyteller knows whereof he speaks inevitably brings the author to the fore of the reader's mind here. Sade, once again, seems to be inserting himself into his fiction.[19] This impression is reinforced by the shift in focalization and narration away from Euphrasie to a more generalized—and now male—'prisoner' and 'wretch' speaking movingly in the first person. But then, abruptly, the pious authorial persona reasserts itself, railing against the 'Culpable authors' who would deny such a prisoner the comfort of religion, a transition which ironically pits Sade against Sade, making him his own worst enemy. It is difficult to say whether this irony undermines or reinforces the poignancy of the previous lines: as Flaubert, a passionate admirer of Sade, argued, 'irony takes nothing

---

[19] The sense of a living death in these lines indeed echoes Sade's prison correspondence, and in particular a letter to his wife written in Vincennes: 'What! It is not enough to be deprived of all that makes life sweet and pleasant, it is not enough not even to breathe the air of the sky, to see all one's desires perpetually shatter against four walls, and to flit through days that are the same only as those that await us when we shall be in the grave?' (Sade, Letter to Madame de Sade, 20 February 1781, in *Lettres à sa femme*, ed. Marc Buffat (Paris: Actes Sud, 1997), 211).

away from pathos. On the contrary, it intensifies it.'[20] In any case, the episode reflects how elusive and protean a figure Sade remains in our imagination, capable of shifting forms in the space of a few words. He teases and evades us, an invisible but inescapable presence.

The tricks Sade plays endure from the first page to the last of *The Marquise de Gange*. In his preface, he admits to 'correcting' fate in his account of the Marquise's murder by not allowing crime to go unpunished at the end of the story. Indeed, while Gayot de Pitaval makes clear that the Abbé married and made a home for himself in Holland, eventually dying 'in good repute' there, Sade decides this is too happy an ending for his villain:

After six months of marriage, Théodore is approached by a stranger at ten o'clock in the evening, on the winding street where he lives.

'You are the Abbé de Gange,' says this mysterious person, 'I have been following you for a long time. *Perish, monstrous scoundrel: I avenge your victim . . .*' And he blows his brains out as he utters these words.

The stranger disappeared without anyone discovering who he might have been. But, whoever he was, he was armed by the hand of God. (p. 172)

While one critic has speculated that this avenger could be the Marquise's son or even Deschamps, her former kidnapper,[21] there is another answer more in keeping with the self-conscious spirit of the novel: the author himself. Béatrice Didier notes of the changed ending that it allows Sade to play the part of 'righter of wrongs' and to reaffirm 'the essentially moral role of the novelist'.[22] But this is an ending devoid of any moral force, undermined by the admission in the preface that it is pure fiction. Sade thereby ensures that justice is both done and undone by the manner of its execution.

Our suspicions about Sade, compounded by the games of hide and seek he plays throughout *The Marquise de Gange*, transform what might indeed have been a 'terribly proper' story into something far more compelling. The sense of unease and uncertainty he creates may moreover make us question our own intentions and motivations as well as his. Does this novel of conspiracy and complicity—between brothers, and, we suspect, between the storyteller and his villains—also

---

[20] Gustave Flaubert, Letter to Louise Colet, 9 October 1852 in *Correspondance*, ed. Jean Bruneau and Yvan Leclerc, 5 vols (Paris: Gallimard, 1973–2007), 2.172.

[21] Trouille, 'The Conflict between Good and Evil', 81.

[22] Béatrice Didier, 'Postface', in Sade, *La Marquise de Gange*, ed. Béatrice Didier (Paris: Librairie Générale Française, 1974), 283.

implicate the reader as an accomplice or accessory to violence? Writing in the context of Sade's overtly libertine novels, Marcel Hénaff suggests it may: 'Between writer and reader—between Master and Master—there is no contractual relationship; it is a relationship of *complicity*. To read is already to conspire.'[23] Although *The Marquise de Gange* may seem worlds away from the pornographic excesses of Sade's most extreme works, it follows the same logic and structure: like Justine, Euphrasie is relentlessly persecuted and tormented until, finally, she dies. Sade's virtuous heroines are born to suffer, and to provide spectacles of suffering for their tormentors and, of course, their readers. At one point in the novel, Euphrasie is driven to delirium by the Abbé's machinations:

her limbs stretch and writhe in every direction; her piercing cries ring out in her prison; she beats her head against the walls; her blood flows . . . it soaks the scoundrel who spills it and who, soon roused like the tiger by the very sight of this precious blood, would doubtless make it flow in an even more abominable manner. (p. 92)

For the Abbé, Euphrasie's bodily agonies make her an object not of pity but desire. If the violence of this particular scene is more likely to repel the intended reader than excite him, there are other moments in the novel when suffering is made more seductive. In the novel's climactic scene, pathos and eros seem to vie for the reader's attention:

In tears, she falls at the feet of these barbarians: those hands clasped and outstretched towards them; that bosom of alabaster, covered only with her beautiful, dishevelled locks; those terrified, pitiful screams cut short by despairing sobs; those tears bathing the weapons already aimed at her breast . . . (p. 163)

If Sade's notoriety alone is enough to make us wary of his intentions, readers familiar with his earlier fiction will find this haunts their reading of *The Marquise de Gange* throughout. In *The History of Juliette*, for example, the libertine Noircueil makes the sensuality of such portraits of suffering explicit:

but beauty, an imbecile would object, touches, captivates; it invites gentleness, compassion: how to resist the tears of a pretty girl who, with hands clasped together, pleads with her torturer? Well! That is indeed what one is

[23] Marcel Hénaff, *Sade, The Invention of the Libertine Body* (Minneapolis and London: University of Minnesota Press, 1999), 66.

asking for: it is from this very state that such a libertine elicits his most delectable pleasure.[24]

Pity, after Sade, no longer seems quite so pure. Nor indeed does piety: when Euphrasie is fervently praying on All Souls' Eve, 'her bosom throbs violently, her gaze, fixed on the heavens, contemplates only her God; from her parted lips, the soul that moments before had so animated her seems to soar towards him' (p. 69).

Were the questions Sade poses about our relationship to the depiction of violence limited to his works only, they would perhaps be less unsettling. After an encounter with Sade, however, readers may start to wonder if their previous confidence in the good faith of more respectable authors may not have been a little naïve. Sade was evidently not the first author to structure his narratives around acts of violence against women. In novels such as *Justine* and *The Marquise de Gange* he is following the template of virtue in distress established by the literature of sensibility. Sade indeed once hailed Samuel Richardson as a model for all novelists for showing that 'it is not always by showing the triumph of virtue that a writer wins over his reader':

when virtue triumphs, things being as they necessarily are, our tears dry up before they even begin to flow. But if, after it has been tested by the most severe trials, we finally see virtue crushed by vice, then our souls will inevitably be torn.[25]

Using the example of Richardson to justify his own method as a novelist, Sade implies that if the suffering of virtue inspires moral sentiments, then the more virtue suffers in any given novel the more moral that novel may claim to be. As cynical as this logic appears, it is nonetheless striking that a novel like *Clarissa* (1747–8) could offer Sade such a valuable model for his own fiction. And while Richardson, in stark contrast to Sade, enjoys a rather sanctified position in the literary pantheon, Sade sees something in *Clarissa* that many readers and critics would rather not: that the very structure Richardson adopts, with its own inexorable momentum towards a violent climax, is suffused with an eroticism inseparable from the violence at its core. Once seen it cannot be unseen: if we were not self-conscious about

---

[24] *Histoire de Juliette*, in *Oeuvres*, 3.415.

[25] Sade, 'An Essay on Novels', in *The Crimes of Love*, trans. David Coward (Oxford: Oxford University Press, 2005), 11.

our motives as readers of sentimental fiction before reading Sade, it is impossible not to be so afterwards.

The Marquise de Gange *and the Gothic Novel*

As great a debt as *The Marquise de Gange* owes the tradition of sentimental fiction, there is a closer antecedent and model—itself rooted in the same tradition—which has hitherto been entirely overlooked by Sade scholars. Its rather lazy categorization as a historical novel (alongside Sade's other late works, *Isabelle de Bavière* and *Adélaïde de Brunswick*) has obscured what it really is: a Gothic novel. Although Sade is often invoked in a Gothic context, it is generally as an early commentator of the genre rather than as a practitioner. His 'Essay on Novels', published in 1800 as a preface to *The Crimes of Love*, is commonly cited among scholars of Gothic literature for its sociohistorical insight that this new form of fiction 'was the necessary offspring of the revolutionary upheaval which affected the whole of Europe'. The praise Sade offers these 'new novels' is not unqualified—he notes, for example, the problems posed by the use of the supernatural—but his appreciation of the genre is evident, and he names *The Monk* (1796) as its finest example, 'superior in every respect to the strange outpourings of the brilliant imagination of Mrs Radcliffe'.[26]

On the rare occasions scholars have sought to bring Sade into the Gothic fold, one has the impression that they have not really found what they were looking for. While E. J. Clery brings together Radcliffe's *The Romance of the Forest* (1791) and Sade's *Justine*, two novels published in the same year, she admits that 'there can be no question of influence either way in this comparison of Radcliffe and Sade' and that the 'shadow dialogue'[27] between the two is of her own construction. One has the same sense of critics willing rather than finding a connection between Sade and Radcliffe when they allude to 'similar plot motifs'[28] such as virtuous heroines in distress, or when they note the striking resonances in the fictional landscapes of castles,

---

[26] Ibid. 13.
[27] E. J. Clery, 'Ann Radcliffe and D. A. F. de Sade: Thoughts on Heroism', *Women's Writing*, 1 (1994), 207.
[28] Maria Vara, 'Gothic Permutations from the 1790s to the 1970s: Rethinking the Marquis de Sade's Legacy', in Avril Horner and Sue Zlosnik (eds), *Le Gothic: Influences and Appropriations in Europe and America* (Basingstoke: Palgrave Macmillan, 2008), 105.

forests, and mountains. Rather than revealing a direct connection between the two authors, however, such shared tropes may simply reflect a shared debt to sentimental fiction. The same may be said of Sade in relation to Lewis: while scholars of the Gothic such as Maurice Lévy and Angela Wright have pointed to similarities between certain scenes and locations in *The Monk* and Sade's *Justine* novels, the evidence of either a Sadean influence on Lewis or a Monkean influence on Sade is far from conclusive.[29]

If Sade did exert some influence on the Gothic novel, it is likely to have been later than the 1790s. As I have suggested elsewhere, a plausible case could be made for Charlotte Dacre's *Zofloya; or, The Moor* (1806), a work heavily influenced by Lewis, although Mary Shelley's *Frankenstein; or, The modern Prometheus* (1818) is perhaps the most obvious example of an English Gothic novel influenced by Sade. Shelley's work features a 'poor guiltless Justine' of its own, an 'exquisitely beautiful'[30] figure of female suffering who, like Sade's heroine, is falsely accused and convicted of murder in an episode which concludes with some very Sadean reflections:

'When I reflect, my dear cousin,' said she, 'on the miserable death of Justine Moritz, I no longer see the world and its works as they before appeared to me. Before, I looked upon the accounts of vice and injustice, that I read in books or heard from others, as tales of ancient days, or imaginary evils [...] but now misery has come home, and men appear to me as monsters thirsting for each other's blood.'[31]

As the example of *Frankenstein* suggests, critics looking for connections between Sade and the Gothic would be well advised to extend their search beyond the 1790s. In many respects *The Marquise de Gange* seems like the missing piece of the puzzle that they were searching for: a genuine example of Sadean Gothic, influenced by both Radcliffe and Lewis, and moreover drawing on some of the same

---

[29] See Maurice Lévy, *Le roman «gothique» anglais 1764–1824* (Paris: Albin Michel, 1995), 350–3, and Angela Wright, 'European Disruptions of the Idealized Woman: Matthew Lewis's *The Monk* and the Marquis de Sade's *La Nouvelle Justine*', in Avril Horner, *European Gothic: A Spirited Exchange 1760–1960* (Manchester and New York: Manchester University Press, 2002), 39–54.

[30] Mary Shelley, *Frankenstein; or, the Modern Prometheus*, ed. D. L. Macdonald and Kathleen Scherf, 3rd edn (Peterborough, Ontario: Broadview, 2012), 102, 103.

[31] Ibid. 113. The case for Sade's influence on Dacre and Shelley is made more fully in Will McMorran, 'The Marquis de Sade in English, 1800–1850', *Modern Language Review*, 112.3 (2017), 549–66.

sources as these English authors. If Sade's novel has so far been over-looked by such scholars, this is perhaps because it lacks the notoriety of his earlier works, but it may also be because it has never been trans-lated into English before, and has therefore remained inaccessible to English readers.[32] This in itself indicates one of the problems that has until recently plagued both French studies of Sade and the *roman noir* on the one hand, and English studies of Gothic fiction on the other: a rigid nationalism, according to which the origins of Sade's fiction are entirely French and those of the Gothic novel entirely English. Jean Fabre, for example, asserts adamantly that 'Sade owes nothing or almost nothing [. . .] to the English practice', but 'extends, revives and appropriates a tradition of *roman noir* which, to simplify, we shall call baroque and French'.[33] Although he mentions *The Marquise de Gange* briefly, his examination—and rejection—of English Gothic as an influence on Sade does not look beyond the 1790s, so the opportunity to bring the two traditions together is missed. He does, however, per-suasively argue that Sade's oeuvre owes a debt to the tradition of *his-toires tragiques*—a claim which the origins of *The Marquise de Gange* within that same tradition strengthens. Fabre's insistence on this form of writing as a purely French phenomenon, however, blinds him to the possibility that it may have exerted an influence—directly or indirectly—beyond France, and indeed on the English Gothic from which he is so keen to distance Sade.[34] Although these violent tales of criminal passions and transgressive love, designed ostensibly to shock their readers into virtue, share many themes and strategies with the 'terrorist' English novels of the 1790s, they have yet to be explored as potential precursors or progenitors of the form.

---

[32] The only Gothic critic to mention *The Marquise de Gange* is Angela Wright, but she incorrectly states that it 'is by contrast told from the perspective of the male villains' and refers the reader to a translation which does not exist: 'The Marchioness of Gange', in Margaret Crosland's *The Gothic Tales of the Marquis de Sade* (London: Peter Owen, 2010), Angela Wright, *Britain, France and the Gothic, 1764–1820: The Import of Terror* (Cambridge: Cambridge University Press, 2013), 172.

[33] Jean Fabre, 'Sade et le roman noir', in *Idées sur le roman: de Madame de Lafayette au Marquis de Sade* (Paris: Klincksieck, 1979), 168.

[34] Rosset's *Histoires tragiques* were certainly read in England during the seventeenth century, providing the source material for dramatists such as Webster and Ford, while other authors of the genre such as Pierre Boaistuau and Jean-Paul Camus were also trans-lated in this period. Some of Pierre Boaistuau's earlier *Histoires tragiques* (1559), a trans-lation of Matteo Bandello's *Novelle* (1554), were also translated and adapted into English, and provided a source for Shakespeare's *Romeo and Juliet*.

For their part, specialists of Gothic literature have generally not looked so far back, or so far afield, when it comes to the origins of the genre. Most guides to the Gothic simply begin with Walpole and move on to Radcliffe and Lewis, paying little if any attention to possible precursors.[35] Even French critics of the English Gothic such as Maurice Lévy have insisted on its Englishness, declaring that the origins of 'the only true Gothic [...] are English and date back to the eighteenth century' and that Horace Walpole 'invented the genre'.[36] In recent years, however, scholars open to a more comparative approach have begun to challenge the 'tyranny of Anglo-American narratives of the Gothic',[37] and to explore the genre as a transnational—and 'translational'—phenomenon. Terry Hale has argued persuasively that the Gothic was not only the cause but the product of 'considerable translational activity' and that 'many of the conventions which we associate with the British Gothic novel today arose as a by-product of the translation process'.[38] He reveals in particular the influence of two of Sade's favourite authors: the Abbé Prévost and Baculard d'Arnaud.[39] Prévost's sentimental adventure novels, including *Manon Lescaut* (1731) and *The English Philosopher, or History of Monsieur Cleveland* (1732–9), and Baculard d'Arnaud's sentimental short stories, *The Ordeals of Sentiment* (1772–80), directly inspired English writers in the 1780s: Charlotte Smith translated *Manon Lescaut* in 1786, Sophia Lee borrowed liberally from *Cleveland* when writing *The Recess* (1783–5), and Clara Reeve drew from two tales from *The Ordeals of Sentiment* in *The Exiles, or, Memoirs of the Count de Crondstadt* (1789). As Hale shows, 'many of the writers engaged in the Gothic experiment began their literary careers as translators', with Smith, Lee, and Reeve 'the main conduits for considerable French input into the development of the sentimental Gothic novel in England'.[40]

[35] Avril Horner, 'Introduction', in Horner (ed.), *European Gothic*, 1.

[36] Maurice Lévy, 'Du roman gothique au roman noir: traductions, illustrations, imitations, pastiches et contrefaçons', in Catriona Seth (ed.), *Imaginaires gothiques: aux sources du roman noir français* (Paris: Desjonquères, 2010), 49.

[37] Avril Horner, 'Introduction', in Horner (ed.), *European Gothic*, 1.

[38] Terry Hale, 'Translation in Distress: Cultural Misappropriation and the Construction of the Gothic', in Horner (ed.), *European Gothic*, 17.

[39] Sade hailed Prévost as 'the French Richardson', and Baculard d'Arnaud as the one author who 'may often be thought to have surpassed him': as he writes approvingly in his 'Essay on Novels', 'Both dipped their pens in the Styx' (p. 12).

[40] Terry Hale, 'French and German Gothic: The Beginnings', in Jerrold E. Hogle (ed.), *The Cambridge Companion to Gothic Fiction* (Cambridge: Cambridge University Press, 2002), 66.

These women translators and novelists in turn influenced the direction of Gothic fiction of the 1790s, and the novels of Ann Radcliffe in particular. Angela Wright draws attention to Clara Reeve's largely ignored second venture as a translator: *The Romance of Real Life* (1787), a translation of some of Gayot de Pitaval's *Causes célèbres* that includes 'The Marchioness of Gange'. As Wright puts it, 'Smith's transformation of Gayot's original character into a heroine of sensibility makes the marchioness an early prototype for the Radcliffean Gothic heroine'.[41] Radcliffe certainly read Smith's translation, and indeed alludes to 'Guyot de Pitaval' in the opening of *The Romance of the Forest*, citing his work as the source for her account of 'the striking story of Pierre de la Motte, and the Marquis Phillipe de Montalt',[42] an allusion all the more intriguing as it turns out to be a red herring. Her decision to announce this as a source at the start of her novel may furthermore have influenced Sade's decision to do the same in his preface to *The Marquise de Gange*; read in this light, Sade's own reference to the *Causes célèbres* accomplishes two goals simultaneously: it allows him both to emphasize the veracity of his own account by indicating its historical source, and to align his work with the Gothic tradition that drew on the very same source. Because of the afterlife enjoyed by the *Causes célèbres* in England, Sade's allusion may therefore not be as singularly French as first appears. It moreover serves not only to signal the genre within which he is working, but to reveal the origins of that genre: with *The Marquise de Gange*, Sade quietly suggests, the Gothic is coming home.

In 1797, an anonymous critic shared the following recipe for 'Terrorist Novel Writing':

Take—An old castle, half of it ruinous.
A long gallery, with a great many doors, some secret ones.
Three murdered bodies, quite fresh.
As many skeletons, in chests and presses.
An old woman hanging by the neck; with her throat cut.
Assassins and desperadoes, 'quant. suff.'
Noises, whispers, and groans, threescore at least.

[41] Wright, *Britain, France and the Gothic*, 57.
[42] Ann Radcliffe, *The Romance of the Forest*, ed. Chloe Chard (Oxford: Oxford University Press, 2009), 1.

Mix them together, in the form of three volumes, to be taken at any of the watering-places before going to bed.[43]

Three years later, Madame de Staël referred to those novels in which 'the aim was to inspire terror with night-time, old castles, long corridors and gusts of wind'.[44] *The Marquise de Gange* certainly has its fair share of Gothic settings, from a bandits' cave in a forest to old castles with dark corridors: the castle of Gange, where much of the novel is set, is moreover said to be 'in keeping with that Gothic style of architecture and design so treasured by those sombre, melancholic souls' (p. 13). Like many of its predecessors it also features a Mediterranean backdrop. As for its cast, its central plot of a virtuous heroine persecuted by a villainous libertine recalls both Radcliffe's *The Romance of the Forest* and Lewis's *The Monk*—particularly as the villain once again wears the habit of a man of the church. There is even room for the supernatural element Sade had earlier condemned in his 'Essay on Novels', with Euphrasie experiencing premonitions of her dreadful fate. Nature too plays its part, with an extraordinary storm scene as she flees from the clutches of the caddish Caderousse. However, when Euphrasie is tricked into spending the night in a brothel, it may seem for a moment that she has wandered into one of Sade's earlier, pornographic novels.

The relationship between Sadean fiction and the Gothic novel, and the shared origins and influences that could shed light on that relationship, have yet to be explored in any detail. Any such explorations that do not take account of *The Marquise de Gange* would necessarily only tell part of the story, however, so it is to be hoped that its publication in English for the first time will be helpful in this regard, and encourage further work on the Gothic as a transnational phenomenon. But as interesting a place as Sade's novel occupies in literary history, there is a much more compelling reason for reading it: it is, first and foremost, a gripping Gothic novel that has been neglected far too long. When David Coward, the translator of *The Crimes of Love*, complained that Sade's 'rambling and very tedious novels'[45] are far inferior to his short fiction, he was referring to the pornographic

---

[43] Anon., 'Terrorist Novel Writing', *Spirit of the Public Journals*, 1 (1797), 229. The same recipe was soon translated into French in *Le Spectateur du Nord* (May 1798).

[44] Anne-Louise-Germaine de Staël, *De la littérature considérée dans ses rapports avec les institutions sociales*, ed. Axel Blaeschke (Paris: Garnier, 1998), 355–6.

[45] David Coward, 'Down with Sade?', *Paragraph*, 23.1 (2000), 12.

works of the 1780s and 1790s. Aside from the fact that there is something ostentatiously ascetic in finding works of such extremes tedious, his comment takes no account of a novel like *The Marquise de Gange*, a work which shares the tone and sensibility of Sade's short stories (which have also been published as 'Gothic Tales'[46]). Sade's last published novel is anything but rambling, and anything but tedious: a taut, tense narrative that builds inexorably to a climax made all the more unsettling by our awareness that it describes the murder of a real woman, not just a fictional character. Indeed, the terrible fate of the historical Marquise de Ganges reminds us that the violence in Sade is never purely fictional, but always born of the real.

---

[46] Sade, *The Gothic Tales of the Marquis de Sade*, trans. Margaret Crosland (London: Peter Owen, 2010).

NOTE ON THE TEXT

La Marquise de Gange was published anonymously in two volumes by Béchet in Paris in 1813. This translation is based on the definitive edition published in the eleventh volume of Gilbert Lely's *Oeuvres complètes du Marquis de Sade* (Paris: Cercle du livre précieux, 1966–7).

SELECT BIBLIOGRAPHY

Works by Sade
(and their English translations)

Les 120 journées de Sodome, ed. Gilbert Lely (Paris: Union générale d'éditions, 1998).

The 120 Days of Sodom, trans. Will McMorran and Thomas Wynn (London: Penguin, 2016).

Adélaïde de Brunswick, princesse de Saxe, in *Œuvres complètes du Marquis de Sade*, 15 vols, eds Jean-Jacques Pauvert and Annie Le Brun (Paris: Pauvert, 1986), vol. 12.

Adelaide of Brunswick, trans. Hobart Ryland (Washington: The Scarecrow Press, 1954).

Aline et Valcour, ou le roman philosophique vertu, ed. Jean-Marie Goulemot (Paris: Librairie générale française, 1994).

Contes étranges, ed. Michel Delon (Paris: Gallimard, 2014).

Contes libertins, ed. Stéphanie Genand (Paris: Flammarion, 2014).

Les Crimes de l'amour, ed. Michel Delon (Paris: Gallimard, 2014).

The Crimes of Love, trans. David Coward (Oxford: Oxford University Press, 2005).

'Dialogue entre un prêtre et un moribond', ed. Jérôme Vérain (Paris: Fayard, 1997).

'Dialogue between a Priest and a Dying Man', in *Justine, Philosophy in the Bedroom and Other Writings*, trans. Richard Seaver and Austryn Wainhouse (New York: Grove Press, 1994).

Ecrits politiques, ed. Maurice Lever (Paris: Bartillat, 2009).

Histoire de Juliette, ou les prospérités du vice, in *Œuvres*, ed. Michel Delon, 3 vols (Paris: Gallimard, 1990–8), vol. 3.

Juliette, trans. Austryn Wainhouse (New York: Grove Press, 1994).

Histoire secrète d'Isabelle de Bavière, Reine de France, ed. Gilbert Lely (Paris: Gallimard, 1992).

Les Infortunes de la vertu, ed. Béatrice Didier (Paris: Gallimard, 2014).

The Misfortunes of Virtue and Other Early Tales, trans. David Coward (Oxford: Oxford University Press, 1999).

Justine, ou les malheurs de la vertu (Paris: Librairie générale française, 1973).

Justine, or the Misfortunes of Virtue, trans. John Phillips (Oxford: Oxford University Press, 2012).

Lettres à sa femme, ed. Marc Buffat (Paris: Actes Sud, 1997).

Letters from Prison, trans. Richard Seaver (New York: Arcade, 1999).

La Marquise de Gange, ed. Jean Goldzink (Paris: Autrement, 1993).

La Nouvelle Justine, ou les malheurs de la vertu, in *Œuvres*, ed. Michel Delon, 3 vols (Paris: Gallimard, 1990–8), vol. 2.

La Philosophie dans le boudoir, ed. Jean-Christophe Abramovici (Paris: Flammarion, 2007).

Philosophy in the Boudoir, or The Immoral Mentors, trans. Joachim Neugroschel (New York: Penguin, 2006).

Voyage d'Italie, ed. Michel Delon (Paris: Flammarion, 2019).

Voyage to Italy, trans. James A. Steintrager (Toronto: University of Toronto Press, 2020).

Works on Sade

Allison, David B., Roberts, Mark S., Weiss, Allen S. (eds), *Sade and the Narrative of Transgression* (Cambridge: Cambridge University Press, 1995).

Barthes, Roland, *Sade, Fourier, Loyola* (Paris: Seuil, 1971).

Beauvoir, Simone de, 'Must we burn Sade?', trans. Annette Michelson, in Sade, *The 120 Days of Sodom and other Writings* (New York: Grove Press, 1966), 3–64; first published as 'Faut-il brûler Sade?', *Les Temps modernes*, 74 (1951), 1002–33, and 75 (January 1952), 1197–230.

Carter, Angela, *The Sadeian Woman* (London: Virago Press, 1979).

Dworkin, Andrea, *Pornography: Men Possessing Women* (New York: Plume, 1989).

Edmiston, William F., *Sade: Queer Theorist*, *SVEC* 2013:03 (Oxford: Voltaire Foundation).

Frappier-Mazur, Lucienne, *Writing the Orgy: Power and Parody in Sade* (Philadelphia: University of Pennsylvania Press, 1996); first published as *Sade et l'écriture de l'orgie* (Paris: Nathan, 1991).

Hénaff, Marcel, *Sade, The Invention of the Libertine Body* (Minneapolis and London: University of Minnesota Press, 1999).

Laugaa-Traut, Françoise, *Lectures de Sade* (Paris: Armand Colin, 1973).

Le Brun, Annie, *Sade: A Sudden Abyss* (New York: City Lights Books, 1990); first published as *Soudain un bloc d'abîme, Sade* (Paris: Pauvert, 1986).

McMorran, Will, 'The Sound of Violence: Listening to Rape in Sade', in Thomas Wynn (ed.), *Representing Violence in France, 1760–1820*, *SVEC*, 2013:10 (Oxford: Voltaire Foundation, 2013), 229–49.

Parker, Kate, and Sclippa, Norbert (eds), *Sade's Sensibilities* (Lewisburg, PA, MD: Bucknell University Press, 2015).

Phillips, John, *Sade: The Libertine Novels* (London, and Stirling, VA: Pluto Press, 2001).

Phillips, John (ed.), *Sade and his Legacy*, special edition issue of *Paragraph*, 23:1 (2000).

Roger, Philippe, *Sade: la philosophie dans le pressoir* (Paris: Grasset, 1976).

St-Martin, Armelle, *De la médécine chez Sade: disséquer la vie, narrer la mort* (Paris: Champion, 2010).

Shattuck, Roger, *Forbidden Knowledge: From Prometheus to Pornography* (San Diego: Harcourt Brace, 1997).

Thomas, Chantal, *Sade, la Dissertation et l'orgie*, 2nd edn (Paris: Payot & Rivages, 2002).

Warman, Caroline, *Sade: From Materialism to Pornography*, *SVEC* 2002: 01 (Oxford: Voltaire Foundation, 2002).

Wynn, Thomas, *Sade's Theatre: Pleasure, Vision, Masochism*, *SVEC* 2007:02 (Oxford: Voltaire Foundation, 2007).

Works on Sade and European Gothic Fiction

Clery, E. J., 'Ann Radcliffe and D. A. F. de Sade: Thoughts on Heroinism', *Women's Writing*, 1 (1994), 203–14.

Cornwell, Neil, 'European Gothic', in David Punter (ed.), *A Companion to the Gothic* (Oxford: Blackwell, 2000), 27–38.

Didier, Béatrice, '*La Marquise de Gange*', in *Sade: une écriture du désir* (Paris: Denoël/Gonthier, 1976), 110–24.

Fabre, Jean, 'Sade et le roman noir', in *Idées sur le roman: de Madame de Lafayette au Marquis de Sade* (Paris: Klincksieck, 1979), 166–94.

Hale, Terry, 'French and German Gothic: The Beginnings', in Jerrold E. Hogle (ed.), *The Cambridge Companion to Gothic Fiction* (Cambridge: Cambridge University Press, 2002), 63–84.

Hale, Terry, 'Translation in Distress: Cultural Misappropriation and the Construction of the Gothic', in Avril Horner (ed.), *European Gothic: A Spirited Exchange 1760–1960* (Manchester and New York: Manchester University Press, 2002), 17–38.

Hall, Daniel, *French and German Gothic Fiction in the Late Eighteenth Century* (Bern: Peter Lang, 2005).

Heine, Maurice, 'Le Marquis de Sade et le roman noir', in *Le Marquis de Sade* (Paris: Gallimard, 1950), 211–31.

Horner, Avril (ed.), *European Gothic: A Spirited Exchange 1760–1960* (Manchester and New York: Manchester University Press, 2002).

Horner, Avril, and Zlosnik, Sue (eds), *Le Gothic: Influences and Appropriations in Europe and America* (Basingstoke: Palgrave Macmillan, 2008).

Le Brun, Annie, *Les châteaux de la subversion* (Paris: Pauvert, 1982).

McMorran, Will, 'The Marquis de Sade in English, 1800–1850', *Modern Language Review*, 112.3 (2017), 549–66.

Phillips, John, 'Circles of Influence: Lewis, Sade, Artaud', *Comparative Critical Studies*, 9: 1 (2012), 61–82.

Seth, Catriona (ed.), *Imaginaires gothiques: aux sources du roman noir français* (Paris: Desjonquères, 2010).

Vara, Maria, 'Gothic Permutations from the 1790s to the 1970s: Rethinking the Marquis de Sade's Legacy', in Avril Horner and Sue Zlosnik (eds), *Le Gothic: Influences and Appropriations in Europe and America* (Basingstoke: Palgrave Macmillan, 2008), 100–15.

Wright, Angela, 'European Disruptions of the Idealized Woman: Matthew Lewis's *The Monk* and the Marquis de Sade's *La Nouvelle Justine*', in Avril Horner (ed.), *European Gothic: A Spirited Exchange 1760–1960* (Manchester and New York: Manchester University Press, 2002), 39–54.

Wright, Angela, *Britain, France and the Gothic, 1764–1820: The Import of Terror* (Cambridge: Cambridge University Press, 2013).

Wright, Angela, 'Gothic Translation: France, 1760–1830', in Glennis Byron and Dale Townshend (eds), *The Gothic World* (Abingdon: Routledge, 2014), 221–30.

Works on The Marquise de Gange

Gambacorti, Chiara, *Sade: une esthétique de la duplicité* (Paris: Garnier, 2014).

Laborde, Alice, 'Sade: la dialectique du regard dans *La Marquise de Gange*', *Romanic Review*, 40 (1969), 47–53.

Lynch, Lawrence W., 'Sade and the Case of the Marquise de Ganges: Sources, Adaptations and Regressions', *Symposium*, 41 (1987), 188–99.

Proust, Jacques, 'La diction sadienne: à propos de *La Marquise de Gange*', in Michel Camus and Philippe Roger (eds), *Sade: Écrire la crise* (Paris: Pierre Belfond, 1983), 31–46.

Trouille, Mary, 'The Conflict between Good and Evil, Faith and Irreligion in Sade's *Marquise de Gange*', *Eighteenth-Century Fiction*, 17 (1) (2004), 53–86.

Trousson, Raymond, 'Histoire d'un fait divers, du Marquis de Sade à Charles Hugo', http://www.bon-a-tirer.com/volume9/rt.html (24 December 2003).

Selected Retellings of the Story of the Marquise de Ganges
(in chronological order)

D. Q. I. S. G. E. M. N., *Les Véritables et Principales Circonstances de la mort déplorable de Madame la Marquise de Ganges, empoisonnée & massacrée par l'Abbé & le Chevalier de Ganges ses Beaux Frères, le 137 mai 1667* (Rouen: Cailloüé, 1667).

Dunoyer, Anne-Marguerite Petit, *Lettres historiques et galantes, de deux dames de condition, dont l'une étoit à Paris, et l'autre en Province*, 7 vols (Cologne [The Hague]: Pierre Marteau [Pierre Husson], 1707–17), vol. 1.

Gayot de Pitaval, François, *Histoire de la Marquise de Gange*, in *Causes célèbres et intéressantes, avec les jugements qui les ont décidées*, 10 vols (Paris: Guillaume Cavelier, 1734–43), vol. 5.

A Select Collection of Singular and Interesting Histories. Together with the tryals and judicial proceedings to which the extraordinary facts therein recorded gave occasion, 2 vols (London: A. Miller, 1744), vol. 1.

Richer, François, *Histoire de la Marquise de Gange*, in *Causes célèbres et intéresssantes, avec les jugements qui les ont décidées*, 18 vols (Amsterdam: Michel Rey, 1772–81), vol. 7.

Smith, Charlotte, *The Marchioness de Gange*, in *The Romance of Real Life, A collection of tales based on 'Causes célèbres et intéressantes' by F. Gayot de Pitaval*, 3 vols (London: T. Cadell, 1787), vol. 1.

Fortia d'Urban, Agricole-Joseph de, *Histoire de la marquise de Ganges* (Paris: Levrault, 1810).

Boirie, Eugène Cantiran de, and Chandezon, Léopold, *La Marquise de Gange, ou les Trois frères, mélodrame historique en 3 actes et en prose, Tiré des Causes Célèbres* (Paris: Barba, 1815).

Dumas, Alexandre, *La Marquise de Ganges*, in Alexandre Dumas, Auguste Arnould, Narcisse Fournier, Pier-Angelo Fiorentino, and Félicien Mallefille, *Crimes célèbres*, 8 vols (Paris: Administration de librairie, 1839–40), vols 2–3.

Gaskell, Elizabeth, 'French Life', *Fraser's Magazine*, 69 (January to June, 1864).

'V' (J. R. Chorley), 'The Story of the Marquise de Gange. A Real Tragedy of the "Good Old Times" in France', *Tait's Edinburgh Magazine*, 9 (1842).

Hugo, Charles, *Une famille tragique*, *La Presse* (17–31 October 1860).

Mazel, Albin, *La Première Marquise de Ganges, sa vie, ses malheurs, sa fin tragique* (Paris: Paul Monnerat, 1885).

Boutet, Frédéric, *Une Affaire criminelle au XVIIe siècle… La mort déplorable de Mme la marquise de Ganges*, in *Œuvres libres*, n° 110, août 1930.

Galzy, Jeanne, *Diane de Ganges* (Lyon: Gutenberg, 1943).

Aragon, Victor, *Diane de Joannis, marquise de Ganges. Sa vie, sa mort tragique d'après des documents inédits* (Montpellier: Camille Coulet; and Paris: Delahaye and Lecrosnier, 1881).

Delayen, Gaston, *La passion de la marquise de Ganges* (Paris: Perrin, 1927).

Vidal, Gaston, *L'ombre d'Amaranthe* (Montpellier: Edition de l'Entente bibliophile, 1959).

Gros, Roger, *L'assassinat de la marquise de Ganges* (Montpellier: Cour d'appel de Montpellier, 1968).

Héritier, Jean, *La Belle Provencale* (Paris: Denoël, 1984).

Further Reading in Oxford World's Classics

Dacre, Charlotte, *Zofloya, or The Moor*, ed. Kim Ian Michasiw.

Lewis, Matthew, *The Monk*, ed. Nick Groom.

Radcliffe, Ann, *The Mysteries of Udolpho*, ed. Bonamy Dobrée, intro. Terry Castle.

Radcliffe, Ann, *The Romance of the Forest*, ed. Chloe Chard.

Sade, Marquis de, *Justine, or the Misfortunes of Virtue*, trans. and ed. John Phillips.

Sade, Marquis de, *The Crimes of Love*, trans. and ed. David Coward.

Sade, Marquis de, *The Misfortunes of Virtue and Other Early Tales*, trans. and ed. David Coward.

A CHRONOLOGY OF THE
MARQUIS DE SADE

1740 2 June: Donatien Alphonse François de Sade, son of Jean-Baptiste François Joseph, Comte de Sade (1702–67) and Marie Eléonore de Maillé de Carman (1712–77), born at the Hôtel de Condé in Paris.

1744 Sent to Provence; stays initially with his aunts in Avignon, then with his uncle, the Abbé de Sade, in Saumane.

1750 Returns to Paris to attend Louis-le-Grand, a Jesuit school.

1754 Enrols at the academy of the Chevau-légers, an elite cavalry corps reserved for the oldest noble families.

1755–63 Serves as second lieutenant in the King's Infantry; commissioned as standard-bearer in the Comte de Provence's Carabiniers regiment, then as captain of the Burgundy regiment; demobilized at the end of the Seven Years War (1756–63).

1763 17 May: marries Renée-Pélagie de Montreuil, daughter of a wealthy judge, in Paris. 18 October: offers Jeanne Testard, an occasional prostitute, two *louis* to take part in flagellation, sodomy, and sacrilegious acts; she refuses. Imprisoned for two weeks in the Château de Vincennes, then confined to a château belonging to his in-laws.

1765 Affair with actress, Mademoiselle de Beauvoisin, whom he takes to the family château of Lacoste, in Provence, and presents as his wife.

1767 Death of Sade's father. Birth of his first son, Louis-Marie.

1768 3 April: takes a beggar, Rose Keller, to his house in Arcueil, where he flogs her and commits sacrilegious acts; she escapes and reports him to the police. Sade imprisoned at Saumur, then Pierre-Encise, before being confined to Lacoste.

1769 Birth of second son, Donatien Claude Armand. Travels to Low Countries.

1771 Birth of daughter, Madeleine-Laure. Imprisoned for debts.

1772 Organizes theatrical performances at Lacoste and Mazan. Affair with sister-in-law, Anne-Prospère de Launay. 17 June: organizes orgy in Marseille with four prostitutes and his valet, Latour. Charged with sodomy and poisoning, having given the prostitutes Spanish fly; sentenced to death and executed in effigy for poisoning and sodomy; flees to Italy with Anne-Prospère. 8 December: arrested and imprisoned in the fortress of Miolans.

1773 30 April: escapes from Miolans; on the run in the south of France and possibly Spain; returns to Lacoste.

1774 Evades police raids on Lacoste, and spends the summer in Italy.

1774–5 Spends winter in Lacoste with his wife, a 15-year-old male 'secretary', six newly recruited female servants of around the same age, and others—giving rise to the so-called 'little girls affair'. January 1775: servants' families complain of abduction and seduction; human bones found in Lacoste garden, which Sade dismisses as a practical joke.

1775 July: flees to Italy again; travels around the country, visiting Turin, Piacenza, Parma, Modena, Florence, Rome, and Naples.

1776 July: returns to Lacoste and writes the *Voyage to Italy*, which he does not complete.

1777 17 January: incensed father of one of the servants at Lacoste shoots at Sade twice, but misses. 13 February: arrives too late in Paris to see his dying mother; arrested by *lettre de cachet* and imprisoned in Vincennes.

1778 Escapes from custody, recaptured after thirty-nine days and returned to Vincennes, where he spends the next six years.

1782 Writes *Dialogue Between a Priest and a Dying Man;* starts work on *The 120 Days of Sodom, or the School of Libertinage*.

1784 29 February: transferred to the Bastille.

1785 Writes an incomplete draft of *The 120 Days of Sodom* in thirty-seven days.

1789 3 July: caught shouting to passers-by that the Bastille inmates are having their throats cut; transferred in the night to Charenton. 14 July: the scroll of *The 120 Days of Sodom* taken during the storming of the Bastille.

1790 2 April: freed from Charenton. 9 June: divorces wife at her request. Begins relationship with a former actress, Marie-Constance Quesnet, with whom he remains until his death. Participates actively in revolutionary politics.

1791 *Justine, or the Misfortunes of Virtue* published anonymously; *Oxtiern, or the Misfortunes of Libertinage* performed at the Théâtre Molière.

1793 8 December: arrested.

1794 28 July: narrowly escapes the guillotine on the day Robespierre falls. 15 October: freed.

1795 *Aline and Valcour* and *Philosophy in the Boudoir* published.

1797–1801? *The New Justine, or the Misfortunes of Virtue* and *The History of Juliette, or the Rewards of Vice* published (years of publication of the latter uncertain).

1800   *Oxtiern* and *The Crimes of Love* published.

1801   3 April: arrested and imprisoned in Sainte-Pélagie.

1803   14 March: after being accused of attempting to seduce young inmates, transferred to Bicêtre, then on 27 April to Charenton.

1804–13 Organizes theatrical performances at Charenton. Has sexual relationship with a young laundress or seamstress, Madeleine Leclerc.

1807   Manuscript of *The Days of Florbelle, or Nature Revealed* seized (and later destroyed after his death).

1812–13 Writes *Adélaïde de Brunswick, Princess of Saxony* and *The Secret History of Isabelle de Bavière, Queen of France*; publishes *The Marquise de Gange*.

1814   2 December: dies; despite his wishes, given a Christian burial, but in accordance with his will no trace of his grave is left.

THE MARQUISE DE GANGE

AUTHOR'S PREFACE

THIS is no novel we are offering here: the awful truth of the events we are to describe may be found in the *Causes célèbres*.* All Europe reverberated with the news of this lamentable episode. Did everyone not shudder when they heard? Did any sensitive soul fail to shed a tear?

But why are the details we lay before you not exactly the same as those recorded in the accounts of the time? This is why: the author of the *Causes célèbres* did not know all there was to this matter; not all—far from it—was revealed in the accounts he consulted. Better informed than he, we have been able to elaborate these events more fully than was possible for someone with so few materials to hand. But why the air of a novel?

Because this is the nature of the events themselves. Because nothing could be more like a novel than this tragic episode, and because we would have adulterated the events had we rendered them any less vividly; but if no lustre has been lost with our brushstrokes, we may also affirm that nothing has been concealed by them either. God forbid we should allow ourselves to paint this canvas any darker than it already is! It would be impossible in any case, even if someone were to try.

We most assuredly protest therefore that we have in no way distorted the truth of these events: to diminish them would have been against our interest; to exaggerate them would have been to heap on ourselves the opprobrium so richly deserved by the monsters responsible for them.

Let those seeking the precise details of the story of the unfortunate Marquise de Gange read us with the interest that truth inspires; and let those who like to detect a little fiction even in strictly historical accounts not blame us for having only introduced a kind where the truth can be found on every line. The bare facts, without the supplementary materials with which we have surrounded them, would not have sustained a reading; and when one knows that the subject one is describing is bound to shock, one is certainly permitted to envelop it with all that may prepare the soul to bear it without too cruel a wrench.

Perhaps we should have laid down our quill immediately after the catastrophe, but as the accounts of the time provide us with the end of the story regarding those villains who made the reader tremble, we thought he would be grateful to learn, not very accurately some may say, what befell the guiltiest of the three. All in good time. But it is so painful to present crime triumphant that if we have not shown it in this light—if we have, so to speak, thwarted or corrected fate—it is to please the virtuous, who will be quite grateful to us for not having dared *say everything*,* when everything in this case serves only to confound the hope, so consoling for virtue, that those who persecute it shall without fail be persecuted in turn.

CHAPTER I

THE testament of Louis XIII, which established a Regency council, annulled by a Court of Justice* decree according to the wishes of Anne of Austria, that monarch's widow; the investiture of this Princess as Regent for an indefinite period; the war which obliged the Regent to arm the French against Philippe, her brother, whom she nonetheless loved very dearly (a disastrous war, which had endured for the last thirteen years); the Regent's choice of Mazarin, who held sway over both this sovereign and all of France; the civil war, an inevitable result of discord, or of boundless ambition among ministers; the dangerous ongoing conflict between the Courts of Justice and the supreme ruler; the arbitrary arrests of Noviac, Chardon, Broussel, etc., carried out and resisted with shots fired, and which left Paris bristling with barricades on that fateful day in which the Cardinal de Retz took such brazen pride;* the court's retreat to Saint-Germain,* where everyone slept on straw; the nonage of Louis XIV, who at the time was only eleven years of age; all these calamitous circumstances offered a less than serene prospect for the early days of the marriage which Mademoiselle de Rossan, daughter of one of the wealthiest gentlemen of Avignon, contracted in 1649 with the Comte de Castellane, son of the Duc de Villars.

These nonetheless were the events of the day, when this beautiful young lady, barely thirteen years of age, first appeared at her husband's side at the court of the young King; and it was there that her charms, her warm nature, and the most celestial countenance soon captured every heart. There was not a lord at this amorous court who did not stake his pride on winning a glance from her, and the young King himself, dancing with her on several occasions, paid tribute to all the young Comtesse's graces in the most flattering terms.

Following the example of all women of virtue, Madame de Castellane, who was singularly devoted to her Christian duties, only took notice of this universal acclaim in so far as it offered her further motivation to be truly deserving of it. But the more an individual is favoured by nature and wealth, the more one sees, all too often, fate assail him with the greatest hardships: this equilibrium is a form of divine justice, serving as both an example and a lesson to mankind.

Mademoiselle Euphrasie de Châteaublanc* was not born to be fortunate: so it was that from a tender age divine decrees weighed heavily on her, teaching her that all the wealth on earth serves only to remind men of the existence of an eternal realm where God rewards virtue alone.

The Comte de Castellane perished in a shipwreck, and his young wife heard the news in the midst of that court, the recent witness of her triumphs, and before long of her tears. Full of respect for the memory of her husband, Madame de Castellane withdrew to a convent to ensure that her youthfulness, now deprived of the protection of her wise husband, did not succumb to any pitfalls; but such prudent reflections do not endure at the age of twenty-two. How many misfortunes nonetheless would this touching woman have avoided if, nurturing these reflections in her breast, she had offered to God the heart she agreed to give to the world. Oh, why is the soul that knows how to love all the objects of creation not inflamed all the more for the Creator himself? How hollow is the former of these emotions, when one has steeped oneself in all the sweetness of the other!

Euphrasie did not care for the tedium of the cloister: keenly pressed to return to a court so worthy of her presence, she listened to its treacherous insinuations and soon rushed to her own downfall, believing she was finding happiness.

How many new suitors appeared when they heard Euphrasie was ready to relinquish the garb of mourning for the roses that matrimony offered her from every quarter!

Madame de Castellane, who had been seen before only as a pretty child, soon merited the title of the most beautiful woman of the age. She was tall, a paragon of beauty, with eyes that could have been Cupid's own, a voice of such dulcet tones, a warm demeanour so indelibly imprinted on all her features, such innocent and natural charms, a mind so fair and gentle! . . . But amidst all this, a romantic quality which seemed to prove that, while Nature had lavished her with all that one needs to be adored, she had at the same time combined these gifts with all that might prepare her for misfortune— a quirk on her part, necessary no doubt, but one which seems to tell us we were created by that celestial power to feel the joy of love even as he imbued us with all that might make us repent of it.

Of all the new suitors who offered themselves to the beautiful Euphrasie, the Marquis de Gange, in possession of a large estate in Languedoc and twenty-four years of age at the time, was the one who succeeded in dispelling from Madame de Castellane's heart the memory of a first husband she had never looked upon, if truth be told, as anyone other than a mentor.

If Madame de Castellane was rightly considered the most beautiful woman in France, Monsieur de Gange equally merited his reputation as one of the most handsome men at court. Born in Avignon, but brought at a very young age to that court, it was there he met Madame de Castellane; the birthplace they shared, and the proximity of their estates, soon led Alphonse de Gange to present both these and his most violent passion as grounds for Euphrasie to choose him. Alphonse appears before her, and is heard; Euphrasie observes all the proprieties—they have such force when love is behind them! Her hand becomes the reward for the Marquis's love, and the wedding is held.

Good heavens! Why did the furies add their torch to the others that were lit at this tender alliance? And why were serpents spied sullying with their venom the myrtle branches that doves had placed upon the heads of these wretches!

But let us not get ahead of ourselves, for softer shades may lighten those with which this fateful story begins. Let us only mix more sombre colours when the truth obliges us.

The newlyweds spent another two years in Paris, amidst the tumult and pleasures of the court and the city. But two hearts in unison soon weary of anything that seems to thwart their mutual desire to flee all that might separate them even for a moment; and, in the euphoria of their passion, they decided to seek refuge in their country estates, and to entrust the little boy Euphrasie had recently had to the care of her mother, who took him back to Avignon to raise him under her watchful eye.

'O my friend!' said the Marquise to her husband after the departure of their child, as they too were preparing to leave. 'O my dear Alphonse. Love is never better than in the country: everything belongs to us, everything is there for us, in those flowery bowers that nature seems to embellish for love alone. There,' she repeated as she held her charming husband in her arms, 'there are no rivals to fear; you need never worry about me, but who can promise that more alluring women in Paris might not end up stealing your heart from me? . . . This heart that is my only possession, Alphonse . . . Alphonse, if I saw it possessed by another I would have my life taken there and then, and seeing it, seeing this heart with your image so clearly engraved on it, what remorse you would feel for not having entrusted me with yours!

You know, dear Alphonse, you know I love only you in this world; still a child, in Castellane's arms, I could not nurture within myself those sentiments of violent passion that you alone have set ablaze in my soul. So no jealousy on that score: mistress of my fate, I saw, I dare say, all the suitors worthy of love that the court had to offer, and of them all only Alphonse de Gange seemed so to me. So love me, dear husband, love your Euphrasie just as she adores you; let your every moment be hers just as all her vows are yours; let the two of us share the same soul: your love, nurtured by mine, will be imbued with all its strength, and you will no longer be able to help but love Euphrasie, just as Euphrasie loves her Alphonse.'

'O my tender, exquisite friend!' replied the Marquis de Gange. 'There is such delicacy in all you say! How could I fail to adore the one who thinks this way? Oh, yes! Let us have just one soul—that will be enough to survive, since we can only do so through each other.'

'Well then—let us go, dear husband, let us leave this dangerous world of seduction and corruption: it is not where love is endlessly discussed that I want to be, it is where it can best be felt. Your fore-fathers' castle seems perfect to me for what we have in mind! There, everything will remind me of all that belongs to you. When I give you heirs I shall gaze on your ancestors and address the Almighty: "Holy Spirit," I shall solemnly tell him, "Alphonse's heart is the sanctuary of the virtues his illustrious forefathers bequeathed him—let them be instilled in his children's souls by the blazing fire within my own."'

They left: the young couple had chosen the ancient and magnificent castle of Gange as their home. The seat of this noble family is situated near the town of Gange, seven leagues from Montpellier, on the banks of the river Aude.* A contented and peaceful town, where the industri-ous inhabitant, from the income gained by his hands, lives in the com-fort that craftsmanship treasures over those effortlessly accumulated riches with which the citizen of the city consumes the fruits of indus-try, destroying them root and branch as he devours them.

Our travellers had spent the previous night in Montpellier, and had left this town at daybreak to arrive in good time at their destin-ation. They were barely halfway when one of the wheels of the coach broke, and Madame de Gange injured her right shoulder[1] as she fell. The Marquis was worried beyond measure. His fear that the remaining

---

[1] Our readers are asked not to forget this detail, as strange as it is true.

distance would exhaust Euphrasie meant he wished to go no further, but what to do in a village where no one had come to their aid? Euphrasie assured him that it was nothing, and, as soon as the damage to the coach had been repaired, they set off again.

'O my friend!' said the sensitive Euphrasie, shedding a few involuntary tears. 'Why must we have an accident just as we are approaching your castle? . . . Forgive your fragile friend, but this sense of foreboding has startled me despite myself! . . . Before I met you I could almost have loved misfortune, but it frightens me when it is shared with you.'

'Dear wife,' Alphonse scolded, 'banish these silly worries: misfortune shall never darken your days as long as you have me to protect you.'

'Alphonse,' the Marquise exclaimed in distress, 'could there ever be a moment when I have you no longer?'

'Only at the end of my days . . . and are we not the same age?'

'Oh, yes! Yes, we shall always live together, and only death shall separate us.'

At last our travellers arrive in Gange; they cross the town; all the Marquis's vassals are under arms; the customary gifts are offered. They reach the foot of the castle's towers; the Marquise looks them up and down; she becomes flustered.

'There is something about these walls that strikes fear in me, my friend,' she said to her husband.

'It was my ancestors' taste—we can knock them down if you wish.'

'Oh, no! No, let us respect everything that reminds us of the virtues of those who built them; the sweet and charming ways of the court we have just left will temper the somewhat sombre thoughts these ancient stones inspire—and will you not always bring beauty to the places that bear witness to our joy?'

The Marquis was expected at the castle—everything was arranged for his arrival. The old and loyal servants of the Comte de Gange, his father, offered their arms to the young couple, and lavished them with those guileless compliments that can only come from the heart. They all recognized, they said, the majestic and dearly loved features of their old master in their young lord's brow, and these kind words pleased the Marquise.

'Yes, my children,' she told them, 'he will resemble the master you cherished: you will love the son as you loved the father—and I shall vouch for his virtues . . .'

Tears streamed down the furrowed cheeks of these honest folk, and they ushered their young master and mistress in triumph through the vast halls where they had so loyally served the one who had preceded Alphonse.

Sweet Euphrasie received another little fright when she heard the echoing footsteps of people walking beneath those ancient vaults, and when she saw those thick doors rolling and creaking on their half-rusted hinges. Overwrought, weary from the road, her bruises aching, once the local physician had assured her she would suffer no ill effects, the Marquise took to bed in makeshift quarters as her own bedroom was not quite ready; and for the first time since her wedding night, she asked her husband to let her sleep alone.

It is in man's nature (this is an eternal truth) to attach more importance than he should perhaps to dreams and premonitions. This weakness comes from the wretched state in which Nature ensures we are all born, even if some have a little more or less than others. It feels as if these secret revelations come to us from a purer source than the ordinary events in life; and the inclination for religion, which the passions diminish but never entirely expunge, inevitably leads us to the conclusion that, as all that is supernatural comes from God, we are, despite ourselves, predisposed to this form of superstition which philosophy condemns and which misfortune tearfully adopts. But actually, why would it be so ridiculous to believe that Nature, which tells us of our needs, which consoles us so tenderly for our misfortunes, which gives us such courage to bear them, might not also have a voice that makes us dread their approach? What! Could she who is always acting within us, she who tells us so clearly all that might save or harm us, not also warn us of all that might tend to our destruction, or that might affect it? I am well aware these arguments will be dismissed as absurd paradoxes, but I know equally well that no one will ever manage to prove that. Now, when a theory is presented and one responds with a joke rather than a refutation, one can, I think, by listening only to reason mock the joker in turn. How many unbelievers would Voltaire have created had he reasoned rather than laughed! And if his sallies are now seen as triumphs, it is because the truth that convinces a reasonable man only makes fools laugh. Whatever the case may be, there is something religious about the opinion we are sharing here, so it should please sensitive souls—and we shall hold true to it until it is proven to be sophistry.

And our touching heroine believed all too firmly in premonitions as she drenched in tears the bed where she slept that first night. She believed in them indeed when, woken suddenly in the middle of that cruel night, she was heard to scream out: *O my husband! Save me from these scoundrels!*

Did these dreadful words come from a dream or a premonition? We do not know, but they were heard nonetheless, and this is how these solemnly held but opposing views of Nature become confused, but where her presence is unmistakable even in our confusion.

Who would be the one to scatter thorns in the blessed path that should have lain ahead of Euphrasie? With her wealth, distinction, beauty, birth . . . who could be so vicious as to make Euphrasie stumble on her dazzling course through life? Who would make the roses wither? Who could be so barbarous as to weigh down with the yoke of misfortune someone who sought only to alleviate the woes of others, and who so graciously counted sensing misfortune—either to relieve or prevent it—among her most exquisite pleasures? Who could so dispel life's illusions in the beautiful Marquise's loving soul? . . . Oh, let us be in no hurry to find out: it is so cruel to have to portray crime; the hues a faithful historian must use to shade it are so dark and so dismal that, rather than expose it, there are often times one would rather leave it to be gleaned or traced from the facts of the case than the dreadful colours with which one is obliged to paint it.

The Marquise was a little calmer in the morning. As one can well imagine, Alphonse visited her quarters as soon as he had been granted permission.

'O my dear Euphrasie!' he exclaimed as he kissed her. 'So who was it that left you so distracted yesterday evening? Why did your tears fall beneath your first footsteps in this castle? Is there something here that upsets you? Do not worry, dear Euphrasie, we shall entertain family, and friends; I have two brothers detained by their duties for a little while longer perhaps, but who will hurry back to meet you. Both are young and charming, both will endeavour to please you, and we shall in time make this seclusion cheerier: neighbours and friends will also come; and if all this is not enough for you, Montpellier and Avignon are not far from here—we shall seek there the pleasures you cannot find here.'

'My dear Alphonse,' replied the Marquise, 'is this home not of my choosing? Are the reasons that led me to settle upon it erased from your memory? You know, dear husband, I concluded my happiness could only exist in a place of solitude where I could have you to myself. Why do you accuse me so unjustly of having changed so soon?'

'But your fretfulness, your unhappiness . . .'

'Evaporate as soon as I see you again . . . so that I no longer even remember what caused them. And how could I remember it? It is pure fancy, Alphonse, I assure you: these are notions that flitter above us . . . notions nigh on impossible to glimpse, let alone grasp, like those will-o'-the-wisps we shall never comprehend. Come, my friend, you can see I am calm—let us explore your castle. I am dying to discover every nook and cranny; let us visit the gardens, the avenues—I want to see it all. Say we shall have a late lunch: the exercise will give us an appetite.'

As soon as the Marquise was ready and breakfast had been taken, husband and wife, followed by some of their vassals, set off on their tour as agreed.

It is worth noting here that for the last eighteen months, in anticipation of his wife's arrival in Languedoc, the Marquis had prepared all that we shall now attempt to describe.

First, they entered the castle's great gallery, which was quite some way from the bedroom where, as we said before, the Marquise had slept that first night while her own was still being readied.

The portraits of the Marquis's family that modestly decorated its walls left a far deeper impression on a sensitive soul than any made by those extravagant paintings, so admired today, which offer only very drab pleasures for the eye, and none at all for the heart.

'Gentlemen,' said the Marquise to the vassals accompanying them, 'while the faddish man today declaims with foolish pride to those who come to admire him, "look at these paintings—this is the Athenian school, this is Cupid entwining the Graces," and so on, I shall content myself with saying, as I embrace you, "Dear friends, these are my forebears; I know they made your fathers happy, and you will love me because of them."'

This majestic gallery, simply decorated as we have just seen, led at its southern end to the quarters intended for Madame de Gange; the other end led to the castle chapel . . . a mystical sanctuary, simply illuminated by a dome, and one which inspired, when one's gaze strayed to the room opposite, the consoling thought that the Holy Spirit whom mortals came to worship could not be closer to his most beautiful creation. Few ornaments, few relics, just the sacred effigy of this great God who sacrificed himself to save mankind, elevated between four silver candelabra interspersed with vases of flowers, and with the image of his mother above him. And how had Alphonse set about rekindling the worship of that saintly woman in the souls of those attending the Holy Sacrament? He had Euphrasie's portrait sent from Paris, and it was this portrait, in the guise of mother of the poor, that they came to adore in the belief that they were looking at a deity.

When the devout Madame de Gange noticed this subtle deception, her sweet and timorous soul reproached her husband a little.

'O my dear wife,' said Alphonse, holding her close, 'I needed the paragon of all virtues—so who else would you have me paint? And is Mary not one of your given names, just as that saintly woman is one of your idols?'

At the other end of the gallery, Madame de Gange's quarters, though simply decorated, were nonetheless the most opulent of the house. Furnishings of green and gold silk, the work and tribute of the good villagers of Gange, were draped over those antique stones laid there almost eight centuries before. A portrait of Alphonse had been left nonchalantly on a table there.

'Oh!' exclaimed the Marquise, seizing it with emotion and placing it on her bedside table. 'As you are putting my portrait in the holiest part of your home, let me adorn the sweet temple of our nuptials with yours.'

Some closets made these quarters as comfortable as one could imagine. One of them opened onto the stairwell of a tower where the archives were kept, and the rest of the house, one of the grandest of the province, was in keeping with that Gothic style of architecture and design so treasured by those sombre, melancholic souls—those for whom reminders of the past offer far more genuine pleasures than our frivolous modern monuments, where all one sees is the superfluous instead of the necessary, the flimsy instead of the solid, and the vulgar instead of the tasteful.

It was the start of autumn . . . of that romantic season, more stirring than the spring: in the latter it seems that Nature is only concerned with herself—a coquette who wants to please, whereas in the former she is speaking to us—a mother saying her goodbyes to her children, leaving them with the sweetest of gifts. The poignant manner in which she lays herself bare for us to miss her all the more; those gifts with which she enjoins us to fill our fruit cellars and stores, while we wait for her to grant us new favours; everything, from the paling leaves that warn us of the fate that awaits us, to those marigolds and poppies that take the place of roses and lilies of the valley—everything about her, as I say, is touching, everything is a reflection of life, and everything she does offers a lesson to mankind.

Immense grounds surrounded the castle; long paths lined with lime, mulberry, and medlar trees, as well as green oaks, split this park of two hundred acres into four small forests, where various animals were left to breed for the pleasures of the hunt.

One of these great copses seemed nonetheless to lead somewhere more interesting: an almost impenetrable labyrinth was laid out with such artistry that it seemed impossible to find a way out once one had entered. The hedgerows that cast their shade over the paths were of lilac, hawthorn, and honeysuckle, of roses and a thousand other shrubs which in the spring would shelter the feathered creatures whose sweet and melodic song inspire those religious reveries in which man gives himself entirely to God, and sees in the eternal miracles that surround him such sweet cause for his worship.

When, after several wrong turns and missteps, one finally arrives at the heart of this labyrinth, a sarcophagus of black marble presents itself.

'This shall be our final resting place,' said Alphonse to his Euphrasie. 'Here, my loyal and dear friend, wrapped in each other's arms, the centuries will roll by overhead without reaching us or taking us with them . . . Does the idea trouble you, Euphrasie?'

'Oh, no! No, my dear Alphonse, for it makes the bond between us eternal, and life's thorny paths will be closed to us, forever leaving only those where God awaits us. But what if the heavens were to thwart such comforting plans? . . . O my friend! How can we know their will? That of men is like a leaf in the wind, and the forces of destruction that will bring us here sooner or later, might they not also destroy any pact we dare make without their accord?'

And husband and wife continued to examine the monument.

The design of this mausoleum was as simple as it was majestic: on a small, granite obelisk crowning its headstone could be read in bronze letters, *Man's eternal rest*. The spectre of Death was prising apart the stone that Cupid and Hymen* appeared to be holding in place, and on that stone one could read, *Eternity, you unfold forever, and it is in God that I understand you.*

Cypresses and weeping willows, veiling the tomb with shade, lent it even greater solemnity. It was as if the swaying of their branches emulated the groans of those who might one day weep at this tomb.

They headed back into the maze, the alleys of which were so perplexing that the path that seemed to lead you out always brought you back to the tomb . . . A consoling image of our pitiful existence, revealing the day when the wickedness of man shall fail against the justice of a God who shall at the last rescue us from his fury!

A few phrases were carved into the bark of the trees. On a sycamore one could read, *Such are the winding paths by which we reach the end of our journey.* A larch offered this: *Nature leads us with ease to our grave, but it is for God alone to deliver us from there one day.*

'O my friend!' said Euphrasie. 'How true these phrases are! How I love the soul who uttered them!'

'It is the one over whom you reign, Euphrasie: how could the Almighty's most sublime ideas not fill the soul which bears the imprint of your image!'

'My dear husband,' said the Marquise as they finally left the labyrinth. 'I find myself in a state I find hard to describe: this imposing forest; these copses that embellish it; the deep solitude one feels in these great, sprawling woods; the absence of statues, sculpted by a now idle hand to offer a respite from Nature's endless movement; this season when everything withers away; the orb that seems to hide itself at this very moment to give the landscape an even more solemn air . . . All this fills the imagination with that sense of religious terror which seems to warn us that true happiness exists, alas, only in the warm embrace of the God who created all we see and admire.'

CHAPTER II

SOME of the local nobility, along with the most prominent burghers of the town of Gange, were gathered at the castle to pay tribute to the young couple.

The lady who had won the approval of the whole court had little difficulty in earning the approbation of the province. Everyone admired her beauty, her sweetness, the consummate ease with which she expressed herself, and above all the precious and rare elegance with which she addressed one and all on matters that might interest them or flatter their pride.

The true spirit of sociability is to allow others to shine; and as one can only do so by sacrificing oneself, there are few people in the world who feel capable of making such an effort.

Monsieur de Gange was held to be the most fortunate of men to possess such a wife, and the more this was impressed upon him, the more the young Marquise seemed to attribute the praise lavished upon her to her husband alone.

Madame de Gange, upon learning the reasons that prevented her mother from joining them on their first journey, seemed more sad than surprised.

'As for my brothers-in-law,' she said to those around her, 'one of them—the Abbé—will surely not delay his visit for long. The Chevalier, obliged to remain with his regiment in these troubled times,[1] may make me wait a little longer for the pleasure of his acquaintance.'

Monsieur de Gange asked a few people to remain behind, and they all sat down to eat.

The Marquise, though a little more at ease, could not hide the melancholic impressions her morning walk had made on her. When she was asked questions, she did not say a word; when she was cajoled, she relented; and the first week was spent exchanging visits.

Winter was approaching; a more intimate and less extensive circle gathered with a view to spending these colder months at the castle.

It is not always in the tumult of the city that life's true pleasures are found. The man of the world, occupied solely with his own existence,

---

[1] This refers to the years of Louis XIV's regency.

seeks only to extract every ounce of pleasure he can from his surroundings. He is selfish by necessity: why would he bother to adopt virtues to please others? Has he time to study them? Has he time to practise them? The semblance of them alone is enough; no one would wish him to do any more than this: were he to take it upon himself to demonstrate more virtues than these he would soon be taken for a slow, dull man.

Living in a narrower social circle, and therefore under closer scrutiny, he must do absolutely everything in his power to pass muster. The microscope is trained on him; nothing escapes it; one can see into the heart's most secret recesses this way. It is no longer duplicity, or guile, that is required of him now; it is candour, it is truth, because he will not fool anyone for long. If he dissembles, he is too close at hand for anyone to be satisfied with merely the trappings of virtue; and if there really is none in his soul, others will hasten to distance themselves from someone who, from the very first day, will contaminate the company he keeps, and cause only harm to those who comprise it.

Monsieur and Madame de Gange were thus as careful as could be to surround themselves only with the kind of people who suited them; and, for the benefit of our readers, we shall say a few words about each of the individuals they befriended.

Madame de Roquefeuille, who owned an estate on the outskirts of Montpellier, had come to visit the young couple because of her former ties to the Marquis's father. She was around fifty years of age, with a sweet and pleasant temperament, and perfectly embodied the spirit of the old court, where she had spent her youth. Mademoiselle Ambroisine de Roquefeuille, her daughter, accompanied her. Eighteen years of age, a pretty face, far more innocence and naïveté than wit, but with all the qualities that make for pleasant company.

The Comte de Villefranche, around twenty-three years of age, was a friend of the Chevalier de Gange, in whose regiment he served; he had come to give the Marquis news of his brother, and had in return been invited to spend the winter at the castle. The Comte, a great admirer of fair ladies, was far from refusing an offer that would bring him the company of his friend's delightful sister-in-law. Villefranche had a handsome countenance, but a gentleness, a decency, that did not always drive him to the fore when there were others keener to make their mark.

An honourable Recollect monk, invested with all the integrity of his order, and a former chaplain to the family, was invited, because of his excellent qualities, to share the sorrows and pleasures of life at the castle; and he was indeed worthy of this in every respect.

Father Eusèbe, so far from sharing the vices of his fellow monks, so close to the Gospel's sublime virtues, an educated man, a good counsellor, an eloquent preacher, deserved, as we have just said, to be welcomed into the most distinguished company. He was almost sixty years of age, with noble features that perfectly captured the serenity of his soul: he had never thought nor said ill of anyone, had almost always made light of the faults people attributed to others, had never in all his days caused a tear to fall but had wiped away a good many, a friend to honest pleasures, in which he willingly partook, he reconciled all those who quarrelled, consoled all those who suffered, with nothing to his name other than his heart, which he called the property of the poor; without fervour, but with a pure faith; worshipping his faith because he found it beautiful, detesting all the abuses it had inspired among men who doubtless understood it very little as they practised it so poorly—men whose blindness he blamed for depravities inseparable from humanity but far removed from Holy God, who wants only our virtues.

It goes without saying that with such a temperament, Eusèbe was very precious to his hosts; this is what made him such a sincere friend to all decent people, and an enlightened guide to the virtuous Euphrasie.

Such men are rare in the world; one has to seek them out, cherish them when one finds them, and above all not slander religion because not all its ministers are made the same way. Such an injustice would be akin to condemning all books to be burnt simply because a third of those we possess are not worth opening.

If religion is the most respectable of constraints, its ministers must be the most respected of men, and any flaws they may have should be forgiven by those who honour the same God these men serve.

Victor was an old valet of the household whom we would not mention but for his longstanding loyalty to his masters, and for the role we shall perhaps see him play in what follows.

Aside from the principal characters of this lamentable tale, who will emerge all too clearly as we describe this tale of misfortune in all its detail, these are the players who shall take to the stage for now.

May our readers, a little reassured by the virtues we have allowed them to glimpse, follow us now with a little less trepidation into the particulars of the sinister events we must unveil!

Everyone had just gathered in the large drawing room, which was lit by a chandelier; Monsieur and Madame de Gange, Madame de Roquefeuille, and the Comte de Villefranche were all playing a game of omber.* Father Eusèbe, standing by the room's ancient hearth, was explaining a point of doctrine to Mademoiselle de Roquefeuille. Six o'clock sounded in the castle keep when a clamour outside signalled the arrival of a new guest. The great doors roll noisily on their heavy hinges; Victor announces Monsieur l'Abbé de Gange, who had yet to visit his brother's home.

'What a surprise!' the Marquis exclaimed, gripping the Abbé in his arms. 'At last, my dear Théodore, so you have remembered you have a brother who has never stopped loving you?'

'Could you think me capable of forgetting you?' replied the young cleric, aged twenty-two, who was not yet bound to take holy orders, and whose demeanour, though quite handsome, seemed more destined for the worship of Mars than that of the altar. 'Oh no, my dear Alphonse, I could not forget a brother such as you, and even less so the duty I am under to present my compliments to a sister. Having never had the honour of meeting her, my delay is all the more culpable, and I would be unworthy of forgiveness were it not for the various affairs which have kept me in Avignon for the last three years, far from all that I hold most dear . . .'

And these words were no sooner spoken than Théodore's eyes met, with as much agitation as astonishment, those of his charming sister-in-law.

'I had a portrait of Madame,' the Abbé continued, casting an ardent gaze once again upon Euphrasie, 'a portrait, dear Alphonse, which you kindly sent to Paris soon after your marriage; but what a difference, and what censure its artist deserves! O my brother, you did not guide his brushstrokes.' And Théodore, having embarrassed his sister-in-law, begged everyone to be seated.

At first they discussed the latest news. The restoration of Charles II in England, his return to the throne of his ancestors, the rise to power of Mazarin, whom the Courts of Justice stooped so low as to harangue on his return to Paris, and various other less interesting events, the talk of the court and the town at the time, were the subject of conversation until it was time for supper.

The Marquis seated his brother between Mademoiselle de Roquefeuille and Madame de Gange with great pleasure, and the most genuine conviviality seemed to reign over the meal.

May we be permitted to take advantage of this moment to offer a rough sketch of this newly arrived character.

Tradition, and some matters of inheritance, had led Théodore to adopt the attire of a vocation that was anything but close to his heart.* The Abbé was simply waiting for an opportunity to throw off his habit, and although his share of the estate was modest, as the laws of the province gave all to the eldest, his brother's generosity in this regard nonetheless allowed him to aspire to a favourable match. But this vocation, among the most honourable and valuable to society, did not suit someone as depraved as young Théodore. The man who desires women only to deceive them, who loves them only to possess them, who takes them only to betray them, and who scorns them when they no longer please him . . . the man for whom nothing is sacred when it comes to seducing them, and who triumphs only in order to disgrace them—will such a man, I say, ever feel the happiness of finding a virtuous woman, someone who could repair the disorder of his desires, and replace that shameful frivolity with the sweetness of those ties that bind when woven by marriage? That would doubtless be impossible, and with this sense of certainty we must admit that, without ever finding happiness himself, the Abbé de Gange would make many women wretched. May the heavens at least preserve from such a fate she who is so closely related to him! We can only hope, but let us not deceive ourselves, or we shall be disillusioned all too soon.

For several years, a certain Abbé Perret had been at the castle; as vicar of the parish he had gained the trust of the Marquis de Gange's father, who had appointed him to administer the castle and serve there as concierge. This man, around forty-five years of age, had spent a good deal of time with the young Théodore in the past, and had inspired the same sentiments in the latter as he had in the late Comte—with the difference, however, that vice was the basis of this alliance. A confidant of the young man's depravities, the Abbé Perret—who aided and abetted them—had acquired some dominion over Théodore's mind that made their association all the more dangerous; and, on this occasion, as the two of them wished to confer, Théodore gave a sign as they rose from the table; Perret took candles to light his protector's quarters, and they closed the door behind them.

'My friend,' said Théodore to his confidant, as soon as they were alone, 'tell me if you imagine there exists in the world a woman more accomplished than my brother's wife? The fate that might perhaps have given me this woman, had I been the eldest, fills me with deep regret that I did not precede Alphonse's arrival in this world by a few years . . . What a difference in fortune! Although, my dear Perret, it is far from certain that the happiness women promise us is to be found in marriage, and I wonder if one is not better off involving oneself with three or four rather than agreeing terms with one alone.'

'Certainly, Monsieur l'Abbé, that would be preferable,' said Perret, 'but these matters are settled, and we cannot change them.'

'No, but unsettle them—that I can do.'

'Oh, you won't do that! Monsieur your brother is so kind! He loves his wife in such good faith!'

'And you believe he is loved in return?'

'Very much so: they are never apart. Their most heavenly moments are those they spend together. If Madame desires something, Monsieur provides it that very instant. Such tender care, such eager solicitude! . . . Regardless, Monsieur l'Abbé, if you imagine my assistance can be useful to you, I am ready for battle—you can count on Perret's zeal.'

'My friend,' Théodore replied, 'I believe such a conquest will be difficult; Ambroisine de Roquefeuille, whom I was next to at supper, offsets the impression made by Madame de Gange a little, but there it would be a question of marriage, and you know that I have no interest in those shackles. Far better to be by Euphrasie's side—all I have to do is meddle and muddle, and that tallies perfectly with the dose of perversity with which it pleased Nature to imbue my constitution. And anyway, do you not think—as I do—that although she is a little older, Euphrasie is a hundred times more alluring than little Ambroisine? I prefer women who fire the imagination to those who only stir the senses.'

'Yes, but a sister-in-law!'

'My friend, I understand all that: a brother I esteem and admire, who, although my elder, treated me so favourably in sharing our inheritance; there is gratitude to overcome, conjugal bonds to break . . . an honourable woman to seduce . . . All this holds me back, I confess; but you do not realize, dear Perret, how easily such impediments could be swept away by the light shining in Euphrasie's eyes—a light like the sun melting the Caucasus's snowy wastes. Do you know that when she was at court, she briefly swayed the King from his violent passion for the beautiful Mancini,* Cardinal Mazarin's niece?'

'Yes, Monsieur, I know all that, and it does not surprise me: Euphrasie is worthy of a king, and should you so desire it, Monsieur, you would prevail over kings.'

'No, no, I shall contain myself, I shall do all I can to be virtuous, even if it means leaving this house. But if my efforts betray me . . . if love prevails, you will acknowledge that it will not be my fault: it is stronger than reason; and, weak as we wretched creatures are, should we not yield to the implacable forces that drive us like reeds in a squall?'*

Perret, whom the Abbé showered with favours and gifts, decided he had too much to gain from these perverse arguments to risk challenging them; he kept quiet, and they both retired for the night.

For the next two weeks, all that the castle and its neighbours had to offer as entertainment was lavished on the Abbé de Gange to distract him from the tedium of country life. There were meals, balls, hunting parties in the grounds, walks along the banks of the Aude—no effort was spared. But nothing could becalm the dangerous impressions Euphrasie was making on Théodore; and, because the young Abbé wished to stifle his passion it burned only more brightly, and he soon sensed the impossibility of resisting the hand that was plunging him into the abyss. Were his efforts genuine? Are we not capable of anything, if we want it enough? He who blames his ill-fated star as he succumbs is but a weakling lacking the courage to take his destiny into his own hands.

'O my friend,' Euphrasie said one day to her husband, when a little tranquillity had succeeded the excitement of the various entertainments. 'Perhaps I am mistaken, but I discern a marked difference between your brother and you. I see in him none of that kindness, that gentleness that is such a part of you! I recognize some virtues in him, but they do not blossom in his soul like those that fill your own; and whereas to see you is to love you, it seems to me he needs to strive hard even to hope to be loved.'

'I put down everything you say to your tenderness for me, Euphrasie; but the Abbé is kind, he is full of wit, and the more you know him the more you will love him.'

'O my friend! Are his ties to you not reason enough for me to grow attached to him? But I still say he is not the man you are.'

'Perhaps you will like the Chevalier better,' said Alphonse. 'His duties keep him in Nice, where his garrison is stationed; but he will return, and I hope that soon, when all four of us are here, we shall enjoy some happy years together.'

'Oh, if my company is enough for you, yours is all I need to be content: it is you alone who will make me happy, and never those with whom you surround yourself.'

At that moment Madame de Roquefeuille interrupted the conversation to see if anyone was interested in joining her to hear Father Eusèbe preach to the Gange parish, as she had not heard him before. The whole castle attended. Eusèbe's theme was divine love. What passion this worthy priest put into his words! How he filled the soul with all that might inspire God's creations with love for their Creator! And how he spurred every heart to the worship of the Holy Father to whom we owe everything! He showed man the gratitude he owes God, who allows him to enjoy the wonders of Creation in all its splendour. He described these without exalting them; he simply showed them, and everyone adored them. As for the unbeliever, he denied his very existence.

'He does not feel then, if he does not believe; he is blind then, if he does not recognize his God. Feeling and love must be one and the same in a sensitive soul,' Eusèbe exclaimed. 'O ungrateful hearts! Can you deny the existence of the God I reveal to you when his hand is all that protects you from the misfortunes into which your stubbornness plunges you? To whom do you owe the fact that you have not been crushed by those your principles corrupt? He alone—and you deny him? He holds a helping hand out to you, and you reject it! I shall not speak to you of his anger . . . You merit it too much for me to frighten you with it: no, I only wish to remind you of his kindness. Hasten to hear the voice of his clemency, and his arms shall always be open to you.'

There are many Protestants in Gange; Eusèbe's reputation was such that many had come to listen to him. They were just as moved as the Catholics: the love of God belongs to all times, all places, all religions; it is the common ground that brings all men together, because every human being with the faculty of reason must necessarily worship and pay grateful tribute to he who gave him life. All virtues follow from the sincere acceptance of this doctrine, which prepares the soul for the sensibility that is home to them all. The atheist's heart alone is empty, and, as it cannot embrace any virtue, it thus naturally opens itself up to vices blind to he who would avenge them.

The only topic of conversation over dinner was the power of Eusèbe's sermon; and it was discussed all the more freely as the worthy Recollect, dining at the curate's house, was not there to take exception to the praise being heaped on him.

The Abbé de Gange alone was rather lukewarm on the subject.

'Some things are so natural and so simple,' he said, 'that I am always amazed when they are made into the theme of a sermon. To preach the existence of God is to suppose there are people who do not believe in him; and I do not believe any such person exists.'

'I do not share your opinion,' said Madame de Roquefeuille. 'Few say so openly, I know, but I believe there are many, and I shall always include amongst them those who are driven by their passions. If they believed in God, would they indulge in anything that offended him?'

'And are there not laws,' said the Abbé, 'that restrain those who are not held back by the fear of God?'

'They are not enough,' replied Madame de Roquefeuille. 'It is easy to evade them! There are so many secret crimes beyond their reach, and a powerful man can defy them with such audacity! What prevents the weak from quaking at the power of the strong, if it is not the consolation that the persecutor who hounds him will, sooner or later, be avenged by a just God? What does the pauper say, when he is stripped bare? What does the wretch say, when he is crushed? "Ah!" one and the other exclaim, shedding tears that the hand of hope swiftly wipes away. "He will be judged as I am, the man who oppresses me; we shall both appear before Almighty God to be judged, and there I shall be avenged." Take not from the wretch this consolation at least. Alas! It is the only one left him—how barbarous it would be to snatch it from him!'

Euphrasie's beautiful eyes, in harmony with the goodness of her heart, approved of Madame de Roquefeuille's every word; but Théodore, distracted, sought to steer the conversation onto less solemn ground; he succeeded, and everyone rose from the table.

These, more or less, were the discussions, the entertainments, the pastimes of the castle of Gange as the chill of winter gave way to the mildness of spring. The state of Théodore's heart was still the same, and he had finally decided to tear himself away from a home that was far too dangerous for him when a conversation with the treacherous Perret revived in him the hope of a conquest that had seemed improbable.

'My friend,' he said to his dangerous confidant, 'now winter is over and I am still no further advanced: marigolds* have given way to roses; everything revives before our eyes, but my heart alone, deprived of sustenance, baulks at this universal regeneration. The same torments, the same anxieties, the same desires, the same helplessness; and why is everything within me dead when everything is reborn in Nature? The more I see Euphrasie, the more I adore her, and the less I dare express what she makes me feel with such intensity. What I am experiencing is very curious, my friend: I do not have the strength to tell her of my love, but I have more than enough to force her to share it . . . Is it confusion? Is it perversity? Tell me that, my dear Perret.'

'My word, Monsieur l'Abbé,' he replied. 'I am not learned enough to explain such a mystery to you. I can well understand that you find the air of modesty and virtue that reigns over Euphrasie a little intimidating; but in that case, rather than shying away from this feeling, it seems to me you should grasp it; and believe me, Monsieur, as you feel all its force, forge ahead—don't hold back.'

'Do you know what I have in mind?'

'No, but whatever it is, be in no doubt that you have in me a man as loyal as he is dependable.'

'I am counting on it.'

'Then explain yourself, Monsieur l'Abbé.'

'We need to rouse these two souls numbed by contentment; when they are less happy, they will both become more pliable; and the jealousy I mean to provoke, by turning the husband bitter or cold, will without fail deliver me the wife.'

'I doubt it will succeed, Monsieur. They are both so sure of their feelings!'

'Because they have yet to be tested. If we lay our traps, they will fall into them; and you will see, Perret, where my plans will lead. It will be in my arms that she spills the tears I shall cause her to shed, and you will admire, though I say so myself, the manner in which I shall wipe them away.'

'And your prudence? Your fear of wronging someone you owe gratitude? Your determination to flee rather than succumb?'

'Ah, how can you expect one to think of prudence when one is driven by delirium?'

'Let us act, Monsieur, let us act, and you will see if I lack fervour when it comes to serving you.'

Let us follow this rogue in his machinations: better to show what he does than repeat what he says—the former will be more interesting than the latter.

CHAPTER III

DURING his stay at the castle, the Comte de Villefranche, a charming young officer in every respect, had allied himself with Théodore, whose wit he enjoyed and whose deportment seemed to him better suited to the profession of arms than that of the Church. For his part, Théodore, who had been hatching plans for the Comte for some time, took every opportunity to ingratiate himself with the young man.

'My dear Comte,' the Abbé said to him one day on one of their solitary walks, 'you seem rather idle in this house; I thought you had your eye on Ambroisine—she is certainly alluring enough to deserve some of your attention; and if you do not want her as a wife, you must say she would make a very pretty mistress at least.'

'I would never dare attempt anything on that score with someone as respectable as Mademoiselle de Roquefeuille, and I am not wealthy enough to aspire to her hand in marriage.'

'Have you made any approach?'

'None, and the reason that stopped me even wishing to do so is that I have sensed nothing in Ambroisine that would justify any such approach. When I arrived here, I thought at first that I had caught her eye; but her indifference restored the peace of mind I should never have relinquished; and now here I am, with nothing to do.'

'You are mistaken: someone of your age, and your bearing, has no business languishing like this in an indolence so deathly for a handsome man. If you are not content with Ambroisine, leave her to my brother, whom I have noticed is far from indifferent to her.'

'What? The Marquis?'

'Have you been taken in by his constancy for Euphrasie? . . . How new you are to love, my dear Comte! One marries out of propriety, and makes other arrangements out of necessity. I assure you that Alphonse likes Ambroisine very much; that she has only spurned your advances because she is besotted with my brother; and if you are a bold and valiant cavalier you really owe it to Euphrasie to provide her with some solace.'

'And so you are suggesting your sister-in-law?'

'It is the most appropriate liaison the house can provide for you; and I offer my services . . . Does Euphrasie not appeal to you?'

'I find her delightful; everything you say suits me perfectly, but I would not have dared attempt anything had you not assured me of the Marquis's infidelity.'

'Give it a try, my friend, give it a try—and let me know how you get on.'

And, with the Comte promising to follow Théodore's advice, the latter turned his attention entirely to the second part of his plan.

The Abbé de Gange's treachery was not satisfied with having his sister-in-law do wrong; for him to profit by it, Alphonse would have to do the same in order for Euphrasie, convinced of her husband's infidelity, to throw herself more readily into his arms . . . But was there not a danger she might end up in those of Villefranche, as this young man was being thrust at her? Oh, the Abbé had little fear of this: he was perfectly confident of cooling the ardour of his sister's infidelity in time if necessary, dispensing with Villefranche, and turning everything to his own advantage.

Perret's soul brimmed with unimaginable delight when Théodore confided his plans to him and put him in charge of all the details.

'My word! What a mind you have, Monsieur l'Abbé,' he exclaimed in his enthusiasm. 'You would have ousted Mazarin had you entered politics.'

'A love as rampant as mine overcomes everything, my friend,' Théodore replied. 'Nothing can withstand its violence: like the wild wind of the north, it destroys, it pulverizes everything in its path; and the more barriers one sets against it, the more strength it gains to break or topple them.'

Before setting the cogs in motion for his second plan, the Abbé thought it would be prudent to judge the effects of the first.

'Well then! Where are we?' he asked Villefranche after waiting patiently for a month.

'No more advanced than the first day,' the Comte replied. 'The woman is unassailable—a pillar of virtue.'

'I wager you are going about it all wrong: with a woman of this demeanour, one should aim one's first blows not at her heart but at her pride. Try to persuade her slyly that it is ridiculous to count for nothing in society when one has graces and charms that are made to please; poke fun at marriage vows. Go further: convince her that the husband she treasures is the first to break his vows, and that Ambroisine has been aloof towards you only since she confessed to you her love for Alphonse—who, for his part, much prefers her to his wife. Prevail upon her mind, and her heart will soon be ablaze.'

'This plan seems dangerous to me,' said Villefranche, 'for if I fail to convince Euphrasie, she will seek an explanation from Alphonse, and then the anger of both will be directed at me.'

'Yes, were I not skilled in the art of befuddling the senses; but you shall see what I am willing to do to serve you, and to convince the pair of them—Euphrasie, that her husband is unfaithful to her, and Alphonse, that you possess his wife's heart.'

'So, let us take to the field—time to do battle; I'm all for it—I find duels most entertaining. I shall slay the husband, no doubt, but that will not gain me an inch of ground on the wife.'

'Not another word, my friend, not another word—you are miles from the truth: for fear of a scandal that would ruin his wife, my brother will not fight, you can be very sure of that. He will leave the castle, go to Avignon on important business, and we shall be masters of the field of battle.'

'My dear Abbé,' said Villefranche, 'circumstances could not possibly destroy all the plans your imagination hatches: so I shall try— I have every incentive, for I confess I love your sister-in-law immeasurably. But if I fail I shall renounce it all. I would rather sacrifice my love than cause the ruin of the woman who inspires it.'

A few more months passed without this first plot yielding any fruit for the Abbé; and so, his patience wearing thin, he put the second into action.

It was now the height of summer. The freshness of the evening had prompted a long walk in the grounds, during which everyone split into smaller groups. By means of the Abbé's intervention, the Marquis found himself, without any ulterior motive, *tête-à-tête* with Mademoiselle de Roquefeuille, while Théodore was with Euphrasie; but the Abbé had arranged matters so well that the two couples were certain to meet at the end of the parallel paths they had taken.

'It seems to me,' said Théodore to his sister-in-law, 'that in the course of this walk, one and all have come to the arrangement that suits them.'

'How do you mean?' Euphrasie asked.

'Oh, yes: the virtuous Madame de Roquefeuille is preaching with Father Eusèbe, and her daughter is with your husband. As for me, I am far from complaining: where else would I rather be than with my delightful sister?'

'I think the first *tête-à-tête* is an excellent match; but I hope you are joking in suggesting some mystery to the second.'

'O most noble and honourable of women!' exclaimed the Abbé. 'What a fortunate disposition the heavens have granted you! People are right to say that those who are incapable of evil themselves cannot conceive of it in others; but as it is very clear that there is a measure of evil in the world, and that this evil must absolutely be committed, so the heavens have decreed for all eternity that some must take their share of the iniquity that looms over all our heads. Your husband bears his share today in the form of his enduring infidelity; it is not chance, believe me, that brings him *tête-à-tête* with Ambroisine. But if you want me to serve you, if you want me to persuade you, swear to me the utmost secrecy, or I shall leave you in the dreadful position of suspecting everything, but understanding nothing.'

'O my brother!' said Euphrasie with the most violent emotion. 'What arms are you wielding to tear my heart apart so? Do you not know how vulnerable it is? Do you not know how dear Alphonse is to me, and that I would rather lose my life a thousand times over than his heart?'

'It is because I know all this, my dear, sweet sister, that I do not want you to turn a blind eye to it any longer. Your husband adores Ambroisine, and he has never felt for you the passion that burns within him for that young woman. I fear that all this may lead him further than one might imagine, so perhaps you should act swiftly . . .'

But at this moment the wretched Marquise's strength failed her . . . She falls to the ground by a tree; her eyes close.

'That's how I want her,' said Théodore wickedly, as he ran to fetch Villefranche, who was waiting for him at a turn in the path. 'Fly to the Marquise,' he told him. 'She has fainted at the foot of that tree; take care of her; seize the moment; she is all yours if that is what you want.'

And, as Villefranche runs to her, Théodore crosses over to the other path where his brother is with Ambroisine.

'We should head over to where your wife is, my brother,' he said to Alphonse. 'I heard some screams over there; I do not know who is with her, nor why she seems to be calling for help, but we should most certainly all go to her.'

'O heavens! What are you saying?' the Marquis exclaimed. 'I thought my wife was with you.'

'Indeed I was, and I had just left her for a few minutes when, on my return, I saw her lying still at the foot of an oak. I looked around for help, and, seeing Villefranche, sent him to her side, and I have come to you to do the same . . .'

And they flew to her as they spoke. At last they reach the Marquise, who is unconscious in Villefranche's arms.

'Hurry, Alphonse,' he cries out. 'I do not know what has put your wife in this state, but I am having a terrible time rousing her.'

Ambroisine unlaces Euphrasie's bodice, and rubs her temple and lips with smelling salts. Euphrasie opens her eyes, and, the moment she sees her husband lending a hand to the woman she believes to be her rival, tears stream down her cheeks.

'What is the matter, dear friend?' Alphonse asks as he covers her with kisses. 'And what caused this alarm and this sorrow?'

'It is nothing, my friend, it is nothing,' says Euphrasie, rising to her feet with some difficulty. 'Let us return to the castle; a little peace and quiet will soon repair all this.'

This prudent woman even wished to hide all that had just happened from Father Eusèbe, who was approaching with Madame de Roquefeuille. Euphrasie wiped away her tears and the conversation took a more general turn.

'We have just negotiated the labyrinth,' said Madame de Roquefeuille. 'I had heard mention of it, but it is the first time I have stepped foot there.'

'It offers an instructive walk,' said Eusèbe. 'It pleases the eye as it nourishes the soul. How delightful are the ideas that came to us there!'

'They are indeed consoling,' said Euphrasie, in a slightly tremulous voice, 'for they show us the harbour where all our misfortunes shall cease, and life is terribly cruel when one has lost all that once made us cherish it.'

'Such sad reflections are not made for you,' said Villefranche quietly to Euphrasie, 'and life should be free of thorns for one such as yourself.'

'I might have thought so yesterday,' said the Marquise, in the same mysterious tone, 'but the last few hours have disillusioned me.'

'May that never be the case when it comes to my love,' said the Comte ardently.

And the Marquise now looked at him with the greatest surprise:

'I thought I had made it clear to you,' she said, 'how much these words offend me, and I do not know why you bring them up again.'

'What is this air of mystery that Villefranche assumes with my wife?' Alphonse, a few feet away, asked Théodore. 'I never noticed it before!'

'That's because there is nothing to notice,' said the Abbé. 'The Marquise can clear all this up in a word, and I hope that by the time we wake tomorrow we shall be in the dark no longer.'

That evening, as he returned to his quarters, the Abbé found a note from Euphrasie on the fireplace with just these words:

I shall say nothing to my husband until tomorrow, but as he will be taking care of business in Gange all morning, come and finish what you have started; and if you really must drive the dagger into my heart, do it without holding back.

As one can well imagine, the Abbé did not fail to attend this appointment: it was so vital for him to see his ruses succeed that he would stop at nothing to ensure they bore fruit.

However, before meeting with the Marquise, he could not avoid some serious reflection upon the manner in which he would conduct himself.

It is a fine moment, he told himself, to declare my feelings. But such rashness may be my ruin. She will reveal all to her husband and, instead of gaining anything, I shall lose everything in an instant. Better, then, to persist in making her culpable with Villefranche: that way I shall firstly rid myself of a rival who, carried away by my encouragement, would end up supplanting me, and secondly, so disgrace the Marquise in the eyes of her husband that he will either abandon or punish her—both results that deliver her into my hands.

This logic was abhorrent, no doubt, but what could one expect of a soul as corrupt as Théodore's?

'Two things seemed very odd to me in the circumstances of our walk yesterday, my dear Abbé,' said the Marquise the moment she was alone with Théodore. 'As for the first of these, the one which affects me the more deeply, this relates to the suspicions you tried to arouse in me regarding the perfectly natural behaviour of my husband with Mademoiselle de Roquefeuille; the second concerns the very peculiar circumstances by which, after fainting in your arms, I nonetheless found myself in those of Villefranche when I opened my eyes. How could you so lightly hand over to a stranger all responsibility for the assistance I had a right to expect from you alone? And how is it that Villefranche took advantage of this on two or three occasions during the rest of the walk to venture certain remarks that I was obliged repeatedly to rebuff? It is for you and you alone, my brother, to shed some light on all of this for me, and I expect this even more out of friendship than the ties which, it seems to me, should bind all our interests together.'

The Marquise, who up to this point had only questioned the Abbé with eyes lowered, now looked up, searching his face in the hope his answers might reveal the mind's construction there.

But the Abbé was too knowing, too sophisticated, to be unaware that a man's facial muscles respond and contort according to the emotions he experiences, and that his eyes and brow are always faithful mirrors of his soul. So he fixed his sister with the same boldness she had shown him, with the difference that while innocence and purity of soul inspired the courage that could be read in the Marquise's eyes, nothing but duplicity, crime, and dissimulation reigned in Théodore's brazen gaze.

'Madame,' replied the Abbé. 'To impose some order on my answers, I shall follow the same you adopted for your questions. Your husband's feelings for Mademoiselle de Roquefeuille astonish you; and as your surprise has turned to incredulity, you compound this now by refusing to face facts . . . Allow me to point out, my dear sister, that the heart's faulty logic is utterly ruinous to that of the mind, and people lose their way each day as much by their blind faith in what they wish to be true as by their obdurate rejection of what they fear to be true. Of all the impulses that prevail over our souls, hope is the most deceptive. Remember the subject of that beautiful painting you so admired in Paris, and which we have on occasion discussed this winter. Hope, as you know, led this man to his death; it shone from a lamp that seemed to expire the moment the spectre enclosed his prey in the tomb. Such is hope in all aspects of life: the offspring of desire, it sustains us for as long as it can; and when the truth reveals the futility of that desire, hope flies, and we are left with our misfortune.'

'This exordium* is sombre indeed, my brother,' said the Marquise.

'My sister, the truth dictates it, and my friendship proffers it to you: believe in my words now. The liaison you fear is all too real; I first noticed it more than four months ago; and neither one nor the other of these two guilty parties succeeded in pulling the wool over my eyes.

The care they took to shield themselves from Madame de Roquefeuille's scrutiny inevitably threw an impenetrable veil over the illegitimacy of their relationship. I confess I cannot comprehend what my brother, a married man, imagines may happen with a woman who is not; and the repercussions of this fateful passion make me shudder! What is beyond doubt is that it is real; and, should you need harder evidence to persuade you, I shall willingly provide it.'

The boldness the Marquise had instilled in her gaze faded by degrees; little by little her head slumped over her chest; her beautiful eyes filled with tears, and her bosom silently heaved with stifled sobs. Her nerves quiver, her limbs tremble: innocence and virtue are easily alarmed; as tender souls never employ artifice themselves, it is so painful for them to imagine it in others that they almost prefer to accept the lie rather than search for the truth.

Euphrasie called on all her strength; she tried to calm herself, but in vain; her sobs suffocated her, and paroxysms of grief made her cry out.

'Alphonse, Alphonse,' she asked, 'what have I done to lose your love and trust? You who loved me so tenderly, you whose only happy moments were those you spent with your Euphrasie . . . Why then do you now condemn her to all the horrors of jealousy, to all the torments of abandonment? Is Ambroisine more beautiful than me, does she love you better, traitor? And you are sacrificing me for her! But you must hate me now, my existence weighs heavily on you; you must wish me dead; and, when the heavens grant you that grace, you will deprive me even of the honour of sharing the tomb that you were once devoted enough to prepare for the two of us. Someone else will take my place; someone else will spend eternity by your side. But if you banish me on this earth, the God who created us for each other will reunite us in his embrace; you will be forced to love me again, when he reveals to you that all my wishes, and my very last breaths, reached out for you even in the midst of your infidelity.'

And Madame de Gange could not stop weeping as she uttered these heartrending words. Her head, half-buried in the handkerchief she drenched in her tears, hid from the fate that tormented her all but a fraction of that exquisite face that despair had robbed of its rosy innocence and modesty.

'Madame,' said the callous Théodore, more concerned with achieving his own ends than calming the dreadful state into which he had plunged his sister. 'It is not your agony that should occupy you now, but finding a way to stop it at its source. You no longer owe your husband any consideration; he has made himself unworthy even of your pity. Thunderous vengeance is what the justice of your cause, and the nobility of your character, demand: the means offers itself quite naturally, and as I elaborate on this I shall answer the second of your questions. The Comte de Villefranche is an honourable man. While we have been at Gange, he has noticed, as I have, your husband's culpable distractions. Ever since, his heart's most ardent desire has been to console you; he told me this in confidence. I shall not hide from you that when I gave my approval to his plan I also offered to make myself useful to him; all of which explains both the service I did him yesterday during our walk, and his overtures to you. Villefranche is kind, he is gentle. Hear what he has to say without fear: this may be the only way to bring your husband back to you. His pride, piqued at the thought of being replaced by another in your affections, will soon make him regret this loss . . . How many women have succeeded by such means!'

'Many coquettes, no doubt, but no honourable women, Monsieur,' the Marquise replied. 'It would cost me too much to try, and I am not sure that I would not rather lose my husband's heart than recapture it by a crime. How he would despise me once he discovered the truth! No, I want to win back Alphonse's feelings through my tenderness, my patience, and the constancy of my affection; I shall hope that time brings what his injustice denies me; I shall hide my tears from him; they would wound him, I am sure, and I would not wish the slightest sorrow to trouble his giddiness even for a moment . . . Although, if I could get to the bottom of this . . .'

'Do not even try,' replied Théodore heatedly. 'To admit you are aware of his wrongs is almost to grant him permission for them; he would only be more dishonest with you, and you would be no happier for it; you would have sacrificed your pride with a serenity you would never regain. As for the plan I have suggested, you are wrong to reject it: it is not a lover I am proposing, it is an avenger; Villefranche will never raise anything that might offend your sense of duty, but he will court you; he will be solicitous, and this alone will so trouble your husband that he will without fail soon be back at your feet. Oh, believe me, Madame! You must stop at nothing to regain the rights injustice has stripped from you. Even if you were weak enough to succumb, your husband would be to blame for it. I am not proposing that you thwart one crime with another, but that you bring the one that is being committed to a halt by all the means that guile and artifice offer an honourable woman robbed of her happiness.'

'But to achieve such an end, is it acceptable to take on the demeanour of a criminal? In any case, who is to say that my husband, delighted to find me as weak as he, will not treat my actions as licence to go further himself? What a triumph that would be for my rival! Oh, no . . . no! My love, my pride, all would be crushed by the scheme you propose: to conduct myself honourably offends neither of these sentiments, and leaves me worthy of his esteem and my own.'

'So be it, but you will undoubtedly lose Alphonse by conducting yourself in this manner, because he is unjust; he will accuse you of weakness; and when one holds someone in contempt, one's love can never be rekindled. My too kind and too virtuous sister, deign hear my advice; it springs from the most tender and sincere friendship. I aspire only to see you happy, and to heal my brother of the dangerous passion that rules him. My only desire is to restore the two of you to each other as soon as possible: this moral severity that constrains you puts this goal forever beyond your reach, and will be your downfall. Think of what you owe my brother, think of what you owe yourself; do not let trivial considerations stop you, not when your eternal happiness is at stake . . .'

'Happiness? Happiness?' the Marquise exclaimed. 'Oh, no! No, there can be none for me anymore. I placed all mine in the matrimonial bonds I freely chose; I placed it in serving the man I loved; he rejects my tenderness, he insults me! Oh, what happiness can exist for me now on this earth? I shall cry over him, I shall adore him still, but he will love no more! O my brother! Can there be a more dreadful torture than this . . .? Alas, only that of the damned, whose endless appeals to the heavens are spurned by the Almighty. So then, you brute, it was only to make me suffer the agonies of hell that you chose to share your life with the one you used to call your angel . . . For you now, she is merely the angel of the underworld, where she prepares torments for man; but I shall never be your torment, Alphonse; oh, no! Never . . . As unfaithful as you are, it would pain you to see me follow your example, and the semblance alone of such an infidelity, by troubling your life, would fill mine with despair . . . I shall love you even in the arms of my rival . . . Perhaps I shall even love my rival herself, as she basks in your love—I shall love her because she makes you happy . . . Oh, what sins I would commit if I cared only about being happy myself! My dignity will avenge me: I shall always have more of that than you, to make you regret having none at all; and if I can breathe my last sigh clutched to your heart—a heart still inflamed by your love for another—you will not hear the slightest reproach.'

'O my dear, sweet sister,' said Théodore with the utmost ardour. 'All you offer me are sentimental sophistries when what I expect of you is courageous resolve. The crime has been committed, it must be repaired: you will make it worse by refusing to put an end to it, and you can only do so if you follow my advice. The idea of warning Madame de Roquefeuille came to me a hundred times; but my heart baulked at such a betrayal. This mother, horrified, would have taken her daughter away; your involvement would have been suspected; Ambroisine would have become miserable, but without any other consequence than her sorrow and your husband's despair, the full force of which would inevitably have rebounded on you.'

'This stratagem would have been dreadful,' said the Marquise. 'I would always have rejected it.'

'Then accept the one I offer you now, or you will become the most wretched of women.'

'But,' said the Marquise, half won over, 'do you really trust Villefranche?'

'More than myself,' replied the Abbé. 'For he will pretend, but feel nothing; while I could not promise,' said Théodore, lowering his eyes, 'to feel nothing if I were to pretend. All I ask is that you give the impression of accepting my friend's solicitude; once you have done so, then you may forcefully reject anything which seems more serious. Once again, have no fear of him: apprised of our plans, he will keep perfectly within their spirit, and will not deviate whatever the reason from anything that might help them to succeed. But hide everything from your husband, reflect deeply on the dangers of seeking an explanation that can only have the direst consequences. If the Marquis notices something, and reproaches you for it, then you will lay down your terms, and he will sacrifice everything for you while you will have nothing to renounce.'

'Well then! I agree,' said Madame de Gange in the greatest turmoil . . . 'O Lord! Sustain me . . . guide my faltering steps along this perilous path, one I cannot help but see as a crime, and which I pursue only to prevent a greater one.'

The treacherous Abbé embraces Euphrasie: he wipes away her tears, calms her down, and all is agreed . . . A wretched and bloody pact in which the unfortunate Marquise is far from foreseeing the woes that will seal its execution.

In any case, it was decided that the Comte de Villefranche would offer Madame de Gange his disinterested solicitude; that, were he to be let into the secret of this dangerous pact, he would swear never to take advantage; and as for Euphrasie, that she would conduct herself with her husband as she always had before—that she would abstain from making any reproach, and from seeking any explanation.

CHAPTER IV

As his first plan of attack posed some risks, Théodore sensed that it was essential to launch the second sooner rather than later, and the next day he visited the Marquis in his quarters.

'I am glad, my dear Abbé, that you stole a march on me,' Alphonse told him. 'I have something to tell you which weighs heavily on my heart.'

'Why have you not told me before?' replied Théodore. 'Do you have a more genuine friend in the world than me?'

'I cannot imagine so,' Alphonse told him. 'That is why I shall take you into my confidence. Until recently, my dear brother, I always thought myself the most fortunate and the most tranquil of husbands, but I fear now my happiness is under threat.'

'And why this fear?'

'What could possibly have caused my wife to faint during our walk the day before yesterday? Why was Villefranche, whom I thought was with you, alone with her when it happened? And why was it that he alone was taking care of her? Did he have something to do with her fit? And if this were so, would I not have reason to be alarmed?'

'Absolutely no reason at all,' Théodore replied. 'Euphrasie loves you too much, and is too virtuous for any suspicion of infidelity to fall on her. Have you any cause to reproach her since you tied your fate to hers? And do you not realize that a woman who has been a model of piety for years does not suddenly abandon it from one day to the next? Besides, Villefranche is an honourable man; he is your friend, and mine; and, invited by you into your home, he would not dream of causing trouble.'

'But that encounter, and that fainting the other day?'

'Are the simplest of matters. I seem to remember your wife explained that same evening the cause of her fright: a noise in the thicket, then a deer crossing the path—these are what led to her fall. I was with her, I can corroborate these facts. Not having the necessary restorative spirits to hand at the time, and thinking I could hear someone nearby, I make haste, find you, and we take her back home . . . I do not understand why you would have me repeat details you know as well as I do?'

'I remember them of course; but what I also remember is my wife's embarrassment when we stumbled upon her, and even more clearly that of Villefranche, when he thought I had noticed the fervour with which he was tending to Euphrasie. A heart as ardent as mine is easily startled; in order to soothe it, it needs something stronger than whatever alarmed it in the first place, and I doubt you can offer me anything of this nature.'

'Such calm depends on you alone,' Théodore replied. 'Put an end to these troublesome fantasies, and your soul will be at rest; trust your wife and your friend, and you will no longer imagine them capable of disturbing your serenity. Nonetheless, I am willing to help you shed some light on the conduct of those who have made you fret; and, regardless of the ties of kinship that bind me to your wife, or those of my friendship with Villefranche, I promise to be impartial.'

'Perhaps they will deceive you.'

'Well then. Do you want a guaranteed way to put Euphrasie to the test?'

'What is it?'

'Make her jealous. Pour a plentiful dose of the poison that consumes your soul into hers: if she has done wrong, she will only be too pleased to discover you have too; if she has not, her anxieties will become so violent she will convince you that you are indeed the only object of her love.'

'But I shall upset her if she is innocent.'

'True, but you will find out if she is guilty.'

'I prefer my doubts to her unhappiness.'

'So resign yourself to uncertainty.'

'It is dreadful, I shall never be able to bear it.'

'So find out, and stop wavering.'

'And who could I use for such a test?'

'Ambroisine.'

'A friend . . . in my own home? And what would such a respectable mother say?'

'I am not saying that matters should go too far; and both mother and daughter must be treated with respect to be sure. Besides, it is perfectly possible to achieve what I propose without Ambroisine being in the know, and without her modesty being compromised as a result: all you have to do is pretend . . . pay her a little more attention which, after all, will have no ulterior motive.'

'And you think that the result of this ruse . . .'

'Will be to prove the innocence or guilt of your wife. These means are infallible: try them without fear.'

'I accept,' said the Marquis, 'but this should not stop you from doing me the service you promised before.'

'Be sure that I shall observe how the Comte and your wife conduct themselves, and inform you daily of the most minute particulars.'

At this juncture, the Abbé thought there was not a moment to lose when it came to warning Villefranche of the role he was required to play.

'The Marquise will hear what you have to say,' he said. 'That much is agreed. Do not rush things though: it is only for a ruse that she has agreed to listen to you; it is to arouse feelings of jealousy in her husband which will restore him to her. She is convinced he favours Ambroisine over her, and has persuaded herself that, by seeming to love you, she will have him back in her arms again. In any case, take advantage of these circumstances—they may turn out well for you. Bring to life the role I have given you to play; become the Marquise's paramour; and even if you owe your happiness to a stroke of fortune, at least it will have lasted for a few days.'

Villefranche did not hesitate. A man of his age, and with his amorous inclination for the Marquise, was never going to refuse such an arrangement. And once all this was settled, the Abbé, seeing the scenes of his play neatly tied together, now turned all his attention to their dénouement.

'My friend,' he said to Perret, as he detailed his opening moves, 'I think that I have successfully plunged this house into total confusion, and that the greatest success will indubitably crown my achievements. All that is needed now is boldness and perseverance.'

'But even if all this works,' said Perret, 'is it not possible that we shall sink just as we are coming into port?'

'Why should that be, if I succeed in subjugating that proud woman?'

'But do you think her virtue will abandon her . . .? Misfortune, far from diminishing strength, galvanizes it in a noble soul; and there are heroines of virtue who can never be made to succumb.'

'Yes, in novels, but this is not one of those; I have a hundred ways to triumph, and I shall employ them all if I must.'

'There are some, Monsieur, that you would not dare put to use.'

'Indeed, I shall dare any which yield me her body, and her heart; but if I could only possess one at the expense of the other, my humbled pride would perhaps not go so far. In any case, we shall act according to the circumstances we find; and I have always observed that fortune favours the brave.'

'Yes, Monsieur, it is a common expression, but not always a very reliable one. There are victims everywhere in this dreadful undertaking!'

'They will all be sacrificed to my goddess, and the gods never complain about the extravagance of the tributes they receive.'

The rest of the conversation turned to the planning of certain measures essential to a successful outcome. Théodore gave Perret his instructions, and they went their separate ways. The promises the Marquise had made to the Abbé de Gange had not put an end to her worries. She had not the slightest suspicion regarding her brother-in-law's conduct; but this ruse that the Abbé deemed essential, this need to test her husband by a form of subterfuge that was so unlike her, spread a sense of disquiet in her soul that she felt in every inch of her body. She had promised to act and say nothing; but the purity of her conscience did not allow her to keep her word with such rigour.

There were two people at the castle who were worthy of her confidence: one was Madame de Roquefeuille, but as this lady could not be informed without such a confession compromising her daughter, she abandoned the idea; the other, Father Eusèbe, was accustomed to guiding her conscience. This venerable character suited her better in every respect, but she could not say everything: to reveal anything relating to Mademoiselle de Roquefeuille could mean the ruin of that young person, as well as the Marquis de Gange, if by chance anything was untrue. For someone of Euphrasie's sound judgement, these delicate considerations were perfectly clear; nonetheless, her heart was heavy, and she needed to unburden it.

She asked Eusèbe to meet her at the castle chapel as she wished to fulfil on bended knee the duties of that holy and honourable sacrament which, reconciling man with his God through the salutary medium of one of his ministers, restores in the soul of the sinner the calm disturbed by his sins: a fine and moving institution of our sacred faith, one which averts, or suspends, the effects of crime by rendering the one who had contemplated it worthy of forgiveness; a cherished symbol of the sacrifice made by the son of God, for we find in this sublime sacrament some of the grace his death granted us.

Euphrasie, dressed now in all the finery that seduces feeble mortals, seemed only to gain in grace from the majesty of the duty she was to fulfil. Embellished for her God, she was embellished by him too: hers was the beauty of the Angels around the throne of the Almighty; a ray of light from that divinity added to her charms, and, like the star shining down on the earth, she owed God alone for her dazzling radiance.

Once this first duty had been fulfilled, Madame de Gange sat with Eusèbe.

'Father,' she said to him. 'I must ask your advice about a matter on which my happiness in life strictly depends. You know of my affection for my husband?'

'I know and respect it, Madame. It earns you the esteem of all men, and makes you an example to all women.'

'O Father, it is not praise I need, it is advice I seek, and I cannot think of any I would rather have guide me than yours.'

And, continuing with all the serenity of a pure soul:

'This tranquillity, which is the foundation of my happiness . . . someone is trying to disturb it, Father: he believes my husband is unfaithful; he plunges a dagger into my heart as he tries to shatter the image engraved there. I cannot tell you who is doing me this cruel service: if he is right, I am guilty of ingratitude; if he is wrong, I am compromising him. Prudence thus prohibits me from a revelation which I think is irrelevant to the facts in any case; but, in order to know the truth, I must tell you of the means I am to employ; it is principally regarding these that I seek your advice. I am supposed to give the appearance of accepting the tributes I am offered. This, I am assured, is the only way to bring my husband back to me, or else lose him forever: if he still loves me, he will fall at my feet, and his innocence will be proven; if he spurns me or becomes irate, his crime, it is said, will be revealed and I shall have to do everything in my power to get to the bottom of it. But can you imagine, Father, what such a course of action costs my heart? Me, pretend to love someone other than Alphonse? Me, lend my ear to words that thrill me only when they are his? Oh, no! No, it is impossible. Tell me what to do, and take pity on my plight.'

'I must begin, Madame,' Eusèbe replied, 'by declaring my utter repugnance at the idea of incriminating oneself in this way. If there was one person in the world on whose good conduct I could pronounce without any doubt, it would assuredly be the Marquis de Gange.

I shall not repeat the words of praise that are already in your heart, and that justice and truth are forever engraving there. Having established this first point, there is no need for me to argue against the advice someone has seen fit to give you, for it is based on an opinion I have already dismissed; I must respond to it nonetheless. Be so good as to convince yourself, Madame, that under no circumstances is it ever permitted to feign a crime in order to reveal or prevent another one. To assent to such a false principle would be to insult virtue not once but twice; indeed, this stratagem is intolerable, and you must reject it . . . reject it, I say, along with the idea that appears to sanction it. Your husband is not guilty, and you should not pretend you are simply to find out whether he is or not; for if he is, your very immoral ruse does not prevent it, and if he is not, it is an affront to him. I shall not tell you to beware the person who offers you counsels and conjectures of this kind: I have never had it in me to suspect evil. No doubt he believed what he told you, and had no qualms about doing so; but you should not base your opinion on the weakness of other people's views, nor take fright at fantasies that may simply have come from the well-intentioned soul of the person who has so alarmed you. Change nothing in your conduct, Madame; may the redoubling of your tenderness for an innocent husband be the only torch you use to shed light on the truth: crimes are difficult to hide; and if your husband is guilty, though I find it impossible to believe, the redoubling of your attentiveness to him will cool rather than kindle his passion. This is the only test to which you may subject him: it will succeed, Madame; more than that, it will reassure you, and you will have evidence of virtue without the need to assume the mask of crime.'

'O Father!' exclaimed the charming Euphrasie. 'What a balm you have spread on my wounds!'

'It is not to me that you owe this comfort, Madame,' Eusèbe replied. 'You deserve it because of the act of piety you performed before opening your heart to me; and you have served the God of peace, whose holy commandments you follow, and who deigned choose me to restore to your soul the tranquillity he owed you for your submission. May this example forever sustain in you the divine love that was the theme of one of my recent sermons! And be assured, Madame, that this merciful God does not endlessly raise his hand to punish the sinner, but forever holds it out to help the unfortunate soul who prays to him.'

From this moment on, Madame de Gange decided to change nothing in her conduct towards the Marquis, but to renounce unequivocally all that her brother appeared to demand of her towards the Comte de Villefranche. She explained this to Théodore, who, knowing of her meeting that morning with Eusèbe, strongly suspected the cause of Euphrasie's change of heart; but he dared not upset her.

'Well then! May whatever ensues prove to you whether I was right or wrong! But, whatever the case may be, Madame,' he said affectionately to his sister, 'see in this only my ardent desire to serve you.'

But as someone as virtuous as Eusèbe could utterly foil the plots Théodore was hatching each day against that most worthy of women, the monster used his influence to blacken the name of this saintly man in the minds of his superiors, who summoned him back to Montpellier before dispatching him to an insalubrious retreat on the border with Italy, where he promptly delivered to God the sincere and pure soul that had led him only to his downfall.

At this juncture, the Abbé sensed more drastic measures would be required to persuade his sister-in-law; and he resolved without further ado to bring into play those he had planned with Laurent,* and which we may, perhaps, soon see carried out. At the same time he made some slight changes to the part assigned to Villefranche, pressed the Marquis with greater urgency to put the test he had suggested into action, and assumed, for the time being, the simple role of observer.

Following the wise advice of her counsellor, the Marquise tried to regain the intimacy she had lost with her husband, but the die was cast: the jealousy that consumed Alphonse, the violent suspicions he harboured, prevented him from sharing with his wife the sweet intimacy that had previously been the source of such happiness for the two of them. The Marquise, remembering what Eusèbe had told her, was no longer in any doubt about her husband's inconstancy, and felt she had to resign herself to weeping in silence, rather than employing the culpable measures her brother-in-law had suggested.

'What is wrong, my dear Euphrasie?' Madame de Roquefeuille asked her one day during a walk she had arranged especially to determine what was behind the sorrow that could be read in her friend's features.

'Alas!' Madame de Gange replied, deeply embarrassed, and keen to withhold any confidences that might lead to dangerous indiscretions.

'Alas! Madame, I blame only myself for Alphonse's coldness towards me, which you must have noticed; and as I do not know what I could have done wrong, I am struggling in vain to find the reason for this rejection. Tell me, Madame, tell me honestly—can you find in me any reason for a change that makes me despair?'

'I have not noticed any, my dear friend,' Madame de Roquefeuille replied, 'but if you believe in the parity of feelings between husbands and wives, let me tell you that you do not know men very well: their injustice towards us is dreadful; the more we let them read in our hearts the feelings that move us, the more they think themselves exempt from reciprocity. One would, dare I say, have to love them much less to be loved much more; a deathly coldness seems to offset all the efforts they previously made in order to please us, and as there is nothing left for them to desire, they are amazed to see that we still want more. Endowed with more sensitive constitutions, our delicate nature takes them aback; little by little their attachment to us weakens, and yet they still have the temerity to complain about the vices prompted by their neglect. Avoid these vices, my dear, let him bear the weight of guilt alone: this is the only revenge for an honourable woman. Your perseverance, your excellent conduct will bring him back to you perhaps; and if he continues to be unjust, at least you will not be able to reproach yourself for having vindicated his wrongs against you.'

'But,' said Madame de Gange, 'you do not suspect him of some attachment that would explain his lack of warmth?'

'No, none: witness—as you are—to his daily conduct while we have been staying at the castle, I have seen no signs that would make me suspicious.'

'In that case, there is nothing for me to do but wait and see.'

'It is the only sensible course of action.'

'Oh, how endless they will seem, these days when I shall no longer be able to call him my friend, when I shall no longer be able to read in his eyes the tenderness that used to make them sparkle!'

'Would you allow me, Euphrasie, to ask him a few questions about this change of heart that concerns you—and which may, perhaps, only exist in your overwrought imagination?'

'Please don't,' said the Marquise. 'I do not wish him to know of my tears . . . if he is not going to wipe them away!'

'Oh, you are too sensitive and too delicate,' said Madame de Roquefeuille. 'Don't think him such a brute: Alphonse loves you; you are all he cares about; your anxieties exist only because of your extreme susceptibility, and I would merely make you miserable if I were to advise you to be less sensitive. Have you confided your worries to anyone else?'

And so Madame de Gange revealed her conversation with Father Eusèbe, and conveyed to Madame de Roquefeuille some of the counsel and comfort she had received.

'Eusèbe is an honourable man,' Madame de Roquefeuille replied. 'I approve of everything he advised, and beseech you to put it into practice; but sadly, we shall see him no more.'

Madame de Roquefeuille then explained to her friend what had happened to this fine monk.

'But what could be the cause of this sudden departure?'

'I do not know. Eusèbe left without saying a word, and without seeing a soul; apparently he has been summoned by his superiors.'

The Marquise reflected on this awhile, then spoke again in an anxious and pained tone.

'Alas!' she exclaimed to her friend. 'As I have no counsel other than yours, I shall listen to no other. Well then! So be it: I shall wait and see.'

'It is the only remedy for your woes.'

'Oh, if time goes by too slowly, sorrow will turn my pain bitter, tears will wither the modest charms he used to find enchanting, and my hope will die with them . . . O my dear lady, how unhappy I am!'

The conversation was interrupted at this point by the arrival of Ambroisine, who had come to beg her mother to bow to the will of the rest of their company, which was to go and spend a few days at the fair in Beaucaire; Ambroisine wanted to leave immediately.

'That's impossible,' said Madame de Roquefeuille. 'Important business calls me to Montpellier; I shall accompany you so far, but,' she turned to Madame de Gange, 'I shall leave my daughter with you. I shall entrust her to your care, as I would not want to do her the disservice of taking her away from her friends and boring her with my business affairs.' Ambroisine throws her arms around her mother's neck to thank her, and thereafter the castle is entirely preoccupied with preparations for a journey which, unbeknownst to all, has been contrived by the Abbé de Gange.

They set off. Madame de Roquefeuille stayed behind in Montpellier, and Monsieur de Gange, Euphrasie, Ambroisine and Villefranche spent the night in Tarascon, where they were to arrange the lodgings they required in Beaucaire.

As everyone knows, this small town, situated on the right bank of the Rhône, takes its name from the square fort where long ago Courts of Love* were held, the remnants of which can still be seen on the mountain that looms over the town—which is equally noteworthy for the residence of the Porcellets family, who were so prominent in the Sicilian Vespers affair.*

Famous for the fair held there each year at the Madeleine,* this town, which is far too small to accommodate all the visitors it attracts at this time of year, would offer a very pleasant stay even without this added attraction; but it is first and foremost during the fair that it merits a visit.

One cannot imagine the vast numbers of people who venture there from all over Europe. The crowds are such that they say, not without good reason, that a flower thrown from a window would not reach the ground. Linked to Tarascon by a pontoon bridge, these two towns seem to merge into one.

A stranger may form a peculiar impression of the way business is done in France from such a tumultuous gathering. Oh, the deals that are done in just seven or eight days! Oh, the hustle and bustle! It seems that the only god worshipped there is Plutus,* and that his gold, rather than blood, circulates in everyone's veins. But if work takes up the whole day, the evenings are nonetheless devoted to the greatest variety of public entertainments: horse-races in the meadows; an abundance of refreshments and ice creams in the cafés; to the right, the magnificent sight of ships from all nations, there to sell or exchange their goods; to the left, dances to the sound of a thousand different instruments; spectacles great and small; fireworks; and walks all the more fascinating because, among that prodigious throng one can hear every language, and see every nation. The same need to trade, and the same desire to make merry, seem to bring everyone together there, and to transform them into one great family of shared interests. There is barely time to sleep; there is barely time to eat. Everyone, even the idle, seems busy, and in the evening, pleasure brings everyone to the meadows—both those who have suffered only losses, and those who sag under the weight of the gold they have just won.

But everything in life has its shortcomings: it was so immensely difficult to find lodgings in such a confined space that rooms were as expensive as they were uncomfortable; and this is indeed what Théodore found when, the day after he arrived in Tarascon with his companions from the castle of Gange, he was entrusted with finding accommodation; as he moreover had particular requirements, reconciling these with what was available only added to his difficulties.

The Abbé lodged the two ladies in a house where the rooms he reserved for them were the only ones available. He had found accommodation for Villefranche, the Marquis, and himself in a neighbouring house and, complaining that this was the best he could do, added he could not find so much as a closet for a chambermaid, let alone space for servants and attendants; and thus everyone other than the masters stayed in Tarascon.

Through the Abbé's treacherous machinations, Ambroisine's bedroom was on the first floor and Euphrasie's on the second. The Abbé had been given two keys for each of these rooms, and while the Marquis, back at the house his brother had found for him, checked that there was no chance of a bed for him there,* Théodore made his aforementioned arrangements for the ladies and returned to give the Marquis the duplicate key for Ambroisine's bedroom.

'Make no mistake when you visit your wife this evening,' he said to his brother. 'This is the key to her bedroom; remember she is on the first floor; the young lady was given the second-floor bedroom as it was less comfortable than the other.'

'I may not visit her,' said the Marquis. 'Until her conduct becomes clearer, I am in no hurry to reconcile with her.'

'But there is still nothing to justify your fears,' said the Abbé. 'Let us keep an eye on her: in the intimacy of these surroundings, it will be easy to clear up any doubts we may have. I have promised to assist you—count on it, my brother, and in the meantime do not treat your wife too severely . . . I do not believe she deserves it.'

'Well then,' said Alphonse, 'I shall see her this evening, but it is still early—let us go for a stroll in the meadows.'

Villefranche and the two brothers set off on their walk. They return at eleven o'clock in the evening, and as the two ladies had remained in their rooms, either to settle in or to ready themselves for the next day, Alphonse heads with his duplicate key to the floor indicated by his brother, expecting to find Euphrasie there. No sooner has he left than Théodore follows him, before slipping past him in the dark; both armed with the keys they require, the Abbé goes to his sister-in-law's room on the second floor, while the Marquis, thinking he is entering his wife's quarters, stops on the first; without suspecting a thing, he enters Ambroisine's quarters and carefully shuts the door behind him.

'Hush!' says Théodore to the Marquise as he enters, seeing her about to go to bed. 'I think I shall be able to enlighten you this evening. Your husband, whose footsteps I followed here without him seeing, has just slipped into Ambroisine's bedroom even though he knew perfectly well that this one was yours. Through this peephole in the floor, known here as a *judas*, we shall see all that unfolds in Ambroisine's room.'

'O heavens! A ray of light! But will I be able to bear what it reveals? O my brother, what a dreadful service you are doing me!'

'I know, but I had to convince you. Had I seen the Marquis head to your quarters, I would have said nothing, but, as I saw him enter Ambroisine's I made haste so you would have a chance to see everything.'

And Euphrasie anxiously rushes to the opening Théodore shows her. What a spectacle for this unfortunate wife! She sees Alphonse close the door behind him, approach the bed where Ambroisine is already resting, and slip in beside her; her strength fails her; she can stand it no longer . . . She throws the first garment she can find over her shoulders and rushes to the stairs, at the foot of which she finds Villefranche alone. She grabs the young man by the arm, drags him into the street, saying simply:

'Let us leave, Monsieur, let us leave. I cannot stay a moment longer in the accursed place where I am being dishonoured . . .'

All this is the matter of a few seconds, and Villefranche, whom the Abbé had briefed on what Euphrasie might discover, offers no resistance. They make for the coaching inn, and hire a carriage for Gange. Villefranche helps the Marquise into it, and off they set.

Now that we have two scenes to follow, let us begin with the one concerning Ambroisine, and leave the Marquise to travel with someone she took for her own safety, but who will perhaps become the cause of her misfortunes.

The moment Mademoiselle de Roquefeuille is woken by the Marquis, whom she never dreamed of seeing in her bedroom, she utters such a dreadful scream that Théodore promptly appears at her door to find out, so he says, what could have caused such a fright.

'What is this, brother?' he says, as soon as the door is opened. 'You did not tell me about these plans.'

'What plans do you mean?' replies Alphonse sourly. 'I have never conceived of any that would be contrary to the respect I owe Mademoiselle, as I have always said to you; and I offer her in your presence my most sincere apologies for the mistake which has led to this imbroglio. But did you not give me this key?'

'Indeed.'

'Did you not tell me that it was for my wife's bedroom?'

'No doubt, but I also added that your wife's quarters were on the second floor, so I have no idea why you are here on the first.'

'But this key?'

'Is for your wife's room on the second floor. Come and try it if you do not believe me.'

The Marquis goes up, the key opens the door. Théodore was too sly to neglect this additional precaution. But what becomes of Alphonse, when he finds no one in the room, and an open peephole in the middle of the floor.

'O good God! She thinks me guilty!' he exclaims. 'And how am I to explain now? Where is she? Who knows where the force of her despair will drive her? . . . O my friend! I am the most wretched of men.'

'Let us fly after her,' says the Abbé. 'We must not waste a minute: perhaps we shall find out where she is.'

'O my dear brother,' the Marquis exclaimed. 'The greatest proof of my wife's innocence is the effect her fear of my infidelity has had on her.'

'Well then! Did I not always say she was faithful?'

While Ambroisine, left none the wiser regarding Euphrasie's disappearance, calms herself down and returns to bed, the two brothers race after the fugitive and begin their inquiries at Villefranche's house. No news: a candle still burning upon the table, clothes carelessly scattered over armchairs, and every appearance of a hasty departure.

'They are together!' the Marquis exclaims. 'And you are wrong to think her alone. But it was my first crime, or rather the appearance of a crime, which prompted hers, and now I am the most unfortunate of husbands. Ill-fated trip! . . . How wrong I was to agree to it! . . . It was as if I foresaw everything that has just transpired. Come, my friend, let us waste no time; let us search the streets; find out everything we can . . . These festivities are proving dreadful for me . . . I was always against the idea.'

The Abbé, never short of tricks, had thought of another which was not certain to succeed, but which he had nonetheless prepared just in case.

He and his brother have barely reached the end of the street where they are staying when a sentry calls out to them:

'*It's midnight, you cannot pass.*'

'But Monsieur . . .'

'You cannot pass, I tell you.'

'Let's go back,' says Théodore. 'Perhaps we shall find an easier way out by our lodgings.'

But they barely make it to the other end of the street before a second sentry calls out the same thing—they cannot even return to their rooms.

'But Monsieur, only a moment ago . . . you were not even here.'

'That's true, Monsieur, we are only posted at midnight.'

'So now we are held prisoner in the street?'

'Yes, Messieurs, until the patrol passes; they will take you to the guardroom, and find out who you are.'

'God's guts! All this is trying my patience,' says the Marquis, reaching for his sword. 'I must pass, or else kill the one who bars my way.'

At this the sentry calls for assistance.

'Let's go, let's go,' said the Abbé, 'and let's not make a bad state of affairs worse. Soon it will be dawn; we shall find a café and rest there until then.'

The motive for this second ruse is easy to guess: the Abbé, who had arranged it by paying and placing the two spurious sentries, had anticipated the Marquise's flight; he wanted by these means to give the two fugitives the time they needed to be beyond reach, so that they might fall more easily into the fresh traps that awaited them.

'Let us resume our search,' said the Marquis as soon as dawn broke. After making inquiries all over, they finally arrive at the coaching inn, where they promptly discover that Euphrasie and Villefranche are together, and on their way to Gange.

Alphonse wants to leave that very minute; but the Abbé, whose only concern is to play for time, points out to his brother that they cannot leave Ambroisine alone in furnished rooms, or their attendants in Tarascon.

'This will never end,' says the Marquis. 'And meanwhile who knows what might happen between my wife and this young man who is already so deeply in love with her?'

'But did you not just say that Euphrasie's reaction was the proof of the store she set by your heart? So why alarm yourself now? Be consistent in your suspicions, and do not fret more than is necessary.'

'Yes,' replies the Marquis, still agitated, 'but bear in mind that when she left she was angry with me, and on such occasions hell hath no fury like a woman scorned.'

They walk on nonetheless; the coaches arrive in Beaucaire; they take their seats with Ambroisine, who was deeply upset that this trip, which she had anticipated with such excitement, had offered her nothing but a disagreeable episode which neither her innocence nor her candour could fathom, and which was only explained to her two or three leagues from Beaucaire by the Abbé—without him revealing the reasons for it.

CHAPTER V

It is difficult to describe the Marquis's surprise when, upon his return to Gange, he found neither Villefranche nor his wife. The Abbé, though better informed, feigned the same astonishment as his brother, and all and sundry seemed dismayed.

'We have been tricked,' the Marquis said to Théodore. 'The two of them are on the run, and it was to throw us off the scent that they had people say the coach they hired in Beaucaire was taking them to Gange. Oh, the cruel situation in which this poor woman and I now find ourselves! She thinks me guilty, and I am convinced she is too. However, I want to find out more—love and pride demand that much.'

And the wretch paced the length and breadth of the castle, shedding tears over all the furniture, all the rooms that reminded him of the happy moments he had previously spent with his dear Euphrasie.

Nothing breaks the heart more than finding oneself alone in those places which had once borne witness to our happiness: everything bears the trace, everything brings to mind, the object of our affection; it is as if she still breathes life into all she once suffused with her beauty; we hear the echoes of the voice that used to enchant us; we fly after them, but all we find is an illusion rent by despair.

One day, when Alphonse was weeping in the chapel beneath his dear wife's portrait (placed, as we have said, above the Christ whose mother it represented), plunged into the kind of wild reveries that bring all our imaginings to life, he thought the eyes of this heavenly Virgin filled with tears as they gazed ardently at him, and that her rosy lips, suddenly paling, parted to utter these halting words: *Death . . . calamity . . . grave.* His agitation intensifies . . .

'O my friend!' he said to his brother. 'She is weeping, her tears flowed over my hands; they fell once more onto my heart . . . She speaks, and my fate is written in the words that escaped her. I must find her or die.'

May we be permitted to leave him in this cruel situation to turn our attention to the person at the heart of it.

Everything had been judiciously, or rather, maliciously calculated in the Abbé's plans. He knew well that if (as was likely) the Marquise decided in her outrage to return to Gange there and then, either alone or with Villefranche, she would inevitably head to the inn to hire a coach. A coachman in Théodore's pocket was therefore to offer his services, and indeed Villefranche, none the wiser as to these details, led Euphrasie straight to this man's coach; and other than one or two declarations Villefranche made to the Marquise, respect and circumspection reigned over this *tête-à-tête*; all was well until the outskirts of Montpellier. But two leagues from this town, in the middle of a small pine wood, the coachman suddenly stops. Though Villefranche demands an explanation, he is simply told the horses need to catch their breath. And now the Marquise cannot help but fret a little . . . What to do? . . . There is no escaping the stubbornness of people from those parts: the more in the wrong they are, the more insolent they become. One has to have travelled about this region to grasp the truth of this principle. Thus they stop for almost a quarter of an hour in the woods; but when two rough-looking men approach, their fears soon mount; and to add to these, Villefranche, having left Beaucaire in haste, had not taken the precaution of arming himself at all: no pistol, and not even his sword.

'Where are you going?' says one of the bandits, approaching the coach with sabre in hand. 'Do you think you can pass through my estates without paying me a visit?'

Villefranche, stripped of the means to defend himself, tries to speak; they pay him no heed.

'Step down, step down, the pair of you,' he is told. 'You are no more than a hundred yards from my palace, so you have no need of a coach to take you there.'

The Marquise, trembling, obeys, assisted by the Comte; the two of them follow their guide who, lifting aside a boulder hidden behind some bushes, politely offers the Marquise his hand to enter what he calls his palace. Four more comrades of the first two are there, and they all gather round to receive their guests properly.

'Do not be surprised at our conduct with you, Madame,' says the leader after allowing her to rest and refresh herself. 'We did not stop you with the intention of mistreating you in any way. You may rest assured of that, both of you; no harm will come to you—we wish to make friends, not enemies. Weary of practising this profession, we are beginning to dread the dangerous consequences of this errant and vagabond life; we are now ready to leave it behind, but the authorities to whom we have been denounced will not believe in the sincerity of our change of heart: we need witnesses. During the fair, we have stopped many travellers and have shown them, as we have you, nothing but courtesy. We are begging all these honourable people to spread the news of our conversion in public: they have vowed to serve us as witnesses and to defend us. Do us the same honour . . . You, Monsieur le Comte de Villefranche, whom we know all about—you have just the influence we need to save us from the punishments we deserve: go to Montpellier, plead on our behalf; we shall keep your lady here as security until, armed with the pardons we require, you return in person to claim her. Until then, be sure that the greatest solicitude and the greatest respect will guide all our conduct towards her; it is only fair to warn you, however, that she is the price of our good grace; she will be returned to you on this condition alone.'

Villefranche wishes to speak, but is not allowed to do so. As for the Marquise, she does all she can to express her objections to this deal, and to prevent Villefranche from abandoning her: it is all in vain, and the Comte must acquiesce; he leaves, escorted by two brigands, while the Marquise, in the midst of her tears and worries, is left alone with the four others.

So that we may thereafter concern ourselves exclusively with Madame de Gange, we shall tell our readers here and now that it was not to Montpellier that Villefranche was led but the gates of Avignon; they left him there, saying that everything he had previously been told was simply to keep the Marquise for themselves alone; that the brigands whose den he had left needed neither mercy nor anyone to defend them—and if he dared take the slightest action for or against them he would be murdered within a week no matter where he chose to hide. They parted as they uttered these words. We shall return to him in due course. Let us return to the cave.

The bandits did not waver from the conduct they had promised to observe with the Marquise; consideration, attentiveness, respectful language were all put to use. But, after three or four days, the leader seemed unable to keep the love that such a beautiful woman inspired to himself: he declared his feelings, but his solicitude waned considerably when he discerned the insurmountable repugnance the Marquise felt for him. Despite all this, she did not think to hide the anxiety she felt at the long delay in Villefranche's return. Poor Euphrasie raised this one day when she found herself completely alone with the leader, whose comrades were on the road.

'Do not worry, Madame,' said the vile man with great arrogance. 'You will not see Villefranche again; my words are as deceptive as my actions, and you will leave here either as a corpse or as my wife.'

But as the brute saw that such a sudden and abrupt proposal might perhaps send the Marquise to an early grave, he tried to reassure her.

'Well, Madame!' he said to her. 'Your suffering moves me, and you will find me perfectly reasonable. I shall willingly promise to take no advantage of a situation in which I could obtain whatever I pleased, but only on the basis of a condition that I hope you will not refuse.'

'What is it?'

'You must copy in your own hand, and sign, this document.'

Euphrasie takes the paper and reads these words:

Unhappy with my husband's recent conduct towards me, I promise and declare to Monsieur Joseph Deschamps, landowner, in whose hands I willingly remain, to continue to live with him in the greatest friendship and intimacy until the death of M. de Gange allows me the freedom to enter into marriage with the aforesaid Monsieur Deschamps, to whom I promise faith, submission and fidelity until that day.

'Has it not occurred to you, Monsieur,' said Euphrasie, 'that I would undoubtedly prefer death to such a commitment?'

'That is up to you, Madame,' Deschamps replied, letting the Marquise see the butt of his pistol. 'This last resort is always at your disposal, but be in no doubt that it shall only be used after another which, I can assure you, will leave you without even the solace of dying innocent.'

'Your words make me shudder, Monsieur.'

'Your resistance, Madame, is more inconceivable than my words; but, believe me, you must make your mind up very quickly.'

There was no reason now for the Marquise to hesitate: if she signed, she would buy time, and perhaps escape; if she did not sign, all was lost. She barely finishes writing before two gentlemen, calling themselves officers of the law, fall on Deschamps, tie him up, and drag him along with the Marquise from his ghastly den. They take the document with them, holding onto it carefully; a coach is waiting for them, and, in under two hours, all four of them arrive in Montpellier. And then something very peculiar happened that the Marquise could not fathom. It was night when they reached Montpellier, and the coach stopped at a *seedy* tavern on the outskirts of the town. Madame de Gange is left with the hostess, and Deschamps and the officers of the law all disappear—except for one of Deschamps's guards who, entering the parlour where Euphrasie is waiting, enjoins her to follow him to the Bishop's residence, where, he says, he is to take her. The Marquise leaves, reassured by this order, and follows her guide with great pleasure . . . They arrive at the palace.

'My Lord,' says the officer, presenting the Marquise, 'this is Madame de Gange; she was with a band of scoundrels when we apprehended her; this is the act by which she was bound to their leader, who has sworn he obtained this document from her without any coercion, and has compounded this testimony with some still more unfavourable allegations about this lady's honour and virtue. Knowing your ties to the House of Gange, we thought we should place the lady in your hands before bringing her to justice.'

At these words, the officer withdraws, and the Marquise is left alone with the prelate.

'This is extraordinary conduct, Madame,' says the venerable pastor.

'I accept,' replies Euphrasie, 'that all appearances are against me; but if you listen to my story, I hope its sincerity will enlighten you.'

And the prelate, inviting the Marquise to take a seat, listened to her as kindly as he did attentively. Euphrasie hid nothing; she merely took the prudent step of blaming her foolhardy venture with the Comte de Villefranche on the malicious rumours surrounding her husband. Her capture by Deschamps was described with the utmost honesty; and when she came to the alleged vices of which she was accused with Deschamps, and to the document which had prompted her confession, she denied everything with that vehemence that belongs only to the innocent.

'Madame,' the prelate replied with that candour and simplicity which is the true hallmark of those who preach the Gospel. 'Your physiognomy would be very deceptive if you are indeed trying to hoodwink me, but the state in which you have been brought here, and the speculation that accompanies you, are such that I cannot allow myself to send you on your way without further instructions: so do not take it ill, I beg you, if in the meantime I have you escorted to the Ursuline convent in this town. You will be treated there with all the respect you deserve; once you are there, we shall each write to the Marquis de Gange, and I promise to do all that he demands of me.'

Euphrasie, who could not criticize such a reasonable course of action, thanked his Lordship, and, in the vicar-general's care, she went that very evening to the aforementioned convent. The letters were written, and this is the one the Marquise dispatched in haste to her husband:

I am, by order of his Lordship the Bishop of Montpellier, in the Ursuline convent of this town. So much has happened to me since we last saw each other! Fly to me as soon as this letter reaches you, but go and see the Bishop before you come to the convent: only he can grant you permission to speak to me. Do not stop loving your Euphrasie: she believes herself as worthy of you as you will always be of her. I may have seemed culpable to you, but how much more you are in my eyes! Make haste so we can shed light on a matter so crucial to our happiness.

It is impossible to describe Alphonse's elation upon reading this missive.

'Yes, my sweet angel,' he exclaimed. 'You love me, and I shall adore you for the rest of my life; you are no guiltier than me, I am sure; we must waste no time in convincing each other of this . . .'

And without further ado, the Marquis leaps into a coach and is taken to Montpellier.

In accordance with the letters from his wife and the Bishop, which he received at the same time, he alighted at the prelate's residence. Once his presence was announced, the Bishop was content, without any further explanation, to sign the order for him to see his wife as soon as he wished; and as he handed him this document, he also handed him the one Euphrasie had signed in the cave.

'As for this declaration,' he said to the Marquis, 'both my duty and my conscience oblige me to pass it on to you, but I must tell you that I regard it simply as testament to this Deschamps's villainy, and as evidence of the extraordinary terror he struck into your wife's soul; it should in no way lead you to presume any guilt on her part.'

Before examining any of this more closely, Alphonse flies to the convent, receives the abbess's permission to see his wife in an external room; and it was here that Madame de Gange said to her husband:

'O my friend, when I saw the cruel spectacle that so clearly proved your infidelity, I listened only to the voice of my despair; it led me into dreadful recklessness, I know, but does one stop to think when one no longer knows what one is doing? . . . Rushing down the stairs I chanced upon Villefranche; I told him everything I had seen, everything that explained the agitation he found me in. Without giving him time to reply, I led him to the coaching inn, and we hired a coach for Gange . . .'

And the Marquise continued to explain all the rest with the same candour she had employed with the Bishop.

'But who . . .' asked Alphonse, 'who revealed to you the mistake I had made? How is it that this hole in the floor was ready in time to observe me in that bedroom, which I truly thought was yours?'

And here the prudent Marquise, not wishing to expose the two brothers, said that she was alone when, surprised by a noise coming from Ambroisine's room, she happened to see the peephole and used it.

'My agitation did the rest,' she added, 'and we left. I say again, my friend, that I cannot speak highly enough of the attentiveness and respect the Comte showed me on the way, and even during our unfortunate encounter with those brigands.'

'That was a dreadful episode,' said the Marquis, appearing more worried by Deschamps's actions than those of Villefranche.

'My dear Alphonse,' replied the Marquise, 'neither should alarm you now.'

'But this note,' said the Marquis, looking over it. 'The vows it contains . . .'

'All with no other purpose than to keep me alive, which I wanted only in order to clear my name: otherwise I would have died in despair. O my friend! Believe in your wife's virtue, a virtue based on her love; it is as steadfast as she is; rip up this dreadful document, it is worthy only of contempt.'

'I shall keep it,' Alphonse replied. 'the manufacture of this paper, the ink you used, all of this may help us find the guilty party one day, and it is vital that we should discover this.'

'So be it! Do as you will,' said the Marquise. 'But let us be reunited as soon as possible, I beg you: I would have thought a word from you would be enough to release me from here so we can be together, without the poison of jealousy ever infecting us again—without, in a word, a cloud to darken the springtime of our life together.'

After further vows of affection, the Marquis returned to the Bishop, who, keeping to himself the reasons behind his actions, handed to Monsieur de Gange the order for his wife's release; and, after a last visit out of courtesy to the prelate, husband and wife promptly left together for Gange.

'What an extraordinary episode!' Alphonse said to Euphrasie, now they could speak more freely. 'Who instigated all of this?'

'I do not know,' said the Marquise, 'but I venture that the same hand is behind it all.'

'Yes, indeed,' Alphonse replied. 'There is one reason alone for all of this, and that is your rash mistake in Beaucaire.'

'But someone prompted that mistake,' said Madame de Gange, 'and that is what is difficult to unpick: the more I try to base my reasoning on something plausible, the more contradictions I see; and after thinking about it long and hard I am still none the wiser.'

'I feel the same,' said Alphonse, 'but let us not wear our wits out with vain conjecture. We are together; I have proved my innocence to you; you have convinced me of yours—let our future belong to happiness, and let us leave misfortune in the past.'

Now that our discerning readers have doubtless recognized the treacherous hand of the Abbé de Gange in this turn of events, it is time to explain the reasons that led him to add further twists to this episode.

Why not let the Comte de Villefranche set off with the Marquise for the castle, then simply have her stopped as she arrived in Montpellier, thereby achieving quite straightforwardly the goal Théodore had in mind? This is the reason: firstly, it would have meant leaving his sister-in-law in the hands of his rival for too long, which would have caused him considerable jealousy; secondly such a step would merely have sullied Madame de Gange with only the slightest of misdemeanours, when the Abbé had it in mind to besmirch her with much graver misdeeds. Thus, by having her stopped by bandits, who would first of all remove his rival, and then by giving her the appearance of taking up with one of these bandits, you will agree that he was springing on his victim a far stronger dose of misfortune than the first scenario afforded; and, as a result, how much more serious, and more severe, would be the means the Marquis used to punish his wife! She would still have been apprehended in Montpellier otherwise, it is true, but only as the companion of an honourable young man worthy of some respect; but escorted to this town along with the leader of a company of thieves, and as his mistress—what a difference! Indeed, we know, and shall know even better soon enough, that none of these subtleties were lost on the treacherous instigator of these infernal machinations, nor any of those that might better secure the total defeat of his victim. But had he therefore anticipated the Bishop's good faith? Oh, of all his ruses, this was without doubt the most straightforward: is virtue's noble simplicity not always the dupe of crime's odious stratagems?

Be that as it may, the scoundrel, who had expected all this to take much longer, was extremely surprised to see the plots his abominable imagination had hatched concluding so swiftly. Indeed, as soon as both husband and wife arrived, he was obliged to join in the general celebration, which posed no problem to a man raised since his youth to be a dissembler and hypocrite.

Such was the state of mind of all concerned when Villefranche reappeared.

This young man, ineffectual but charming, and still secretly in love with Madame de Gange, evinced the deepest concern for the fate of his friend's wife, and this was the reason for his visit. He said that despite the threats made against him were he to try to find the lady from whom he had been so cruelly separated, he had nonetheless retraced his steps; he had, he said, found the cave, but no one was there; not knowing how to continue his search, he returned to Avignon with the idea of explaining what had happened to Madame de Gange's mother herself; he rejected this idea, however, for fear of making public an episode that the family would doubtless much prefer to remain secret; in the end, it was by chance that he learned that Madame de Gange was back at the castle, and he had rushed there to reassure himself of the good news.

They hastened to explain to the Comte what had happened, and having done all that courtesy demanded of him, he announced his departure for the next day. They begged him to stay; he was happy to bow to their wishes; and the joy at this would have been universal had a letter from Madame de Roquefeuille, now informed of all that had happened, not urgently summoned her daughter home. The lovely Ambroisine thus left, showered with the compliments and regrets of the rest of the company, who could not help but lament the departure of such a charming young person, regarding whom Madame de Gange was now perfectly reassured.

'It seems to me,' said Théodore to Villefranche a while later, 'that you made poor use of the marvellous opportunity I contrived for you to be with my sister-in-law. You will admit it is rather clumsy to allow a woman to be dragged off by some thieves when she should be clasped tight in your arms alone.'

For the scoundrel was far from revealing that it was his malice that had led to this villainy, and his jealousy that had put an end to it . . .

'Oh, believe me, my dear Abbé,' Villefranche replied. 'I could have done no more, but as I said, your sister is unassailable: I know of no more modest and virtuous woman in the world; forever confronting me with the ardent love that consumes her for her husband, she left me without a glimmer of hope.'

'It is time to make amends for this, my friend. Now you are back, with an invitation to stay; you have a free hand, and I promise to continue my efforts on your behalf. You have to crush this arrogant beauty; you have to humble this savage virtue which resists you more out of pride than inclination. Do not underestimate yourself, my dear Comte: as handsome a cavalier as my brother may be, are you not the better man by far? A little perseverance, and you will succeed. Is it not droll,' the Abbe continued, 'that it should take a man of the cloth to teach a dashing young cavalier of your rank how to go about seducing a woman? What's this, my friend? Even at your age you still believe in their virtue? Be in no doubt that it is only ever want of opportunity—and as soon as it knocks, they know perfectly well how to make the most of it; you will have a thousand opportunities yourself, each more certain than the last, and I promise to help you seize them.'

'I agree to all this,' said the Comte. 'The obstacles, the refusals, have only stoked my passion, and I am more smitten than ever.'

'O my dear Perret,' said Théodore to his confidant, a few days after Villefranche's return. 'How poorly fortune has served me once again! Once the Marquise was in Montpellier, I had wanted all means of writing to be taken from her, and for the Bishop to give no word of her; all of this, you say, had been promised, but the promise was not kept. By these means, Alphonse would have roved the world over without finding her; wearying of this hopeless task, he would in the end have given up, and I would have become my sister's master!'

'It was my Lordship's oversight,' said Perret, 'for I impressed this important requirement on him, stressing the necessity of apprehending a sister-in-law who was gallivanting with young officers and bandit chiefs. Be that as it may, Monsieur,' Perret continued, 'you may rest assured: this proud woman's reputation has been desperately tarnished by my efforts; her escapade has been reported; I have spread the news everywhere.'

'So much the better,' said Théodore. 'That's something at least: there is often plenty to gain from defaming a woman; there are many who only succumb to debauchery because everyone already believes them to have done so already. The results of slander are always most propitious to plans such as ours; the poison of human spitefulness spreads with more energy than any other, and its wounds are the most difficult to heal. We must put it to constant use; and besides, will my brother not abandon his wife once he believes she has dishonoured herself? And will this abandonment not pave the way to my happiness?'

'But if she catches us . . .'

'Never. No one is more skilled than I in the art of hiding behind circumstances, or of contriving new ones from a grain of truth. The Comte is not as in love as I would like.'

'What's this, Monsieur? You want another man to be in love with the one you adore?'

'Oh, Villefranche's love does not bother me in the slightest; I shall extinguish it when the time is right, and if I nurture it now it is only because I need to ruin the pair of them. Don't worry, Perret, unless I am much mistaken you will soon witness some peculiar events.'

This was the state of affairs when Madame de Châteaublanc, Madame de Gange's mother, arrived at the castle: word of her daughter's escapade had brought her there, and she appeared keen to hear the whole story. The Abbé would dearly have loved to be the one to oblige her; he would have done so in his own particular way, and the impression he would have given Madame de Châteaublanc would no doubt have served his schemes; but what dangers, on the other hand, would have lain in store had a more truthful account already reached this respectable mother's ears! Madame de Gange thus related the facts herself, and these were corroborated by Alphonse. Although her daughter was guilty of nothing other than a little imprudence, her mother held her largely responsible.

'My dear child,' this tender mother said affectionately, 'remember that no matter how honourable a woman may be, she must never give the slightest grounds for suspicion: virtue, for her, is a flower even a zephyr's breath can bruise; the public, always naturally inclined to believe the worst, often condemn a woman more for the vices she appears to have than for those of which she is truly guilty. The latter are a matter of conscience—her good character, the quality of her education should protect her from these; the former are a matter of opinion, and without very careful attention, it is difficult to win over that of the public. But this is unjust, you may tell me: so it is, but all men share this flaw. You cannot offer them an opportunity they are bound to exploit.'

'O my dear mother,' the Marquise exclaimed. 'How deep are the wounds of this undeserved slander!'

'You must cauterize them at their source,' Madame de Châteaublanc replied. 'This is why the most stringent precautions are essential for a young woman; and it is only if she has a perfect understanding of her faith that she will succeed in protecting herself from all the dangers she faces. There is no true morality without religion: religion shores it up, supports it; and how could it do anything other than triumph over all the traps laid by men when it combines the fear of temptation with the reassuring hope that the Almighty will one day reward all its virtues?'

And this respectable mother, not wanting to appear to reproach her daughter unduly, contented herself with offering some simple advice that the Marquise received with tears of gratitude.

'My brother,' said Théodore to Alphonse, while Madame de Châteaublanc was staying at Gange. 'I do not like this woman: she enjoys her daughter's confidence far more than we do. If your wife inherits from Madame de Nochères, as seems to be certain, you will see Euphrasie come to some arrangement which will prevent us from sharing in this immense fortune until your child has reached his majority.'

'All the more reason to humour her,' said the Marquis.

'All the more reason to do away with her, if we are bold enough.'

'But, my friend, it is not at the very moment of my reconciliation with her daughter . . . when I love my dear wife more than ever . . . it is not, as I say, at this very moment that I am going to inflict on Euphrasie the pain and grief of depriving her of a mother.'

'My dear Alphonse,' said Théodore. 'As ever, I find your reasoning poor when it comes to defending your interests. What does this mother have to do with you and her daughter? By tying the knot with one, did you wed the other? And doesn't it happen all the time that one adores the daughter while abhorring the mother?'

'That's rare.'

'But it happens.'

'That may be, but would the pain felt by the woman I love, arising from the pain inflicted on the woman I don't, be any less real? And would I not always live in dread of its consequences?'

'And would the harm that old woman can do us not cause you a more violent pain than the one your wife might feel for the loss of her mother?'

'What? The *loss*? What on earth do you have in mind?'

'It is true, I have said too much: with a soul as timorous as yours, it is better to keep one's counsel, or dissemble; besides, I admit my words were fiercer than my thoughts on this. I have no intention of making an attempt on the life of your wife's mother; God forbid such an idea should ever enter my mind! But one could for a while place her at some remove from the world, somewhere safe, and act—or have her act—in the interim; one could take, in a word, the necessary precautions to deprive this woman of the means to ruin us, or to encourage your wife to do as much.'

'My friend,' said Alphonse, 'you know I trust you; do as you wish, but do not say a word to my wife; she must not suffer in the slightest from the plans you put in place—that is all I ask.'

'Fine, leave me in charge of this venture, and I guarantee it will unfold just as we would wish.'

The Abbé, endowed with his brother's authority, could not have been a more charming companion to Madame de Châteaublanc; he was the one to show her round the castle, to take her for nearby walks; and as one can well imagine, the traitor, now more at ease, did not demur from allowing some suspicions to linger over the charming Marquise.

'It certainly appears we were the dupes in all this,' said Théodore to Madame de Châteaublanc, 'but it is difficult to convince oneself Euphrasie was particularly pure by the time she escaped Deschamps's clutches. I would dearly like to believe she had no part in all this; but a brigand does as he wants with a woman when he threatens her with pistol in hand. As regards Villefranche, your daughter is not so easily excused, and without her acquiescence, their attachment would not be so intimate. Watch the two of them closely, and you will see if there is any doubt about this.'

'I have great difficulty believing all you are telling me, Monsieur,' said Madame de Châteaublanc. 'I know my daughter's virtuous modesty; she is incapable of the things you suspect. Esteemed by all of her first husband's family, has she joined yours only to see her reputation tarnished within it? The pleasures of the court, where my daughter spent her early years, provided her with far more opportunities to err, and she never took advantage of a single one.'

'But this story with the brigand—how do you justify it, Madame?'

'The facts nullify the charge: my daughter had to choose between death and infamy; she is alive, thus she is innocent.'

'Thus she is guilty.'

'No, Monsieur, thus she is innocent: she would have killed herself had she been forced to succumb.'

'Well then! Delve deeper into the rest, Madame, that is all I can say. But be in no doubt that her escapade in Beaucaire, her detention in Montpellier (mysteriously ordered by the Bishop), Villefranche's sudden return—be in no doubt, as I say, that these weigh heavily against your daughter. Moreover, the remorse she has shown, and the pain further reproach would cause my brother—because of all this I ask you to keep our conversation secret . . . the future will prove to you one day if it is your naivety that deceives you, or my anxiety that misleads me.'

'I see as you do, Monsieur, the reasons to keep quiet about your suspicions, and all the more so the grounds on which you base them; but I have no cause to be so quick to see evil in a young girl's conduct . . . a girl who has never given me a moment's alarm; so, before changing my mind, I shall wait for proof worthy of destroying the esteem and affection I have always felt for her.'

Although these opening exchanges were designed to throw a little cold water on the relations between these two characters, the Abbé, sensing that in the interests of his stratagems he needed to remain on a good footing with this woman, continued to be pleasant, and made no further mention of such a serious subject.

Madame de Châteaublanc left after a fortnight, without revealing any of what had transpired between herself and Théodore, and, unfortunately in one regard, though very fortunately in another, Villefranche had done nothing in the meantime to justify the suspicions the Abbé would have been delighted to see take root in her mind.

It was around this time that the Marquis received a letter from the Chevalier de Gange, his brother, signed and dated in Nice, where his duties still detained him. He assured Alphonse in his letter that he would see him again soon; his eagerness to meet his sister-in-law, of whom everyone spoke so highly, would ensure his swift expedition of all those matters that might yet delay the pleasure.

This new character, whom it is now time to introduce given the importance of the role we shall soon see him play, was the youngest of the family; more wicked than the Marquis in what follows, he none-theless had less wit and finesse than the Abbé; the latter was his close friend and confidant, and he rarely made any decisions without Théodore's intervention. To describe all three in one fell swoop, we shall say that the Marquis lent himself to evil, the Abbé counselled it, and the Chevalier committed it.

One cannot help but tremble to see the enemies that will soon encir-cle the sweetest, most charming, and most virtuous of women; but let us not get ahead of ourselves—there is much to tell beforehand.

Every year, on the eve of that day consecrated by the Church to commemorate the dead, a lugubrious and solemn celebration which dates from great antiquity and is rooted in the tender piety and reli-gious respect the man of sensibility owes those who have walked life's path before him and left behind only mortal remains . . . every year on this day, as I say, Madame de Gange had, since her arrival at the castle, gone to the labyrinth to visit the tomb where her husband wished to be immured with her: a more intense emotion than usual seemed to lead her there this time.

It was about five o'clock in the evening when she arrived alone as was her wont; a thick mist shrouded the air and veiled the sun's dying rays as it plunged into the waves; on this calm and mild evening she could hear the imposing tolling of those bells by which men, shatter-ing the stillness of the air, seem to share their tears of sorrow with the Almighty. This plaintive sound, which joined the mournful calls of the night-birds, lent this sombre setting all the pathos and solemnity it seemed to invite: it was as if one could hear the moans of those who were to be remembered . . . as if their spirits were whirling about their tombs, prying them open to greet you.

Euphrasie, dumbstruck, does not move for a few minutes, and only emerges from this state of apathy, precious fruit of the most exquisite sensibility, at the piercing whistle of a barn owl* swooping over her. Overwhelmed by this assault on her senses, she falls to her knees, her two hands clasped together over the tomb.

'O Lord!' she exclaims with the contrition of an intense and pas-sionate soul. 'If you have further misfortunes in store for me, allow me to escape them today by placing me in this final resting place, where the dear husband you gave me shall in time join me: this way I shall at least reach it pure and worthy of his grief; you will extend his days on earth so he retains for all eternity the image of the one who died worshipping him. But if this worldly thought offends you, O Lord, take all of Euphrasie's capacity to love for yourself: it is only fitting it should belong to you alone, as it is you alone I owe the few happy moments I have experienced until now. Hold me close to your heart, O Lord! Mine was always filled with your image; I only knew of your existence from the love that blazed within me for you. Oh, if the heart of man is your temple, this is because it is also the hearth where the flame of holy ardour burns. Deign hear my prayers for the family I have lost ... for my first husband who guided me through my early years; and when I am reunited with them by your command, deign, as you did with them, keep me close to you, so that I may follow their example and see you throughout the boundless eternity of the passing centuries—an eternity which no longer strikes fear in the feeble mind of men when one can devote it to blessing and glorifying you forever.'

Euphrasie, uttering these last words, so relinquishes her physical faculties that she barely seems to cling onto life; her bosom throbs violently, her gaze, fixed on the heavens, contemplates only her God; from her parted lips, the soul that moments before had so animated her seems to soar towards him; and as she only exists in him, so she can only be reborn through him.

O you monsters! You who choose this moment to complete her ruin, come see the anguish that unites her with the God your crimes shall appal; and if the view of this celestial angel does not stop you, then all the tortures in hell are too paltry for you.

Théodore, acquainted with his sister's habits, suggested to Villefranche that this would be the ideal moment for the conquest to which he aspired.

'She is there,' said the traitor. 'Her soul, made tender by devotion, will open up more easily to love: go, my friend, slip softly into this labyrinth, seize the moment; if she is praying, she is yours; I cannot promise anything if the height of her fervour has dissipated. Be for her the serpent who tempted Eve: she too was praying at the time.'

'What do you make of those prayers your wife offers without fail every year in the labyrinth?' Théodore asked the Marquis a moment later. 'As for me, I do not mind admitting I find them unedifying. If I were married, dear brother, I assure you I would not like my wife to wander in the woods, all alone, at this hour. Try as I might, I cannot help but have my suspicions about that Villefranche. I have hidden these from you as much as I can, but they keep returning. In all decency he owed us an explanation as well as a visit after the Beaucaire escapade. Listen, brother, do not accuse me of wishing to sow discord in your marriage; I do not need, it seems to me, to defend myself on that score—you know that I am incapable of such a thing; but even if you see no dishonour in having an adventuress in the family, I warn you that I do not wish to be brother-in-law to a woman whose imprudence, or weakness, gives rise each day to the gravest suspicions. In any case, arm yourself and let us head over to the tomb.'

'In truth, brother, your mind is forever seeing evil everywhere: you even go so far as to suspect it now in the most virtuous and pious of acts.'

'O my friend! Do you not know that it is beneath the deceptive appearances of modesty and religion that the most cunning coquettes conceal their vices? I hope I am mistaken, and doubtless I am; but as this is a perfect opportunity, let us seek the truth . . . Where is Villefranche? The two of us were supposed to go hunting this evening in the grounds; where is he? Why did he not keep his word?'

'All right, I shall do as you please,' said the Marquis, placing two loaded pistols in his pouch; 'but remember that this will be the last time I indulge your fantasies.'

'So be it, I am of the same mind, and if this test does not succeed, I swear I shall not ask for another. But let us hurry: the night is approaching, and the day that remains is barely enough to shine its light on your Euphrasie's innocence, or shame.'

They had barely entered the labyrinth when one of the trees bearing those mottos we mentioned before in our description of this maze, offered this to the Marquis, who halted before it:

BEWARE THE TRAPS LAID BY THE WICKED

'This motto is peculiar,' said Alphonse. 'It takes me aback . . . I had forgotten about it.'

'It makes me tremble,' said the Abbé. 'Might it not be a horoscope for the steps we are taking? And might this precious advice not lend weight to my suspicions?'

'This warning is for one of us,' said Alphonse. 'If you are wicked, I should be wary of you.'

'Let us move on,' said Théodore.

They continue . . . And here they are, near the dreadful place where all will be revealed.

'Carry on without me now,' said the Abbé. 'I shall wait here: I would not want anyone to think I provoked actions you alone have the right to take. Go then, but be careful: there is no evil in discovering a crime, but there is a great deal in punishing it oneself. Leave justice for the courts—leave that dreadful burden to them.'

The Abbé rests against an old oak, and the Marquis continues alone. He barely reaches the row of cypresses and willows, their branches bowing over the tomb, when through the leaves he spies Villefranche holding Euphrasie in his arms, and smothering her mouth with the most criminal of kisses. Without taking a moment to notice Euphrasie's vigorous resistance, to see that this rogue's mouth is stifling her cries of outrage and despair, he throws himself on his brazen rival, handing him a pistol as he takes aim with the other.

'Defend yourself, you scoundrel,' he tells him, 'or I shall blow your brains out.'

Villefranche, dumbstruck, takes the weapon, fires at the Marquis, and misses. Alphonse steadies himself, and the villain is left to wash away his crime in Stygian waters: he expires . . . Euphrasie falls on his corpse . . . She swoons.

'Here, brother,' the wretched Alphonse cries out. 'Come and enjoy the infamy you counselled; come and relish the horror of my fate. I no longer have any cause to doubt you now: there she is, complicit in this traitor's debauchery . . . Look at her, covered in the blood that has dishonoured mine; see the shame spread over her adulterous brow, the veils of death that already cover her. Oh, how she deceived me every day of her life! Leave them . . . they wish to die together; and let this tomb bury both my despair and those who caused it.'

But the vile Théodore did not relinquish his victim: he wanted to punish her, but not yet destroy her. He gives her smelling salts, and revives her; he lifts her to her feet, but she does not have the strength to walk; she falls after a few steps. The two brothers hasten back to the castle to summon a coach for her. By the time they return, she is unconscious, and it is only with the greatest difficulty imaginable that they manage to get her home, consumed by a burning fever.

CHAPTER VI

'WHAT a deceitful creature!' Alphonse said to his brother, as soon as they were alone. 'How well she feigns religion, virtue, decency, and how well her face, with its air of sweetness, fools people all the more! But one can discern, in those seductive features, the mask of hypocrisy— I must have been blind not to recognize it straight away. Oh, how I would pity men, if all women resembled this one.'

'My friend,' said Théodore, 'I fear you were too hasty; I advised prudence, and you listened only to your passions. What are we going to do now? A dead man! A guilty woman!'

'We must bury the first and imprison the other,' said Alphonse. You will stay here, and take care of everything, and as for me, I shall seek refuge in Avignon* from the repercussions of this duel. Do not let the secret out, forestall any inquiries, and keep me informed of every circumstance without fail.'

'And what will you tell the mother, to justify her daughter's detention?'

'I shall reveal her conduct.'

'You cannot do so without dishonouring yourself.'

'Are you therefore going to conclude that I must suffer the further ignominy of allowing this woman to go free?'

'That is not at all what I mean, but this, I think, is the prudent course: you must send Madame de Châteaublanc to me here with her grandson . . . As soon as she has left Avignon, spread the word that important matters have called her, and the child, to Paris. I shall take care of the three of them, once they are in my grasp. This precaution of mine is all the more essential as Madame de Nochères, that very wealthy relation of hers, will make her will in favour of Euphrasie; if your wife is unhappy with us, she will leave everything to her mother and son. It is vital therefore, as you sense yourself, that we take precautions. There is more to this, brother, than vengeance: we must think of our interests. Once Madame de Châteaublanc is in our hands, and thought to be in Paris, she will be forgotten; she is not well known in society, and we can feign her demise. Thereafter the assets left by Madame de Nochères will unquestionably revert to your wife, whose unsound mind will be very easy to prove after her recent conduct; and then we shall be master of those assets until your son reaches his majority.'

'All that is well conceived, dear brother, but there is many a slip between cup and lip! I see so many difficulties in what you say!'

'I shall overcome them, be sure of it.'

And off they went to bed, without even checking on the dreadful state in which the most innocent, most virtuous and most unfortunate of women had been left.

How the passions harden the hearts of men! How can anyone say with certainty they are inspired by Nature when they categorically break all her laws! The heart of man, stirred by them, resembles a ship battered by a storm, swept away by the winds in all their fury. Thereafter, the heart becomes prey to impulses that are no longer natural, as they derive from an utterly foreign cause; without this cause, it would be calm; it can no longer be so when this cause acts upon it; but as foreign as it may be, does it not still belong to Nature? Most certainly not: to insist so would be to claim that God, the driving force behind Nature, wishes to do both good and evil—untenable in a perfect Being. But, the atheists will say, if God is all-powerful, why does he allow evil?* To make us worthy of resisting it, something we always have the power to do by his grace. But why not grant this grace to all men? Because not all know to ask for it, or because not all are worthy of obtaining it. Sophistry, those immoral individuals will tell you. Far less so than your arguments, for if an evident sophistry exists, it most certainly belongs to he who dares claim a divine and perfect Creator as an author of both good and evil. No, evil is not in Nature, it is in man's depravity, when he forgets its laws, or when he loses all sense of the true meaning of these laws: is there a man in the world capable of committing a crime in cold blood? . . . Of course not. Who is the man who commits a crime? One carried away by his passions; one who, defying Nature, and straying from it, can no longer be a man of Nature. But evil is necessary to Nature. No, it is an accident of Nature, but not a necessity: if I leap into a river, and I drown, this death is an accidental consequence of my action, but it is not necessary, for there was no need for me to leap into the water. Let us remember therefore, that all of man's poor arguments come from his passions alone: when they lead his heart astray, they disturb his mind; when he learns to suppress them, or control them, he soon sees them in a clear light again. They are only hidden by the darkness into which his passions have plunged him.

But let us end this digression into which our story led us, and pick up its thread, as painful as it may be to pursue.

'I am going to the Marquise's quarters,' said Alphonse upon rising. 'I am curious to see how brazenly she makes excuses for her ignominy . . . Do you wish to accompany me, Théodore?'

'It would not be my place: I would get in the way of the explanation. Be gentle but firm: listen to what she tells you; forgive her, if she is in the right; no mercy, if she cannot clear herself of what you saw with your own eyes yesterday.'

'I defy her to exonerate herself.'

'O my friend! Do you not know how trusting love is? She will prove to you that you did not see a thing, because she knows full well that one always believes a beloved wife; she will come out of this examination as pure as you had the weakness to think her in her escapade with Deschamps, to whom there is no doubt she granted all her favours.'

'Ah . . . do not open fresh wounds when I am still trying to heal from those I have just suffered.'

'I have to be cruel to be kind with you, so I shall be; I have to be bold to make the scales fall from your eyes, so I am; if you still want to be deceived, you will be; it is so pleasing to make excuses for the one we love, so gratifying for our self-esteem to be placed in such a situation, that one can no longer conceive of any infidelity—and you are by nature so weak!'

'I shall soon convince you I am nothing of the sort,' said Alphonse, gripping his brother's hand and charging towards Euphrasie's quarters. He is stopped, however, at her door, and told the Marquise had endured a very bad night and needed some solicitude.

'Vice is owed none,' said Alphonse, pushing the chambermaid out of the way, and pulling apart the curtains of his wife's bed. 'Get up, Madame,' he said harshly, 'and answer me.'

'I shall obey you, Monsieur, no matter how much I am suffering.'

'I think it unlikely that you are suffering as much as you make others suffer.'

And the Marquise, without replying, hastened to find a dress.

'Take this one,' said Alphonse, indicating the one she had worn the day before. 'It is still stained with the foul blood you wanted to mix with mine. These spots, forever before your eyes, will help you remember your crime; it is the only attire appropriate for the tomb in which I shall bury you.'

'Oh, may I enter it at least without having lost your esteem.'

'Have you done anything to deserve it?'

'I have done nothing to lose it; and if I am no longer worthy of your love, believe at least that I am worthy of your respect.'

'That is to take arrogance far indeed.'

'Oh, far less, no doubt, than you take injustice!'

'So I should not believe my own eyes?'

'Appearances are often deceptive, Monsieur, in such moments of crisis. It was for you, alas, that I was invoking the Almighty, when a man I barely recognized grabbed hold of me—a wicked man who forced me into the compromising position in which you discovered me.'

'I could not read your mind, and I caught you by surprise.'

'But if you could not read my mind, why do you suppose it to be guilty?'

'Because the facts prove its depravity.'

'So then, you believe that a wife who has always been faithful to you, a wife who has adored you . . . who adores you still—you believe her guilty of the greatest of crimes against you simply because appearances are against her?'

'What? Does what happened here not follow on from your escapade in Beaucaire? Is it not a consequence of your liaison with Villefranche?'

'But how can you say, Monsieur, that it follows something that never happened in the first place? As I have vindicated myself regarding the first part of this false accusation, why would you allow the second to stand when it is nullified along with the first? If you retained some suspicion of Villefranche, why did you receive him upon his return? Of the two of us, who is at fault, I ask of you here and now? He follows me into the labyrinth, where I went to pray for you and my ancestors. Who sent him there? Who told him I was there? What, Monsieur? Do you really imagine it is at the very moment I am imploring God on your behalf, when my heart brims with tenderness for you alone, when my only thought is of you, when I am overcome with the joy of seeing you relinquish those dreadful impressions of me . . . you believe, I say, that at such a moment I would be guilty of the utmost treachery and duplicity? Oh, no! No, my dear Alphonse, you don't believe this,' said this touching woman, throwing herself in tears at her husband's feet. 'You don't believe your Euphrasie is guilty, because she could not possibly be, because the heart that belongs to you could not burn for another, because I shall adore you until my dying breath, and because the woman who would betray you could love you no longer as soon as she ceased to be worthy of you. Love me, Alphonse, love me, and never believe Euphrasie capable of profaning the altar at which I worshipped your image.'

This divine woman, at her husband's feet, tears streaming down her rosy cheeks, still flushed with the fire burning in her veins, her bloodied dress seeming to exonerate rather than incriminate her; the distraction with which she puts it back on, her beautiful hair strewn over a bosom of alabaster, with some of her locks curling around the finest waist in the world; the truthfulness intoned by that sweet voice; one beautiful hand raised to the heavens, the other holding her husband's; that noble agony, inflicted unjustly on a proud soul not stooping to justify itself—all of this . . . all of this effaces the earthly aspect of this angelic woman, revealing her to mortal eyes as the divinity of innocence and virtue.

When Alphonse felt his hands drenched in the tears of the woman he had idolized, he trembled; wanting to stifle . . . to hide at least the surge of sensibility to which he succumbed despite himself, he rises, paces the room like a man demented, steels his soul, which was urging love and repentance; then, violently pulling his wife up:

'Follow me, Madame,' he told her. 'You have lost the power to deceive me; you fool me no longer.'

With these words he opened the door to the closet, where there was a staircase leading to the tower holding the archives:

'Follow me, I tell you. I shall find a room that suits you better than this one: the Marquise de Gange's quarters can be those of an adulteress no longer; crime, symbol of death, must bury itself in the same darkness.'

Euphrasie, whose tears are stopped by this redoubled cruelty, wishes to take some personal effects or clothes with her; the Marquis refuses.

'You will be given all you need, as soon as you are settled in this tower,' he said with furrowed brow. 'Be calm, Madame, you will be treated there with more kindness than you deserve.'

She obeys, and follows her husband; but as she passes by her bed, she grabs Alphonse's portrait, which had never left its place there:

'Oh, as for this,' she said ardently, 'no one shall steal this from me.'

'Let go of this portrait, Madame,' said Alphonse, trying to take it from her. 'You are no longer worthy of it, as you have betrayed the man it represents.'

'No, no, I did not betray him, and no one will take his image from me,' said the poor wretch, pressing it to her heart. 'It will be my consolation in the cell to which you have condemned me; I shall tell it of the proofs of my innocence which you refuse to hear; it will be more just than you, it will listen to me.'

But the painting, damaged in the struggle, drops to the ground; the poor soul lunges at it, like a distraught mother whose children are being taken from her; she picks up the canvas, clasps it to her breast, and climbs the stairs.

The chamber where she is to be locked away, situated above the archives, is as round as the tower at the top of which she finds herself; a skylight high above her, covered in iron bars, lets into this sombre den barely any rays of a sun of which no man has the right to deprive another. A table, two rickety chairs, and, nailed to the wall, a bedstead covered with two paltry mattresses—such were all the furnishings allowed this woman, who until now had known only luxury and opulence.

'Someone will visit you once a day, Madame,' said Alphonse as he withdrew. 'It will be to bring you clothes and food; if you utter a single word to the woman who will serve you, your door will not open again. Adieu . . . May your stay in this cell restore your soul to virtue, and make me forget, if that is possible, your sins.'

'Monsieur,' said the Marquise, 'shall I be allowed to write to you?'

'You will write to no one, Madame. As you can see, we have left nothing in your room that would allow you to do so. Here are a few works of piety—learn from these the sentiments that should never have deserted your heart.'

Euphrasie throws herself at the door when she sees her husband ready to close it: she reaches out with both arms, without saying a word . . . O the eloquence of silent suffering! You no longer reach the heart that ought to hear you; your ardour melts in the torrents of injustice . . . Euphrasie, pushed away by Alphonse, falls back from the door, which slams shut, and all one can hear within are sobs of despair and piercing cries of agony.

'I would never have thought you capable of such strength,' said the Abbé, seeing Alphonse return. 'But you have done what you had to do . . . Henceforth, no regrets.'

'O my friend! If you had heard her, perhaps you would have lent some credence to what she said.'

'What's this? Do you not know that it is when women are at their guiltiest that they justify themselves most eloquently?'

'O my brother! It was as if her tears fell on my heart—I feel them there.'

'You need some distraction, Alphonse. Avignon will be a safe haven for you; it is a delightful city; go and spend some time there; I shall take care of everything here at the castle. Above all do not forget to send me Madame de Châteaublanc and your son: I have explained just how vital this is. The opportunity to see her daughter will more than justify the trip. Explain nothing before she leaves: I shall say what needs to be said once she is here.'

All is put in place, and the Marquis leaves without seeing his wife again—without even deigning to ask the woman charged with looking after her for news.

The very next day, Théodore walked up to Euphrasie's room.

'My dear sister,' he said as he entered, 'I am deeply moved by your situation. You see now where imprudence has brought us; I am quite convinced that is all there is to it. Was Alphonse not guilty of the same sin as you in Beaucaire? He was, however, no more culpable than you are here: and who can promise never to do anything imprudent in the course of a lifetime? But what makes me despair is not to be able to alleviate your fate; he left me such precise orders! He even wanted you put in the humid dungeon that serves as a cellar for this tower. It is to my insistent appeals that you owe these more salubrious conditions. But what do I see? A bed without curtains, paltry mattresses, and not so much as an armchair! Such trifles are up to me, and you will have them immediately. I am unfortunately not master of the rest; but my brother will relent, believe me; we shall convince him in the end; have confidence in me, and you will soon see the fruit of my labours.'

'So my husband is no longer at the castle?'

'He feared for the repercussions of his duel; Avignon will provide him with refuge for a while, and before long you will see everything return to normal.'

'O heavens! My husband is in danger, and I am the reason for it! Good God! Let your wrath strike me and spare my husband.'

'What a soul you have, Euphrasie! What is this? Still you pray for the one who persecutes you!'

'He believes he is in the right; he is my husband, I must respect even his injustice. One day perhaps he will know the woman who loved him with such dignity: my reward awaits where his blindness ends.'

'What surroundings!' said the Abbé, looking around the room. 'Is this really where the perfect model of grace and virtue should draw breath? (Then, still as affectionately:) So the Marquis forbids you to write?'

'He took away the means to do so: but in any case what would I write that I have not already said to him? If he did not wish to see my innocence in my heart, would he read it any better in my words? This deprivation only upsets me because it means I shall receive no letters from him: it would have been such a comfort to shed tears over the treasured lines his passion once moved him to write! What can we do, my brother? I must be deprived of everything. It is only my thoughts that cannot be banished: for as long as I live, they will be of him, and, no matter the woes I endure, they will always be my consolation.'

'Perhaps,' said the Abbé distractedly, 'perhaps one day you may find consolation of a more palpable kind . . .'

And, not wanting to go too far at first, he took leave of his sister-in-law, promising to provide her with all that might be agreeable to her, with the exception of anything the Marquis had expressly forbidden.

Thereafter, Théodore took over all the administration of the castle: farmers, tradesmen, servants—all were under his authority. As there was no shame in his brother's duel, he did not conceal it; he said that the Marquise had left in secret and gone to Avignon to be reunited with her husband, and was likely to travel on to Paris to solicit the Cardinal's pardon for him. He had taken Rose, the only woman serving Euphrasie, into his confidence, and so from this moment on the traitor held the woman he had won through trickery and infamy entirely in his possession; but as he believed prudence necessary for the consummation of his crimes, he contained himself, and did not visit his captive for over a week.

The Marquise alleviated her solitude with the devotional books her husband had left her. One has to have experienced the dreadful plight of a prisoner to be able to convey it.

> While around him everything changes in a trice,
> He stays in the same moment each day of his life.
> Is that living? O Lord! 'Tis barely existing.
> La Chaussée*

It is cruel indeed to see the days passing by in the same manner, to say to oneself, through tears, tomorrow I shall do exactly what I did today; there will be no variation for me; it is the darkness of the tomb that envelops me already; all that separates me from the dead is the awful despair of being alive; here I am, indifferent to all the events of my life; numb to all the sentiments of the soul; all its affections are now blunted, I remain a stranger to them all; this sweet gift of nature, this heart, the reason I exist, is already frozen in my chest, impassive to love, to hate, to hope. The beating of this automatic heart is but the swinging of the pendulum preparing me for oblivion; and as he no longer has the gift of love, the wretch in his cell who has also lost the gift of life is all but a cadaver . . . To whom will he speak? To whom will he call in the terrible silence into which misfortune has plunged him? . . . To God alone! . . . Culpable authors, unbelieving barbarians, wallowing in those criminal pleasures your dangerous doctrines condone, take not from the unfortunate the only joy that can offer him some peace; leave him this God who reaches out to him; sustained with far nobler thoughts, the righteous hope this divine Creator inspires will at least console him for all that your dangerous pleasures steal from him.

The Marquise de Gange, who even in the midst of life's seductions, had never wavered in her piety, now found in religion all the rewards it provides to those who respect it; she devoured the books her husband had left her; our holy scriptures offered her peace, calm, and contentment. Let those who seek them as she did, read with care the Books of Job and Jeremiah, the admirable Psalms of David, *The Imitation of Christ*, and they will see if the words contained in these sublime writings are not indeed those of a God. Remembering this God who died to save us, let them model themselves on the patience, the kindness which marked the last moments of this unforgettable sacrifice: at that moment they will be convinced of a truth so consoling for the unfortunate, which is that all of life's joys are not worth the ray of hope the Almighty grants the man who weeps and prays. It was at that moment, as I say, that Euphrasie found in this manna from heaven the courage to bear her plight, and to cry out along with the Prophet King: 'O Lord! You are my sole refuge against the evil that surrounds me: deliver me from the hands of my enemies as they assail me from all sides.'*

The Abbé finally appeared once again at his sister's door; and, congratulating himself on seeing his orders followed in relation to the favours he had promised:

'Well then, my dear Euphrasie,' he said to her. 'Are you a little more comfortable? . . . Ah! I think of your exile from the world as I do that of the angels of heaven, who draw near to the Almighty's boundless dominion. What delights will compensate you one day for the deprivations you bear for a moment!'

'I am counting on it, my brother,' the Marquise replied, 'and I confess those are the only thoughts that bring me peace since I have been in this cell.'

'How I would love to make your stay here more pleasant still!' said the treacherous Abbé, gazing at Euphrasie with eyes ablaze.

'Oh, what could be a greater comfort for me in my tribulations,' Alphonse's wife replied, 'than that which the Almighty provides?'

'Far be it from me to take away the source of your happiness,' said the Abbé, 'but I nonetheless think it might be possible to provide you with some distraction.'

'And how?'

'You see that I have been left the absolute arbiter of your fate . . . If you were to take pity on mine, do you not think I would find a way to ease yours . . .?'

Here the perspicacious Marquise, who thought she understood Théodore, averted her gaze with an anxiety that was impossible to disguise.

'I do not follow you, my brother,' she said to him softly. 'My fate, you have said, is determined by Alphonse, and can only be eased by him . . . What would you dare do without his permission?'

'I would dare love you, Madame,' said Théodore, throwing himself at the Marquise's feet. 'I would dare swear to you a love that will end only with my life, and that began the first moment I saw you.'

At this the Marquise, utterly resolved to reject such declarations, was nonetheless thrown into confusion: she could see the wretched abyss into which her refusal would pitch her; and, on the other hand, what insurmountable repugnance she felt for the criminal liaison this man had dared propose! To betray her duties, her husband and her virtue in one fell swoop was an impossibility for her: her emotions were in turmoil, but her decency, her faith, her feelings did not fail her:

'Leave, Monsieur, leave,' she told Théodore defiantly. 'I thought I had a friend in you, and now I see only a seducer . . . Leave, I tell you, I shall find a way to withstand the burden of my sorrows . . . Perhaps I can bear it still . . . If I were to compound it with such a crime, it would be more agonizing to me than the most dreadful of tortures.'

'I do not believe, Madame, that you are thinking clearly,' said the Abbé, withdrawing. 'Never mind, I shall leave you to your reflections, persuaded that circumstances will change them in my favour.'

'There are none that could make me forget either your wickedness or my husband,' said Euphrasie, 'and I can imagine none that could ever lure me into crime.'

CHAPTER VII

I⊤ would be easier to paint than to describe Théodore's confusion at
finding himself treated thus by a woman whose woes he had expected
to drive into his arms.

'What pride!' he said to Laurent, bemoaning the scene he had just
experienced. 'My friend, what must I do to crush this arrogant creature?'

'The very opposite of what you are doing, Monsieur,' his confidant
replied. 'Once she starts to treat you this way, you can be sure you will
triumph over her only by following her example: she is cruel, so be
the same towards her; take away all the comforts you procured for her,
and deprive her of something new each day; let her know that her
hopes rest on you alone, that you alone are the key to her happiness,
that you alone can reconcile her with her husband, and finally, that
you alone can bring her innocence to light. You will then see submission replace pride in her heart of stone, and necessity inevitably force
her into the only arms she will feel are still willing to embrace her.'

'Your advice is sound, but harsh too, my dear Laurent.'

'What? Should one waver in your situation? What do her misfortunes matter when set against your desires? Should one not always
put whatever matters to oneself before whatever matters only to
others? In a word, is it my place to lecture you—am I not your worthy
student?'

'You are right, my friend. Henceforth I shall show no mercy, and
listen only to Cupid, but I must take it one step at a time: a torment
today, an attempt tomorrow, and so on until she surrenders.'

'Yes, that is by far the best way,' said Laurent, 'but what if she
doesn't surrender?'

'Impossible, my friend. This is a fortress we shall breach in the
end: the besieged will capitulate—an assault will be the very last
resort.'

'It would be better . . . yes, Monsieur, it would be better, all things
considered, if she capitulated; she will, you can be sure of that.'

'I am counting on it . . . Send me the woman taking care of her, so
I can pass on my instructions.'

'Rose,' said the Abbé upon seeing Euphrasie's turnkey, a girl
around thirty years of age and a member of the household since her

childhood. 'Go tell your mistress that in light of the new orders I have just received from her husband, she must be reduced to the same situation she found herself in before my goodwill came to her rescue; you will remove absolutely everything from her quarters—the portrait, the books, the furnishings—and leave only a single mattress on the bed.'

'But Monsieur,' said the compassionate Rose, 'these orders are so severe. Madame will fall ill . . . She has barely recovered from her last fever . . . I swear to you, Monsieur, this will kill her.'

'I know, Rose,' the Abbé replied, 'but pressing circumstances oblige us to act in this way: the duel is causing a stir; it is only by acknowledging his wife's crimes that my brother can justify this unfortunate bloodshed; and if anyone were to come here, we would have to prove, by the severity of the conditions in which the guilty party is being held, the part she played in this misfortune. You can see the sense in this, Rose—you are too sharp-witted not to grasp it.'

'Oh yes, Monsieur! But the price of these circumstances makes me despair no less about what their consequences might be; and Madame is so good, so kind, so resigned to her fate.'

'If she stirs you to pity, I shall send you away: you must see in her nothing but her crime, which is so serious it should extinguish any feelings of compassion that might diminish their horror. Are you not aware, Rose, that she was Villefranche's avowed mistress? That this rogue was utterly brazen? That he dishonoured her in public? That, in a word, my brother caught the two of them in the act? That is what she did not tell you, Rose, and what she is doubtless hiding from you.'

'Oh indeed, Monsieur, I didn't know all this . . . Betraying such a good master as Monsieur le Marquis! That's awful! My opinion of her will change now, you can be sure of that.'

'Then go and carry out my orders without showing the least mercy, and afterwards come and tell me what effect they have had on her.'

There are moments in life when even the greatest scoundrels reflect, when remorse still rumbles in their hearts, and when they would perhaps reverse their course were their passions not driving them on: in such moments it is as if Nature is reclaiming the rights that crime wished to steal from her; the wrench of this conflict alone would be enough to strike fear into the wise; indeed, there would be no conflict at all if those determined to be guilty did not confront virtue with crime. If reason triumphs, such a man is fortunate. He becomes the most pitiable of men, however, if the passions overwhelm him: repentance returns a second time to make his wounded heart listen; it is too late . . . men hold him in contempt, the law deals with him, a vengeful God looms, and this wicked man can only blame himself for his suffering. But Théodore, hardened, does not waver: his soul, open to infamy, allows not a single ray of virtue to penetrate.

'Well then, Rose,' he said, when this girl returned from the tower. 'Have my orders been carried out? . . . You are crying, Rose! I thought I had convinced you this weakness was out of place.'

'That's all well and good, Monsieur, but how can I stop myself crying when I see my mistress in tears?'

'So, how did she react to what you have just done?'

'With angelic resignation, Monsieur. She wanted me to remove far more things than you had ordered me to take; she did not even want me to leave a mattress on the bed. "This wood will do for me," she said. "I do not need anything in the world, now I have lost my husband's heart: it is a coffin I need, a coffin . . ." And her eyes flooded with tears . . .'

'Did she mention me?'

'No, Monsieur. I described your regret at having to carry out these punishments; she replied that she could well believe it.'

'And not a word of complaint against me?'

'Not one, Monsieur.'

'Right! Tomorrow, instead of the meals you bring her, you will give her only bread and water.'

'O Monsieur! I could never do such a thing.'

'Well then! I shall do it myself if you refuse. You would have to be a wretch yourself to take pity on a monster who has just brought about her husband's exile, her lover's death, her family's dishonour, and who knows what further tribulations these heinous crimes may yet bring. Have you reproached her for these abominations?'

'Oh no, Monsieur. Where virtue shines forth so clearly, how is one to suspect evil? Alas! I would feel I was insulting her to accuse her of such horrors; and if I were to talk to her of such a crime, the virtue would gleam in her eyes, demanding its rights, to come to her defence and seal her triumph.'

'Rose! I can see you are not the woman I require. Abbé Perret will fill your post far better, and I shall see to it now.'

But worthy Rose, who sensed all that the Marquise might lose from such a change, chose to play her part in order to be useful to her mistress; and, having Théodore repeat a second time all the crimes of which the Marquise was accused, she gave the impression she was converted by the evidence he so wickedly described, and promised to carry out word for word all that he ordained.

After a few days of this regime, the Abbé wished to mount a fresh assault. He enters, and, struck by the Marquise's despondency, pity stirs within him for a moment; but a heart as corrupt as his does not allow it to take a firmer hold.

'Madame,' he says to his sister-in-law, 'I have come to express all the sorrow I feel at the execution of my brother's orders; but it appears that the matter of the duel is still not resolved, and that this new severity he has imposed is designed to convince others of the very great part you played in this affair.'

'So, Monsieur,' said the Marquise coldly, 'you are accusing my husband of committing a second injustice to mitigate the first.'

'You take forgetting your sins to an extreme, Madame, when you excuse them by such words: one is capable of anything when one takes brazenness so far.'

'O Monsieur. Would you agree to lightning striking the guiltier of the two of us?'

'No, Madame, for I would be vexed to see you perish in front of me.'

'This cunning subterfuge unmasks you, Théodore; it exposes your soul, and you will certainly not succeed by it.'

'Why then this agitation, when you can ease all this hardship with a single word?'

'Then I shall say this word, as long as you do not object to me acquiring my husband's consent first.'

'What is the point of all these sly evasions?' asked Théodore. 'Such a request for consent would not chime well with the feelings I have revealed to you, Euphrasie. These feelings are beyond the power of words to convey: to adore you is my most cherished commandment; to express it my greatest happiness; I breathe for you alone in this world; say the word, and your misfortunes will cease. Relinquish the vain hope of winning back my brother's heart: he is too bitter, and you will never prevail. Can I not therefore take care of you in all the ways he should have done? If the law prevents us from finding happiness in France, there are other countries where we can live, and my home shall always be wherever you allow me to live with you. Follow me, Euphrasie, follow me, and my happiness is assured if you believe me capable of contributing to your own.'

'So then, everything you have just done is not by order of my husband after all? In that case, it is a very clumsy stratagem to make me fall into your traps.'

'No, Madame, no—all the wrongs I have done you are by your husband's orders; any happiness shall come from me alone.'

'Well then. I shall not buy it at this price: your plots against me are revealed, Monsieur; perhaps I am as skilled in untangling them as you are adept in weaving them. This art is the resource of the weak; it is Nature's gift, to protect them from all that the strongest might employ against them. So I have seen through you, Monsieur; now it is for you to do as you will, but be in no doubt that I shall resist your ruses and your efforts with all the strength the heavens have given me to defend myself.'

'I beg you, Madame,' the Abbé replied, 'to think of me more kindly, as you did before. You love your husband—well, I alone can restore your place in his soul, I alone can restore his heart to you, and I shall forever ruin you in his eyes if you do not satisfy me in return.'

'So, you cruel and reckless man: you wish me to regain my husband's heart by doing everything possible to make myself unworthy of it?'

'These sacrifices will be nothing to him—he will not know of them. You deprive me of everything even when you have nothing to gain.'

'If I am so unfortunate as to fail to regain my husband's esteem, I shall at least have my own; I shall have that clear conscience that consoles us for any hardships that may lead us to a peaceful death; I shall have your esteem too, Monsieur. One hates, I know all too well, those who refuse to be complicit in crime, but one cannot help but respect them.'

And the Abbé, furious, locks up his wretched victim himself as he leaves.

Théodore from that moment changed tack: he returned to the Marquise all the comforts that had been taken from her, and filled her cell with anything he thought she might find agreeable: books, paper, ink, flowers, birds—everything she loves is lavished on her; a great show is made of serving her only those dishes she is known to enjoy; and Rose, each morning, asks her what she would like.

'Well then! What does she think of me now?' he asks Rose. 'Is her aversion for me abating?'

'I cannot conceal from you, Monsieur, that Madame seems as indifferent to the kindness you do her as she was to the cruelty it pleased you to show her. "Rose," she tells me with the greatest composure. "The motives that make my brother behave in this way are so well known to me that I can no more credit him for his generosity than I can reproach him for his ill treatment. In any case, I hope for no other joy in the world than to see my husband, and it is not through his brother that I shall be granted this favour . . . I must resign myself, my sweet Rose, and you can see that I am indeed resigned to everything. You cannot imagine, my dear, the consolation self-esteem and religion can bring to a sensitive soul. The injustices of others often become delights for us. To be in the right is so pleasing to one's pride in oneself that one would almost prefer the role of victim to that of persecutor. In the garb of the most humiliating misfortune, I am far happier than one would imagine: when I am one day restored to my husband, as is my hope, he will be grateful to me for not allowing myself to be cowed by my woes." That is what Madame says, Monsieur.'

Rose here was trying to fathom what the Abbé's goal might be in his extraordinary conduct towards Euphrasie. She had done likewise with her mistress; but as the two of them were so circumspect, albeit for quite contrary reasons, she was none the wiser; and so Rose, not daring to say any more, resigned herself to obedience.

'So then, Madame!' said Théodore at last, when he reappeared at his sister-in-law's door. 'Are you a little happier with me?'

'No, my dear brother,' replied this charming woman, as she smiled. 'No, I am no happier with you, because all of your actions have the same motive, and this motive is too criminal for me to be content with any of the conduct it has inspired.'

'O my dear sister, what a deluded idea you have of womanly virtue!' said Théodore. 'Marriage, a pact that unites husband and wife, can only hold strong for as long as each of the conjoined is willing to submit to it. The moment one of these breaks the pact, its strength is divided and thus no longer the same; thereafter, one of the two is much to be pitied. And yet, I ask you if it is reasonable to think that the purpose of civil and religious laws could ever have been to cement a link in a chain which renders one of the two contracting parties unhappy. A pact can only be conditional: it is nothing but abuse or tyranny if it ceases to be so; and indeed some legislators understood this so well that they established divorce. And yet, if the introduction of divorce is a masterpiece of wisdom and prudence in any government, why don't they all introduce it? And why don't the subjects of a government that has not introduced it throw off a yoke that becomes one only through the negligence of legislators? The wise man foresees the law before it exists; he anticipates it, and pays it tribute as if it did exist. Believe me, my dear sister, anything that deviates from this is absurd, and harmful to the population, as it prevents men and women from fulfilling elsewhere the goal that Nature demands of them, and drowns the gift of procreation in floods of tears. The obligation, in a word, to remain under the yoke of marriage when it offers us only thorns, seems to me as criminal as all those vices that extinguish life, and I have no doubt that hell awaits the individual who willingly refuses that which Nature grants us only to serve her.'

'Everything you have just said, Monsieur,' the Marquise replied, 'is simply what is known as the logic of the senses. When a woman is joined in matrimony with her husband, as soon as she has willingly agreed to those bonds, she must respect them for as long as her husband is alive, and anything that might be contrary to this will inevitably plunge her into adultery. Some honourable and powerful political reasons may on occasion have led sovereigns to loosen the knots they tied; the interests of their subjects doubtless legitimized their divorces. Crime is nothing for a sovereign whenever the interests of his people demand or prescribe it; but among private parties such as ourselves, nothing attenuates the force of evil, and no law can stand in its way. Thereafter, divorce once again takes on all the bearing of crime that political interests had masked. What do you expect to happen to children who no longer have a mother, when this fickle mother leaves them? As soon as she has brought other children into the world, she will inevitably neglect her first ones. In a word, inconstancy alone, and thus libertinage, is what drives a husband or wife to seek a divorce: thereafter, its effects are as criminal as its cause. As soon as a discontented wife separates from her first husband because she wishes to find a second, there is nothing to stop her then finding a third, a fourth, etc., etc. And yet, what example can be made thereafter of this immoral woman? We owe her our contempt; and if we owe her a second debt, it is of course not to marry her. The climate, the inconstancy natural to men, may have led certain countries to adopt divorce, I grant you; but whenever a people does not have these reasons, it must never be permitted.

'Examine, if you will, this oddity from the perspective of the emotions. What value can the vows of a woman have in the eyes of a second husband when she was unable to keep them with her first? And do you think he can ever be happy, this husband living in fear? This fear will be swiftly followed by coldness: and where is the joy in a marriage between husband and wife when one of the two neither esteems nor loves the other? What difference do you see, in a word, between a divorced wife and an unfaithful one? And if the latter receives our contempt, why would this not also be the just deserts of the former? If a wife's lack of loyalty towards the husband to whom she has sworn to be faithful is a crime, it remains so even under the hollow authority of the law; for whether the crime is a matter of law or simply of a woman's will, it remains a crime in either case—whether it is the wife who wants it, or whether she has sought a freedom which is itself inherently criminal. Some peoples have allowed theft: does that make the act any less criminal in your eyes? No, of course not. It is the act itself one must consider, and not the motives of the legislator who permits or prohibits it. A thousand reasons might have led him to authorize this peculiarity; none can condone you for exploiting it. The man who stifles the sacred voice of his conscience, simply because some grounds or other led a legislator to diminish what this conscience reproaches him for, is as guilty as the man who stifles this voice simply because his passions require it. One cannot compromise with one's conscience; look deep within your own, Théodore, and see if it counsels the infamy into which you wish to drag me. No matter the situation, remember that a man ceases to be virtuous the moment he justifies his failings either by his sophistries or by his passions.'

And this touching creature, serving thus as an apologist for virtue, seemed to radiate all its charms. But as the man she was addressing was dissolute, she inflamed rather than soothed him.

'O dangerous creature!' the Abbé exclaimed. 'Stop being in the right if you want to persuade me, for you become more enchanting only while making me a thousand times more wretched.'

Here, the kind and tender Marquise affectionately took Théodore's hand.

'This is how I love you, my brother,' she told him. 'Master your passions; remember these become our greatest enemies when we do not know how to rein them in. How do you not blush at loving your brother's wife? And what opinion would you have of her, if she gave in to this culpable fervour? If you could only imagine the celestial pleasures one tastes when one triumphs over oneself! It may be pleasant to be delighted with others, but believe me it is a hundred times more so to be delighted with oneself: this pleasure is ours and ours alone; the other depends on the whims of men, and you know the value of those. Reconcile me with my husband, I beg you, my dear brother. If you only knew how much the idea of being thought guilty by him makes me suffer! So be frank with me yourself for a moment: you know perfectly well I am innocent; prove to him that I am—I want nothing more than to convince him of this. Do you not realize you will find in so great a deed as many delights as you could hope for in corrupting me? O my friend, do not speak to me of the pleasures of vice when they occasion such remorse.'

But when one has read the conclusion of this lamentable tale, when one is left in no doubt as to the perversity of the monster we are obliged to put on the stage, his indifference to the earnest candour, and the touching naivety with which this admirable woman has just expressed herself, will come as no surprise.

'You ask the impossible of me, my dear sister,' he said to the Marquise, whose beautiful eyes fixed him and seemed to demand a better response.

'The impossible?' Euphrasie asked.

'Yes, my sister—the impossible. You are innocent, you say, and it is because of this that your heart's desire is to be happily reconciled with my brother. This reasoning is specious no doubt; but if you are guilty, as your husband and I have every reason to believe, how can you expect me to take on this negotiation?'

'And why do you destroy my hopes over an unwarranted supposition?'

'This is the very epitome of the duplicity your husband will never forgive. He would a hundred times prefer the confession of your sins, and a plea for forgiveness, to this guilty insolence in crime.'

'One can only demonstrate guilt with proof: where is yours?'

'I have it: it was to me that Villefranche confided his love, without heeding all my efforts to dissuade him; it was to me he proved the hold he had over you. Let us not revisit, if you please, the document signed in Deschamps's lair in the course of that journey, though that evidence alone would have been enough to condemn you. Let us confine ourselves, shall we, to your exploits with Villefranche: what was the meaning of his return here, or that walk in the labyrinth, or the rendezvous arranged there, as proven by a note you signed that was found in the dead man's pocket?'

'Can you show me this note?' Euphrasie asked firmly. 'At this moment all I ask is limited to this one thing: show me this note.'

'Your husband took that document, as he did the one from the cave: they are, he said, necessary evidence for the separation he intends; they will only come to light before your judges. I would have hidden all this from you for the rest of my life; I would even have halted their effect, if you had looked more favourably on my love. Your rigours justify my own, and from now on I shall attend only to my brother's interests.'

'Good heavens!' exclaimed the Marquise, shedding a torrent of tears. 'What point is there in pleading with you, when I am cast with such composure into the most calamitous of misfortunes.'

Her tears cease; the violence of her agitation dries her eyes, now wild with the most alarming delirium; the muscles of this exquisite face no longer lend themselves to its charms, but to contortions of despair; her limbs stretch and writhe in every direction; her piercing cries ring out in her prison; she beats her head against the walls; her blood flows . . . it soaks the scoundrel who spills it and who, soon roused like a tiger by the very sight of this precious blood, would doubtless make it flow in an even more abominable manner.

'This was all that remained for you to do,' Perret tells Théodore when he learns of this dreadful scene. 'Success almost always depends on the force with which one strikes the final blows; you have crushed her with slander, and she must either give in or die of sorrow. Leave her alone in this state for a while, abandoned by the whole world, alone with her thoughts . . . There is no doubt you will profit from this surfeit of suffering.'

This repugnant conversation had barely concluded when a great commotion was heard in the castle courtyard. The Abbé is informed that Madame de Châteaublanc and her grandson are about to arrive.

Théodore rushes off to meet them.

'Madame,' he says to Euphrasie's mother as he holds out his hand, 'I think it is of the utmost importance that you allow neither your servants nor your coach to stay here at the castle.'

'That was my intention,' said Madame de Châteaublanc. 'My son-in-law has informed me of everything.' The order is promptly given to her attendants to seek refreshment in the town before returning straight back to Avignon. 'You will take me to my daughter, will you not, Monsieur?' Madame de Châteaublanc then asked. 'I am desperate to see her.'

'Please allow me, Madame,' the Abbé replied, 'to begin by taking you to the quarters prepared for you; my brother was most insistent about doing this first, and I shall reveal his reasons for this as soon as you are settled there.'

'My daughter will come and find me?'

'I imagine so, Madame.'

And as they spoke they walked, with Laurent ahead of them, to a bedroom far removed from those that were usually used at the castle, and prepared like a prison cell, with the exception of its beautiful furniture and pleasant arrangement.

'This is a very beautiful chamber,' said Madame de Châteaublanc, 'but what is the meaning of these bars and bolts?'

'My brother's orders, Madame,' said Théodore, 'and I now have the honour of explaining the reasons for them, if you would be so good as to take a seat.'

And while Perret entertained the child, showing him around these quarters, the Abbé spoke thus to his sister-in-law's mother:

'There is no point in hiding from you, Madame, the extent of your daughter's guilt in this cruel episode; and sadly we are now armed with all the documents that prove her crimes. These first and foremost are the reasons why she has been detained by her husband here, and why it is impossible for you to see her until everything has died down: the slightest scandal could ruin us all; and knowing your tender affection for Euphrasie, we were fearful of you, Madame. You would have proclaimed her innocence, and the greater the commotion you would have made, the more you would have forced us to prevent its repercussions by publicly declaring your daughter's guilt. This would have resulted in a thousand dreadful difficulties for your son-in-law. He thus thought it best to hide you away, and, realizing he could not do so without constraints, prepared those that you can see—albeit rendered more tolerable, as you may judge for yourself, by every comfort and convenience he could muster. Such are your quarters, Madame, and you will be served in the manner to which you are accustomed, but locked away at all times along with your grandson, and absolutely forbidden to see your daughter, whose fate is the same as your own. To cover your tracks, the moment you left Avignon the Marquis spread the word that you were travelling to Paris to obtain Cardinal Mazarin's pardon for the duel which arose from your daughter's vices, and which brought guilt on my brother. The course of action he has taken pains him no doubt, but you can see how necessary it is.'

'Yes, Monsieur,' Madame de Châteaublanc replied. 'I can appreciate that. But the importance of any matter must remain within the bounds of propriety and decency, and you will admit that you have failed in those duties towards me today. To behave in the way he has, my son-in-law must doubtless have other motives than those you describe; otherwise, your allegations would seem very feeble. I shall not hide from you that these machinations only make me believe all the more in my daughter's innocence, rather than the crimes of which she is accused; and this refusal to let me see her lends decidedly more weight to my suspicions. Never mind, I can only curse my own weakness: that is the reason I fell into such a crude trap; and now you may do as you will, Monsieur—I shall not complain until the time comes. But as for my religious duties, Monsieur—how shall I fulfil these?'

'This is Monsieur l'Abbé Perret, vicar of the parish, Madame,' Théodore replied, 'who in the absence of Père Eusèbe, the chaplain of the castle, comes to the chapel to celebrate the Holy Sacrifice on those days the Church ordains it for its flock.'

'Shall I see my daughter there?'

'No, Madame.'

'So she does not go to mass?'

'She prays in her bedroom; and as devout as she is, she has yet to complain about the severity we are obliged to show her.'

'And thus the sins of which you suspect her, wrongly perhaps, make her commit the very real ones of neglecting the duties her faith imposes upon her.'

'We can pray to God wherever we are, Madame, and this region as you know is full of honest people who invoke him even in the wilderness.'

'One should not, it seems to me, say such things robed in a habit such as yours.'

'This habit, simply a matter of custom in our House for the youngest son, does not commit me to anything, Madame; no bond ties me to the Church.'

'So be it, but let us return, if you please, to the vital matter we were discussing before. My son-in-law and you, Monsieur, are thus both quite convinced of my daughter's guilt?'

'Certainly no one is better placed to know than we. Her liaison with Villefranche dates back to the fateful trip to Beaucaire: while this young hothead is bringing her back, a bandit chieftain stops them; Villefranche is separated from her, and your daughter, led to this thief's lair, becomes as culpable with him as she had just been with her lover. This complicity in lechery finally reaches the ear of our relation, his Lordship the Bishop of Montpellier. He has your daughter apprehended, and only releases her in the end out of consideration for my brother. Euphrasie finally returns to the castle; her seducer wastes no time in showing up here; their liaison resumes . . . You know the rest, Madame.'

'But, to dare the kind of vengeance against my daughter her husband is wreaking, is it not essential, Monsieur, to be as sure of the crime one alleges as one is of one's own existence?'

'I agree, Madame, but when what we have seen is reinforced by written proofs as clear as those we possess—I believe, Madame, that there can be no doubt.'

'But surely you can show me these written proofs?'

'Only the copies are in my possession; the originals are in my brother's hands.'

'Then at least show me these copies.'

And the Abbé promptly took from his pocket a note containing these words:

Tomorrow, All Souls' Eve, I shall go as is my wont to pray at the mausoleum in the grounds; be there too, my dear Comte, and you will become the God I shall adore, as no other is more sacred to me than you. Do not be seen by the Marquis or the Abbé; they both have eyes like hawks. I am sending you a kiss to match my love for you: that, I think, should give you a true idea of the ardour of an embrace that burns with all the fires of the most intense passion.

After this note, the Abbé read out the declaration written and signed in Deschamps's cave.

When Madame de Châteaublanc was acquainted with these documents she was so stupefied for a moment that she found it hard to recover.

Composing herself nonetheless shortly after:

'I believe that these words, Monsieur,' she said firmly, 'may well serve in every respect as true monuments to horror and iniquity: either they belong to my daughter, and according to such a hypothesis, they could hardly be more dreadful; or they are counterfeit, and if this second supposition is true, can you imagine Lucifer's hand tracing anything more shocking?'

'The truth, it seems to me,' Théodore replied, 'is more in evidence here than any lies; some things are so horrible that they are beyond invention.'

'Yes, but some are too shocking to believe. There is such evidence in my daughter's favour, Monsieur, to counter yours! Her limitless affection for Monsieur de Gange, whom she chose over the whole court; her irreproachable conduct; her faith, so at odds with the blasphemous phrases of the alleged note written to Villefranche; that sincerity, that candour which set her apart—all of this, Monsieur, all of this exonerates her of the horrors of which she is accused, and I would rather believe in slander than adultery. Whatever the case may be, Monsieur . . .' Madame de Châteaublanc added, breaking off a conversation in which she was left in no doubt as to the presence of a guilty party who was either very dear, or very dangerous. 'Yes, Monsieur, whatever the truth may be, I need to rest awhile, and I beg you to retire. Carry out your orders—I shall go along with them as I am the weaker here. But the heavens, which leave no crime on earth unpunished, will avenge virtue sooner or later for the outrages by which crime seeks to crush it.'

The Abbé summons Rose.

'Here, my child,' he tells her, 'is another boarder sent by my brother. You will show her the same consideration you have your mistress. You will serve her and her grandson in this bedroom, and you will take care to lock the door whenever you leave these quarters. As for you, Monsieur l'Abbé Perret, you will be at Madame's beck and call for as long as she requires your services. If Madame judges you fit to tutor her son* you will do so, and as for you, Madame,' said Théodore, withdrawing with the vicar, 'I shall have the honour of paying you a visit when it pleases you to grant me permission.'

They leave, and Rose, thoroughly drilled, remains behind with Euphrasie's mother.

'Another two or three such boarders,' the Abbé said to his dear Perret, 'and our home will start to resemble a fortress. They say that Mazarin is having some built—I have half a mind to offer him this one.'

'You are fortunate, Monsieur l'Abbé,' said Perret, 'to be able to make light in this way no matter the difficulties life throws at you—even the thorniest ones.'

'Thorniest? How so?'

'It seems to me that this woman is not so easily persuaded by the powerful evidence we have shown her.'

'Who cares? We have her—that is all that matters. In Avignon, they think she is in Paris, and I guarantee you that in Paris they would never imagine her to be in Gange.'

'But,' said Perret, 'you never told me of this note written to Villefranche: in what infernal den was it made?'

'In my own,' Théodore replied. 'Even the Marquis is still in the dark about it. I wrote it myself, then found a skilled forger in Nîmes who needed only a line of my sister's handwriting to be able to copy it in an instant.'

'So you only showed the copy?'

'The original will only leave my pocketbook when it is necessary. But enough of this. What is essential now is to prevent any communication between these two women: keep driving home the importance of this to Rose. You, keep a close eye on the mother; offer her some pious sermons; and I, I shall take care of everything as far as Euphrasie is concerned.'

CHAPTER VIII

THE watchful Abbé realized that, just as the mother knew her daughter was at the castle, it would become very difficult to prevent the daughter hearing of her mother's arrival. Could he really count on Rose to keep such a secret? Are criminal accomplices not always dangerous? There were signs that Rose had a kind heart and affection for her mistress. Nothing could be more alarming than these hints of virtue to someone plotting a crime; and the imperious manner in which Nature thus reasserts its laws should be enough to stop all those who seek to break them.

The Abbé therefore concluded that it was far simpler, as well as easier, to provoke a rift between two women unable to see each other than it was to count on the discretion of a girl able to see them both. Consequently, after a few days, he paid a visit to Euphrasie.

'Madame your mother, and your son, are at the castle,' he said as he entered.

'My mother! . . . My son! . . . O good God! What a ray of hope you have brought me!'

'Do not be in too much haste to bask in its light,' said the treacherous Abbé. 'This ray is not as pure as you seem to presume. Madame de Châteaublanc is here, but she is appalled by you, and absolutely refuses to see you. Your husband had her read the wretched documents which comprise and prove your crimes, and her fury could not be greater.'

'But what slanders are you alluding to now?'

'What? You still deny it?'

'Let us be clear, Monsieur: the document from the cave was only written to keep me alive, so I would have the means to defend myself; the letter to Villefranche is a forgery; I never wrote it.'

'Pardon, Madame, but such obstinacy damns you far more than it vindicates you: some gentleness, some moderation, some contrition would be infinitely more to your advantage; they would demonstrate a noble soul; the contrary approach reveals a soul accustomed to vice, one which believes that it can efface its crimes by denying them, and shield itself from punishment or opprobrium by blaming others for the horrors it has committed. Such extraordinary deceit always comes at a great cost to the accused, and never works in their favour. This is not how remorse expresses itself, and the guilty can only move us by showing remorse.'

'So then, according to you, to merit the esteem of others one has to incriminate oneself for crimes one has never committed?'

'No, but when a crime has been committed, one has to confess to it, not exacerbate it by persisting in its denial. But let us abandon arguments whose logic is hollow, often false, and always pointless. Your mother has read the note to Villefranche, which you deny with such audacity.'

'I did not write this note; I shall not allow myself to be accused without defending myself, and my silence would be as great a crime as the one that has been laid at my door.'

'You shall defend yourself in court.'

'Then I ask to be taken there immediately.'

'Be in no doubt your husband will bring you before it soon enough. In the meantime, content yourself with the knowledge that your mother refuses to see you, as she is now fully convinced of your crimes.'

'If that is so, then why did she come to the castle?'

'For some documents she needs for the trip she is making to Paris to resolve, if possible, the wretched duel which you provoked and which may, without some placatory effort, forever exile your husband to a foreign country.'

'Is she not vexed at least that I cannot see her?'

'No, because this refusal comes from her.'

'And so my whole family is against me? Could I suffer a more dreadful fate if I were guilty? And is it not cruel that innocence should suffer all the horrors, all the torments that belong to infamy alone? But you were, it seems, offering me your services as a mediator to absolve me of an imaginary crime, just as long as I were willing to commit a real one?'

'I make you the same offer at the same price.'

'So the price of your virtue is my guilt?'

'Be assured that the action you fear is far less reprehensible than the one you have already allowed yourself; consider that you would be expunging a very great crime with a rather petty one.'

'I see no difference between the crime for which you reproach me and the one you wish me to commit; indeed, as you are my brother-in-law, the latter evil seems far greater to me.'

'You have not done my feelings justice: I want only your heart, Madame, and we have proof that Villefranche demanded much more of you than that.'

'There was nothing between Villefranche and me, and I want to love my husband only: the first part of my reasoning refutes your accusation; the second proves the impossibility of the reward you demand as the price of your services.'

'Well then, Madame! Let us remain as we are; my mission is complete. I was to relay your mother's farewell—I have done so. If there is anything in particular you wish me to pass on either to her or to your son, I shall take care of it, and withdraw as soon as you have given me the order.'

'What's this? I shall not see my son? It is cruel of you to speak of him to me: if I was not to see him, better that I remained ignorant of his presence here. What have I done to you, you brute, for you to treat me so harshly?'

'Given the relish with which you plunge the dagger into other people's hearts, it is rather odd, Madame, to hear you complain you have been treated too roughly yourself.'

'O my son! The caress of your hands will not wipe away the tears your father makes me shed each day—tell him at least how much I adore him; when he sees that tender innocence in your face, perhaps he will believe in mine, and these tears I cannot spill over you will flow no more if you succeed.'

It was late; the Abbé withdrew, and readied himself for the next morning, when he would strike the same blows at the mother that had just torn her daughter's heart apart.

'Madame,' he said as he entered her quarters, 'although my brother advised me not to let you see your daughter, the desire to bring you together, to reconcile you, drove me to her door to see if she would agree to visit you. Imagine my surprise when I encountered only resistance from this defiant spirit. "My mother is here only to redouble my woes, or tighten my shackles," she said. "I do not wish to see her. She would reproach me for things that are stronger than I am, and which I cannot bring myself to regret: is any woman mistress of the feelings in her heart? Without offending anyone, I can now at last confess my love for the tender soul taken from me by my husband's jealous rage; I have only his memory to console me, and I am in no mood to suffer reproaches I believe I in no way deserve. My mother is going to Paris, you say, to resolve my husband's case: may she succeed—on that I pledge my most sincere vows to the heavens; but as soon as my husband is safe, I shall beg him to accede to our eternal separation. One should not oppress another heart simply because one no longer possesses it. Nothing could be more atrocious, more unjust than the prison where I am locked away: does anyone have such a right over someone who is yet to stand before a judge? And to shield from the law an individual one believes should be brought before it is to offend those very laws with a culpable acknowledgement of their inadequacy, is it not? Sovereigns perhaps are given this power: as authors and defenders of the law, they have the right to correct their own work; but this right, which they alone may enjoy, does not belong to any family.* Yes," she continued insolently. "Yes: this one step, taken before the courts, would soon grant me the separation I crave." '

'I am obliged to believe everything you tell me, Monsieur,' Madame de Châteaublanc replied, 'but I confess I would have dearly loved to hear this from my daughter's own lips.'

'And so, Madame, the reward for my consideration is to traduce me as an impostor?'

'It is so painful for a mother to hear such declarations! Well then, Monsieur! As I am in a dreadful position, unable to discover the truth for myself, I ask only one thing of you: that you swear an oath on this Christ placed here in my room . . . that you swear, as I say, before and by him, that all you have told me for the last two days is nothing but the truth; that the note you showed me was truly written by my daughter to the Comte de Villefranche; that the document from the cave bears the same stamp of authenticity; that, in a word, you have not deceived me in any way.'

'I would never have imagined, Madame, that you would put me to such a test; but as you deem it necessary, I shall submit to it.'

And the monster, for whom no crime was of any consequence, raises his hand, pronounces before God every word Madame de Châteaublanc dictates, and proves by this boundless villainy the unfortunate truth that only the first step comes at a cost in crime; once this is taken, one no longer refuses oneself any excesses, and no longer denies oneself any atrocities. May this shocking example hold back those who stifle the cry of their conscience! Oh, let them stop at their first transgression; let them reflect on all the dangers of a second, on all the evil that necessarily follows, and, held in check by the moral principles inculcated in childhood, and by the holy faith that nurtured them in those early years, they will avoid a great many misfortunes.

'Come, Monsieur. I believe you now,' said Madame de Châteaublanc. 'We always cast doubt on that which pains us. A sweet illusion maintained my hope; you have torn that from me, and I must accept it.'

And this devout and tender soul, throwing herself at the feet of the same Christ, witness to Théodore's perjury, cried out in tears:

'O Lord! Give me the strength to bear such cruel agonies; deign convert above all my daughter's heart by restoring one day the virtues that were my greatest happiness in life.'

At that moment the child, seeing his grandmother in floods of tears, buried himself in her bosom:

'Why are you crying, grandmamma?' he asked, holding her tight in his little arms.

'O my dear boy,' she replied, giving him a kiss, 'may you never know what it costs to stop loving she who was our pride and joy!'

The man observing this violent paroxysm of grief seemed unperturbed by it . . . It must therefore be true that crime extinguishes all the soul's faculties; how much of an enemy to himself is the man who lets such a destructive poison take hold!

A fair interval elapsed in this state of affairs, during which the Abbé saw these ladies out of courtesy alone, and with no further revelations to sour his visits. But the Marquise craved an explanation too desperately not to use every means at her disposal to arrive at one. She did all she could to sway Rose and win her loyalty; and this honest girl, despite all the risks she ran, promised to arrange an opportunity for the two ladies to meet.

One can well imagine that the mother, informed of her daughter's desire to see her, and recognizing from this alone some of the Abbé's deceitfulness, supported Rose in all her efforts in this regard. Soon it was simply a matter of ensuring the success of an enterprise made all the more perilous by the fact that Perret never fell asleep on watch, and was as willing to serve the two brothers as Rose was to sacrifice herself for the mother and daughter.

Preparations were made for this dangerous escapade. Euphrasie was to head down to her mother's quarters, the door to which Rose would leave slightly ajar.

It was the month of January. The charming Euphrasie rises with a shiver; she passes through her former bedroom, and for a moment casts her eyes, brimming with tears, on a place that had once borne witness to her happiness. Swiftly tearing herself away from a setting that inspires such painful memories, she crosses the gallery leading from her bedroom to the chapel. She had nothing to guide her steps: Rose's wise precautions ruled out a lamp.* The darkness of these vast halls was only broken by a few pale glimmers from the stars shining in the sky that night, transforming the portraits hanging on the gallery walls into phantoms. This sickly light, barely penetrating the antique panes of glass, was more frightful than helpful. Beyond this gallery, even this feeble assistance faded away: one had to pass through a long corridor where no light penetrated. Madame de Châteaublanc's quarters were at the far end. A candle left at the door offered a quivering light as pale as the one which had guided Euphrasie's steps there. This poor creature, trembling more than ever, was leaning heavily against her companion's shoulder when, all of a sudden, a rough and heavy hand seized Rose by the arm.

'Where do you think you're going?' thunders Perret. 'Straight back to your room, or I shall tell Monsieur l'Abbé.'

But Euphrasie hears not a word: she has fainted in Rose's arms, and is carried back to her tower in this state with Perret's help. Rose stays behind to tend to her, while the vicious accomplice to that unparalleled monster locks the mother's quarters before revealing all to his master.

'Monsieur,' he tells him, 'there is no torment too cruel for that disloyal turnkey. No punishment would be too severe, I beseech you: all this is the result of a plot hatched over a very long time. Where would we be, Monsieur, if these two women had been reunited?'

Théodore hastens to his sister's quarters.

'So, Madame, you wish to exacerbate your detention and your crimes?' he said in a rage. 'What possible motive could have led you to corrupt a young girl, and to reconcile with a mother . . . so utterly set on leaving without seeing you?'

The Marquise, who could not answer without compromising the girl who had come to her aid, said only that she had forced her turnkey to open the door and take her to a mother she still adored, and whom she wanted to put straight.

'In that case, you shall be punished,' said Théodore, who, with no obvious candidate to replace Rose, chose simply to reprimand and keep her rather than separate her from Euphrasie as a punishment. 'Follow me, Madame,' he told his sister. 'This room is too comfortable for you. I shall find you one less conducive to your nocturnal wanderings.'

So the barbarous Abbé, dragging his sister along with that ferocious anger only crime inspires, plunges her into the dungeon of that same tower, where there is barely any air to breathe, and only a little hay upon which to rest.

'Rose, take the keys for Madame's room,' said the Abbé, 'and if I find you have made poor use of them again, this same dungeon will serve as your tomb.'

The wretched Marquise, resigned to all of this, offered no resistance to her tormentor's brutality other than noble courage: tears would have been an admission of defeat; she shed not a single one; and, like the early Christians pursued for their faith, the doors to her dungeon closed to the song of those Psalms in which the holy king asks God to forgive his enemies.*

O religion! These are your delights—there are no earthly woes for those your arms console. Indeed, why grieve at the torments one suffers, when the certitude of being reborn in the peaceful embrace of God offers us such an exquisite future!

'Your foolhardiness this night, Madame,' said Théodore as he entered the bedroom of his victim's mother, 'tallies neither with your age nor your good sense. Knowing the compelling reasons that force us to hold you in this unfortunate captivity, what could possibly be driving your attempts to escape it?'

'The desire to know more, Monsieur: I am far from convinced, and I need to be.'

'Yet more suspicion, Madame, even after the vow I made you?'

'The person who needs to be forced to make a vow may well be culpable of the abomination that leads to it. I absolutely have to see my daughter, and I shall not leave this castle without doing so.'

'After such a firm resolution,' replied the Abbé, 'I only ask, before I accede, that you wait for my brother to respond. I shall immediately dispatch a man to ride to Avignon, and I shall follow the orders my brother gives to the letter: I am but the instrument of his will, and I swore to him I would enforce it.'

'But on what grounds, pray, must I be answerable to my son-in-law? And what gives him the right to hold me prisoner in his castle?'

'You came here of your own free will, Madame. The rest is simply a precaution to ensure the peace and tranquillity of the family, and one that I already impressed upon you as necessary.'

'Write then, Monsieur, by all means, and I shall willingly wait for a reply.'

Théodore penned a letter in haste.

The accounts we have consulted provide only an extract of this letter, but the reply, as it is given below, is recorded in its entirety.

Avignon, 25th January 1665.

A very great change in our affairs has arisen that will force us to alter our plans too. All the reasons that led to the detention of my wife and mother-in-law evaporate in light of the important business I shall now disclose.

Monsieur de Nochères, who died three days ago, has left his immense fortune to my wife.* Any further ill-treatment will drive Euphrasie to make arrangements for this inheritance that are all the more inimical to our interests, for twenty years from now her son will be in line to inherit it. If she were to take action against us, we would thus be divested of the child's guardianship for the next twenty years, and consequently of the right to benefit from his assets. But there is one way we can have everything . . . as you have already guessed . . . And the Chevalier de Gange, who came here when he arrived with his regiment, is urging me to take it; but I have loved this woman, I have cared deeply for her mother . . . Besides, I am not as strong as you, my friends, when it comes to all these Machiavellian plots of which ancient Rome and modern Florence still offer us so many examples . . . I shall say no more: the Chevalier assures me that you understand, and that you are capable of seeing this through. What more do you want me to say? The choice is either this, or a general reconciliation that would restore these ladies' good humour, and see them return to Avignon well-disposed towards us and no longer inclined to take steps that would see this fortune pass before our eyes but beyond our reach. I send you my love, as does the Chevalier, who is impatient to see you.

This letter, sealed to keep it from prying eyes, was delivered to Théodore in the messenger's pouch.

The Abbé read it with Perret. How surprised and vexed they must have been when they received this news!

'The course your brothers have allowed you to glimpse would certainly be the surest and best,' Perret said. 'And in your place, I would not hesitate for a moment: here they are, already hidden from the world; it would only take one more step for them to disappear from it entirely.'

'Certainly,' Théodore replied, 'and I can assure you I would not have the slightest qualm about doing so; but let us not undermine our own interests when our only thought should be to serve them. I recognize the danger of allowing disgruntled women to receive such a generous inheritance. It is a safe bet that, until the child reaches his majority, the two of them will do everything imaginable to ensure that this fortune remains intact in the boy's coffers, and that we cannot pilfer so much as a single *obole*.* But if we get rid of her . . . in the first place, can we even be sure we could do so safely? Or secondly, that a board of guardians will not be appointed to safeguard the inheritance, and oppose any form of peculation on our part? Will the friends and relatives of the deceased not join forces to protect it? Neither my brothers nor I have particularly strict principles when it comes to spending wisely; there would be concern we might embezzle the funds; those responsible would secure them, and we would have far less control over the inheritance than we would with my sister or her mother as its trustees. Euphrasie, still madly in love with her husband, will always do far more for him than for her own son—or so I think at least. We have embittered these ladies, I know, but there is nothing so tractable as women: their hearts are naturally so kind, so tender, their temperaments so fickle, and their minds so flighty, that the line between love and hate, or between hate and forgiveness, is very fine indeed. I am therefore minded to release them immediately, console them, mollify them, and send them off as soon as possible to Avignon, where the Marquis will do his best to placate them. I shall accompany them myself, and be in no doubt, Perret, that this plan will succeed better than any other.'

The bold Perret, always inclined to extreme measures, had a face like thunder once he realized the chance to commit a crime was being snatched from him. He shook his fearsome head three times, swearing as he replied:

'You are too good, Monsieur l'Abbé, you are too kind; remember this, for you will regret it, because sooner or later you will be forced to resort to the most severe methods, and these may no longer be available to you.'

'My friend,' said Théodore, 'you know me well enough to be sure I am not frightened by the course of action that has been suggested, but by the certainty that it will achieve absolutely nothing and work to our detriment rather than to our advantage. All you need to know is that you will not be displeased with me when the time comes.'

And Perret, very reluctantly becalmed, left to feed like a serpent on the venom he could not discharge.

Sweet Euphrasie was kneeling in prayer to the God of beneficence and mercy, as this was her only hope for a little relief from her woes, when Théodore entered the room.

'Everything has changed, Madame,' he told her, 'and to avoid any delay in passing on the happy news Alphonse has just sent me, please follow me to your mother's quarters so she can hear it at the same time.'

Euphrasie, whose soul had matured after being so tested by misfortune, bore this change of circumstances with the same serenity that had sustained her in her troubles, and followed her brother into Madame de Châteaublanc's quarters. But confined for too long, that soul now cracked, and she fell tearfully into her mother's arms. Madame de Châteaublanc felt the same surge of tenderness. Sensitive souls speak the same language; she and the young child drenched Euphrasie with their tears, and for some time none of the three could utter a word.

'Compose yourselves, ladies, I beg you,' said Théodore, 'and pay heed to the important matters I have been instructed to relay to you.'

They settle, take a seat, and listen to the Abbé.

'Without being gifted with the wisdom and prescience of the Almighty himself,' said Théodore, 'it was very difficult to doubt that Euphrasie was guilty of the crimes my brother and I had laid at her door. Villefranche's declarations condemned her: he bragged of his extraordinary triumph over the most virtuous of women; he took his brazenness so far as to take me into his confidence, and to compromise my sister in a thousand different ways. Backing up these half-proofs, the dreadful calamity in these grounds, the fate that made my brother a witness to it, and finally the note found in the pocket of the deceased together offered a mass of evidence. Who would have remained unconvinced in the face of such corroboration? And who would not have been appalled, let alone someone as jealous as my brother? He acted against you, Madame,' Théodore continued, looking at Euphrasie, 'in two different ways but for the same reason. He implored me to persuade you I had the same feelings for you as Villefranche: initially, in order for me to see if you were naturally inclined to err in this manner; and subsequently, for me to gain your confidence, and (had we found ourselves on more intimate terms) to elicit from you the facts of the case. I put these two plans into action, and now declare in public that they served only as dazzling proof of your innocence. Each day I dutifully reported our every conversation to my brother who, still convinced of your crimes, paid no heed to anything that might have vindicated you. As Madame de Gange's confinement was beginning to cause a stir, he dispatched Madame de Châteaublanc to Gange to avoid blackening his good name, and had the word spread in Avignon that his severity towards his wife had the backing of her family and, given that he was sending his mother-in-law and son to her, that this treatment was not as harsh as it pleased certain people to suggest in a town where, as everyone knows, slander travels with the same ease as the squalls that buffet it each day. After some time had elapsed, I was to arrange the interview which your impatience precipitated, and which I had only deferred with the best of intentions; and, on the basis of your explanation, I drew a firm conclusion—one with which my brother promised to be satisfied once and for all. It was in this interval,' the Abbé continued, addressing Madame de Châteaublanc, 'that you insisted upon an oath from which I did not feel I should demur, given the evidence I had of the authenticity of the documents in my possession. Here are the originals of those documents: we need not dwell on the first one, from the cave, as we know of this already; all we were after in relation to this was moral evidence—its physical existence was never in question.'

They therefore paid far more attention to the other document: the two ladies studied the letter avidly, devouring every word.

'What artistry!' Euphrasie exclaimed.

'Do not worry, Madame,' said the Abbé. 'This document was indeed found in the pockets of the deceased, but it is most certainly a work of the blackest slander, fabricated by Villefranche himself with the help of a nearby forger—one who, recently convicted of similar crimes, confessed to this one himself. It is therefore clear that Villefranche kept this note in his pocket to provide an excuse for his misconduct if he was ever caught out, and, if possible, to save himself by ruining you; no doubt he thought that, with your adoring husband, you were sure to be forgiven more easily than him. As a result, there is no longer any evidence against you, Madame: you are completely vindicated, and all that remains is our bitter regret at the conduct which such grave suspicions obliged us to observe with you. I now have another kind of balm to apply to your wounds, O sister dear: Monsieur de Nochères has just died, leaving you a fortune which, as you know, is considerable. I have no more to say, so permit me to be the first to congratulate you on such a delightful—and universal—change of fortune as far as all your interests are concerned.'

The traitor then rose, shedding tears as false as the heart which appeared to inspire them, and embraced these ladies and his nephew, whom he apparently congratulated with the best will in the world on this unexpected fortune, adding that the offspring of such virtuous and worthy women would doubtless put it to the best possible use one day.

As a little peace and calm were necessary after such developments, the Abbé left these ladies only to serve them a few hours later the most splendid meal, where joy, serenity, and happiness succeeded all the anxieties that had consumed them for so long. There they discussed and settled their plans, which led all and sundry to leave for Avignon the next day.

When a violent crisis has broken the ties that bind any company together, it is rare that perfect harmony is restored as swiftly as it took discord to sow division: people fear each other, watch each other, spy on each other, and a kind a coolness marks the first few days of reconciliation. This was the case for our travellers: they spoke little, and reflected a great deal. The ramparts of Avignon came into view at last; and the conviction that their arrival in this town meant the breaking of our prisoners' shackles furrowed their persecutor's brow even as it effaced his victims' frowns.

They went their separate ways. Madame de Gange was to stay with her mother, while the Abbé joined his brothers, whom he promised to bring to these ladies without delay.

While they are all settling in, our readers will allow us to give them an idea of what this town was like in the seventeenth century.

Avignon, famous for being the residence of the supreme pontiffs for seventy-two years, under seven successive popes from Clement V to Gregory XI, restorer of the Holy See to Rome, is situated upon a plain as fertile as it is pleasant. Situated on the east bank of the Rhône, this town might, given such a position, have been a great commercial trading post; and so it would have been, were it not for the listlessness, the sluggish indolence, of its inhabitants, almost entirely nobles, lawyers, or clerics, who could barely countenance the presence of any merchants in their midst. As a result, the number of consumers without shops to supply them inevitably, sooner or later, brought poverty to a region where gold, always kept far from the town, was no longer in harmony with the goods that could be exchanged for it.

It was Innocent VI who, to protect himself from the forays of the Archpriest Cervoiles,* a bandit chieftain, girdled the city with those magnificent walls so admired by travellers. This pope had another motive, however, for the building work, which was to demonstrate by this extravagant act the sovereignty his predecessor, Clement VI, had acquired over this beautiful region when Joanna of Naples, daughter of the good king Robert, had sold it to him for the price of eight thousand florins[1] in 1348—an acquisition all the more remarkable as Joanna no more had the right to sell it than the pope had the right to buy it. Sovereignty cannot be ceded, and he who buys it reveals thereby his inability to acquire it: the rights of the occupier are always the most powerful of all, for the invader's right is earned by force; and this right at the very least was one that neither vendor nor buyer enjoyed at the time of the Comtat's cession: besides, our kings have never baulked in the slightest at seizing control of this region whenever they needed it, or whenever they wished to punish the popes.

Upon their return to Rome, the pontiffs left vice-legates behind in Avignon to represent them; as they were only posted there for six years, these men, like Egyptian pashas, cared only about making money, selling everything they could lay their hands on. Some wives also shared the authority of these vice-regents; all favours came through them—another flaw in the administration which, when combined with the absence of trade, inevitably led to the ruination of a region that, given its location, should have eclipsed, or at least depleted, all its neighbours by drawing them in with the sweet lure of its fertile ground.

The town's garrison comprised merely the vice-legate's guard of honour—a further reason for its impoverishment, as it prevents a town from hosting the troops who contribute to its riches, pleasures, and security. The Avignon troops were the town's cooks, butlers, and valets, and as their service was neither long nor tiring, at least their masters did not have to do without their manservants for long.

Another reason for the people's malaise in this region was the indulgence of its sovereign, who raised no taxes.

While adding to the wealth of the richest, the complete absence of taxes plunged the people into indolence, as without the burden of

---

[1] Forty-eight thousand francs in French currency.

levies there was no need for them to work. Besides, was it not inevitable that creating an enclave of such a moribund State within another so full of vitality and industry would lead to its ruin?

All the peoples of France had their government; Avignon alone had none. A place where everyone does as they please, and business carries on as well as it can. However, no sovereign was a greater despot than the vice-legate: no appeal was possible against any of his orders; all of the tribunals' rulings were suspended once the vice-legate had passed judgement. And yet, what are laws in the eyes of a sovereign who suspends them whenever he pleases? The kings of France used to say: 'I want it.' The legate used to say: 'I command it.'

But, in order to bring the poverty of this beautiful region to its very limit, would you believe that French farms collectively paid two hundred thousand francs annually for the Comtat's inhabitants *not* to produce either tobacco or cotton? And this to the absolute delight of the vice-legates, who understandably preferred an arrangement that guaranteed them money to an industry whose products were far from assured. Had they remained in the region, the money they gained would at least have been shared out; but after six years, as we have said, they disappeared with the funds they had seized.

Plenty of dukes and princes could be seen in Avignon at the time, a kind of tribute the government collected instead of taxes. For it cost money to assume these titles, which were only awarded by bulls similar to those used to appoint bishops. It was as if the popes, no longer able to make kings, made up for this by creating great lords at least.

The Inquisition was in force in the Comtat, but was less severe than it was in Spain; as a result, many Jews could be seen there. The same oddity can be observed beyond the Alps and the Pyrenees. It appears that a natural impulse leads the fearful to draw closer to those they fear, as if to placate or observe them. As well as this harsh instrument of the Church, there were nonetheless some dispensations, and some places where allowances were made; the Church deserves some credit for establishing in all the regions under its control places where the sinner could take refuge, and be given time to absolve himself before appearing before his judges or peers.

As for the rest, entertainment of every kind, walks, balls, church concerts, afternoon tea in convent parlours, and above all scandalmongering were the dearest pastimes of the people of Avignon. Their profound idleness inclined them to this sort of vice, and it certainly suited their temperament perfectly.

Every age, and every country, has its own fashions. Amongst the ladies of this region, it was to love not their husbands, but instead, as in Italy, to have three or four lovers of various kinds, among whom the *sigisbée*,* who carried the lady's fan and gloves while trotting along-side her sedan chair,* was very much in vogue.

Upon arriving in Avignon, it was not long before one was acquainted with all the local intrigues: the mistress of the inn, as she served you, would immediately bring you up to date with everything that you could, should you so wish, find out for yourself during your stay there; she would often say even more than was really the case, for among the lazy, gossip is never very far from slander. The people of Avignon had every flaw that those with nothing to do always have—not the least of which was their passion for politics.

This, in a word, was the town where the Marquise de Gange was to spend a few years with her mother, who lived there, and where we shall see her exposed to new events—the work, as ever, of those seeking her downfall.

CHAPTER IX

THE day after Madame de Gange's arrival in Avignon, the three brothers went to pay her a first visit. The Marquis conducted himself marvellously well: self-interest, at this point, spoke to him more loudly than any other feelings he harboured in his heart.

'A thousand of the most sincere apologies, Madame,' said Alphonse, 'if all that the violence of my love has brought you is misfortune. How is one to guard against jealousy when one is in love with someone of such beauty? We were deceived by the tricks, the ruses, of a hothead whom I can only despise even as I remember him now, for he is the one I hold responsible for all my injustices towards you. Is it too much to hope that my remorse might in time efface my wrongs?'

'I dare speak for my charming sister in this regard,' said the Chevalier de Gange, who had not seen this exquisite woman without being profoundly stirred, 'and I hope she will not give me the lie.'

'Never fear, my dear brother,' said Euphrasie, as she tenderly embraced her husband. 'Why would I dwell on misfortunes that had no other cause than the love of this tender husband? And how could the pain he attests in regard to all that has happened fail to dispel any rancour from my heart?'

They turned to the business of the inheritance; the Marquis offered his services; Madame de Châteaublanc thanked him, and said without any bitterness, without a hint of resentment, that people she trusted had already taken charge of everything in that regard, and that there was no need for her son-in-law to trouble himself with this.

Alphonse's features took on a sombre and thoughtful air at this juncture; he bowed, assuring her coldly that he had made his offer only out of a desire to save his mother-in-law and wife the worry, but that whatever these ladies decided to do would be perfectly fine.

Next they spoke of acquiring a handsome mansion on the Rue de la Calade, where the whole family could spend its winters together; and the Marquise, without rejecting the idea, wished to delay its execution until the outstanding income from the inheritance had been recovered. Madame de Châteaublanc was of the same opinion, which therefore prevailed.

'So we shall see each other only on formal occasions,' said Alphonse rather coldly. 'That is very irksome indeed for those who love each other. However,' he added to his wife, 'the last thing I want is to upset you, and your desires shall always be the laws I follow.'

'Besides,' said the Chevalier, still deeply moved in the Marquise's presence, 'we shall spend our summers together in Gange.'

'Oh, I hope so,' said Alphonse. 'And I trust also that the unpleasantness my dear Euphrasie suffered in that castle will soon be forgotten in the company of a husband who shall never cease to adore her.'

The whole family dined at Madame de Châteaublanc's house, and went that evening to a ball at the home of the Duc de Gadagne, who was playing host to all of Avignon.

The Marquise, who was expected, had attracted the whole town; she appeared in the midst of this circle like the spring sun which wintry clouds can no longer conceal. That air of languor she exuded; that delicate sway of a supple and narrow waist, which brought to mind a branch of roses ruffled for a moment in the breeze; those locks of brown hair daintily braided on the noblest head; the slightest gestures lending grace to her every movement; the dulcet tones of her voice, which only made itself heard in order to speak with wit and kindness; in a word, this combination of so many charms produced a universal gasp of admiration when she entered the salon; and even her rivals sang her praises—a very rare triumph for a pretty woman, but one which was unanimously conferred on the alluring Euphrasie, forever securing her the title of the greatest beauty Avignon had ever seen.

A descendant of Laura,* and a poet in vogue amongst good company at the time, whispered these impromptu lines in her ear the moment she entered:

> Once upon a time in this fair city,
> Laura, they say, was the fairest lady,
> Oh, but for the graces of Euphrasie,
> She would have attained immortality.

People there knew something of the Marquise de Gange's misfortunes, but with the gallantry of the Avignonnais prevailing over their penchant for slander, they allowed themselves only a few muted comments in passing. The Abbé and the Marquis left before supper; Madame de Châteaublanc had not attended, so Euphrasie had only the Chevalier to escort her home, and as it was still early, he asked to talk to her for a moment or two.

'The tributes that have been lavished upon you could not be more flattering,' the Chevalier told her. 'But what commends you even more is to merit them in the way you do.'

'All these courtesies are simply a matter of form,' Euphrasie replied. 'This is the first time I have appeared in Avignon since my arrival from Paris. People are very curious here; they wanted their curiosity satisfied, and felt they had to praise me—that is the only reason for all the compliments you would have me take to heart, but my husband's alone are the ones I aspire to receive, and I shall never crave any others.'

'He was barbarous enough to refuse you the justice that was your due,' said the Chevalier. 'And, as far as I was from you, I can assure you I shared in your woes.'

'Who has not experienced some petty moments of injustice in life? I had been rash, and deserved to pay the price for that.'

'Very well, but you will admit that the penalty exceeded the crime, and that my brother went, it seems to me, far further than was necessary.'

'I shall never share your opinion as long as it means finding fault with Alphonse: the one we love is always in the right; to excuse him is a duty; to forgive him a pleasure.'

'What a soul my dear sister has, and how fortunate is the man who has captured it.'

'You can see that is not so, Chevalier, for Alphonse certainly did not believe he was fortunate with me.'

'You have suffered greatly through all this?'

'I see my husband again—all is forgotten.'

'But this Villefranche behaved very badly.'

'There are aberrations one forgives the young: you will agree he has been severely punished for his.'

'My brother had some trouble settling this matter. He must have told you that he only received his letters of pardon a few days ago.'

'I imagine it was out of tact that he made no mention of this.'

'What a generous heart you have!'

'It is the fruit of love. He was a friend of yours, Villefranche?'

'Yes, we served in the same regiment. I liked him well enough, but his crimes against you have revealed how wrong I was, and I confess I shall never forgive him these.'

'When life ends, animosity should fall silent. It is torturous in the extreme to hound the memory of the dead. When someone is no longer here to defend himself, do you not think there is weakness, I would even dare say cruelty, in going so far as to despise his ashes? Hatred is a burden so heavy that sooner or later it destroys itself. Let us leave it then at the grave; let it be enveloped in the shroud of the one who inspired it. Is it not enough to have hated thus far? We should do the same when our own final hour approaches: at such a dreadful moment, I think I would forgive even the one who was about to take my life—I would not want the spirits of my ancestors to wander filled with bile in search of my persecutors. Would I be worthy to sit at the feet of a merciful God if I had failed to show mercy myself?'

As she uttered these words, a faint tremor jolted Euphrasie's nerves, and she paled as she turned from the Chevalier's gaze. And indeed, to whom . . . to whom, great God, was she addressing these words? One would have said a God was using her as a mouthpiece, forcing her to say something she apparently wished to keep to herself.

'Madame,' the Chevalier resumed, 'what is certain is that I wish I had been there. The Marquis is jealous, the Abbé very severe; you needed a peacemaker.'

Here, the Chevalier seemed to wish for more details about the Marquise's detention, but she steadfastly refused.

'And why,' she asked, 'recall sorrows, when one is surrounded by people who are doing all they can to help one forget them?'

'Ah!' said the Marquis's brother passionately. 'How I should like to turn them into pleasures . . .! Allow me to take my leave, Madame; I have taken advantage of your goodwill, and I am starting to fear I am in great danger in your presence.'

'Come now, Chevalier,' said Euphrasie in the most charming and playful tone. 'Do not cast a shadow over a conversation that can end only in friendship for me—a friendship that I swear to uphold, and that you shall always deserve.'

The Chevalier withdrew; and when Euphrasie went to give her mother a kiss before going to bed, she told her of the conversation she had just had, confessing that she liked this brother far more than the other one; that she thought he had some wit, a pleasant manner, and above all a gentleness of character which had quite disarmed her—and which would, she imagined, have spared her a great many torments had he been by his brothers' side throughout all those events at the castle.

Madame de Châteaublanc did not seem taken with this idea, and said her daughter's misfortunes gave her every reason to be wary of anyone and everyone.

The next day, the whole town appeared at Madame de Gange's door. This mark of respect was polite etiquette in Avignon, but on this occasion there were two additional reasons for it: curiosity, and the astonishing stir Euphrasie had caused at the Duc de Gadagne's ball. She repaid these visits one by one with her family, and while she was busy securing the five hundred thousand francs of the Nochères inheritance and putting it to use, everyone did their best to amuse and entertain the beautiful Marquise.

The Chevalier had not hidden from the Abbé the deep impression their brother's wife had made on his senses.

'She's an angel, my friend,' he told him. 'I have never seen anyone to rival this woman. Such graces, such sweetness, such wit, such kindness! How did you manage not to lose your head over this woman when she was under your lock and key?'

'Because trust should never be betrayed,' said the Abbé, 'and besides, such cruel duties were imposed upon me!'

'You should have refused them. You had her sleep on straw, you wretch!' said the Chevalier. 'She should have been resting on a bed of roses! Oh, how I would have softened the blow, but people like you, men of the Church—or destined to be—you are capable of such severity . . . But this is not the spirit of the Gospel, my dear brother, and you will make a dreadful priest.'

'I shall not make any kind of priest,' said Théodore. 'You know full well I can marry if I wish to, and you may rest assured I shall not condemn myself to dreary celibacy . . .[1] So, you have fallen in love with Euphrasie, that much seems clear; and you have done me the honour of making me your confidant.'

---

[1] We cannot labour this point enough, although we are far from certain of it, and the memoirs of the time do not say whether or not the Abbé de Gange had joined holy orders. But the author, already pained that these same memoirs have obliged him to make that scoundrel, Perret, a vicar of the parish, and now faced with the choice of enlisting the Abbé de Gange in holy orders, did not wish to lay himself open to the accusation that he chose to do so with the sole and culpable intention of casting ridicule on one of the most respectable orders in our society.

'I love her very much indeed, but as you know yourself, this shall be the most forlorn of passions. Not a word of this to the Marquis: with his boundless jealousy, there would be one scene after another, and to see this angelic creature shedding tears for me would be no consolation. Well, my friend, I say again—how could you possibly have spent so long with this woman without falling in love with her?'

'I am more sensible than you, my dear boy—that is my only excuse. But do you not think Alphonse has been rather cold towards her since our return from Gange?'

'I noticed that too: the Marquis finds it difficult to shake off his first impressions. Besides, this inheritance is worrying him—and in fact it does give food for thought, don't you agree? As long as this woman does not waver, there is nothing to fear; but if she takes precautions—and be sure her mother will make her—if she does, as I say, we won't have even a hundred *louis** for a meal; and it is hard for both of us, at our age, to be dependent on an allowance paid by a brother who, loyal as he may be, is far from acceding to all our desires. What can we conjure up, my dear Théodore, to prevent this woman from seizing it all on behalf of her son?'

'My word,' said the Abbé, 'I see only one way, and that is to lay ever more traps in Euphrasie's path, concealing ourselves so well that we evade all suspicion. When she falls into them, as she inevitably must, this should excite the Marquis's jealousy more than ever; let the scandal we shall foment around each stumble ruin his wife's reputation. Let this series of crimes force the Marquis, as he sees her disgracing herself again with every guilty step, to have her legally removed from the administration of the inheritance, so that one of the three of us can take charge of it. And the Marquise, deemed by then to be either mad or debauched, having totally lost her husband's trust, having been shamed before the whole province, will once again be banished to Gange; then we shall see about the rest.'

'Good,' said the Chevalier, 'but we have to take great care over some of this. If the Marquise comes to suspect us, instead of preventing her from taking action we shall end up prompting her to do so, and all our efforts will have been wasted. Secondly, the mother has a very keen eye, and if we are exposed, our fears will be realized more swiftly still.'

'And that is why,' the Abbé replied, 'we must take great pains to disguise ourselves.'

'Yes, but this woman I adore . . . must we really continue to make her wretched? Besides, the nets in which we seek to catch her will be cast by men who will make me die of jealousy.'

'O my friend! It is gold we need, and we must do everything in our power to acquire it. Don't you know that with gold one can have whatever one wants—and women even more beautiful than Euphrasie?'

'Impossible—there isn't another on this earth to rival her, and all the treasures of Europe would not procure me one I loved as much.'

'This fervour will melt away: we know only too well what comes of such passions. Believe me, my dear Chevalier, let us serve our interests first—we shall talk of love once we are rich.'

'Well then, let us sum up: what is your final decision?'

'To do everything in our power to ruin this woman so that her husband no longer has even the slightest esteem for her. Must I say the word? So be it! My friend, we have to prostitute her in Avignon, then have her return to Gange steeped in ignominy and despair.'

'And, for the hundredth time, what about the mother?'

'There are a thousand ways to get rid of her. At her age, if we bide our time, we can pass her off as a madwoman; once declared incompetent, she would be removed as guardian.'

'We could do better than that,' said the Chevalier, 'but let us keep to the plan you suggest, and above all disguise ourselves so well that we become unrecognizable . . . But my love . . . my love . . . in the midst of all this?'

'May well have a very happy ending: that at least is how I see it now, but you will keep me apprised of everything.'

'I give you my word.'

And they parted with the firm resolution of taking immediate action, according to the infernal plans they had just concocted.

The Abbé, as we can see, let nothing slip in the course of this conversation. He was too sharp and shrewd to declare himself a rival to a brother worthier than he; but he certainly hoped to profit from the traps he would once again lay for his sister-in-law, and to bring his former plans to fruition.

Among the few to enjoy the honour of being welcomed into Madame de Gange's home was a certain Comtesse de Donis, whose husband was born into a Florentine family that settled in Avignon at the time of the popes. If this woman possessed, in terms of nobility, all that was required to be received in polite company, her morals were far from meriting the opening of any doors. But her innermost self was couched in such profound hypocrisy, and her words chimed so well with the role she wished to play, that she fooled everyone. Her husband, dead for some years, had left her widowed and without children at an age when physical charms still justify the passions. Madame de Donis was barely forty years of age, with a pretty face and a fortune substantial enough to occupy a distinguished rank in the town. She was certainly thought to have a few lovers, but her liaisons were conducted so secretly that no one dared slander her; and once one had heard her speak, it would doubtless have been harder to believe in her depravities, even after seeing them with one's own eyes, than in her virtue. Women of this sort are far less rare than one might imagine, and always far more dangerous than brazen coquettes: one can protect oneself from the latter, but never the former.

Madame de Donis, the Abbé de Gange's mistress for three or four years, seemed to this dangerous man to be well placed to serve him in one of the treacherous plans he was hatching against his wretched sister-in-law. He shared it with her. For Madame de Donis, any ruse or vicious act was a thrill, and as she saw she could indulge in this one while shrouding it in the same secrecy she did everything else, she accepted without hesitation. What you are about to read was the result of a plot to which the Marquis's involvement seemed essential.

Madame de Donis, as we have already mentioned, had managed to pull the wool over Madame de Châteaublanc's eyes, and was spending time with her and her daughter in the greatest intimacy. One day she opened up to the latter:

'I am vexed,' she told her, 'at the disharmony that seems to have come between the Marquis de Gange and yourself. His behaviour is beginning to cause talk in the town; and yesterday in particular, at the Duc de Gadagne's, people seemed astonished that he would not deign even to stay with you.'

'But this is down to some business and family interests,' said Madame de Gange, 'that in no way change our feelings for each other. Though we are staying in two houses rather than one, we love each other no less, and I hope that you will see us reunited under the same roof this winter.'

'So be it, but in the meantime people gossip, make things up, look for reasons where there are none, and you know how high society is, especially here in this town. Should I even tell you this? People think they have detected a little coolness between the two of you. Tell me the truth, my dear Euphrasie, open your heart to me in confidence: what could be the cause of this alteration everyone has noticed? You owe it to your happiness as much as your honour to resolve it. I beg you, in the name of the friendship I have always shown you, speak to me about this as candidly as I have in raising it with you.'

Now the Marquise, whose heart was being touched at its most vulnerable point, throws herself into Madame de Donis's arms and confesses that Alphonse's disaffection is all too real; she protests at the same time that she does not know what caused it, but would give her life to know and to bring it to an end.

'Do you wish me to speak plainly?' asked Madame de Donis. 'I think your husband is very jealous. The Villefranche affair, which many people know of here, reveals the great depth of Alphonse's jealousy: in such cases, husbands inevitably become either colder or more hot-headed. It appears yours has settled on the former, but there are ways to bring him back to you.'

'Some have proposed ways that fill me with horror.'

'An infidelity, no doubt? Oh, I am far from suggesting such treachery, my dear. When my husband was alive, circumstances similar to your own led me to act in a manner that I am going to advise for you too. It succeeded for me: listen before you reject it, and try it if it suits you. When a husband seems to have lost his taste for the bonds of matrimony, one has to catch him again on the gossamer wings of love. Stop being the Marquis de Gange's wife for a while. Become his mistress: you cannot imagine how much a shrewd woman can gain from this change of role. I shall whet his appetite to make him agree to this ruse. A dark chamber at my house will receive the two of you; he will know it is you, but to make the scene more alluring, you will pretend not to know it is him. You can be sure that this encounter will rekindle the flames of love. Give in to him, if he urges you: where is the risk, when you know you are falling into your husband's arms? You will see him in ecstasy . . . in that delirium that never comes when routine holds sway. When the spell is broken, and the candles are relit, he sees the woman he thought was his mistress in his ardent and beloved wife; and he thereafter rediscovers in the bonds of matrimony the red roses of passion.'

It was not without turmoil that Euphrasie had been listening to Madame de Donis; the most chaste of passions flushed her cheeks with that delightful mixture of modesty and sensuality. Stifled sighs stirred her exquisite bosom, and made her heart beat like a dove as its playfellow draws near.

'But, my dear lady,' she said as she composed herself, 'is there nothing dishonourable in this?'

'Nothing: the aim of all this is to restore to you the one given by law.'

'Nothing unseemly?'

'Far from it: what could be unseemly in assuming with one's husband the form that first seduced him? This ploy, an immeasurably guilty one when undertaken with another man, becomes a virtue in this case because your sole purpose is to remind your husband of the most chaste of bonds.'

Euphrasie accepts. The day is fixed. To maintain an air of mystery, they are not to arrive at Madame de Donis's home before evening. The Marquise arrives at nine o'clock.

'He is here,' said the Comtesse. 'He thought it a charming ruse, and is delighted to put it into action. Play your part well: remember above all that he believes he is with Euphrasie; but Euphrasie must not say anything that reveals she is with her husband. Draw on all your skill for this scene, and I guarantee it will succeed.'

A very sombre chamber had been prepared. Though the Marquise was sure as could be that no one but her husband would be within, she trembled all the same as she entered. No light penetrated this isolated sanctuary; no sound could be heard there, and the Marquise had been told to speak softly.

'Is that you?' said a quiet voice, hushed in the same manner. 'Is that you, my angel? How exquisite it is to see each other this way!'

'It was so hard for me to lend myself to this, but what wouldn't one do for the man one loves! Do not take advantage of my weakness, at least.'

'I won't, but you will allow me to exercise my rights.'

'So you believe you have some over my heart?'

'Oh, the most absolute of all: my love grants them.'

'How that word "love" delights me in such a setting.'

'Let us waste no time in proving it.'

'So you are breaking your promises already?'

'I only promised to love you . . . What's this? You resist me?'

'Ah . . . can I for long with the only man I love in the world . . .?'

'Well then! Do not struggle against the ardent proofs of the same love that consumes me too . . .'

And the credulous Euphrasie, obliviously clasped in a criminal embrace, is on the verge of granting to matrimony that which crime would so profane.

Suddenly a door, different to the one by which she entered, opens with a crash . . .

'Treacherous creature!' said the Marquis de Gange, lighting his way with two torches that dazzle the Marquise and blind her to the young man fleeing in haste. 'Guilty and deserving of all my wrath . . .' the Marquis raged. 'So this is how you compound your depravities, without even trying to hide them!'

But Euphrasie, retaining her composure, charges into Madame de Donis's rooms, her husband rushing after her.

'What is the meaning . . .' she said with that noble courage that comes of virtue. 'What is the meaning, Madame, of these dreadful scenes you have inflicted on me? Was it not you that hurled me into this trap, and was it not with my husband that you arranged this encounter?'

'Such hypocrisy!' said Alphonse, still in a rage. 'I may not have been with you, but nor was I far away. Did you say a single word, in the midst of your *tête-à-tête* that proved it was me you were addressing?'

'And how could she have done?' the Comtesse jumped in. 'She knew full well she was with the lover she had begged me to let her see at my house—which I allowed, but not without warning her husband.'

'Hussy!'

'Silence, Madame, silence!' Madame de Donis continued. 'I took no pleasure on this occasion in acting against you but for a husband I needed to convince of your ill conduct; and when, after your repeated entreaties, I granted you a rendezvous with your lover under my roof, it was only so your husband could see with his own eyes the unconscionable extent of both your debauchery and your duplicity.'

'Accursed monster!' screamed Euphrasie, paling with fury. 'What infernal abyss unleashed you for the misfortune of virtue.'*

'Hold your tongue, Madame,' said Alphonse. 'This fervour will no longer do; perhaps it would be appropriate for virtue. Here, it only serves to cast the vice that sullies you in a still more hideous light. Do not make a scene, Madame, it will redound on you, and you need fear no outbursts from a jealousy . . . that died with my love. I leave you in contempt. Go home in peace and above all quiet: discretion and better conduct may still preserve the last shreds of your reputation—it will be ruined, along with mine, if you allow word to get out.'

'I shall obey you, Monsieur,' said Euphrasie, still containing herself despite this violent shock. 'Yes, I shall obey you; but this esteem you wish to strip me of again—a fresh wound I owe entirely to the barbarous hands of this despicable creature—I shall wrest it back, Monsieur, I shall wrest it back. Believe me, I shall find a way, through irreproachable and exemplary conduct, when these monsters no longer hound me . . . I shall find a way, I say, to force you to restore to me that which I never deserved to lose.'

And addressing the Comtesse:

'Make up some plausible reasons for ending our friendship, Madame; but above all may I never see you again, or the effects of my vengeance will eclipse those of your duplicity.'

The Marquise returned home, determined to say nothing, for she was quite convinced that, after such a wretched episode, she might well be more likely to be convicted than exonerated. Following this reasoning through, she thought she should appear in public as usual, and this she did.

However, through the efforts of the scoundrels whose handiwork it was, this episode did not pass by without a stir. This was what her tormentors wanted, and now, emboldened by the success of this ruse, they began to hatch fresh plans.

To prevail upon the Marquis, we strongly suspect that Madame de Donis, at the behest of the Abbé, did not tell Alphonse his wife had thought she was with him during this encounter—thus presenting Euphrasie in the most unfavourable light possible. One can imagine how fresh and damning this evidence must have seemed to the wretched Alphonse, and how much strength he must have taken in the conviction that such scenes would, slowly but surely, lead his wife to the end which his disaffection, and his interests, demanded.

There were at this time in Avignon two very charming young men, gifted with great wealth and handsome appearance, but of that type that later became known as *roués*, which is to say individuals who, taking advantage of all the gifts they have received from nature, have the temerity to treat women as beings created solely for their passions.

These men do not stop to think of the harm they do to society, luring gullible wives into adultery, or seducing girls into libertinage who, once corrupted, bring vices and often crimes of their own into the world, and soon turn on their seducers the poisoned darts with which the latter were foolish enough to arm them . . . A cruel truth which, by demonstrating above all the pressing need for moral instruction, should allow the pure of heart to hear the voice of their own preservation. How illogical are those who strive only to destroy morals by their example or by their writing, for they are paving the way for the very misfortunes that will punish them!

One of these young men was named the Duc de Caderousse, the other, the Marquis de Valbelle; though richer than the Chevalier de Gange, being the eldest sons of their respective Houses, they were no less close to him for all that, and following Théodore's advice it was to these two that the Chevalier confided his intentions after some earlier overtures.

'You saw my sister at the ball yesterday?' de Gange asked, while dining with them at the most famous restaurant in town.

'Indeed,' said Valbelle, 'there is not a woman in Avignon to rival her. If what you require of us now accords with what she inspires in us, you will be serving her up on a plate.'

'That's not it, my friends—I will not be serving you at all. On the contrary, you will be doing me a great service, and what will seem all the more extraordinary to you is this: I am madly in love with this woman and yet I wish to do her reputation as much damage as I possibly can.'

'My word!' said Caderousse. 'I would have thought that the moment she becomes your mistress her reputation will be tarnished enough. You certainly possess, my friend, all that one needs to dishonour a woman.'

'That's not quite it either: either I am explaining myself badly, or you are rather slow to understand me. If I do what you say, I shall have this woman on my ledger; but I need her to be on yours while I seduce her: I must have the profits while you bear the costs.'

'Valbelle,' said Caderousse, 'I rather like this role; indeed, you will agree it is almost better for a handsome fellow's reputation to be credited with a woman than it is in fact to have her. Come, I shall work on my part,' the Duc continued, 'but you will guide me, Chevalier—you will tell me everything I need to do; and in the meantime, you will reveal what has led you to carry on in this manner.'

So de Gange told his friends the whole story behind the inheritance, explaining the legitimate fears he and his brothers shared that Madame de Châteaublanc's guardianship of the child would only be to their detriment, and would further tighten their purse strings for another twenty years; he added that the appearance, or actuality, of wrongdoing on the part of the Marquise de Gange and her mother would allow the brothers to distance these two women from the administration of the inheritance; and through all this, with his friends' help, he would most certainly possess the Marquise, and consequently, would thus be serving both love and his own interests, something that was not always very easy to manage in one fell swoop. To sum up then, they would take turns to play the Marquise's alleged lovers while he would be her true one; the victim of these charming plans would then be dispatched to some tower to lament to her heart's content the loss of her reputation, her honour, and her inheritance.

'This is the most infernal plan one could possibly devise,' said Valbelle, 'and I think it is fair to say, Chevalier, that you surpass us in the learned art of betraying and ruining women.'

'My friends,' said de Gange, 'some things are truly regrettable, but their necessity obliges one to ignore the unpleasantness. As I love this woman, I must have her; and as she wishes to be richer than me, I must ruin her. There is no justice, no equilibrium in the world if those who desire have nothing, and those with nothing to desire do not share with others.'

'But what will the Marquis say to all this?' Valbelle objected.

'He will come to terms with it: he will have as many women here as he could wish for, and more money than he could imagine. You can see how much I want to serve my family. Oh, believe me, my friends, I am far more methodical and rational than you think.'

'If you ever want to prove it to us,' said Valbelle, 'I would not rely on the reasoning you have just applied. Be that as it may, it shall be done. The Chevalier has handed out our parts: you will go first, my dear Duc, and I shall follow.'

'That suits me perfectly,' said Caderousse, 'but if it so happens that an opportunity presents itself while I am working on your behalf, I'm not going to come and fetch you simply for you to take the spoils.'

'That is nonetheless what I wish you to do,' said de Gange, 'and it is why I'm afraid all this may end up with us falling out. In any case, let's not play out in advance the delightful fable of the Oyster and the Litigants.* It is quite possible that none of us will swallow the pretty little fish. Let us see what unfolds, and set sail on these rather stormy seas.'

A few bottles of Hermitage and champagne sealed this disastrous pact, and they then turned simply to the matter of its execution.

The imminent carnival, a typically noisy and lively affair in Avignon, was immeasurably helpful to the Chevalier's plans, which Théodore enthusiastically approved when these were shared with him. They decided they should begin by introducing the Marquise to the treacherous Chevalier's criminal accomplices, so the Abbé invited them into her home. With all the qualities necessary to please and partake in high society, they received a warm welcome from Euphrasie.

As the Duc de Caderousse's mother was hosting a ball two days later, the young lord did not neglect to invite the Marquise.

Although truly modest and truly virtuous, Madame de Gange, who was in the prime of her life, did not shy away from any pleasures as long as they were in keeping with her duties: it is moreover worth remembering that this was part of her plan following her misadventure at the Comtesse de Donis's house. In any case, she desperately needed some respite from the woes that had just assailed her; as her surroundings urged her to do so in such good faith, she accepted with all the grace imaginable.

No matter how pretty a woman may be, she still likes to make the most of her charms by appearing in all her finery, and the Marquise had a gift for showing that, in an honourable woman, a little coquetry can go together very well with modesty, and indeed finery with religion: are there not holidays when its ministers provide an example of this? What pleases the eye always strikes the soul. Religious fervour might perhaps be diminished were altars not strewn with flowers, and vestments not often covered in gold.

Madame de Gange thus finds herself at the ball, the most elegantly dressed and most beautiful woman there. The Marquis and the Abbé had remained at Madame de Châteaublanc's house; the Chevalier alone was there to offer the Marquise his arm. Her appearance was greeted with the same excitement as her debut at the Duc de Gadagne's house. Those gathered there recalled that she had danced with Louis XIV; that for a moment the young king had favoured her over the beautiful Mancini. All eyes were on her for much of the evening, and she received countless requests for the honour of the next dance.

Only Caderousse, keen to throw others off his scent, seemed utterly uninterested in her, while the Chevalier's love was hidden beneath all the decency he could muster.

Around eight o'clock in the evening, the Duc de Caderousse innocently invited the Marquise to take some refreshment in a room at some remove from the one where people were dancing; the Chevalier followed her. Over all the dishes offered her, the Marquise, who was rather hot, chooses a consommé; it is in a golden bowl, and it is Caderousse who serves it. Euphrasie no sooner tastes it than a dark veil extends over her brow: she falls onto a sofa, unable to resist the lethargic slumber that overwhelms her. That very instant she is snatched and bundled into a four-horse coach that sets off at full pelt towards the village of Cadenet,* home to the Caderousse estate, where the ancient castle that gave the family its name can be found, seven leagues from Avignon on the Aix road, looming over the Durance on its towering foundations.

The jolting of the coach wakes the Marquise; she lowers the window, and wants to stop, but the two men accompanying her, their disguises and masks lit by the moon, prevent her from calling out, one of them covering her mouth with his hand, the other firmly grabbing her neck.

'O good God! What is happening to me?' asked the Marquise, sitting back in the coach despite herself . . . 'What will become of me? Why must I always be the victim of my own imprudence . . .'

'Do not worry, Madame,' said a voice she did not recognize. 'Nothing terrible is going to happen to you, or at least nothing too distressing for a pretty woman.'

'But is this outrage Monsieur de Caderousse's doing?'

'No, Madame, he has nothing to do with this.'

'So it is my brother-in-law? They were the only two with me when I took that sleeping potion.'

'It is neither of the two individuals you have named.'

'Was I not at the Duchesse de Caderousse's ball?'

'You were, Madame.'

'But was the Chevalier de Gange not with me?'

'He was, Madame.'

'And yet they were not the ones who had me abducted.'

'No, Madame. A powerful philtre* was put in the broth you chose. Everything changed in an instant: a gentleman who is deeply in love with you stole you away, and just as the Chevalier de Gange and the Duc were rushing to get help, this same gentleman carried you to this coach and placed you in our care. We are very close to our destination: there, Madame, you will meet your abductor; there you will see at your feet the man you believe has wronged you, and there you will do as all women do and forgive the criminal entirely in favour of his crime.'

'I shall forgive nothing,' said the Marquise in despair. 'I do not want to hear anything, or understand anything, I just want you to set me down here in the middle of the road, where I can surely find someone to help me escape the indignity that awaits me.'

'Set you down here, Madame, in the perilous Lourmarin valley? Where Protestants take refuge and mercilessly slaughter those who bother them?'

'I shall have less to fear from them than from you: they defend their rights, you violate mine; these same men you invoke to frighten me live on the same earth I do; I have never had reason to complain of them; they worship the same God I do, and do not offend him as you do. Let me go, let me go, I say, or I shall call out to them for help.'

The only outcome of this threat was that two elegantly designed wooden shutters were carefully raised over the coach windows, the coachman was urged to make haste, and the Marquise was held more firmly than before.

'So be it, I shall resign myself to my fate,' said this unfortunate woman. 'I made a mistake, I must be punished for it. Holy Saviour, I beg for your mercy. You shall protect me from these terrible dangers. Your goodness would never abandon weak and wretched virtue. Ah, you would no longer be the avenger of crime if you allowed it to triumph over virtue.'

They journeyed for another hour, arriving in the middle of the night. The coach came to a halt in a very dark courtyard, and as the Marquise alighted all she could see were tall ramparts that almost obscured the staircase she was made to climb, escorted still by her two guards. She reached an enormous bedroom and was locked carefully inside. Every precaution had been taken to prevent her from being able to open the windows, and the most chilling silence reigned over the castle.

CHAPTER X

WITH such a vivid imagination, and such recent memories of her woes, it is not difficult to imagine the distressing reflections to which Madame de Gange succumbed. How many sighs came from her oppressed heart . . . how many tears drenched her cheeks as she contemplated her terrible plight! Cruelly agitated, she wandered around this great chamber, unable to discern its dimensions, when she thought she spied a small door ajar. It was still night, and the room was lit only by some faint and fleeting beams from a pale moon constantly hidden by the squalling clouds. She flies to this door . . . misfortune grasps wildly at anything that chance presents: a spluttering lamp reveals a glimpse of a chamber on the other side of the door; she enters . . . But what hideous object greets her eyes! There on a table before her, she sees an open cadaver, almost entirely ripped asunder, on which the castle surgeon had just been working . . . for this is his laboratory. Euphrasie recoils with a bloodcurdling scream. She loses her way, stumbles . . . only terror is keeping her alive; were it not for the intense agitation making her heart pound she would die . . . But there is no way out . . . no means of escape left; and without her so much as touching it, the door by which she entered this terrible place closes behind her.

'Ah!' she cries out, trembling. 'This must be a victim of these monsters, and now the same fate awaits me . . .! How can I escape?'

Standing still, pressed weakly against the wall, she barely dares breathe. The lamp suddenly expires, a thousand phantoms appear before her, and as if nature wanted to add to this wretched woman's anxiety, a storm breaks . . . she hears a dreadful clap of thunder, and throws herself to her right . . . So it is that sometimes the heavens work on our behalf when they seem to be against us: Euphrasie's movement pushes her against a spring that extends to open another door. A narrow corridor reveals itself. Desperate to flee the present danger, without a thought for the still greater horrors that might lie ahead, she hurtles down it . . . There is a staircase at the end of the corridor: she descends it without seeing where she is or where she is going. She finds herself in the castle courtyard. The foul weather has driven away the porters: there is no one at the gates; she shakes them, the locks give, and they open . . . Euphrasie is free.

Ah! how inevitable it is that crime's inadequate precautions betray it at every step!

The thunderstorm intensifies. What will become of Euphrasie, dressed elegantly, but lightly, as indeed one would be, for a ball? There is nothing to protect her from the dangers to which this new turn of events has exposed her, but she knows only too well those that threaten her in the house she is leaving behind; she presses on in haste . . . There is no track, no path, not even a tree: the road she should have taken is far behind her. The storm is far from abating: the thunderbolts rumble on; the electric sparks, flashing across the sky, shock the ether as they ignite it, the very image of a war raging in the heavens. Thunder, harbinger of death, rolls in the valleys beneath the castle. Almost blinded by the lightning as it blazes only to plunge her into greater darkness, Euphrasie is beset with obstacles at every step; her delicate feet catch on the thick roots of the vines as she dashes hither and thither through them.

The clouds finally break, spewing torrents of rain upon the earth that nonetheless fail to extinguish the fires that fall with them. A hundred yards away, the flames from a luckless cottage consumed by a lightning bolt terrify Euphrasie even more as they bleakly illuminate the tortuous paths she is taking, revealing nothing but precipices all around. And with this calamitous spectacle come the plaintive howls of the wretches whose belongings have been devoured by this misfortune. Their suffering cries, accompanied by the bells tolled by locals out of foolish superstition, and by redoubled bursts of lightning, seem to sound a warning that Nature, incensed by man's crimes, will plunge him back forever into the abyss from which he emerged by God's grace.

Euphrasie, tottering, buffeted both by the gale and her own terror, resembles a young willow battered by a storm. She finally stumbles to the ground in furrows brimming with water that make her miss her step; she cries out for death to come to her aid. She calls on the lightning, as its bolts fly down all around her . . . a young doe pursued by huntsmen, waiting to expire in its final resting place.*

She hears a sound. Someone is approaching. This plaintive, pitiful creature no longer knows whether she should welcome or fear whoever may be heading towards her.

'What do you want of me?' she wails. 'Is it me you're seeking? If it is to kill me, leave me to die here instead; Heaven will grant my wishes, and I would prefer to perish at its hands than yours.'

'Come, Madame, come,' she is told. 'You caught us unawares; you were nearly our downfall, but stronger shackles will preserve us from the fate your rashness almost brought upon us.'

At these words two men seize her; they wrap her in the coat they are carrying, and take great care in escorting her back to the castle. She enters it once more; one of her guards leaves; the second, after taking her back to the room where she had previously been, returns with a light. But who does she see before her? So it is true that the heavens never abandon virtue . . . It is Victor, the Marquis de Gange's loyal valet, whom we mentioned at the start of this story; dismissed over some trifling misdemeanours, he had entered the Duc de Caderousse's service: he recognizes his former mistress.

'What? It's you, Madame la Marquise?' he said, throwing himself at her knees. 'O good God! How am I going to deliver you from the dangers that surround you?'

'Where am I, then?'

'At the Duc de Caderousse's, Madame—the finest master in the world, no doubt, but also the most depraved man of the age. The men who brought you here told me everything other than your name. The Duc had you abducted in Avignon; you are four hours ahead of him, and he is returning here only to submit you to his criminal desires. You are lost, my honourable mistress, lost, if I fail to extract you from this hell. But how am I to do that? Alas, he will kill me, if I allow you to escape, and you . . . you, Madame, will be defiled if I do not save you.'

'O Victor!'

'Do not implore me, I have made my decision: between my life and your honour, I should not hesitate for a moment.'

'Good man! . . . have my guards left?'

'They should have, but how can we leave in the state you are in? Fortunately my wife is here in this house. Let's go to her: you will take her clothes, leave yours with her, and I shall accompany you . . . But, in sacrificing myself for you, understand that I can never return here.'

'O Victor! Do you really think I could ever abandon you for a moment?'

'Let's make haste then: there is not a minute to lose.'

They go down to see Victor's wife, the castle concierge. The change of clothes does not take long; they rush out into the courtyard, and pass through the gates a second time.

'One moment,' says Victor, stopping on the other side. 'We must be careful not to return to Avignon by the same road the Duc is taking to his castle: otherwise we are bound to run into him. Let us hurry down the mountain, take the ferry across the Durance, head straight to Aix, and find a coach there to take us to Avignon. But will you survive such a long expedition on foot?'

'Come now! Does one tire when one is fleeing misfortune? Let's make ourselves scarce, and don't fret about me.'

They set off . . . Madame de Gange takes every sound she hears for her abductor's coach. Victor reassures her, and they arrive at the ferry. But they cannot cross the torrent: swollen dramatically by the storm, it is flooding the countryside all around; and no matter how much they entreat the ferryman, he refuses to take the risk for people who, in any case, seem of no particular importance. They have to wait for the waters to subside, but how long will this take? . . . Where are they to stay in the meantime?

Two hundred yards away, to their right, they see a squalid smugglers' tavern. Between taking shelter there and retracing their steps, there is no middle course: if the first plan raises fears of the worst company imaginable, the latter risks a far more dangerous encounter with her abductor. Madame de Gange wishes to wait in the boat, but the man in charge only allows her to do so for a couple of hours before making them leave. They therefore have to make do with the humble inn.

'Ah!' Victor exclaimed, recognizing from afar a fearsome individual smoking in the kitchen doorway. 'O heavens! Where are we? The man you see there is one of the Duc's henchmen: a scoundrel who, in return for services rendered to this lord, has already twice escaped the punishment his crimes deserved. I am sure he has been sent to track us down . . . Where can we hide? . . . Where can we flee? . . .'

They see a ramshackle lean-to just to the left of the tavern door; from there they would be able to hear every word said in the inn by the bandit and the two lackeys who did not leave his side.

'Let's hide in there,' said Victor. 'At least we shall know what to expect from these dreadful men.'

Euphrasie agrees; the two of them huddle under bundles of straw, and anxiously lend an ear . . .

'We missed them by an hour,' says the chief to his companions. 'They must have been hidden in the boat . . . What a loss for us! The Duc promised us two hundred *louis* if we could bring her back. He'll have Victor cudgelled to death, but as for the Marquise, she's ruined: it doesn't really matter—she's a far from respectable woman. Her husband only duelled with Villefranche because he found him in his wife's bed. And not long before that, when she was on the run from Beaucaire with the same lover, and Deschamps—my chieftain at the time—took her down into his cave, did he not have his way with her? And she went along with it too . . .'

'Oh, she's a right old Jezebel.'

'Yes,' says the chief, 'that's how these lovely ladies make the most of the public esteem they enjoy. If it had been one of our women, people would simply say she's a hussy: it's as if the poor aren't entitled to a reputation; but with these Marquises, these Duchesses, you have to choose your words carefully; they do worse things than our women, and yet you still have to pay them respect.'

'They say she's pretty, this one,' said the third of these comrades.

'If it weren't for that,' the chief replied, 'the Duc wouldn't be paying us so well for our services. Oh, she's a ruined woman all right,' the brigand continued. 'No one will ever want to see her in Avignon again.'

'Well then!' said the third henchman. 'Her husband will have her locked up. She's young—she'll be given time to learn her lesson. All these women should be kept under lock and key—they're the ones who ruin the others, and that's why there's so much lechery in these parts. But let's carry on with our search: let's head to the other ferry—they might be there instead.'

'God's guts! I tell you I'd gladly bring her back to the Duc: he's a good man, and there's no harm in him taking advantage of all these women's follies. Why did she come in the first place?'

Our bandits paid what they owed, and on their way out passed so close to the lean-to that one of them nearly fell onto the bundles of hay covering the Marquise and her guide.

Once they are gone, our two fugitives head back into the countryside, climbing to slightly higher ground to observe what is happening at the second ferry; they finally see the bandits retrace their steps and take the road back to the castle. They make their way along the riverbank and ask to cross. As the waters have receded a little, the man in charge agrees; then, paying them closer attention:

'Aren't you among those the Duc sent after the woman who's run away from his castle?' he asked. 'Some folk you may have seen too told us they had been sent to hunt them down, and to stop them if they came this way.'

'By God!' said Victor. 'Those are our orders too: he dispatched my wife here and me for the same reason. We work for him too, you know.'

'Hurry,' said the boatman. 'I think the woman you are after is on the road to Aix; she took the other ferry.'

'Right,' said Victor. 'We'll give chase and won't stop until we have her.'

'Get on, get on, my friends—anything for the Duc: he's a fine lord, and pays well.'

They cross, they reach the other side, and at last the Marquise is on the road to Aix.

'O my dear Victor!' said Euphrasie, as soon as she sees the river between herself and her abductors. 'How can I repay you for what you have done for me?'

'Madame,' said Victor, refusing a precious ring the Marquise tried to give him. 'The man who is fortunate enough to protect virtue assailed by vice needs no reward other than the one he receives from his heart.'

'But did you hear the horrible things those people said?[1] So this is where the slightest imprudence can lead a respectable woman![2] O my dear Victor! What a lesson!'

'You will triumph over all this, Madame,' Victor replied. 'And the light I shall shed on everything will give me the pleasure of helping you in that regard.'

The Marquise was tired. Her stamina, sapped by anguish and distress, was starting to fail her. She and her protector climbed into a cart headed the same way, and it was in this fashion that they entered Aix. As soon as they reached the Cours,* they parted ways with this pitiful escort, and Victor led the Marquise to the finest inn in the town. They had barely arrived when who should they lay eyes on but the Marquis de Gange! Euphrasie is fit to faint . . .

'Am I deceived?' said Alphonse. 'What? It is you, Madame! . . . in this state . . . accompanied by a man I banished from my home! And

---

[1] We have reported these remarks word for word to show the extent to which Madame de Gange's enemies manipulated public opinion in order to achieve their perfidious ends.

[2] If some of our readers were to ask what the moral purpose of this work might be, we would reply with this wise reflection by the Marquise.

it is in this disguise that you take flight? And, under the pretext of going to the ball, here you are traipsing around the whole province? Can you imagine the worry you caused your mother and all your family? And so fate would have it, Madame, that whenever we meet it is only for me to upbraid you in the manner your misconduct deserves.'

'O Monsieur, deign hear me before you condemn me.'

'Well then, let us hasten to my room: and there, you can take your time and tell me all about this peculiar episode . . . As for you, Victor, have no fear. That you accompanied Madame is enough for me to reward you: you will tell me what I can do for you.'

'The honour of serving you, Monsieur le Marquis . . . Oh, be in no doubt you have a truly honourable wife.'

They enter the Marquis's room and Euphrasie, having shed very bitter tears, tells her husband in the greatest detail all that has happened to her, prudently hiding nonetheless the part the Chevalier played in these events.

Let us not tax our heroine with dishonesty: it is permitted to hide what it would be imprudent to reveal; but it is always very criminal to cast the facts in a misleading light.

The Marquis severely reproached his wife for perpetually falling into every trap laid for her.

'You can see,' he said, 'that once again you risk placing me in the same position with Caderousse that caused all that trouble with Villefranche.'

'Avoid that at all costs,' said Euphrasie. 'Let us forget an episode which would ruin me if word got out: from now on, I must rely on my good conduct to protect me from any further calamities.'

'O traitor! You said as much at Madame de Donis's house.'

'Guilty of imprudence alone in each case, believe me when I say I shall now be stricter than ever regarding anything that might lead me into the same pitfalls. Give Victor his reward, Monsieur, I beg you. The grounds on which you had him dismissed from Gange in no way detract from the noble deed he has just performed. I vouch for him.'

The Marquis paid Victor well, placed him and his wife in service in Aix, and it was then simply a matter of returning to Avignon; husband and wife arrived there without exchanging a word.

'Here is your daughter, Madame,' says Alphonse to his mother-in-law. 'She will explain everything, and it will be for you to judge.'

The Marquis withdraws after these words, leaving these two women to their discussions.

The first thought that occurred to Madame de Châteaublanc was that this had been yet another trap.

'I do not doubt it,' says Euphrasie. 'And what seems peculiar to me is that Alphonse has still not overcome any of his unfortunate impressions of me. He was as cold as ice on our return home.'

'Someone is poisoning him against you,' said Madame de Châteaublanc. 'You have your duties to fulfil, my daughter—let nothing stand in the way of those. The truth will reveal itself sooner or later, and we shall triumph over our enemies.'

'I fear,' said Madame de Gange, 'that this inheritance will only add to their rancour.'

'But what rights could they have over it? Nochères left the five hundred thousand francs to you because he wanted them to pass to your son.'

'True. But my husband would, perhaps, have preferred this will to be as favourable to him as it is to me. Perhaps he wishes to receive the revenue until my son comes of age.'

'With the way your husband and his brothers conduct themselves, our dear child might well lose out under his administration.'

'Monsieur de Gange is incapable of . . .'

'I think so too, but he is weak, and his brothers hold sway over him.'

'O mamma! I would be sorry to fall out with my husband . . . if you only knew how much I love him!'

'And I, my daughter, would be sorry if your son ended up with nothing. In any case, let us proceed as diplomatically as possible, and trust that my reflections, and those of our advisers, will soon provide us with the means to ensure the right balance in all the different aspects of his important matter.'

CHAPTER XI

AN hour after the Marquise's escape from Cadenet, the Chevalier de Gange and the Duc de Caderousse arrived there with the most criminal intentions. One can imagine their astonishment when they learnt of Victor's betrayal. His wife was shown the door the moment Euphrasie's clothes were discovered in her quarters, and strict orders were relayed to every corner of Caderousse's estate.

'Well, this is the greatest calamity two honourable gentlemen could suffer,' said the Chevalier, 'for you will acknowledge we could not possibly have been in greater agreement. I relinquished all my rights prior to the defeat of our enemy. From that moment, nothing has come between us.'

'One never falls out when one conducts oneself in this manner,' said the Duc, 'but such debonair lovers are rare indeed. Still, if the most essential part of our plan has not been carried out, we must hope the rest of it will be. Let us return to Avignon and spread the word about our exploits at the ball. What do I really care whether or not we defile this woman, so long as it appears she has been defiled? I told you, my friend: I am as happy to besmirch this woman as to have her; my interests are satisfied either way, and that is all I consider.'

'And for my part, I shall compensate you—be sure of that. Let us go and find Valbelle: it is his turn; perhaps he will be less unfortunate than you.'

As soon as our young gentlemen had returned to the capital of the Comtat, they joined Valbelle and Théodore for what they called a confabulation, and the first item that was agreed was to give this episode the greatest possible publicity while nonetheless casting a veil over the role played by the Chevalier, who doubtless did all he could to come to his sister's aid. The second point was to insinuate Valbelle into the lady's company in order to add to her suitors, though to bide their time over this to avoid any suspicion of malice or spite.

'In any case,' said the Abbé, who had revealed this new plan, 'let us see what unfolds in the meantime. The Chevalier, who will arouse no suspicion, or very little at least, will maintain his current good footing with his sister-in-law; perhaps the lull I am suggesting will create new opportunities, and new ways of seizing them.'

This opinion prevailed, and it was left at that.

The Chevalier wasted no time in paying his sister a visit.

'I was there only to come to your aid,' he told her affectionately.

'So I was told, and so I believe,' Euphrasie replied. 'When it comes to anything that might bring about my ruin, my dear brother, I would certainly never accuse you of having any part in it.'

'What upsets me is that this episode is causing a great stir, and, with the sincere attachment I have for you, this slander could not pain me more.'

'I am touched by the interest you take in me.'

'You must know it could not be keener.'

'Ah! Your brother's is fading fast . . .'

'But all these things make a husband fret: no matter how absurd such prejudice against you may be, it exists, and must be acknowledged. How will you make people forget this upsetting episode?'

'By utterly respectable conduct: with limitless prudence, I shall win the public over; people quiet down when the truth is revealed.'

'Slander is so much in fashion in this damned town.'

'Oh, how sorry I am that I came here! Unfortunately, I cannot leave it yet.'

'Because of this inheritance?'

'All the various business related to it needs to be concluded.'

'Five hundred thousand francs, or so I have been told.'

'More or less. I fear my husband is vexed at not being named as I was in this will.'

'He is too fair-minded for that: it was for Nochères to decide; he did what he believed was right. Besides, you and Madame de Châteaublanc can repair much of the damage . . .'

Euphrasie, who understood perfectly what the Chevalier meant, lowered her gaze and changed the subject.

'I should no longer receive the Duc de Caderousse, do you not agree, brother?'

'I suppose it would be unwise; it would be better not to see him. But Valbelle, who had nothing to do with all this—Valbelle, who is courteous, pleasant, and discreet, may continue to pay you visits. You should not isolate yourself: that would cause even more gossip.'

'Nonetheless, I do not wish to attend any balls.'

'Such a precaution is excessive, but I cannot blame you for it.'

The Marquise maintained this perfect restraint for almost a year, during which time the Chevalier continued his constant and assiduous courting of Euphrasie. And the Abbé, as jealous as he was treacherous, fuelled this passion, assuring him that he would prevail in the end. But the Marquise's extreme reserve offered no signs of such a future: she was somehow able to kindle his ardour without ever giving him the slightest hope; and in this subtle manner she thought she could create an ally, a protector close both to a husband she still adored and to the Abbé whom she continued to fear, but without ever allowing this man the slightest hold over her. Théodore often reproached her for this preference.

'You have forgotten, Madame,' he told her one day, 'just how much I love you. You no longer remember that I have placed all my hopes of happiness in your hands.'

'But it seems to me, my dear brother, that when you revealed the reason which once made you speak in such terms, you promised to forget this madness.'

'Since you raise that occasion,' said the Abbé, 'I must now reveal the grounds for my actions. It was not,' Théodore continued, 'without great suffering that I observed the disharmony between you and your husband. No matter how much I wanted to possess you, it was never my intention to do so at the price of your irrevocable separation from Alphonse: I wanted, as far as possible, to reconcile my love with the proprieties, by persuading my brother that you had done nothing wrong in the various misadventures that befell you. I thought I would achieve my goal; and, although there was no doubt you were guilty . . .'

'Me? Guilty?'

'Yes, Madame, you are: it is impossible to exonerate you. Despite this, as I say, I wanted to defend you.'

'O heavens! What new horrors are these!'

'No, Madame, no—I shall simply remind you of the old ones . . . I repeat, Euphrasie, you are guilty: all I said in your favour was born of my tenderness for you, not of the truth. The note found in Villefranche's pocket is very clearly in your hand; it is still in my possession; it can be produced whenever it is required. The document you signed with Deschamps is further proof of your delinquency, and sufficient to bring about your ruin. Nonetheless, you have seen my own conduct. I led you myself into your husband's arms; I sacrificed myself for you. I expected some appreciation, but you are an ingrate: you favour the Chevalier over me; you succumbed to the Duc de Caderousse; you cover yourself in vice and ingratitude. I am the only man before whom you maintain this masquerade of virtue, and yet you expect me not to be angry? What recklessness though! For you know that with just one word I can destroy you in my brother's eyes; and be in no doubt that I shall say this word, and produce these proofs, if you persist in this coldness which is so dangerous for you, and so unjust to me . . .'

The Abbé, who can contain himself no longer, now throws himself passionately at the feet of the woman he adores: he implores her to offer some token at least for the impetuous passion that consumes him. What a predicament for the Marquise! Here she is in the same situation this madman inflicted on her in the castle of Gange: if she sours him against her, she makes a dreadful enemy of him; there is no doubt this man will avenge his loss by turning her husband against her and alienating the Chevalier, whose faults she does not perceive, whose temperament she still appreciates, and whose help she trusts will redeem her in the public eye. If she manages to anger Théodore further by a cold and contemptuous silence, would she not be admitting to the crimes she had in no way committed? On the other hand, does she have it in her to submit? What a quandary!

'O Monsieur,' she said to the Abbé, insisting he adopt a different posture to the one his love had forced on him. 'O Monsieur, how wicked and deceitful you are: wicked, most certainly, as you threaten to ruin me if I do not agree to dishonour myself; deceitful—can you deny it, as you now claim that something you proved was false before leaving Gange is genuine? How does a man who aims to please dare show himself to the woman he wishes to seduce while wearing two such hideous masks? When you court a woman, do you not hope to be agreeable to her? If you do, Monsieur, would you conduct yourself in this manner?'

'I have nothing to say to this clumsy subterfuge,' said the Abbé. 'It shows me all the treachery of your heart; I need nothing else. I shall abandon you to your reflections, Madame, but remember that you now have in me the most mortal enemy.'

'So be it! So be it!' said the Marquise, holding him back against his will. 'Then accuse me in front of my mother and your two brothers if you dare. Stop using these secret and slanderous measures. I shall invoke a family tribunal: that is where I wish to answer your slurs against me; if you have the audacity to defend them there, if you man-age to convict me, I shall yield to you; but you will no longer speak to

me as you do now should you fail to persuade those before whom
I wish my case to be heard of my crimes.'

'Deceitful creature,' said the Abbé. 'You know full well I can do no
such thing without appearing to be guilty myself, and this is why you
defy me. No, I shall not do what you wish me to, and the measures
I shall employ to ruin you will be more reliable than those you think
will save you.'

Poor Euphrasie trembled: it was as if she sensed what this monster
had in store for her; it seems to her that hell's furies, before her very
eyes, are lifting the bloody veil cast by the future.

The scoundrel left and (if we may be allowed the liberty of con-
densing certain moments in his life which best reveal him, even though
some time passed between these conversations) went to tell the
Chevalier that he was wrong not to press Euphrasie—that he had
discerned in her the most decided inclination for him.

'You are sure to triumph, my friend, if you are willing to turn up
for the fight. Oh, this battle would have been over a long time ago had
I been in your shoes!'

The gullible Chevalier, convinced by what he has just heard, flies to
Euphrasie's side, but, aside from a few courtesies, leaves her with as
little hope as before.

For over a year, the Marquise de Gange lived such a cloistered life
that no slander could possibly sully her. The Caderousse affair had
done her considerable harm, and as a result of the efforts made by
those who wished to ruin her, this episode had been so embellished,
and so distorted, that the public were only very warily beginning to
come round a little.

Valbelle was virtually the only young person in town whose visits
the Marquise, in the company of the Chevalier, still received.

'Come,' said de Gange at last to his accomplice. 'Amiability and good
behaviour are reaping us no rewards with this woman, and she is winning over the public while wasting our time: we can no longer allow
a reputation we wish to destroy to blossom anew. People will end up
believing she is virtuous, and that would be disastrous for our plans. Let
us not give the wounds time to close: we must tear them asunder while
they are still bleeding. It is your turn, Valbelle, as you know: try to acquit
yourself better than Caderousse, and the victim will be sacrificed.'

'But how to go about it?' asked Valbelle. 'Everything must be so
consummately arranged this time that she cannot escape us.'

'Certainly, but remember to respect the same terms I previously agreed with the Duc.'

'I promise, but only with great reluctance: I cannot hide from you that my love for your sister deepens the more I see her. What a paragon of virtue, of piety, of candour! What a combination of graces and sweetness! My friend, she is an angel the heavens have placed in the midst of demons, but only to test her. Her lucky star, that beacon of virtue which always triumphs, will deliver her from our criminal hands as pure as she fell into them.'

'I doubt that,' said the Chevalier. 'Our nets are too well cast: she will free herself from one trap only to fall into another, and we shall always remain in control. Speaking of which, what are we going to conjure up this time?'

'I don't know: this startled bird will be hard to lure from her cage.'

'You are wrong,' said Théodore. 'We shall still reap the fruit of the trust we have inspired, and that alone will work in our favour.'

No sooner were these resolutions taken than Madame de Châteaublanc received a letter from those dealing with her business affairs inviting her to meet them immediately in Marseille to take possession of a country property, part of the Nochères inheritance, near the town. Their letter advised Madame de Châteaublanc that this transaction was unlikely to detain her for more than a week. The lawyer briefing her on these matters was offering to accommodate her in his own home—situated, he said, on the Cours.* Euphrasie's mother, already apprised of these matters, prepared to leave the next day, without even thinking of proposing to her daughter a journey that could only be tedious for her; and as her absence was to be so brief, she did not even think to write down her address there. She simply said that she would be staying on the Cours, and that she would write if by any chance her trip had to be extended.

Euphrasie seemed perturbed for a moment at the prospect of being alone in Avignon, particularly with her husband away for a few days in Gange, but Madame de Châteaublanc comforts herself with the knowledge that the Chevalier will not leave her side; and this rather too trusting mother leaves without the slightest apprehension.

Two days later, de Gange went to see his sister-in-law. This prudent woman's first action was to entreat him not to bring her any visitors.

'As my husband is away from Avignon,' she told him, 'I must be more circumspect than ever.'

Gange praised her for this vigilance, the traitor telling her that this should henceforth be the basis of all her actions, and that she would have avoided a great deal of misfortune had she always conducted herself with such prudence. The Marquise thanked her brother tenderly for taking such interest in her, and could not resist opening her heart to him:

'O my dear Chevalier,' she told him with that natural candour and innocence that made her so touching. 'Why is the burning love I have for my husband met only with coldness?'

'You have been too carefree in your conduct,' Gange replied, 'and you know that this led to some little misjudgements which—without you ever having been guilty—nonetheless gave that impression. Only time can heal all this. You know Alphonse's temperament: he is trusting, he is kind, but such people always fly into a fury when they are deceived; they need to be handled more carefully than others. Count on my help, Euphrasie: I shall do all I can to win back for you a heart you so utterly deserve.'

The charming Marquise, no longer able to suppress a torrent of emotion, buried her head tearfully in the Chevalier's chest; and these tears, born of conjugal tenderness, of gratitude and virtue, moistened the brow of crime and deceit unabated. This deeply depraved heart did not melt at the shedding of these precious tears; the pain and disarray of the woman who wept them served only to fuel the guilty passion of one of her cruellest enemies. The Chevalier disguised his feelings to resemble those which his sister was pouring out to him. He embraces her, consoles her, and, further encouraged by these simulacra of a friendship she believes to be so pure, Euphrasie talks to him about the Abbé.

'He seems angry with me,' she tells the Chevalier. 'He dredges up old slanders, and seems more persuaded than ever of my guilt. Oh, what a torture it is for innocence to be treated thus!'

'I believe,' said de Gange, with an air of the utmost candour, 'that Théodore is in love with you.'

'Oh, no! No,' said the Marquise, rejecting an idea that discretion dictated she dismiss. 'Do not think any such thing, my brother. The Abbé, more severe than you, sees crimes everywhere; nonetheless, no one should know better than he that I never committed any of those he imputes to me.'

'Then suspect him of avarice, at least,' said the Chevalier, 'and remember that self-interest is a god he serves all too well: this is the real reason for his bitterness; it has its roots in the matter of this will. The Abbé, reliant on an allowance as I am, is nonetheless far more upset than me that this inheritance is not in the hands of the Marquis, as it would have put our brother in a position to do us a great deal of good.'

'I understand that,' said Madame de Gange, 'but we had to obey the testator's intentions, and my mother was not at liberty to deviate from these.'

'The Abbé, like Alphonse, will overcome his prejudice against you,' de Gange replied. 'And in any case, remember you will always have me here as your protector and most loyal friend.'

That is how the traitor dared to speak even as he was unearthing the abyss into which he was about to plunge this poor woman.

Oh, if treachery and duplicity are terrible vices, what dreadful blackness do they assume when crime in all its horror brings them to bear on virtue?

Madame de Châteaublanc had been absent for almost a week, and so, were she to remain true to her word, it was about the time her daughter might expect her return. Madame de Gange was therefore making ready to provide her with a warm homecoming when a troubling letter arrived to disturb this pleasure. Madame de Châteaublanc required her daughter's presence, and was begging her to come very quickly to a house on the Cours, the address of which was indicated in a manner which could easily be misconstrued. Guided solely by her eagerness to be of use to her mother, Euphrasie hastens into a coach bound for Marseille (as her own had been taken by Madame de Châteaublanc), and alights at the address where she expects to find the dear object of her concern. She walks up to the house with that kind of confidence which forges straight ahead without a second thought. Imagine her surprise at being received by Monsieur de Valbelle, who happens to be staying in the house of his uncle, a famous naval officer of the same name away on an expedition with the Duc de Vivonne.

'To what good fortune, Madame,' Valbelle exclaims, 'do I owe the pleasure of seeing you in this town today?'

Euphrasie, baffled, does not know how to respond.

'Monsieur,' she says, letter in hand, 'I thought I was paying a visit to my mother, who has just fallen ill in this town. It seems to me this is indeed the address she indicated.'

Valbelle quickly reads the aforementioned letter, and sees *at the end of the Cours*, and not *on the Cours*: he shows this to Madame de Gange who, deeply agitated, wishes to leave that very moment and search for the house indicated.

'This is a large town, Madame,' said Valbelle, holding her back. 'Be so good as to allow me to carry out this search myself, and to offer you my home in the meantime.'

'Monsieur,' said Euphrasie. 'It appears you are alone here, and decency forbids me from accepting your hospitality.'

'No, Madame, I am not alone,' the Comte eagerly interrupted.

And, taking her by the hand, he shows her into a room where there is a lady of around thirty-five years of age.

'This is Madame de Moissac, my cousin,' Valbelle continued, 'who will be your hostess in this house.'

But the young Comte, realizing that here was an opportunity more pressing than any exchange of niceties . . .

'My cousin,' he says to this woman, 'I think the best way to oblige Madame at this time would be for you to go and find out where Madame de Châteaublanc is staying yourself so that we can then accompany Madame de Gange there—for I can see she is growing ever more anxious.'

'O Madame, what an imposition! But we can go together if you wish.'

'I would not put you to this trouble, Madame,' said Valbelle. 'You are tired, and the walk could be a very long one: allow my cousin to take care of this for you.'

'It would be a pleasure,' replied this cousin, 'for it will allow me to share with Monsieur de Valbelle the honour of serving such a charming and honourable lady. Wait here patiently, the two of you, and rest assured that, even if I have to walk around the city three times over, I shall not return without having seen Madame de Châteaublanc.'

At these words, this respectable cousin hurries off to begin her search. Madame de Gange, still agitated, refuses to sit down.

'Well then, Madame,' says the Comte, who understands perfectly well the cause of her anguish. 'As you apparently think me too redoubtable to spend even an hour or two alone in my company, let us take a walk by the port: you have yet to see this magnificent spectacle, and it is bound to interest you.'

'Forgive me, Monsieur, but at this moment my only concern is my mother.'

'But it will take a good two hours for my cousin to find the right house. We shall be back well before then, and I can see that you would be ill at ease spending these two hours doing anything but walking, or perhaps resting: I would favour the latter myself, as it would allow me to take care of you in greater intimacy.'

'Well, then, Monsieur, let us leave then. Let us leave—I shall gladly take the walk you have proposed.'

This indubitably seemed the wiser course. They set off, and Madame de Gange, absorbed by all the sights that were pointed out to her, could not help but marvel at them.

Indeed, what painting could be more captivating than this assortment of individuals from all nations, brought together by trade in a hive of activity; on one side one sees ships being unloaded; on the other, the goods they had on board being carried to the grasping merchant, who receives them with a raging thirst for gold and a keen appetite for profit; meanwhile, a poignant contrast reveals a wretched convict on the same shore, who, with the identical aim of growing richer, failed to use honest means to reach his goal; there is shame on his brow, and pain in his eyes; to distract himself he makes the best use he can of the talents he has. Music playing here and there along this magnificent quay, that horde of curious bystanders and busy traders colliding with each other this way and that . . . everywhere, in other words, the good cheer, the utter exuberance of these lively and industrious people, who nonetheless only give themselves over to pleasure when they have first taken care of business—all this, no doubt, serves to make the port of Marseille one of the finest spectacles in the world, and Madame de Gange admired it without dreaming that she had herself become a subject of public admiration; indeed this *tête-à-tête* between such a pretty woman and one of the most fashionable and charming young men of the age seemed curious to many onlookers.

The poor woman was enjoying the distraction for a moment without suspecting that her enemies, pursuing their twin aims of seducing and dishonouring her, had orchestrated this walk purely to parade her. She was, to her great embarrassment, approached and maliciously greeted by various individuals of her acquaintance, among whom were several young nobles from Avignon: Caumont, Théran, Darcusia, Fourbin, and Senas all recognized and accosted her, smiling at her gallant and in some cases congratulating him very quietly on his good fortune. The Marquise even thought she saw the Chevalier de Gange, but when she wished to approach him Valbelle held her back, assuring her that she was mistaken, and that even if she were right, it would be better to avoid him than join him: rather than wait for an explanation, the Chevalier would perhaps begin by condemning her behaviour and upbraiding him for doing something which, as Madame de Gange could see, had no other motive than decency and honour. They therefore continued their walk, and when the two hours granted to Madame de Moissac for her search had expired, they headed back to Valbelle's mansion.

Madame de Moissac had returned.

'I had a great deal of difficulty finding what I was looking for,' she said, 'but in the end I succeeded: Madame de Châteaublanc is staying in the very house which had prompted the discussions that brought her here, as this proved more convenient when it came to dealing with the matter. One can reach this house, one of those *bastides*[1] as we call them in Marseille, by a street *at the end of the Cours*, and these were the words that misled you in the letter. I have had the honour of seeing Madame your mother; she is better and seemed upset at the misunderstanding about the address—for which she entirely blames herself. She is impatient to see you.'

'O Madame, how great a debt I owe you!' said Euphrasie. 'All I ask of you now is to be so good as to take me there straight away.'

'Certainly,' said the Comte de Valbelle. 'Neither my cousin nor I shall abandon you now, but allow me nonetheless to point out that it is late, and that since you arrived here this morning you have not had so much as a bowl of soup.'

'Oh, no! No, we shall leave straight away, I beg you,' said Madame de Gange. 'I do not want to trespass on your kindness any further, and you can imagine how keen I am to be at my mother's side.'

'So be it! Madame, we are at your service,' said Valbelle, as he ordered horses for one of his uncle's coaches. 'You and my cousin are both too tired for another expedition on foot: let us be on our way.'

They set off towards the quarter in question as planned. But when Madame de Gange notices they are leaving the town behind, and that night is falling, she starts to worry; her soul is cloaked in the same darkness that will soon enshroud the imposing spectacle of nature

---

[1] The name for the country houses which surround this town.

outside, and her furrowed brow already betrays all the agitation of her heart.

'This house seems a long way to me,' she said.

'I did point that out to you,' replied Madame de Moissac. 'I would not have returned a second time on foot either for love or money.'

After an hour, they arrive at last.

This *bastide*, utterly remote from the others, was surrounded by fig, orange, and lemon trees which hid it from view on all sides. The main entrance faced the countryside; the garden entrance led directly to the sea, whose shimmering surface had by now melted into blackness.

As soon as they alight, the coach speeds off; these ladies, alone with Valbelle, enter a low and dimly lit room. The cousin withdraws, and so Madame de Gange finds herself standing between the criminal and his crime.

'O Madame!' said Valbelle, throwing himself at the feet of the lady he both affronts and adores. 'Will you forgive the most violent love for the error into which I have led you? In this house, which belongs to me, you will find not Madame your mother but a man most ardently enamoured of your charms. This passion which burns for you justifies all these ruses; and whatever a lover does, he is only ever guilty of love.'

'What can you expect of me, Monsieur?' said Euphrasie, with as much boldness as pride. 'You know the matrimonial bonds that tie me, and you must respect them. In light of these, any hope on your part is a crime, and not to be entertained.'

'O Madame, is there any reasoning with great passions? Do not dream of destroying the one that burns in me for you, and do not remind me of those obligations driven from my mind by your eyes: consider that we are alone here, that the woman with us is under my command and no relation of mine, and that she will use force if I command it. The remoteness of this house, the darkness concealing the ways out—everything, as you can see, Madame, everything serves my desires here, and you are lost if I allow your charms to overwhelm me: do not attempt to withhold their possession from love, abetted by force. If you resist, I shall surrender you to the waves you can hear roaring close by; a small barque will carry you to the shores of Africa, where your savage virtue will be treated with no great respect.'

'O Monsieur,' Euphrasie exclaimed, 'you dare call this barbarous feeling love, when it blinds you to the point where you will only grant my life at the price of my dishonour! So be it! I shall not hesitate: these ferocious men to whom you wish to abandon me will be less cruel than you—I choose this second course, so let us waste no more time. But no! I see you are reverting to gentler sentiments. Listen to them, Monsieur, do not spurn them. Oh, how sullied the two of us would be by the infernal scheme you have the temerity to propose. And if I were to give myself to you—what would remain after the sacrifice of your victim? Could you still adore the wretch whose throat you will have cut? And, as for me, could I have any feeling other than hatred for the man who will have served as my executioner? Let us treat each other with more respect, more decency than that, Monsieur. Let us be worthy of the regard in which we hold ourselves: we can do so through sentiments contrary to those you wish to indulge; we would only end up hating each other, despising each other, if we were to act on those you have dared to conceive. You love me, you say: prove it by taking me to my mother, or to the governor of this town—on this condition, I shall forgive you; on this one alone, and thus by deserving my gratitude, you may perhaps inspire a gentler sentiment from me one day . . . But let me be free, let these doors open, and let me leave a house where the Marquise de Gange, insulted by Valbelle, could only view him as the most contemptible of men.'

These words, uttered with the greatest spirit, made such an impression on the Comte's soul that he took the weeping Marquise in his arms, sat her down, and begged her to be calm.

'At this moment, Madame,' he told her, 'the extraordinary power of your sublime virtues prevails over that of your charms. The light shining in your eyes strikes me down—you have stolen it from the heavens, and a feeble creature like me cannot but be cowed by it. Nonetheless, Madame, it is absolutely impossible for me to renounce the feelings that consume my soul; as much as I respect you, I cannot stop myself from worshipping you, and so I am granting only half your demands. I am going, Madame—I am leaving you alone. Come down, Julie, come down. Take the greatest care of Madame, prove to her she is alone in this house with you, and let her own eyes persuade her that I am returning home this instant. But see this as a truce, and one I shall break in two days. I shall return the day after tomorrow, at the same time, and hope to find you more favourably disposed towards me. If I am mistaken, then nothing will weaken my resolve, and I shall obtain through violence what love will have denied me. Until then,

Julie, I forbid you to allow Madame to go outside. Be in no doubt that you will answer for her with your life.'

And so, without another word, Valbelle sets off in his coach, which was waiting for him twenty yards away, and returns in haste to Marseille, leaving the Marquise in the most violent turmoil.

'Madame,' said Julie, as soon as she was alone with her. 'For my part I owe you a great many apologies for the harm I caused you by pretending to be someone else. I was never Madame de Moissac, nor Monsieur de Valbelle's cousin; my name is Julie Dufrène, and I own furnished lodgings in Marseille, where I can take you if you wish to escape the dangers that threaten you here. I know I shall attract all of Monsieur le Comte's wrath, but I shall have righted the wrongs I have done you, and that is enough for me.'

'What's this, Madame? Despite the strict orders of the man seeking my downfall, despite the risks you run, you really want to offer me refuge?'

'Absolutely, Madame, I must—and I do it without a qualm.'

'But in that case, why not take me to my mother?'

'I was never ordered to find her, Madame; but once I manage to get you safely back to my house, we shall be at greater liberty to devote ourselves to that.'

'And why would you think Valbelle will leave me in peace at your house?'

'But you will be there only for the time it takes to find Madame de Châteaublanc's address: by the time he reaches it you will be gone.'

'In that case, why sleep here? We should leave right now.'

'That would be impossible tonight: I live at the other end of the town, almost two leagues from here, and we will not find a coach at this hour to take us home. In any case, you can rest assured: we are alone; I hold all the keys; we shall leave at dawn.'

Madame de Gange accepted this delay with some difficulty but there was no choice. Julie prepared supper for her, settled her in a very pretty bedroom, then lay down on a trestle bed by the alcove where the woman she had been entrusted to guard was resting.

At this point it is worth noting that the scheming Julie, very generously paid by Valbelle and the Chevalier, was at the beck and call of them both; and the latter gentleman, an equal partner with his friend in every regard, was in no way straying from his plan to possess the Marquise himself, and to play his part in shaming her afterwards too.

Madame de Gange was far too agitated to fall asleep that night; the darkest thoughts afflicted her. Wandering over the thorns that life had strewn in her path, she chose to lose her way amongst them rather than avoid or escape them. It was as if she were leaving her existence in the hands of the furies, and that the thread of this unhappy life was being spun by the daughters of Erebus from Megaera's serpents.* It was to suffer that she was breathing now, without resisting or fearing it; indeed, she was savouring it . . . an agonizing state of the soul, fortunately unbeknownst to fools, which misfortune transforms into pleasure.

All of a sudden, she hears the sound of oars cleaving the waves; cries of terror coming from the shore . . . a boat making land. Euphrasie barely has time to throw on her clothes and wake Julie.

'We must run, we must run,' she screams at her. 'What? Can you not hear that dreadful noise? They are storming the doors.'

Julie, who had been given no warning of this, rises quaking, and while she is fleeing as fast as she can:

'Do not worry, Madame,' she tells the Marquise. 'It is not us they are after. I think it must be pirates from Algiers who often ravage these shores. We shall be long gone by the time they break in.'

But they have barely made it through the gates when they hear their pursuers violently forcing their way into the house. Fortunately, the men do not find who they were looking for, and the two women soon reach the town.

The supposed pirate was none other than the Chevalier de Gange. There is no need to repeat the reasons that had brought him there—they are all too obvious. By neglecting to warn Julie, he had recklessly precipitated an escape he had not in the least anticipated. Finding no one, he returned that same night to Marseille, where we shall soon see him reappear to execute the other part of his plan, which he imagined Julie must be working towards as she was no longer at the house.

As for our two women, they were making all possible haste to Julie's house, where they arrived at five o'clock in the morning.

Euphrasie is offered a room, and as she sees several women already up and about in the house, she ends her night feeling a little calmer. However, she is woken up early when she hears men's voices and some very peculiar noises; there was even someone trying to get into her room, but she had taken the precaution of locking it before going to sleep. She rises, calls Julie . . . but imagine her surprise when she sees, in the light that enters when she opens the door, a man rather the worse for wear, who then proceeds to climb into the bed she has just vacated . . . She tries to escape . . . Julie appears and stops her.

'What do you want, Madame?' Then, pointing out the man: 'Has Monsieur not behaved himself?'

'What are you saying? Who is this man? What is he doing here? . . . Ah, I see I am still in the hands of traitors.'

Then, furiously pushing Julie away:

'Let me leave, I say—you are all hell-bent on ruining me!'

'No, no, Madame,' her two brothers say as one as they barge in . . . 'Not on ruining you, but on wresting you from the infamy in which you endlessly mire yourself. Julie, have some of your companions come up here: it is only right that they should congratulate their new colleague.'

Five or six despicable creatures then entered in peals of laughter, convincing Euphrasie that misfortune, having pursued her remorselessly, has now led her to one of those houses of ill repute that political authorities tolerate only to avoid greater evils.

Meanwhile, by order of the two brothers, a commissioner is summoned. He states for the record: (i) That the house to which he has been called is a place of prostitution; (ii) That those ladies present all work in this vile place; (iii) That the lady before him is, according to the sworn testimony of her brothers-in-law, without question the Marquise de Gange; (iv) Finally that the man lying on the bed is, according to his own testimony, a sailor in the navy who most certainly spent the night with the Marquise. All these depositions are signed, the report is completed, and the Marquise, unable to withstand the horror of these abominable procedures, is thrown unconscious into a coach between two men she has never seen before, and who, without saying a word, return her to her mother's house in Avignon.

'Well then, my dear, sweet mother,' said this unfortunate woman tearfully as she threw herself into Madame de Châteaublanc's embrace. 'Well then! Here is your daughter once again in the depths of despair. Those barbarians! . . . They will only relent when they have seen me perish; they see me only as a victim whose blood they thirst to drink. The web they weave around me will be rent only by Death's trusty scythe!'

When Euphrasie is a little calmer, she tells her mother everything that befell her; she makes this respectable mother shudder when she reveals all the traps laid to ruin her.

'The Chevalier,' she said, 'this young man who was so charming, who I thought was my friend, was amongst my accusers; he has perhaps done me greater harm than the rest.'

It was then Madame de Châteaublanc's turn to reveal what she had been doing all this time:

'I was only in Marseille for eight days, my dear daughter; I had already left by the time you reached there. I had sent you, upon my arrival, the precise address of the house where I was staying on the Cours. It seems that the letter you received in place of mine was a counterfeit, since the directions were unclear and told you of an illness I never had. This forgery told you to come and find me, when I on the contrary wrote that I would join you. These abominations are unparalleled, my daughter, and they force us to take decisive and prompt action. Be in no doubt, it is the will which has made them desperate, and this love they feign, these traps they lay, have only one object: to give you the appearance of a woman incapable of receiving and managing an inheritance on behalf of her son. Let us thwart all these ruses, and ensure we are soon beyond their reach.'

These two women, as wise as they were prudent, were hatching their plans when something happened to render them all the more urgent.

CHAPTER XII

THE devout Marquise de Gange, for whom all religious duties had become genuine pleasures, was at the Saint-Agricole parish one day, fulfilling one of those sacred acts by which men and women, with the guidance of the clergy, see before their very eyes the divine mystery of the eternal alliance that, for man's salvation, the son of the Almighty himself willingly contracted with his Holy Father. An ineffable sacrifice no doubt, as that celestial Being condescends to appear before those he saved in a crude form which, far from diminishing the merit of such a solemn humiliation, renders it all the more noble and sublime for the pure soul who appreciates it.

Euphrasie was praying when a man in pauper's rags interrupted her and begged for alms . . . She raises her eyes and, for some reason which she herself cannot grasp, immediately lowers them again to her book.

'No, Madame, no,' says a man she in no way recognizes in a low voice. 'Oh, please no. Do not extinguish the pity I have just inspired in your charitable soul. Do not rely on my words, Madame—be so good as to see for yourself the pitiful hovel to which my poverty has reduced me.'

And this wretch's eyes were brimming with tears. Euphrasie sees them and says:

'Lead on, my friend, lead the way—my porters will follow you.'

The order is given: Euphrasie steps into her sedan chair; the beggar walks ahead, and she follows. Finally, he stops in a narrow, remote street where it is evident from the few decrepit buildings that only the most desperate penury has found fragile shelter here. The pauper stops at the humble entrance of one of these rickety homes, the porters open the coach door for their mistress, who had decided to leave her maidservants behind; she follows her guide, who heads down a long alley leading to a kind of cellar, where the beggar falls to his knees the moment his benefactress enters.

'O Madame la Marquise!' he says in a voice weakened by hunger. 'Will you not condemn for his folly the man who fell into poverty only to receive his deserved punishment by God's hand for the crime in which he sought to ensnare you? O Madame, when you recognize the despicable Deschamps, will you stoop to save him? It is not for myself that I beg, O my respectable lady! My infamy renders me too unworthy of your pity . . . No, it is not for me, Madame, but I dare implore you to extend that generous pity to the miserable creatures you see here, plunged with me into misfortune by the righteous anger of the heavens.'

The Marquise looked up and saw on some rotten floorboards an octogenarian gentleman twitching in the throes of starvation, whose breath, bereft of warmth, sought nonetheless to revive a sickly infant who could no longer suckle at the withered breast of the wretched mother stretched over the feet of the man who had brought her husband into the world.

'Here is my family,' Deschamps continued. 'Here are the creatures my crimes drive to the grave. It is on their behalf alone that I intercede: should the innocent bear the punishment of the guilty? Refuse me anything, as you must, Madame, but save the lives of these wretches whose hands already have the pallor of the grave, yet still have the strength to reach up to you. May their spirits not recoil in horror from the eternal darkness in which I bury them as well as myself. For three days not a single morsel of food has entered this shelter; I shall lose all that I hold dearest in the world and, left alone with their ashes, I shall behold nothing but my crime.'

At this point the infant's piercing cries were joined by the mother's piteous moans and the old man's parched groans.

The Marquise had been wronged, without question, and cruelly so by the man who dared to beg for her help now, but in a soul such as hers resentment vanishes when misfortune makes itself known.

'My friend,' she told Deschamps, 'you have caused me as much pain as you possibly could, but what you show me here causes me even more. You only attempted to inflict hardship upon me . . . Now I see it overwhelm you. I forgive you. I only have thirty *louis* in this purse . . . but here they are. Support your family, become upstanding once more—it is at the school of misfortune that man learns to do so. Seek only remorse in the time that remains before the grave, and you will be worthy of resting there when you have no more tears to shed over the life you have led.'

'O Madame!' said the man with a sublime rush of gratitude to his saviour, Euphrasie. 'Do not leave, I beg you, before I have named the instigators of my crime . . . What a source of illumination I can be for you . . .! In the name of God, please hear me out: it is the only way I can repay you for all your goodness towards me.'

'Silence, Deschamps, I order you . . . If it appeared that I had bought your confession, what merit would I have in your eyes? You did the bidding of wicked men. I do not need to know them: such a revelation would debase them in my heart—their crime has already brought them low enough. It would make me no happier, nor would it make you as happy as I would wish you to be. Each year on the same day you shall go to my notary to collect the same sum I have just given you. That sum shall no longer be paid should the names of those who corrupted you escape your lips.'

'O paragon of all virtues!' exclaimed Deschamps, dragging himself and his wife after Euphrasie, whose footsteps they drenched in their tears. 'The virtues you have shown us today are equal to those shown by our divine Saviour, who blessed his executioners on the cross.'

The Marquise leaves, and orders Deschamps to stay at home. No sooner is she at the door than the Abbé de Gange appears.

'Where did you come from, Madame?' he asks her insolently. 'Should a woman like you be seen in a quarter such as this?'

'I shall always take pride in being where I can bring succour to the poor.'

'You will not hoodwink us again, Madame,' Théodore replied sharply, 'and we know what brought you here. You were no doubt looking for, and finally found, that Deschamps—you have just left his home. I have followed your every step since you left the church, and it is now clear what led you to this den. You still fear this brigand, and have doubtless come to buy his silence, so I am all the more convinced of your misconduct with him. Deschamps is impoverished, that is true: his sins have plunged him into the penury in which you found him, but you should not have gone to see him, and by doing so all is revealed. Go home, Madame: the world and your family shall soon know you all too well. You will hear from me shortly.'

'I look forward to it, Monsieur,' said Euphrasie stepping into her chaise. 'Yes, I look forward to it with the tranquillity of innocence, while you announce it with the trepidation of crime.'

'You see, my loving and honourable mother,' said the Marquise when she arrived home and described all that had just passed, 'the traps are multiplying with every step I take: we must hurry, hurry on with our plans—we can delay no longer.'

Indeed, the next day, Madame de Gange sent for her notary. She made a will, in which she declared Madame de Châteaublanc her heir and placed her in charge of the estate of the young de Gange, then aged eight and the only child her husband had given her;* and although this will was made in secret, the next day Madame de Gange summoned members of the noblest families of Avignon and several magistrates, solemnly declaring before them that, were she ever to make a will other than the one she had dictated to her notary the previous evening, she formally disavowed any such subsequent will, and wished only the first to be executed.

This declaration, indisputable proof of Madame de Gange's sad forebodings, caused a great stir in Avignon and immediately changed the Gange brothers' plans. 'There is only one course of action left to us,' they said to each other, 'and that is to have this will, swiftly followed by this declaration, revoked; and it is only with the greatest delicacy that we shall succeed now. Let us put an end to all the slanders, and make up no more of them; let us bring the mother and daughter to Gange, and there we shall see what can be done.'

As a result of this new plan, the three brothers came to see the Marquise, and lavished on her what appeared to be the most heartfelt tokens of esteem and friendship.

'Let us forget all that has passed, my dear Euphrasie,' said Alphonse. 'We have been duped, as you have, by all those scoundrels who seem to have given the word to wreak your ruin. But the justice we do you is absolute, and believe me, O my dearest friend—you never lost either my heart or the sincere esteem of my brothers.'

The virtuous Madame de Gange, who for so long had not heard such flattering, such comforting words from the mouth of the man who was so dear to her, eagerly clutched at hope, which is always so enticing for an unfortunate soul. She tearfully threw her arms around her husband's neck.

'So did you really believe,' she asked, 'in the imaginary crimes of a wife who has never ceased to adore you? Oh, how exquisite is the justice you now do me! This is the first day of happiness I have seen dawn for a very long time. What would you have Euphrasie do in the world if you deprived her of the only thing that keeps her alive? Oh, yes! Yes, my dear Alphonse, swear that you will always love me, and that, together in the tomb you prepared for the two of us, we shall prolong the joy of our love even beyond this life.'

Madame de Châteaublanc, whose fears were now banished, whole-heartedly joined in this reconciliation, saying quietly to her daughter:

'Well then, my dear child—now you see the results of the steps we took.'

The whole family embraced, celebrated, and the next day a great banquet set the seal on this happy reconciliation.

That same day they discussed returning to Gange: Madame de Châteaublanc would be their first guest, and the day of departure was set for a week or so later. It was decided that the Marquis and his mother-in-law would travel to the castle ahead of Euphrasie and her brothers-in-law to prepare the most resplendent of welcomes for this dear wife.

When the Marquise arrived, all the young girls of Gange presented her with flowers. She walked beneath the bowers of the olive, lemon, and orange trees that lined her path. Oh, the poor wretch! She resembled those victims bedecked in finery only to be sacrificed.

All the Marquis's vassals had contributed to a magnificent feast which they laid out at the entrance to the estate, and at which they served their guests with distinction.

The sincerity and courtesy of this welcome dissipated all of Madame de Gange's fears, and two months passed in that sweet ecstasy of happiness to which misfortune always clings fervently when convinced its woes are at an end, like the sailor coming into harbour having been violently tossed about by stormy seas.

Madame de Gange was utterly duped by these false appearances: she believed in the perfect calm she so badly needed.

When Madame de Châteaublanc and the Marquis sensed that tranquillity had been perfectly restored, they returned to Avignon where they were both called on business. Euphrasie, left alone with Théodore and the Chevalier, discerned no alteration in the friendly dispositions of her brothers-in-law. They allowed themselves no reminders, no reproaches, not so much as a jibe; all was now sweetness and light. The Marquise, in seventh heaven, appeared to have been given a new lease of life: she seemed to everyone a thousand times more beautiful than she had been before. It is as if Nature redoubles her efforts within us when she is ready to summon us back to her breast, as if she wants, with her last gifts, to make us worthy of the Supreme Being to whom she will lead us by the hand.

One day, in the midst of this sweet serenity, the Chevalier ventured to talk to his sister about the will she had made in Avignon. He proposed that she revoke it, arguing that, as all her husband's esteem and tenderness had been restored to her, allowing the will to stand would lead others to suspect that she did not feel as he did, and such reticence would bring accusations of duplicity. The perfidious logic of this traitor managed to sway the Marquise, who no longer had her mother by her side, and, without revoking her formal declaration, she made a new will in her husband's favour.

Thereafter, the Chevalier could not have seemed happier, but this in itself is remarkably hard to understand—something which no account from the time can explain, and which proves that criminal conspiracies always lead to blind confusion: the Chevalier, who must certainly have been informed of the formal declaration made before all the persons of note in Avignon the day after the first will was signed, either decided it was unnecessary to raise this, or forgot about it, so that this last act signed in Gange by the Marquise was entirely null and void.

But let us not suspect Madame de Gange of any duplicity whatsoever in this matter: no such infamy could besmirch so pure a soul. This touching mother was under as much of a duty to her son as to her husband, if not a greater one. By doing what the Chevalier wished, Euphrasie ensured her own safety without running any risk to her son, as the Avignon declaration annulled any subsequent documents she might be made to sign. By not doing so, she would have been engulfed once more in all the woes from which she had only just been delivered. In light of all this, she felt quite entitled to buy a lasting peace at a price which cost her scruples nothing: all the fault in this episode lay with the Chevalier who forgot, and none with the wife who signed—one made a foolish mistake, the other simply took a precaution that was utterly essential to her peace of mind.

We owed this vindication to the most unfortunate, and at the same time, the most respectable woman imaginable; and as there is no evidence to support it, we are obliged to draw a realistic conclusion based on her heart and our own impartiality.

But the Abbé was not so easily fooled upon his return from a few days in the country.

'You are a dunce,' he told his brother. 'What we have in our hands is only good for the fire. Euphrasie has made a mockery of us: we need to ask her to retract the public declaration made in Avignon and to take violent action if she refuses, because if she reveals your proposal, and lays on the table the document that resulted from it, she will make us look like suborners.* She and her mother now hold terrible weapons against us. This resembles the last round of a card game when the players risk it all: one of the two will be left ruined. Euphrasie is doubly culpable here: extraordinarily so in the first instance for the declaration she made before all the nobility and the magistrates of Avignon, in whose eyes these proceedings clearly make us look like spendthrifts, slanderers, and rogues . . . and secondly for the way she carried on with you yesterday, which is nothing less than an abominable confidence trick, and one that proves the utter duplicity in the soul of this treacherous woman. So, no middle ground: she must either retract her public declaration in Avignon, or she must perish, if we wish to have any peace for the rest of our days. Moreover, all is lost for them the moment her eyes close: whatever measures she has taken, the will in favour of Madame de Châteaublanc will no longer be allowed to stand as it will be to the detriment of the Marquis for no good reason. He must be named his son's guardian: as long as that is the case, no other judgement could possibly be pronounced . . . Will they try to mount a challenge? When we put an end to this woman's days we shall say she killed herself; this will prove she was mad and consequently incapable of making a will. We shall reveal her conduct, show Villefranche's letter, the words she wrote in Deschamps's cave, the visit she recently paid the same man, the report by the commissioner from Marseille. This, I believe, should be more than enough evidence to prove the complete loss of her wits. It is perfectly clear that a legal act cannot be allowed to stand when it is signed by a woman who frequents the lowest dives in the provinces, who allows herself to be abducted at a ball, who arranges secret meetings in the grounds with her lover having traipsed around all of Languedoc with him— a lover who, to top it all, happens to get himself killed a little while later in her castle. Oh, no! No, no more niceties now, my friend; let us show her the wording of the act that is to annul the public declaration in Avignon. If she signs it, all well and good; but if she refuses . . . no mercy.'

The next day the new act is presented to the Marquise; she refuses to sign it, but with all the meekness imaginable, saying that she had acquiesced to all the Chevalier had asked of her, but that her sense of duty, her sense of honour, prevented her from doing more.

The two brothers withdrew without another word. This silence worried the Marquise: she became distracted, and melancholic.

These monsters did not act for a week; behaving towards her with the greatest delicacy and cunning, they tried at the end of that interval to ensnare her once again . . . It was to no avail.

Madame de Gange had shown throughout her life that she was a good wife; now she had to demonstrate that she was a good mother, and this she did.

O hell's furies! Lend me your torches! They alone can shine a light on the horrifying scenes we have yet to paint. Let our readers be assured at least that as far as the facts are concerned we are simply transcribing word for word the court documents; that it would be impossible to add to the abominations they contain, and that they come at a greater cost to the man of honour who describes them than to the scoundrel who perpetrates them.

On 7th May 1667, the Marquise de Gange, feeling unwell, felt the need for some medicine. A pharmacist from the town of Gange prepared the tonic himself and left it in the castle kitchens. It is not known whose hands it fell into thereafter, but when the Marquise said she wished to take it she was told it had not yet been delivered. It arrives at last. It is given to the Marquise, who is told that, because of the inordinate amount of time the tonic had taken to prepare, someone had been sent to fetch another from the town. The Marquise picks it up, and raises it to her mouth, but the medicine looks so black and so turbid that she does not wish to take it. Perret volunteers to return to the pharmacist to have another tonic made up . . .

'No, no,' says the Marquise. 'I have pills which have the same purgative effect—I will take some of those.'

She finds these in a small coffer to which she alone has the key, and swallows them. The brothers are immediately informed of this circumstance but say nothing.

That evening, the Marquise invited several ladies to come and have tea at the castle. She did the honours with all the grace and insouciance one could imagine; she ate well, and seemed perfectly cheerful throughout. Her two brothers-in-law were at the meal, but others observed they were very distracted and preoccupied; the Marquise cajoled them for it, but to no effect.

After tea, the Abbé showed the ladies out. The Chevalier meanwhile stayed by his sister's side, and the Marquise shared some very charming thoughts with her brother about the restored calm she was now enjoying, which she said she could attribute only to him. To all this, de Gange, still thoughtful, said not a word. The Marquise took his hand.

'What's this, Chevalier?' she asks him. 'You no longer love me? So your coldness would have me fear, or is it that you wish me to understand that my misfortunes are not yet at an end . . .?'

'No, indeed they are not,' says the Abbé, storming in like a man possessed, a pistol in one hand, and in the other the tonic Euphrasie had refused that morning. 'It is time to die, Madame: there shall be no mercy for you . . .!'

At that same moment, the Chevalier draws his sword . . . The Marquise thinks it is to defend her . . .

'O my dear Chevalier,' she exclaims in the most touching and poignant way. 'Protect me from this evil man's fury . . .'

But from his reaction, and his wild eyes, she sees only too clearly that he is a second executioner, and that she will be the victim of them both. This dreadful certainty gives her the strength to throw herself at the foot of her bed . . . In tears, she falls at the feet of those barbarians: those hands clasped and outstretched towards them; that bosom of alabaster, covered only with her beautiful, dishevelled locks; those terrified, pitiful screams cut short by despairing sobs; those tears bathing the weapons already aimed at her breast . . . O heaven almighty! Who could fail to be disarmed by this heartrending spectacle?

These monsters were not.

'It is time to die, Madame,' Théodore told her for the second time . . . 'Rather than trying to move us, thank us instead for allowing you to choose the manner of death that shall put an end to a creature as guilty . . . as duplicitous as yourself. Choose then, I repeat, either fire, steel, or poison, and give thanks to the heavens for granting you this favour.'

'What? So it is you? It is you, my brothers, who want me dead?' said this poor woman, still at their feet. 'And what have I done to deserve this death, and to suffer it at your hands? O Chevalier! Let me plead for my life. Do not go through with this barbarity—let me die when I am ready for the grave . . .'

'Hurry, Madame,' this brutal man replied. 'It is time: nothing about you moves us any more, you have gone too far . . . Quickly, choose your death, or we shall combine all three to put an end to you.'

'O heavens! Is there nothing other than my blood that can satisfy your vengeance? And must it be you who spills it . . .?'

But this wretched woman, seeing that the depths of her despair are only redoubling her murderers' rage, gathers all her strength, takes the glass, and swallows the fatal draught . . . The Chevalier, noticing the dregs still at the bottom and thus diminishing the strength of the poison, grabs the vessel, shakes it, and stirs the sludge with the point of the sword he still has in his hand.

'Go on, drink,' he tells his sister. 'Drink from the poisoned chalice.' Euphrasie, trembling, takes it again . . .

'Give it here, give it here,' she says. 'I shall obey you . . . it forces me to hasten the end of my torments; by swallowing the death in this vessel, I shall see my torturers no more . . .'

So she says: but her strength fails her. She brings the draught to her lips, but a cry of repulsion makes her disgorge it despite herself. It spills onto her breast, which is immediately tainted, like her lips, a green tinged with black . . .

O Nature! So in this moment you let this heavenly woman's most alluring features be pitilessly tarnished by crime?

'As your vengeance has been satisfied,' said the Marquise, in the most affecting tones, 'as death is already flowing through my veins, do not refuse me the consolation of a spiritual guide, so I can offer God the soul I received from him. You kill me as criminals, but I, I wish to die as a Christian: I want you to go to heaven, so you can beg forgiveness for your fury . . . the fury you wield to slay your victim.'

At these words, the two scoundrels withdraw, and their cruelty extends beyond the grave: as if they wish to rob their sister of the last solace she implores, it is the Abbé Perret, that savage beast . . . whom they summon to fulfil this sacred office.

As they leave, the two brothers close the doors behind them and allow a little time to pass between their departure and Perret's arrival. The Marquise hurries to make the most of it. She hastily slips into a *white taffeta* petticoat[1] and rushes over to a window which is only twenty-two feet above the stable-yard. At that very moment Perret arrives. Seeing her leap forwards, he pulls her back by the strings of the underskirt she had just thrown on, and as this rights her fall, she lands on her feet instead of her head. Perret, without shame, and desperate at the sight of his prey escaping, grabs the large flowerpots lining the window and hurls them at Euphrasie, who receives only

[1] See the text of the *Causes célèbres*.

glancing blows from them. She picks herself up, calls for help—but who? . . . who is coming to her aid? . . . Alas! It is that poor Rose, now wife to the castle coachman. She rushes over to her wretched mistress.

'O Madame!' she says in tears. 'What have those monsters done to you? Oh, if only I could have visited you . . .! I always feared they would be the end of you . . . My dear lady, my poor mistress . . .!'

And Rose drags her to one of the nearest houses in the town, the home of someone named Desprad, whose daughters were alone there at the time.

When she arrived there, the Marquise forced a lock of hair into her mouth, and this brought up a good deal of the poison she had swallowed. But the young Desprad ladies, whose candour, kindness, and virtue had always typified the decent and honourable citizens of Gange, lavished further succour on the wretched Marquise. One of them remembers some antidote kept in a case, has Euphrasie swallow a little, and this brings up the rest of the foul contents of her stomach.

The Chevalier and his brother arrive shortly after, having heard their sister is at Desprad's house. With blasphemy on their lips, and weapons in their hands, they hurl insults at anyone offering their sister assistance, threatening to kill on the spot anyone who does not share in their fury. The Chevalier takes charge inside the house; the Abbé takes guard outside.

'What is this?' they exclaim. 'You come to the aid of a creature lost to debauchery, whose hysterical ailments so consume her that she leaps through windows to chase after men? It's iron bars that this adulteress needs, not help.'

Then, addressing the young Desprad ladies:

'Only those who resemble her could possibly take an interest in her.'

Meanwhile, the Marquise, parched with thirst, asks for a glass of water. The barbarous de Gange brings it to her, and smashes it against her face.[1]

The Desprad ladies call for a surgeon. Théodore promises to go and fetch him, but this is only to delay the arrival of any such physician, and to give the poison plenty of time to act in the meantime.

The Chevalier, now alone, wants the ladies of the house to leave; they refuse at first, and only agree in the end at the insistence of the Marquise, who is afraid they will fall prey to his rage.

---

[1] We would not have dared include this horror were it not to be found word for word in the *Causes célèbres*.

As soon as she is alone with him, she tries to mollify him once more.

'O my brother!' she tells him, throwing herself at his feet. 'What have I done for you to treat me with such savagery? You, who always seemed so gentle to me . . . you, who I always favoured with such candour and sincerity? The veil of death is already stretching over my weakened eyes, let it envelop me without another hand being laid on me—it shall be the matter of a few days at most. If you are afraid I shall spend my few remaining moments making this bloody scene public, I swear to you I shall never say a word about it. Why would I at this dreadful hour wish to besmirch myself with a lie? Save me, save me . . . I ask you in the name of all that you hold dearest in the world.'

'No, you shall die—I told you, the die is cast. Your death is necessary to the whole family . . .' But the Marquise, outraged, rushes impetuously towards the door in an attempt to escape into the street . . . The brute beats her to it, and pierces her breast with two blows from his sword.[1] She staggers, she cries for help, the madman persists, inflicting five more blows, the last of which, thrust into her shoulder, breaks the blade, which is left jutting from the wound.

At the sound of these screams, the Desprad ladies rush back with the surgeon's wife, there in place of her husband, who could not be found. The Abbé, not far behind, steers her away, and looks to dispatch his sister with the pistol he still holds in his hand but is thwarted; as he sees more joining the crowd, he makes his escape, dragging his brother with him, and the two of them disappear, pursued by the serpents of crime and the agonies of remorse.

More help then arrives: the Marquise's blood is staunched, her wounds bandaged; it proves difficult to remove the blade still stuck in her shoulder.

'Pull, pull, and brace yourself against me with your knees,' says the brave Marquise. 'You must pull the blade out and hide it—otherwise it will betray de Gange: I forbid you to name him . . .'

And this was the heavenly creature these scoundrels were destroying! The blade comes out at last; it is buried, and the Marquise is taken back to her quarters.

This fateful day soon caused a great outcry. Madame de Gange, loved by all, received visitors from more than ten leagues around.

---

[1] See the Trial.

Alphonse is informed; he remains calm; for two days he does not stir
from Avignon, and continues to go about his usual business and
pleasures. This bizarre conduct arouses suspicion, as one would
expect. At long last, he arrives; Madame de Châteaublanc and her
grandson have made it there before him.

'*O my dear Alphonse*,' said Euphrasie, seeing her husband enter her
bedroom. '*Look what those barbarians have done to me: why did you
leave me in their hands . . .?*' Dreadful memories suddenly made the
Marquis shudder . . .[1] 'Alas! These reproaches wound you, Monsieur,
but my condition prevents me from casting a veil over an atrocity that
is already too well known. I would have liked to die, and your brothers
to have fled, before the scandal broke . . . That is now impossible, and
to be obliged to accuse guilty parties who must be dear to you is more
distressing to me than death itself.'

Everyone was crying, except the Marquis. Euphrasie, in unimaginable pain, asked them all to leave.

The next day, before anyone else had entered his wife's bedroom,
Alphonse came to her.

'Madame,' he said, 'I fear you have brought all this on yourself.
There is still time: you refused the proposals that were made to you;
do not take this crime of stubbornness with you to the grave. I shall
send for the notary—retract your Avignon declaration.'

'No, Monsieur, I cannot,' said the Marquise firmly. 'Things will
stay as they are; I shall not change a thing.'

The fear of arousing suspicion prevented the Marquis from
renewing his demands and, worried lest others might read in his
soul the secret he needed so desperately to hide, he left, maintaining
that his wife was not as ill as had been thought and that he would
return soon; but he was not seen again, and his brothers were
already far away.

Madame de Gange, sensing her last moments approaching, asked
once again for the succour of religion . . . But imagine her surprise to
see this being offered by the Abbé Perret! He brings her the solace of
the holy table.* The Marquise, frightened, does not want to consume
the host unless the curate takes half himself: he agrees, and Madame

---

[1] It is important to remember here the words she spoke in the dream she had on her
first night in Gange, after hurting the same shoulder now pierced by the sword.

de Gange thus satisfies all the requirements of this Holy Sacrament, as distraught as she is to have it administered by such a man.[1]

Five days after the event, the magistrates from Toulouse arrived to investigate the case. To allow the guilty brothers time to escape, Madame de Gange, with an overabundance of discretion truly befitting her soul, asked the judges to be so good as to wait until she was at her mother's home in Avignon before attending to such a serious matter—something she could not undertake with any peace of mind in a house that so terrified her. Her request was granted.

Sensing the next day that her weak state might not allow her to withstand the journey, she wanted to surround herself in her last moments with all that was most dear to her: she was helped into fresh attire as she lay in her bed, which was decorated all around with flowers; then, once she had her mother, her son, the Desprad ladies, two or three cherished friends from the town, and her most loyal servants (among whom Rose was not forgotten) all seated around her, she spoke in the following terms with all the assurance, all the strength that, much to crime's despair, virtue always retains:

'O my dear mother,' she said solemnly. 'Here I am arrived so young at that formidable moment when the soul, separated from the body, flies back to its God and leaves behind its mortal remains. I thought this moment would be more frightening than it is: I like to believe that it only seems tranquil to those who have not squandered this life, and who, seeing it merely as a testing path that the hand of God obliges us to follow, have with high hopes avoided the pitfalls along the way. In our last moments we feel the urge to cast a swift glance back, from the day of our birth to the day of our death; and one may count oneself fortunate, it seems to me, if one sees over this long span only rare joys and frequent sorrows. After such a severe trial, it is truly consoling to believe one has at least some additional rights to the benevolence of that just God who waits for us only to console us; one would be sorry, I think, to have lived a happier life. Alas! If I see, in this stern examination of my life, that I have not done all the good I would have liked to do, I have at least not done the evil of which my tyrants accused me. I owe these confessions to those who are listening here. It is not pride

---

[1] The incomplete accounts of the time do not tell us why Madame de Châteaublanc, who was at the castle by this time, did not demand a different priest to administer the Sacrament for her daughter. We can only attribute this to the shortage of priests in a small town like Gange, where almost everyone was Protestant.

that speaks them, it is truth that dictates them: it is a pleasure to show innocence where the wicked supposed there was guilt. O my mother, who would have thought you would raise your dear Euphrasie for such misery! Who would have told you that all the care you lavished on her would soon become an inducement to crime. May the dear child I leave you (she kissed him as she said these words) . . . may he one day console you for your daughter's woes! And you, my son, don't let these frightening scenes change in any way the love and respect you owe your father: he will need consolation one day, not reproaches. He was not culpable for my death; he was not among my executioners; his hands are innocent, they did not cut the thread of my days . . . Oh! Should I complain if it is broken? Woven by misfortune, it would have endured only to submit me to even greater trials. Why does the dying man weep over the end of his existence? He is wrong to do so: had he journeyed further in life he would have encountered only more tribulations; he should thank heaven for ending them. Oh! Does the God who created us not know when to destroy us? Given that all he does is just, why complain of his decrees? Let us adore him and not cry. O Lord! You know I have always placed my trust in you; at every moment your hand was there to wipe away my tears. It cannot be to shed still more that you dry up the source of those I wept when offering you my earthly woes. It is with this sweet trust that I fly back into your embrace; deign receive me, and place me one day between this tender mother and this innocent son I leave behind, not without concern, to journey at such a tender age down life's thorny path. Protect him, O Lord, from the misfortunes that assailed me; preserve him from deserving them one day; allow me to believe, O Lord, that all those you had destined for my family have been exhausted through me. O you who attend to me now, pray for unhappy Euphrasie; let the pure and innocent hands of this sweet child be raised along with your own to the heavenly vault to plead that the friend you are hearing for the last time shall find there some consolation at last for her woes.' She then seized the crucifix with the most poignant ardour.

'Alas!' she continued as she pressed it to her heart. 'Did he not suffer more than I, this God who sacrificed himself for us? Misfortune entitles one to his kindness. It was through misfortune that he became worthy of his glorious father: it will be through misfortune that I shall become worthy of his ineffable goodness. Oh, what serenity does blessed religion bring the soul of a devout Christian! It is in these last moments that all its sweetness is felt: it is as if its torch offers to those who revere it the joyous harbour where its founder, Holy God, awaits. Almighty God, may those gathered around me enjoy an equal share of your good graces! I have received the most touching and devoted care from them: if they were the instruments of your kindness when they came to my aid, you owe them some protection. Come closer to me, mother: I want my days to end in the arms of the woman who gave them to me; I want you to deliver me again, into this second life I shall spend by my God's side. And you, my son, receive the last goodbyes of a mother deprived of the sweet responsibility of an education that I would have guided only for you to avoid the wickedness that has killed me. Never dream of avenging me . . . Oh, what reason could I have to complain, as I am being plucked from this life only to begin a better one? Take my portrait from this castle, and when you look upon it . . . you, my mother, remember a daughter who dies treasuring you, and you, my son, remember the mother who gave you life and loses her own adoring you still.'

Everyone dissolved in tears; all one could hear were sobs of grief and cries of despair. It was as if this angel, flying up to the heavens, was taking with her all the splendour, all the wealth of the world, and as if this world, stripped of its crowning glory, would crumble without the lustre from the radiant star which had made it so beautiful.

This celestial woman, above all praise, so worthy of gracing another world, left the one into which she was born thirty-one years after arriving there, and almost two hours after the last words we have just heard her pronounce.

Her body was opened up: the blows from the sword had not been fatal; it was the violence of the poison alone that led her to the grave. It had left her intestines burnt and her brain blackened. She was embalmed and laid in the chapel for two days for the public to pay their respects . . . in that same chapel where the Marquis had one day seen tears fall from her portrait.

They came from all around to shed their tears over the lady whose hands had wiped away so many. The third day she was taken back to Avignon and placed in the tomb of her forefathers . . . She breathes there still: virtue never dies.

Madame de Châteaublanc concerned herself solely with ensuring the inheritance of her grandson and the pursuit of her daughter's assassins. The Marquis de Gange was put in prison and conducted his own defence. As there were only suspicions and few clues, the court went no further than to strip him of his nobility, ban him in perpetuity, and confiscate all his assets. But these suspicions, and these clues, almost became convictions when it transpired that he had reunited with the Chevalier.

As for the Chevalier and the Abbé de Gange . . . close enough to the coast to find a skiff, they had set sail and made their escape. The court in Toulouse condemned them both to be broken alive on the wheel[1] and sentenced the Abbé Perret to the galleys in perpetuity.[2]

The Chevalier was at the siege of Candia;* the Marquis did not take long to join him, and it was at that famous siege that the two of them, serving the Republic of Venice, finally met a just, if too glorious, punishment for the dreadful crime with which they had sullied themselves. Alphonse was killed in the blast of a bomb and the Chevalier perished in a mine explosion.

Heavenly vengeance was for a moment suspended over the Abbé. He went to Holland where a young Frenchman in Utrecht introduced him to the Comte de la Lippe,[3] whose confidence he gained so completely that this gullible man, who did nothing without consulting him, entrusted him with his son's education.

Gifted with all the talents that Nature should only accord those who will not misuse them, Théodore raised this child very well. There was in this household a very pretty young woman whom this monster had the audacity to seduce, in contempt of all he owed his benefactor; he even dared ask her hand in marriage, but the Dutchman refused because of the assumed disparity in birth.

'Who are you?' Monsieur de la Lippe asks him one day. 'I shall decide accordingly.'

The imprudent Abbé, thinking he would inspire pity rather than revulsion, names himself . . . he admits he is the wretched Abbé de Gange . . . The all too recent crime so horrified Monsieur de la Lippe that he wished to have him arrested: and would have done so had his wife not prevented him.

---

[1] The judgement of the Toulouse court was delivered on 21st August 1667.
[2] He died before reaching the galleys.
[3] This House possessed a sovereignty in Germany.

'Then leave my home this instant, at least,' said Monsieur de la Lippe to the scoundrel, 'and leave me alone to fret over the principles with which you may have poisoned my son's heart.'

The Abbé thought he could conceal himself in Amsterdam; the young lady he had seduced joined him there; he married her.

But his crime had not been punished and it had to be: it is at the very moment the criminal believes he has escaped heavenly vengeance that it pursues him and strikes.

After six months of marriage, Théodore is approached by a stranger at ten o'clock in the evening on the quiet street where he lives.

'You are the Abbé de Gange,' says this mysterious person, 'I have been following you for a long time. *Perish, monstrous scoundrel: I avenge your victim . . .*' And he blows his brains out as he utters these words.

The stranger disappeared without anyone discovering who he might have been. But, whoever he was, he was armed by the hand of God.

Oh, if there is one thing that consoles the unfortunate, it is the certainty that the hand that crushes them will soon suffer the same fate!

APPENDIX

THE HISTORY OF THE MARCHIONESS DE GANGE, WHO WAS BARBAROUSLY ASSASSINATED BY HER HUSBAND'S BROTHERS (1744)*

IT has been observed that there never was a man who had not in his heart the seeds of every vice; that is to say, be a soul born with never so good dispositions, and have all the advantages of education, yet upon certain emergencies, where the passions happen to tyrannize, he is capable of perpetrating the most horrid crimes, even those which are shocking to human nature.

'Tis thus we may account for the extreme barbarity of the Abbé and Chevalier de Gange, in assassinating the innocent Marchioness de Gange through the instigation of violent passions, even contrary, as it would seem, to the bent of a good natural disposition. Such horror I feel in attempting to relate this tragic story, that I fear lest the pen should drop from my trembling hand, or that I shall be at a loss for words strong enough to express the ideas of my mind. A poet would say the sun, who beheld such enormous crimes, shrunk back from the frightful spectacle. But as there is no serpent so odious, nor monster so hideous, but an artful imitation may render agreeable to the sight; and objects which are too terrible to be calmly looked upon in the original, may please in a picture or description: so notwithstanding the horror of the following story, I flatter myself to be able, by delineating it naturally, though not with the most delicate pencil, to present an image which will equally please and affect the mind.

The Marchioness de Gange was an accomplished beauty; and though of no distinguished birth, yet as the fortune of her grandfather by the mother, which she was to inherit, amounted to upwards of 20,000*l.** she was thought a proper match for persons of the first quality. She was the only daughter of the Sieur de Rossan of Avignon: her mother's grandfather was named Joanis Sieur de Nocheres. It seemed as if nature had designed that the lustre of her fortune should be eclipsed by that of her charms. In her youth she went by the name of Mademoiselle de Chateaublanc, which was the title of one of her grandfather's estates.

Upon the death of her father, she was put under the care of this grandfather. Love and avarice, the two reigning passions by which the world is governed, rendered her an object of desire to all the great matches in the province. The possession of an exquisite beauty, joined to a plentiful fortune, appears but too evidently the sovereign good to which the hearts of the generality aspire. Besides these external and so highly valued endowments, a remarkable sweetness of temper, a peaceful calmness and serenity of mind, animated her charms.

At the age of thirteen years she married the Marquis de Castellane, grandson to the Duke of Villars. He was descended from an illustrious family, a comely personage, and of a happy natural disposition. He had been educated at court under his mother the Marchioness d'Ampus, and distinguished himself in all the manly exercises. Their marriage was solemnized in the year 1649. He brought her to court, where she made a shining figure on that great theatre, which seems purposely formed for such accomplished beauties, who may there receive the suffrages of the most refined and delicate tastes, and homage from those who are themselves the objects of homage to all the world besides.

Louis XIV, who was then in the prime of youth, appeared struck with her beauty, on which he could not forbear bestowing high encomiums. He would needs dance with her in one of those balls where gallantry and magnificence were united. She acquitted herself with so much grace, and appeared in a dress so well adapted to her beauty, that the whole court gave testimony in her favour: from that time she became better known by the name of the *Fair Provincial*, than of the Marchioness of Castellane.

The King did her the same honour a second time at another ball, where she still appeared with new graces; they sprung up under her steps, and accompanied her in all her motions; a phrase, which though not new, seemed calculated on purpose for her. The Queen of Sweden admired her beauty, and declared that in all the kingdoms she had surveyed, she had seen nothing equal to her; and that if she had been of the other sex, her heart and affections had been at her devotion.

In the midst of all these applauses, which were bestowed upon her charms, none was more sensible than she, of the emptiness of this her so much envied felicity: she told a lady, with whom she was intimate, she perceived it all to be but vanity; vanity of vanities. I know full well, that, notwithstanding this moralizing, she is recorded for adventures of gallantry in the archives of that time; but this I likewise know that the more judicious give no credit to those histories, especially as they never were made public.

As nothing is more worthy [of] admiration than the variety with which nature has distinguished the several beauties of the female world, curiosity will hardly be satisfied with being barely told in the history of a heroine, that she was handsome; nothing less will satisfy the imagination, than to know what was the form of those handsome features; because it is in the face where beauty particularly resides, the rest being but concomitants to this; it is here the character lies which distinguishes one fair from another; all the other beauties inherent in her person are considered as such, only because, as Monsieur Fontenelle* observes, they belong to a fine face.

To descend then to a particular detail of the Marchioness de Castellane's perfections; I shall begin with the beauties of her person. Maynard* has given an exact portraiture of this lady, which is reckoned a masterpiece of its kind. Her complexion, says he, was of a dazzling white, enlivened with the finest vermilion which the hand of nature ever drew: without being too glaring it was uniformly united, and softly blended itself with the ground of her complexion; her hair jet-black, and naturally formed in ringlets heightened its lustre to such a degree, that it was impossible to look upon her without admiring that curious mixture of light and shade. Her eyes, large and well opened, were of the colour of her hair, the soft and piercing beams with which they sparkled, was the principal reason that few or none could contemplate her with steadfast regard. A simple glance from her seemed to penetrate you with its light. The little size and turn of her mouth, the rosy tincture of her lips, the uniformity and beauteous whiteness of her teeth, raised in conjunction with her eyes that first impression, which seems to answer the idea we have, when we say beauty is the finest spectacle of nature. The regular disposition of her nose gave her an air of grandeur; the round turn of her visage, the sprightly bloom and vigour which health diffused over all her body, the air of her head, which resulted from all together, was so graceful, so charming, that it inspired even those who had no poetical imagination, to regard her as a goddess; or to speak in the Christian style, as a most lovely image of the Divinity.

Her make was correspondent to the beauty of her face: by her arms, her hands, and all of her that was presented to the eye, one could see that nature had designed her for a masterpiece of her productions.

Let not the reader imagine that this portraiture I draw is of my own invention. I have taken it from a sketch I found in a book that was printed at that time.[1]

Whence is it that such a beauty raises not our minds to the Creator? Why should so finished a piece of workmanship so entirely engross our senses, as not to leave the soul at liberty to ascend towards the divine Author? Great indeed must be the dependence which the soul has upon the body, since it suffers itself to be so easily captivated by corporeal objects. Instead of exhibiting a beauty to flatter and attract men's sensual regards, I would rather consider it as an argument to confound the atheist.

> Vous, à qui notre foi paraît une imposture,
> Qui doutez des secrets que son voile a couverts;
> Qui ne connaissez point de maître en l'univers,
> Et croyez qu'ici-bas tout roule à l'aventure:

[1] A faithful Narrative of the principal Circumstances relating to the deplorable Death of the Marchioness de Gange, at Rouen, 1666.

Pouvez-vous voir du ciel la brillante structure,
Le constant mouvement de tant d'astres divers,
Le retour des étés & celui des hivers
Sans convenir qu'un Dieu préside à la nature.

Que si pour vous tirer de votre aveuglement
Ces fortes vérités sont un faible argument,
Je veux bien vous guérir de votre erreur mortelle:
Incrédules esprits, accourez en ce lieu,
Quand vous verrez Philis si charmante & si belle,
Vous avouerez qu'elle est le chef d'œuvre d'un Dieu.*

[You, for whom our faith seems a deception,
Who doubts the mysteries its veil conceals;
Who sees no master in the universe,
And believes that down here all is just chance:

Can you see the heavens' dazzling design,
The constant movement of so many stars,
The return of summer, and of winter,
And not know a God rules over Nature.

And if, to rescue you from your blindness,
These firm truths are too weak an argument,
I can still cure you of your fatal error:
You unbelievers, fly here to this place,
When you see Philis, her charm and beauty,
You will admit she's the work of a God.]

The Marchioness de Castellane joined to the exquisite beauty of her person a singular goodness of disposition, a tenderness of heart and commiseration towards the infirmities of others; a mind easy, sociable, rather judicious than lively, more solid than showy. In a word, never was diamond set in a finer bezel, never did mind animate a finer body.

She was just arrived at that happy and flourishing state of life wherein her beauty in spite of herself procured her a kind of adoration from all who beheld her, when she received the melancholy news of the shipwreck of our galleys in the Sicilian sea, and that her husband the Marquis de Castellane was buried in the merciless waves.

The loss of so tender a relation, wounded her heart with anguish, more easy to be conceived than expressed. Yet she remained some time at court with her mother, where her grief served to give a new lustre to her beauty: and from thence she removed to Avignon, whither she was called by the urgency of her affairs.

As she had never been a mother, and was just in the bloom of her youth, she seemed by her widowhood to re-enter into her virgin-state; and her beauty being in its highest glory, she was in danger of being exposed to a crowd of suitors, who would have been soliciting her to marry, had she made her appearance in the world. To avoid their importunities, she chose to retire into a convent, where she made herself known only to her more intimate female friends, and to those with whom she had connections in business.

But, as she was not made for a solitary life, in that tribe of illustrious admirers, who longed to join their fortune to hers, she hearkened to a proposal of marriage made her by the Sieur de Lanide Marquis de Gange, a young man about the age of twenty, of a distinguished family, Baron of Languedoc, Governor of St. Andrew,* and sufficiently furnished with the gifts of fortune. He was for a man just such another as the Marchioness was for a woman, as to figure and gracefulness of person; to see them both, you would have said they were made for each other. Love, which united them from their first interview, inspired all the world with that opinion.

Their characters however were widely different, as far as pride is from gentleness, a haughty spirit subject to capricious irregularities, from a mind uniformly equal; humble modesty, from bold confidence, yet such a confidence as was accompanied with knowledge.

Dissembled tenderness, which cast a veil over the faults of the husband, sweetened the first days of their marriage. All the world applauded an union, which seemed so promising and happy. It was in 1658 their nuptials were celebrated; the Marchioness de Gange being then in her 22nd year. La Bruyère says, he remembers it was the wish of a certain company he was in, to be in the state of a fine woman from 18 to 22, and after that to return to manhood. And indeed from 22 we date the critical period of beauty; after that, its charms begin to lose their force; though in spite of these general remarks it must be owned, there are numbers of women, who preserve all the lustre of youth still many years after that era.

Of this number was the Marchioness de Gange. But, notwithstanding all her charms, which gave such high delight, the scene was quickly changed, and to this sunshine of life, wherein two yoke-fellows are sufficiently happy, while they are together, and can never have enough of each other's company, succeeded days, wherein a certain lassitude begins to be felt; which, if not timeously* prevented, soon brings on disgust. This is what determined the Marquis to cease from being so assiduous about his wife, and go more abroad in the world.

The Marchioness followed his example: but as she had a large fund of virtue, she aimed only at innocent recreation, without having any designs upon those of the other sex, with whom she conversed; and no sooner did she perceive them grow too officious, than she shunned their company for that of others, who saw her with more indifference. This conduct, however innocent, was misrepresented by the husband's friends, who took occasion from thence to inspire him with jealousy.

This passion seized his mind with all its direful effects, that is, with disquietudes, dark and lurking suspicions, perturbation of mind, and a thousand other painful feelings, that wring and tear the heart to pieces.

As jealousy is the common topic of ridicule, and no man would be ridiculous with his good will, the Marquis concealed his anguish, and suffered it to prey upon him in secret. Besides, the Marchioness giving no handle to just suspicion he even dared not to speak out his sentiments to the world. But his gloomy sorrows grew at length into an habitual ill humour, and he never presented himself to the Marchioness but under a sullen and discontented aspect. Thus all the pleasures of that lady were alloyed with bitterness. In this manner she passed away several years without enjoying one serene peaceful day. Such were the preludes to her disaster, when the Abbé and Chevalier, her husband's brothers, who were destined to be the artificers thereof, came to reside with the Marquis. As they act the barbarous part in this tragic history, it is proper to bring the reader acquainted with them. The Abbé had in him the spirit of a devil, that is, he was wicked and malignant in the superlative degree; he was debauched withal, libertine, impious, profligate, taking these epithets in their utmost extent. He had tied himself down to no religious order; having chosen that neutral state, as what favoured most his licentiousness. He was a man violent, imperious, headstrong in his passions, and would needs have all the world yield to him. It is needless to say he was capable of the greatest excesses, since of that the reader will be but too fully convinced in the sequel. To conclude, he hardly deserves the name of a man, but ought rather to be denominated a cunning artful demon, who could turn himself into every shape, to compass his diabolical ends, even into that of virtue itself, assuming the character of amiable generosity and benevolence, gentle, officious, complaisant, with a heart compounded of all vices.

The Chevalier was of a middling soul, formed for being governed; one of those low geniuses which tamely bow their necks under the yoke. Of him the Abbé disposed as he pleased, not so much as deigning to give him a reason for the laws which he imposed upon him; nay he sweetened the ascendant he had over him with so much art, as to govern him without letting him know he was governed.

'Tis indeed no great wonder that so weak a man suffered himself to be thus easily led, when we sometimes see great geniuses become mere tools to the crafty purposes of others; 'tis only laying hold of their blind side, and by using a little address you may lead them too at will. Of this the Marquis de Gange is a glaring instance: though he was a man of knowledge and discernment, the Abbé had him entirely under management, by making him believe he was devoted to his interest, and capable of supporting by his counsel the dignity and splendour of his House; giving him a high idea of his capacity for managing his fortune, and laying out his revenues to the best advantage: thus he left the Marquis the bare name of master of the family, and transferred all the authority to himself.

The Abbé no sooner saw the Marchioness than he felt the first impressions of love, giving himself up entirely to the influence of the soft enchantment, like a man who had no mind to combat his passions. He presumed that the authority of which he had possessed himself would lead him to his end, especially as he was officiously zealous to please the Marchioness, prepossessing her husband in her favour, representing her virtue to him in so advantageous a light, that he quite extinguished his jealousy, and gave his heart and soul a prevention* of esteem and tenderness towards her.

The Marchioness saw her situation quickly changed, and her first joyful days of marriage again arise. She received the advances of the Marquis with a heart cured of its coldness, which was about to degenerate into aversion; and they were for some time mutually happy.

The Abbé was not willing the Marchioness should be ignorant to whom she was indebted for this happy change of her condition. He communicated to her in confidence, that it was he who had turned the heart of the Marquis in her favour; and was at great pains to make her sensible that he had the absolute command of him, and was the source of the happiness she now enjoyed.

The Marchioness at first sight conceived an aversion to the Abbé. She was uneasy to think she should be under so great an obligation to a man who she dreaded might make a wrong use of it; however, she signified to him, that she was sensible of the pleasure he had done her, but in so cold a manner, that her air seemed to give her words the lie. He was mortified to find her heart so little touched with these impressions of gratitude, which he thought such a favour would have produced; but as he had a considerable share of vanity, he flattered himself to be able by assiduity to gain upon her affections in time. But, finding the Marchioness still carry towards him with indifference, and showing him only outside civilities, he resolved to open his mind to her more fully.

Having notice that she was gone to the country seat of a certain lady of her acquaintance, he set out after her. As he was a man of most agreeable conversation, the soul of every company where he came, he was at first well received by all; he shone in his usual way by the many resources he had from wit and genius.

In all the various subjects of conversation that were introduced, his passion prompted him to display all the talents he was master of, and make the most of them. The day after his arrival, there was proposed a hunting-match, and the ladies to be of the party; the Abbé offered to be the Marchioness's squire, hoping by that means to have an opportunity to disclose his mind to her freely, and without interruption. Accordingly when they were in the fields at a proper distance from the rest of the company, he began to open his mind to her, without that air of timidity which love usually begets; he made her a blunt declaration of his passion, representing himself in the warmest expressions, as the most amorous man alive. He was too much transported to leave room for the Marchioness to doubt his being in earnest. She presently changed colours, and appeared in the utmost degree of surprise; yet she thought it prudent to conceal her anger, and put on a cold forbidding air, as if she had not deemed him worthy her resentment.

'Master Abbé,' says she to him, 'you know how a woman, in my situation, ought to receive such a compliment; pray ask your own heart what answer I ought to make you, and save me that unnecessary trouble.' Though these words of themselves imply no great degree of contempt; yet the air which accompanied them breathed it in the strongest manner. They entered deep into the heart of the Abbé, and stung him to the quick; however, he soon recovered himself out of his confusion, and altering his tone of voice, thus replied with abundance of assurance: 'Do you know, Madam, that your happiness is in my hands, and that whenever I please I can make you the most wretched woman upon earth? It will be an easy matter for me to undo all that I have done; nor have I any apprehension that it is in your power to prevent me, because I am well assured that whatever you may say, whatever expedients you may use, you will not be believed. Therefore, Madam, for the sake of our mutual quiet, let us not take cross measures; do you fall in with my wishes, and you may expect to enjoy smiling and serene days.'

The Marchioness, without elevating her voice, rejoined with the same coldness as before, 'Sir, I would have you learn to esteem me, if you have learned to love me; and know, that the terror of enduring the most unhappy destiny in this world, shall never make me do anything in prejudice of my virtue.' To gratify her aversion, and punish the vanity of the Abbé, she added: 'Was I capable of such a weakness, you would be the last man for whom I would have the inclination.' The Abbé could not brook this language, he grew red with anger, and left the marchioness to rejoin the company. During the rest of that day he was in the worst humour imaginable, nor with all the art he was master of, was he able to disguise it. His pride thus baffled and confounded, represented him to himself as the lowest of all mortals. So little was he in his own eyes, that nothing was ever seen so humble. He returned abruptly in the evening to Avignon, and left all the world to conclude that he was under some violent discontent.

When he was alone he renewed his courage and hopes, still flattering himself to be able to vanquish the Marchioness's virtue. Thus not in the least disheartened, he continued to impress the Marquis with a high idea of his lady's honour, and fidelity, which he represented as equal to her beauty. The Marchioness by consequence remained happy, though without any abatement of her aversion to the man who was the author of it; still carefully shunning all opportunities of being with him in private. Meanwhile the Chevalier was no less sensible than the Abbé of the Marchioness's charms; far from having the same dislike to him as to the Abbé, she loved his company, and opened to him the secrets of her heart; not that she had any impression of criminal love for him, but she could not help being pleased with the sweetness of his manners, and the comparison she made between the two brothers rendered the Chevalier the more agreeable in her eyes.

All these civilities from a lady of so much merit and beauty, flushed him with hope. The Abbé soon found out the rival in the brother, and observing that while he was shunned, the Chevalier had free access to the Marchioness, took occasion from thence to conclude that he was the happy object of her affection. He resolved therefore to be a spy upon the two lovers; but after all the pains he was at, could perceive nothing to make him suspect the Marchioness's virtue.

This rivalship, however, nettled him extremely. He long deliberated with himself how he should behave, and at last determined on the following scheme. Being sensible it was in vain to try his power over the Chevalier, and that love was too stubborn to be managed by dint of authority; he talked to him in the following manner. 'I find we are both in love with the Marchioness; let us therefore behave in this affair like brothers: for my part I will by no means stand in the way of your happiness; if you can carry your point, good; if not, I expect you will quit the field, and leave me to try if I can be more successful; we understand one another too well to quarrel on her account.' This expedient he thought fit to take, only because having failed himself, he was willing to have the experiment made, whether the Marchioness was susceptible of any impression, or if her virtue was not quite impregnable. The Chevalier was touched with the Abbé's generosity, and declared that he was ready to make a sacrifice to him of his passion. 'No,' says the other, 'I shall be overjoyed to see you happy; being so far master of my inclinations, as to suffer nothing to come in competition with friendship.' Upon which they embraced each other.

The Chevalier thus disengaged from his rival brother, renewed his civilities to the Marchioness, who received them so long as she thought love had no share therein: but she no sooner perceived passion to be concerned, than she treated the Chevalier with the same indifference as she had done his brother. He never durst directly explain his sentiments to her, but contented himself by zeal and officious assiduity, to show her very glaring signs of love. She affected to take no notice of it; and after a very long course of obsequious attendance, he was no farther advanced than the first day. Not to leave him the smallest glimpse of hope, she even showed him signs of contempt, though in that she deviated from her known character; and as the Chevalier happened now and then to blunder in his expressions, she would take occasion to sneer at him, though she had no turn for raillery, and was more apt at other times to palliate such faults than censure or ridicule them.

The Chevalier despairing of success in his amour, resolved to conquer his passion, and spoke of it to the Abbé, who encouraged him in his resolution; from thence he was naturally led on to utter some sentiments of disgust against the Marchioness, and appeared disposed to rank himself among her enemies. The Abbé then re-entered the lists, and finding he was not able to recommend himself to the Marchioness, by reinstating her in her former good fortune, he thought it high time to change his conduct, and practise upon the distempered mind of the Marquis, who seeing only with the Abbé's eyes, had taken no notice of the Chevalier in his assiduous visits to his lady, and imputed those of the Abbé to an honest design of observing her behaviour. He began now to poison his soul with direct insinuations to the Marchioness's dishonour. Hitherto, he said, he had depended upon her virtue; but that a late discovery had opened his eyes. He then proceeded to relate to him a story, to which she had given rise, by allowing a young gentleman to toy with her in a company which she frequented. He let fall his whole venom upon this innocent freedom which she had indulged; and so perverted the mind of the husband, that his passion entirely got the better of his reason; he even went the length of reviling and abusing her, without so much as allowing her a hearing. The Abbé took care to blow the coal, and added fuel to this fire of jealousy, which grew every day into a fiercer flame. He forgot himself so far as to insult the Marchioness. And when he had infused into the husband's mind all the spiteful suggestions against her, his malice could invent, he gloried in his successful villainy, triumphed in the hellish revenge he had taken on an innocent lady, who had made him her enemy only because she had too much virtue to yield to his criminal solicitations. She gave herself no trouble to undeceive the Marquis with respect to the conduct of the Abbé, because she knew she would not have been heard.

Yet such was the impudence of the man, that after having raised this storm, he resolved to renew his attacks upon the injured lady, and to try if he might not yet hope to gain her over. However careful she was to shun him, he watched an opportunity of finding her alone, and as she was taking a turn in the garden, obtruded himself upon her with all the assurance imaginable. 'Why, Madam,' says he, bluntly accosting her, 'shall you and I be always thus at odds? Will you oblige me still to make war upon you? Will you never be convinced that it is for your interest that we be friends? And while it is so easy for you to gain me, and to reinstate yourself in your husband's affections, will you be thus resolute in persecuting me?' She heard him out with perfect composure of mind, and immediately turned her back upon him, treating him with that disdain he so justly deserved.

Much about this time happened the death of the Sieur de Nocheres, to whom she was heiress. The plentiful fortune which he left was the reason that the Marquis could not go so often to Gange as he was wont to do. He went to Avignon to settle his affairs, and carried the Marchioness with him.

Here an attempt was made to poison her, by presenting her with a dish of cream mixed with arsenic; but as the quantity was but small, and given in an aliment, which serves for an antidote against that poison, its effects proved not fatal, though she suffered considerable pain. All those who ate with her were affected in the same manner. She then called to mind her horoscope which had been cast for her at Paris, where an astrologer, who was reputed a man of skill, if there can be any skill in so vain a science, foretold her that she would die a violent death.

The adventure of the poisoned cream made a considerable noise at Avignon; but after a while, according to the fate of such stories, it was entirely hushed, and no more heard of. The Marchioness, whom it so nearly concerned, was one of those who spoke of it with the greatest coldness and indifference: she ought, however, to have taken it as a warning from heaven, to make her for the future be more upon her guard. Her succession to the Sieur de Nocheres's estate happened seasonably for her relief; it gained her esteem from her lord, the Abbé paid her more regard, and advised the Marquis to do the same; as for the Chevalier, who was born to imitate others, a mere echo to the Abbé, he followed the example of his leader.

The Marchioness did not suffer herself to be deluded by these fair appearances, she still saw the hearts of her enemies to be the same, and that their change of behaviour was only owing to her change of fortune: she therefore thought fit not to alter her conduct with regard to them.

It was proposed after this, that they should go to Gange to pass the autumn. This place was at the distance of seven leagues from Montpellier, and nineteen from Avignon. The Marchioness, who, from a secret presage, whereof she could give no account, dreaded her residing at that castle, formed a resolution to make her will before she set out. This design she put in execution, constituting her mother her heiress, leaving it in her option to settle the succession either upon the son of the testatrix, who was six years old, or upon the daughter who was five.

Though this will was secret, she made an authentic confirmation of it in the presence of the magistrates of Avignon, and several persons of quality, before whom she declared that in case she should make any other testament posterior to this, she formally disavowed it, and insisted that this alone should stand good; which she expressed in the strongest and most emphatic terms. From this we may easily conceive how highly she must have been incensed against her husband, and that the particular distrust she had of the perfidious Abbé had contributed not a little to make her take this hasty step.

Before her departure she likewise distributed among several friars, mostly Recollects, a score of *pistoles*,* in order to their saying mass that she might not die without the sacraments of the Church. And when she charged them to pray to God for her, she did it with so much earnestness, that it looked as if she had a near prospect of her end.

When she took her leave of her friends, she spoke to them with such tenderness, and was so melted into tears, that it had all the air of a last adieu. All were deeply affected with the parting; to those especially, who were related to her by the ties of friendship, it bore a rueful aspect.

All histories are full of signs, the forerunners of great misfortunes; which would tempt one to think, that those who are doomed to a wayward fate, do sometimes foresee the approaching evil, without having the power to fly from it, and reach forth their necks to meet the instrument of death.

The Marchioness being arrived at her husband's seat, was received by Madam de Gange, her mother-in-law, with great demonstrations of friendship. This lady lived, for ordinary, at Montpellier, and was come to Gange, only to pay a visit to her son: she was a woman of singular merit. The Marquis himself, and both the brothers, contributed their utmost to give the Marchioness an agreeable reception: they seemed to outvie each other in their endeavours to wear off the uneasy impressions which she had received. Whenever they addressed her, it was in the most insinuating terms of friendship, with the most inviting marks of courtesy: they were no more the same persons, so much were their former manners transformed into the most obliging, complaisant deportment. The Abbé and Chevalier presented themselves no more to her under the guise of lovers, they were but too sensible how odious they were to her in that character. They had now recourse to artifice, and acted the part of vile dissembled respect, with so much address, as to impose upon the undesigning Marchioness, whose mouth always spoke the language of her heart: she was so far trepanned* by these fair appearances, as to believe she was about to enjoy not only a state of easy quiet, but even of high delight and satisfaction. But the scenes were soon shifted: her mother-in-law returned to Montpellier, and the Marquis being gone to Avignon about business, she was left alone in the hands of the brothers, who, whatever disguises they put on, were her implacable enemies at heart, and only watched an opportunity to wreak their revenge upon her, for not entertaining their criminal passion. There is ground to believe that the Marquis, before his departure, held a consultation with his brothers, wherein were formed those terrible resolutions, that ushered in the following most tragical catastrophe. In all the steps of this complicated villainy, the two brothers acted in concert; but the Abbé still led the way, and gloried in outdoing the Chevalier.

They continued to affect their former obsequious complaisant deportment, and entered so much into the spirit of their parts, that had they studied under the most refined Italian master, even Machiavel himself, they could not have carried on the disguise better.

The Marchioness, whatever diffidence she ought to have entertained of these two hypocrites, saw them act the farce so long, till she thought it natural; suffered herself to be won by these advances of civility, and came at length to believe that sincerity was at the bottom. When they found their insinuating manners had succeeded, the Abbé then artfully began to bring into conversation the testament which the Marchioness had made, and gave her to understand, that while it subsisted, the union between her and her husband could never be firmly cemented, since he would still think she retained against him some remains of her old grudge; and therefore as he designed to live with her in a thorough good understanding, it was necessary to remove that obstacle, which was so great a bar to their mutual felicity; and upon her making this sacrifice, she would see her husband and his relations all conspire to make her happy, and establish her in absolute sway over all the hearts of the family. Soft persuasion dropped from his lips with so much efficacy, that the lady, whose predominant quality was good nature, revoked her testament, and made another in favour of her husband. The Abbé undoubtedly thought it not necessary, for the validity of this last testament, that she should retract the declaration she had made before the magistrates of Avignon, else he would have required this of her; he thought the forms in law were fully answered, and that he had now accomplished the design of his dissimulation. He prepared therefore for the unravelling [of] the plot, in which this horrid tragedy was wound up; he addressed the Chevalier in such language as was most likely to inflame him, in spite of the sentiments of nature, to that pitch of barbarity, with which he himself was inspired; and that was necessary in order to make a sacrifice to their bloody revenge of this innocent victim.

The Marchioness happening some time after to be out of order, signified her inclination to use some physic, May the 17th, 1667. The physician of the place made up for her a potion, which she was to take that day: when the medicine was brought to her, it looked so black in the glass, and withal so thick, that she could not think of swallowing it down; and chose rather to use a dose of pills she had in her casket, and to which she was accustomed.

There is all the reason in the world to suspect the two brothers had mingled a dose of poison with the potion. As they knew not at first but she had taken it, they sent twice or thrice that morning to inquire of her health; waited with impatience the effects of their baneful medicine, and were not a little astonished to hear the Marchioness had no complaints.

At length they were undeceived, and entered into the barbarous resolution, that, however this first attempt had failed, they would consummate their crime, though it should cost them never so dear.

The Marchioness being advised to keep her bed, invited some ladies of the place to come and bear her company; who accordingly waited upon her after dinner. She entertained them with all the good humour imaginable, and never appeared more cheerful; the Abbé and Chevalier, who were of the party, discovered great distraction of mind, seemed to be musing on some deep design, and, for a while, bore no share in the conversation. The Marchioness rallied them for being so absent; upon which the Chevalier, who sat at the foot of the bed, recovered himself a little, and began to retort upon her, while the Abbé calling home his roving mind, put in a word now and then to humour the joke.

Their constrained air failed not to be taken notice of by the company, who inferred from it, that they must have somewhat more than ordinary in view. There was a collation served up to the ladies, whereof the Marchioness performed all the honours, and ate heartily. The Abbé and the Chevalier touched none of it. At length the ladies withdrew, and the Abbé accompanying them to the gate, while the Chevalier remained alone with the Marchioness, still absorbed in his former reverie, whereof she could not fathom the reasons. But the mystery, which she was at great pains to unfold, too soon cleared up of itself.

She saw the Abbé re-enter her chamber, reaching forth in one hand a pistol, and in the other a glass full of blackish liquor, thick and foul, his eyes inflamed, his physiognomy quite changed, and all his features distorted by the violent passion with which he was agitated. It required no common resolution to stand the shock of this frightful spectacle; she imagined she saw his hair raised high on end; and has since declared, that no idea she had ever been able to form of devils or furies came near to the horrid appearance of that execrable monster, disguised in human shape. He made fast the door, and drawing near her bed, paused a while, darting dreadful looks upon her, as if by that dumb show he meant to give her intimation of all the horrors he was preparing for her, and damp her soul with the frightful anticipations of death, before he disclosed his direful purpose.

The Chevalier, whose fury spread an expression in his looks no less terrible than the other, though somewhat different, started up at the same time, and presented his naked sword. In these two devils incarnate, the Marchioness saw a lively image of hell. She imagined however, at first, that the Chevalier had drawn his sword only in her aid; but she was soon undeceived by his ferocious aspect, which was insupportable to her.

At length, the Abbé opened the scene, and pronounced these terrible words, without greatly elevating his voice, but in a tone firm and resolute: 'Madam, you must die; choose you pistol, or sword, or poison?' 'Die?' CRIED THE MARCHIONESS! 'Why, what crime have I committed? You then, it seems, have the ordering of my death, and are to be my executioner! How have I merited this so violent fate, which drives you to such an excess of cruelty?' Finding that all access to pity was shut against her in the heart of the Abbé, she hoped there would be some remains of compassion in the Chevalier's breast, and that he would not prove a very tiger like his brother: to him therefore she turned her lovely eyes, and, in accents that might have pierced a heart of flint, thus bespoke him: 'May I not hope, my dearest brother, to soften you to pity in this my extremity; heaven forbid, that you too should prove inexorable? Have you the heart to think of being yourself my executioner? Is it thus you forget all the tokens of friendship I have given you? Can your rage against me be so implacable, that nothing less will appease you than my blood?' Besides many other marks of friendship, at which she now hinted, she had often lent him money, sometimes even to the pinching of herself: and had lately given him a bill of exchange for 500 *livres*.

Far, however, from making any impression upon the Chevalier by this tender expostulation, she read nothing in his looks but menaces of present death. In that mirror of his soul, she saw her doom sworn and denounced, even before he spoke his answer, which, to cut off from her the smallest degree of hope, he thus delivered, in the same air and tone which the Abbé had assumed: 'Madam, 'tis done, take your choice, or if you will not, we will choose for you this instant!' Then the Marchioness, with an entire command of herself, casting upon them a glance of indignation, which must have brought them to themselves, had they not been past all reflection; and lifting her eyes, as taking God to witness their horrible perfidiousness, reached forth her hand to the glass of poison, which the Abbé presented to her, clapping his pistol at the same time to her throat, while the Chevalier pointed his sword to her breast. She gulped down the fatal draught, her forehead all drenched in sweat; and letting fall some drops on her bosom, the corrosion was so violent, that in a moment the skin from the most lovely white grew black and livid, and her rosy lips were transformed into the same baleful hue.

The Chevalier perceiving that she had left in the bottom of the glass the thickest of the potion, composed of arsenic and sublimate diluted in aqua fortis, scraped together these remains with a silver bodkin, and bringing it to the edge of the glass, gave it the Marchioness to drink off. 'Come,' says he, 'Madam, you must swallow down the rest of this holy water.' Which she did; but kept it in her mouth without swallowing it; then leaning her head to the pillow, and shrieking out as in prospect of immediate death, let go that remainder upon the cloths, at the same time addressing the barbarians in these words: 'In the name of God, since you have now glutted your revenge by taking away my life, carry not your barbarity so far as to destroy my soul too; send me a confessor, that I may die as a Christian, and not like one without hope.'

Upon this they withdrew, and making fast the door after them, went to the vicar of the place, who had been a domestic of the family twenty-five years since, and desired him to attend the Marchioness, who was a dying.

What appears surprising is, that in this terrible revolution that happened in her soul, she still preserved all her freedom of acting. Scarce were they gone, when she attempted to make her escape. As she was in her smock she flung on a petticoat, and getting to the window which looked to the courtyard of the castle, made an effort to throw herself down from thence the height of twenty-two feet.

The priest just arrived in that very moment. She had taken her measures so ill, that she would have fallen with her head foremost, and in all probability dashed herself in pieces, when the priest catching hold of the end of her petticoat, turned her body into such a proper direction, that she fell right upon her feet, on a hard stony ground, where she received no other damage but to mangle her feet a little, which were uncovered. The weight of her body, which had taken its swing, tore the petticoat which the priest held by the extremity, and left a shred of it in his hand.

The priest, who was devoted to the Abbé and Chevalier, to prevent her escape, let fall a large pitcher full of water, which stood by the other window adjoining to that through which the Marchioness had passed: he had done her business effectually, had the pitcher lighted upon her head; but it happened to fall two inches short of her.

As soon as she found herself on the ground, she thrust the end of her hair hastily down her throat a great way, and provoked herself by that means to vomit; which she did without any difficulty, because she had eaten a great deal before.

After she had thus eased herself, she bethought her of making her escape. Finding the courtyard shut up on all sides, she went to the quarter of the stables, where she flattered herself she might get out; but she found these too made fast. Thus all the advantage she had by this elopement was to be confined in a prison larger than her chamber. By good luck, she spied one of the grooms: 'My friend,' says she to him, 'for God's sake save my life, I am poisoned; open to me your stables, that I may go in quest of assistance.' The groom, melted with pity, took her in his arms, conveyed her into his stables, and put her into the hands of some women, whom he met by the way.

Meanwhile the priest was gone to apprize the two inhuman brothers of her escape. They resolved not to leave their work unfinished: while she was running here and there for shelter from her executioners, they came up after her crying out that she was mad, that she was subject to fits of the mother.* The populace seeing her in disorder, her hair dishevelled, her feet bare, and almost in her smock, was inclined to believe her case really was what they represented.

At length, the Chevalier overtook her near the house of the Sieur des-Prats, about the distance of 300 paces from the castle: thither he made her enter by force, shutting himself up with her, while the Abbé planted himself at the door, with a pistol in his hand, threatening to kill the first who durst approach without leave, for that he would not suffer his sister-in-law to be made a spectacle to all the world. His true design, however, was to prevent anybody from giving her aid, that the poison might have time to work its effect.

The Sieur des-Prats himself was abroad, but they found his wife at home, in company with several young ladies. One Mrs Brunel, wife to the minister of the place, who was of the number, found a way imperceptibly to convey to the Marchioness a large box of orvietan,* whereof she took some doses, while the Chevalier, who was walking up and down as her guard, had his back turned. Another of the ladies gave her a large glass of water, which she was going to drink off with great eagerness, to quench the fire which the poison and the orvietan had kindled in her bowels; but the Chevalier, still firm in the cause of inhumanity, withheld from her this relief, by breaking the glass between the Marchioness's teeth, and told the ladies they would mightily oblige him, if they would not be witnesses to his sister's disorder, nor encourage her in her whimsies; that he was there to take care of her, and would not leave her, till he saw her better, wherefore he begged they would retire and leave her entirely to his management.

The Marchioness thought she would try once more to soften the Chevalier; and desired the ladies to leave them together, that she might have more freedom to deal with him effectually. Upon this they withdrew into another room.

Then the Marchioness, all in tears, threw herself at the Chevalier's feet: 'My dear brother,' says she to him, 'will you not recall my sentence of death? Is there no possibility of exciting in you some sentiments of pity?

Do but regard me in the quality of one, who comes to you unknown, to implore your aid; sure you will not withhold from a sister those sentiments of humanity you would not deny to a stranger. Here I swear to you by all that is most sacred, that I will henceforth cancel all remembrance of your past behaviour, and will do all in my power to give it a favourable construction in the eyes of the world. Had I done you the smallest injury, I could have submitted to the most cruel punishment you was capable to inflict. But now that I am conscious I never injured you in the least, let me conjure you, my dearest brother, in the name of GOD, to grant me this one, this last request, to leave me at the gates of death, and while I have still as much breath remaining as to beg for mercy, Oh, grant it for heaven's sake.'

This prayer, accompanied with all the motives of persuasion, which beauty in distress can inspire, was thrown away upon the Chevalier, who was quite inflexible, and served only to inflame his cruelty the more. He took his sword, which was a short one, and used it as a poniard,* giving the Marchioness two stabs with it in the breast. Whereupon she, flying to the door, cried out for help; while the monster, pursuing, gave her five more stabs in the back, and the weapon breaking short, he left the piece sticking in her shoulder.

The Chevalier, after all this shocking barbarity, went out to the Abbé, who was watching at the gate, with these words: 'Abbé, let us away; the business is done.' The ladies immediately entered the room in the utmost consternation to see the Marchioness extended on the ground, and swimming in her blood. From her quickness of breathing, they concluded she was in the agonies of death, and were enraged at themselves beyond measure for not having prevented this sad disaster.

They imagined, however, there was some possibility of her recovery, and begged from the windows that a surgeon might be called.

Upon hearing this, the Abbé apprehending the Marchioness might still live, came to give her the finishing blow. He advanced towards her in violent transports of fury, presenting his pistol to her breast: the weapon misgave, and Mrs Brunel turned it aside, by laying hold on the Abbe's arm, who, seeing himself crossed in his design, turned short on that lady, and gave her a great box with his fist on the head, and using his pistol as a club, was going to dispatch the Marchioness outright, when all the ladies fell upon him like so many lionesses, overpowering him with blows, and gave him a convoy into the street.

After this they returned to look after the Marchioness: one of them, who had some skill in surgery, staunched the blood of her wounds, after having wrenched out the stump of the sword, encouraged by the patient, who bid her not be afraid of hurting her, but lean her knee against the wounded shoulder, to give her the more force. They applied the first dressings to her wounds, which were not judged mortal; the Chevalier, in his disorder, not having aimed his stabs at those parts where was most danger. After having perpetrated their crime, he and the Abbé took the advantage of the night to make their escape, it being then past nine in the evening: they arrived at Auberas, a manor belonging to the Marquis, about the distance of three miles from Gange.

There they rested themselves a while; reproaching each other bitterly, for not having consummated their wicked deed, insomuch that they were ready to cut each other's throats. They had some thoughts of returning to finish their sacrifice; but were deterred by reflecting on the danger they must run, by putting this design in execution, since they foresaw it would have been impossible for them to save themselves from being arrested. They resolved therefore to take no further thought but how to escape the punishment they deserved.

The consuls of Gange, hearing of what had happened, came, with assistance, to offer their service to the Marchioness, which she gladly accepted; they planted a guard round the house of the Sieur des-Prats. But, as in great disasters, by I know not what fatality, it often happens, their succour came too late.

As soon as the news of this horrid assassination came to be spread abroad, those of distinction in the neighbourhood waited upon the Marchioness, to testify their deep concern for her misfortune; the Barons of Semenez and Sinestous presented themselves amongst the first, pierced with the most tender sentiments of grief on her account.

Baron du Tressan, the Grand Provost, went in close pursuit of the two assassins; but they had taken ship near Agde, towards that quarter which is called le Gras de Pataval. We shall see what became of them afterwards.

Physicians and surgeons were sent for from Montpellier, to attend the Marchioness, who had all necessary assistance. As for the Marquis, he was at Avignon when they brought him the news of his wife's assassination. He did not expect to hear of this bloody catastrophe being brought about with such terrible and alarming circumstances. Though there is ground to believe that he had concerted her ruin in conjunction with his brothers, yet he had doubtless reckoned upon their effecting it by the silent method of poison. But hearing how it was, he expressed the utmost horror of the action, and broke forth into imprecations against his brothers. He swore they should have no executioner but himself. This, at least, was behaving in such a manner as he ought to have done.

It was observed, however, that he deferred his journey to Gange till the day following, after dinner; though, methinks, had he been innocent, he could not have made too quick dispatch in flying to his lady's aid. Besides, he saw some of his friends at Avignon; and, what is pretty singular, mentioned not a syllable to them of that fatal accident. 'Tis common for people, when they are under any pressure, to communicate their griefs to all those who are disposed to hear them; they even seek opportunities of disburdening themselves of their affliction, by imparting it to others, who may help them by their sympathy. Perhaps the Marquis was diffident of himself, and had some apprehension lest he might betray his guilt in giving the narrative of this assassination.

Upon his arrival at Gange, he desired to see his lady; of which a friar informed the Marchioness: she received him with all the demonstrations of tenderness that the best of husbands could have expected; only had some kind expostulations with him, upon his seeming to have abandoned her.

Such a reception, supposing him guilty, as there is but too much ground to believe, according to the striking evidences that were laid before the parliament of Toulouse, must have been one of the severest punishments he could have suffered. After so horrid a crime, to find nothing but goodness and tenderness in the heart of the person, who was the object thereof, is to hold up a mirror to the author, where he sees himself in the most odious light. What was transacted in the Marquis's breast was visible to God alone, so well he knew to form his looks. I may apply to him what is said of that hardy Lacedemonian,* who suffered the fox to eat into his bowels, rather than betray his theft by crying out; even so the obdurate Marquis was gnawed with pangs of remorse, while he showed an air of ease and unconcern.

The Marchioness, on the other hand, was so delicate, that upon reflecting that she had used terms rather too harsh in upbraiding him for leaving her to the mercy of her deplorable destiny, she frankly asked his pardon, and reached forth her hand to him in the tenderest manner; for that he ought to impute those hasty words to the excess of her illness, rather than to her being wanting in esteem for him. All the world admired these overflowings of goodness in the injured lady, which could be attributed to nothing but an extraordinary degree of native virtue, improved by the influence of religion.

The Marquis had the assurance to take advantage of this excess of conjugal affection in his spouse, and to demand of her the revoking of that declaration, whereby she had confirmed her first will at Avignon, because on account of it, the vice-legate had refused, at the Marquis's request, to register the will she had made at Gange.

But to this she replied with great firmness of mind, that she was resolved not to meddle with her will at Avignon. It was a high instance of imprudence in the Marquis, to call it no worse, to open afresh those wounds, which the assassins had given the Marchioness by extorting from her that will at Gange; it inflamed suspicions against him, which were already but too strong: and we have reason to believe, that the Marchioness then began to open her eyes, though she took no notice thereof to him, her piety not allowing her to act unsuitably to her usual character of good nature.

The Marquis introduced no more conversation on that head for the future, and continued his assiduous attendance on the Marchioness, who was still in the Sieur des-Prat's house. She was very solicitous to be removed to Montpellier, where she might be in the way of proper medicines and advice; but her physician told her it was impracticable to remove her thither, in the case she was in, without imminent hazard of her life.

Madam de Rossan, the Marchioness's mother, accompanied with some persons of distinction in Avignon, came to visit the Marchioness the day after her husband's arrival. She was in the utmost surprise to find him with her daughter, and to see them in so good understanding. Being fully persuaded that he was the ringleader of the detestable plot, she could not bear the thoughts of his being about the Marchioness; she stormed with indignation, and notwithstanding all the entreaty of her daughter, could not be prevailed upon to stay with her above three days, not being able to overcome the violent conflicts, which the sight of him raised in her breast.

The Marchioness expressed her desire to partake of the sacraments of the Church; having first declared, in terms that spoke a truly Christian spirit, that she heartily forgave her assassins, and made a sacrifice to religion of all revengeful sentiments. But how great was her astonishment, to see the same priest, whom her murderers had sent to assist her at death, present himself to her with the holy viaticum in his hand! At a time when her profound reverences and love to her God were awakened, her soul was possessed with jealousy and dread of the minister: she desired he would participate of the host with her; lest, under the veil of that adorable mystery, deadly poison had been concealed. To satisfy her, the priest communicated with her on the half of the host which he gave her.

Then in the presence of that God, who was exhibited in the symbols of the sacrament, she once more protested her hearty forgiveness of all her enemies in general, and of her assassins in particular; calling God to witness the sincerity of her heart.

The insensibility with which she received the compliments people paid to her beauty, during the course of her illness, telling her, what was indeed the case, that she never looked more lovely, is a proof how much she had eradicated out of her mind those seeds of vanity, which are so apt to shoot up in the heart; especially when nursed by those flattering charms of person, which she possessed in so eminent a degree.

She was at great pains to infuse into the tender mind of her son, sentiments of virtue and piety, persuaded that no teaching could impress them more strongly, than that of a mother lying upon a deathbed. Such a one represents the truth without any disguise; tenderness of blood uniting with the ties of Christian charity, inspire her with lively animated expressions, which hardly ever wear off the mind of a child, the impression always returning with the idea of the dying mother.

She strove, with all her might, to crush the sentiments of revenge that rose in the breast of her son, and taught him, on that head, the purity of Christian morals.

The parliament of Toulouse appointed M. de Catalan, counsellor of that parliament, their commissioner to repair to Gange, and interrogate the Marchioness. Upon his arrival, he was told she was inclined to sleep, so that he could not see her that day. He saw her the day after, and made all the company withdraw, that he might confer with her more freely. He was at great pains to make her sensible, that it was fully consistent with Christian forgiveness, to inform against the authors of so horrid a crime, on whom justice called for vengeance. She signified to him how much it was contrary to her inclination to be at Gange, where so many occasions of terror presented themselves to her mind, which made her long to be removed elsewhere. Though she had nothing else to affect her, but the image of the cruelties she had suffered in that place, this alone was sufficient to strike her imagination continually. M. de Catalan told her, she should be gratified in that article, as soon as her health would permit.

After this her distemper increased, she passed the night in racking pains. The next day, being May 5,* about four o'clock in the evening she expired, amidst a circle of bystanders all dissolved in tears; on many of whom the mournful spectacle made so deep an impression, that they have since lamented her death with as lively expressions of sorrow as at first.

Thus died the Marchioness of Gange, whose beauty and virtue rendered her one of those miracles of her sex, who appear from time to time upon the face of the earth, as spectacles that seize, strike, and captivate at once. Who would have imagined, that one endowed with such endearing qualities, should have fallen a sacrifice to a pair of assassins?

Immediately after her death, M. de Catalan having issued out a warrant for seizing the Marquis de Gange, he was arrested in his castle. He said he was ready to obey, that he was designed to prosecute before the parliament the murderers of his wife. His effects were sealed up by authority, and he himself conducted to the prison of Montpellier, where he arrived at night. The whole inhabitants of the city came crowding to the windows, which were greatly illuminated, to gaze upon such an infamous monster, and he was exposed to all the hootings and hollowings of the populace, who looking upon him with horror, loaded him with imprecations.

All the ladies of Montpellier and Avignon seemed to consider the disaster of the Marchioness de Gange, as their common cause; it occasioned public mourning, and an universal desolation: it looked as if all the world had been related to that unfortunate lady, not only by the common ties of humanity, but by those of the nearest consanguinity; and they spoke of revenging her death, as a particular calamity to every family.

Her body was opened, and it was found that she had not died of her wounds, but of the malignant influence of the poison, which had burnt up her entrails, and blackened her brain. She must have been of a very strong constitution, to be able to hold out against a violent poison for no less than nineteen days. Nature in giving her beauty, had at the same time given her a body fitted to preserve it long, as if she had designed her to subsist for many years upon earth a spectacle of her curious skill. It was hoped for some time she would have recovered; in regard that she never appeared more charming than the very day on which she died, her eyes never sparkled with greater lustre, her complexion never showed more lively, nor her speech more firm; but these were only the flashes of a taper, collecting all its force, when it is just about to expire.

The Lady Rossan entered on the possession of her daughter's estate. She declared her intention to prosecute the Marquis with the utmost vigour, till the death of her daughter should be revenged: all her words breathed nothing but resentment.

M. Catalan interrogated the Marquis twice, and the second time detained him in the examination for eleven hours together. He was conducted to the prison of the parliament of Toulouse, and an indictment drawn up against him with great care and exactness. [...]

The public cry was loudly raised against the Marquis: however, his case, short as it was, furnished the judges with much subject of reflection.

But, as they were inwardly persuaded of his guilt, and yet did not think there was a sufficient degree of evidence to convict him, and therefore durst not condemn him to capital punishment, they pronounced sentence August 21, 1667, 'condemning the Abbé and Chevalier, for the aforesaid crime, to be broke alive upon the wheel; the Marquis to perpetual banishment, with the forfeiture of his nobility, and confiscation of goods to the King; and the priest Perrette, after being degraded by ecclesiastic power, to the galleys for life.' Perrette was fastened to the chain, but died by the way. All the ladies murmured aloud against the judges, for condemning the Marquis to a punishment, which to them appeared too gentle. This murmuring was, perhaps, the reason that the Marquis de la Douze, who was accused some time after of poisoning his wife, was condemned to capital punishment: there were only strong presumptions against him, any more than against the Marquis.

The Marquis and Chevalier repaired to Venice: they demanded of the Republic to serve against the Turks in Candia, the capital of an island in the Archipelago, to which it gives name. It was besieged by the Turks for two and twenty years. Their service was accordingly accepted of, and they were sent over to that island, where they signalized* themselves greatly. Some time after, the Chevalier was killed with the bursting of a bomb; and the Marquis survived him but a few days, being buried in a mine, which was sprung under him in one of the out-works of the place: too honourable a death for men stained with the infamy of so foul a crime! A death, which, if we may judge of it from the idea of the Marshal de Villars, is one of the happiest: that General hearing, in his last illness, that the Duke of Berwick had his head shot off by a cannonball, at the siege of Philippsburg, where he commanded, cried out: 'My Lord of Berwick was always extremely happy!'

As to the Abbé de Gange, he fled over to Holland, to the Count de Lippa, sovereign of Viane, a district two leagues distant from Utrecht: he was acquainted there with a gentleman, a friend of the Count, who introduced him to that lord, as a French gentleman of distinguished merit: he changed his name, and embraced the Protestant religion.

The Count finding him, upon conversation, to be a very knowing man, and well versed in the *belles-lettres*, and the polite arts, committed to him the education of his eldest son, then about nine or ten years old. By the sentiments which he instilled into his pupil, and the care he took of his improvement, he made him an accomplished prince. By this means he gained the esteem of the Count and Countess, and of that Prince's whole family; he carefully concealed his birth, and to avoid curious enquiries, suffered himself to pass for a person of obscure parentage. He had, however, a constant source of disquietude, which gnawed upon him within. Some French refugees, who wanted to settle at Viane, and there build houses, asked permission of the Sieur de la Fare, chief justice of the place, who goes by the name of the Drossard: he told them they must apply to the Count, and that it would be no loss to them, if they had the Sieur de la Martelliere's interest with that lord; this was the name the Abbé de Gange had taken. But this new Protestant, fearing lest he should be discovered, if the French settled at Viane, dissuaded the Count from granting the petition of the refugees; his credit with the Count and Countess being arrived to such a height, that they took no step, without first consulting him. Here he fell in love with a very agreeable young lady, a relation of the Countess. By his artful address, he soon kindled in the lady a mutual flame, and aspired to marry her. The Countess, whatever esteem she had for the Sieur de la Martelliere, could by no means approve of this match; and told the young lady, she never would suffer it. 'The Sieur de la Martelliere,' says she to her, 'is a very worthy man, but he is a kind of Melchisedech:* for as long as he has been with us, we have not been able to discover who or what he is, and we cannot but suspect him of mean birth, since, being of a nation which stands not much upon hyperboles, he never yet durst call himself a gentleman; his manners, 'tis true, are noble, his sentiments polite, and becoming a gentleman, but all this ought not to induce you to disparage yourself, by a match so much below you; when he goes from us, he shall have a recompense proportioned to his services, but we will never interest the honour of the family in his favour.' To this remonstrance the young lady durst make no reply, yet she persisted in her resolution to wed the Sieur de la Martelliere. She repeated to him this conversation: upon which, after some deliberation, he was infatuated by his passion to take a most foolish measure, for a man of parts. He flattered himself, that by discovering his parentage, he would bring the match to bear, and that the esteem he had acquired in the family, would counterbalance the horror, which the knowledge of his former crime might inspire. In this confidence, he demanded an audience of the Countess, and was no sooner alone with her in her closet, than he fell upon his knees before her: 'Madam,' says he, 'I flattered myself, hitherto, that your Highness would honour me with your good will, nevertheless 'tis you who this day stand in the way of my happiness. Miss —— honours me with her esteem: wherein, Madam, have I offended you, or what can be laid to my charge for these several years since I have had the honour to be in your service?' She replied: 'My spouse and I are very well satisfied with you; be but so just to yourself, as to confine your ambition within due bounds; forget not yourself so far as to pretend to a match, to which we could not consent, and you shall have no reason to complain of our ingratitude. Hitherto we have not been able to find out your parentage, and what can we infer from your concealing it so industriously, but that it is so obscure, that you are ashamed to own it?' Upon this the Sieur Martelliere rejoined: 'Madam, could I make myself known to your Highness, without incurring your displeasure, you would soon see I am not unworthy the honour to which I aspire on the score of my birth: yes, Madam, you will be convinced of it, when you hear I am the unfortunate Abbé de Gange, whose notorious crime makes him but too well known. Rigid is the penance I have undergone, and since I had the honour to be in your service, I have proved by my conduct, how opposite my sentiments are to that horrid action, at which I shudder as oft as I think of it.' 'What!' cried the Countess, 'are you that abominable Abbé de Gange, whom I have heard of with so much abhorrence? O heavens! What a monster have I been harbouring in my house? Whom have we entrusted with the education of our son? I tremble to think what barbarous hands he has been in.' The Count de la Lippa had the same sentiments, when let into the secret, and was just upon the point of ordering him to be laid under an arrest; but suspended his angry purpose, at the solicitations of his son. The Sieur de la Martelliere was obliged to quit Viane in all haste; a strict charge being given him, never more to appear in sight of the Count and Countess. The lady was in agony, every time she reflected on the risk she believed she had run. The young Count, however, had learned nothing from his governor but the purest morals, and he saw them confirmed by the example of his teacher. From hence the unhappy Sieur de la Martelliere retired to Amsterdam, where he became a master of languages; thither his mistress went after him, and they were secretly married. The young Count had the generosity to remit supplies of money to his tutor, which enabled him to subsist, till such time as he came to the possession of an estate by his wife. His good behaviour procured him admittance into the Protestant consistory; and he died among them some time after in good repute. We are credibly informed by a friend of his, to whom he made himself known, that he had told him in confidence, the Marchioness de Gange often appeared to him in the same attitude she was in when he came to offer her the choice of the three kinds of death; he believed it was really she, and at those times he felt himself torn with cruel pangs of remorse; than which it was impossible, he said, to endure any pains more terrible, at the very thought whereof, his bowels were racked with horror, and convulsed within him.

EXPLANATORY NOTES

3 *Causes célèbres*: Sade is referring to Gayot de Pitaval's *Causes célèbres et intéressantes*—a highly popular collection of true crimes reprinted several times in the eighteenth and nineteenth centuries. Sade had a copy in Charenton, but had also read it years earlier in the Bastille (see Introduction, p. x) and it was his main source. An English translation published in 1744 is provided in the Appendix.

4 *say everything*: Sade's dictum in his pornographic works such as *The 120 Days of Sodom* and *The History of Juliette* was *tout dire*, so its inclusion here suggests a sly wink to the reader.

5 *Court of Justice*: a reference to the *parlement de Paris*, the jurisdiction of which covered at least a third of the country during the Ancien Régime. At the time of these events, there were a further eleven provincial *parlements*.

the civil war . . . brazen pride: an allusion to the Fronde (from the French for 'sling'), a rebellion against Anne of Austria and Mazarin led by the nobles in the *parlement de Paris* over taxation. The arrest of Broussel, a leading figure in the *parlement*, on 26 August 1648 led to a public uprising in Paris the following day. The detainment of other judges including Charton and Novion was also ordered that day, though the latter narrowly evaded arrest. Cardinal de Retz, another important figure in the Fronde, rather inflated his own role in the 'day of barricades' in his famous memoirs.

Saint-Germain: Saint-Germain-en-Laye, where Louis XIV established his court in 1666 before moving definitively to nearby Versailles in 1682.

6 *Euphrasie de Châteaublanc*: Sade changes the first names of his protagonists: Mademoiselle de Châteaublanc's first name was Diane; the Marquis de Ganges's first name was Charles, not Alphonse. Alphonse was one of Sade's middle names.

8 *Aude*: a mistake by Sade as Ganges is on the banks of the Hérault, not the Aude.

14 *Hymen*: the Greek god of marriage ceremonies.

19 *omber*: from the Spanish *hombre*, a card game popular throughout the seventeenth and eighteenth centuries. It was played with forty cards and, usually, three players.

20 *Tradition . . . heart*: the position of *abbé* (abbot) at this time was only nominally clerical, and had become an honorary title that allowed the holder—often the youngest son of an aristocratic family—an income.

22 *Mancini*: Anna Maria Mancini (1639–1715), niece to Cardinal Mazarin. Louis XIV fell in love with her, and wanted to marry her, but never consummated their relationship.

reeds in a squall: a reference to 'The Oak and the Reed', one of Aesop's fables retold by Jean de La Fontaine.

25 *marigolds*: the French word for marigold is *souci*, which also means a worry.

33 *exordium*: the beginning or introductory part of an oration or treatise.

45 *Laurent*: the narrator here alludes to Perret by his first name, suggesting the same conspiratorial intimacy this character shares with the Abbé.

48 *Courts of Love*: medieval tribunals presided over by noblewomen where disputes between lovers were adjudicated and matters of love debated.

Porcellets family . . . Sicilian Vespers affair: Guillaume III des Porcellets (1217–88), Baron of Sicily and Provence, was the only Frenchman to survive the Sicilian Vespers rebellion of 1282 which saw France lose Sicily to the local rebels.

the fair . . . Madeleine: the Fair of La Madeleine in Beaucaire, held every summer since the Middle Ages, was the largest commercial fair in the Mediterranean region in the seventeenth century. As Graham Robb notes, 'the fair was said to make as much money in a week as the port of Marseille did in a year' (*The Discovery of France* (London: Picador, 2016), 259).

Plutus: the Greek god of wealth.

49 *while the Marquis . . . checked that there was no chance of a bed for him there*: the French is rather confused here, to say the least.

68 *barn owl*: Sade uses the more evocative name of *oiseau de la mort*, or bird of death, for barn owl.

72 *Avignon*: the Comtat (or county) of Avignon was a papal enclave and therefore outside the jurisdiction of the Kingdom of France.

73 *atheists . . . evil*: atheists, indeed, like Sade. The narrator here is taking the opposite position of the libertines of Sade's earlier fiction. Dubois, for example, tells Justine, 'if evil does exist here, either such disorder is ordered by this God, in which case he is a barbaric entity, or else he is unable to prevent it, and then he is a weak God' (*Justine, or the Misfortunes of Virtue* (Oxford: Oxford University Press, 2012), 224).

79 *While . . . La Chaussée*: these lines are very freely adapted from Pierre-Claude Nivelle de La Chaussée's *Mélanide* (1741).

80 *the Prophet King . . . all sides*: there is no exact match in Psalms for the quotation that follows the reference to David here, but it is perhaps closest to Psalm 31: 'Deliver me from the hand of mine enemies, and from them that persecute me'.

96 *her son*: an apparent slip by Sade here as this should be 'grandson'.

101 *does anyone . . . family*: this was an issue close to Sade's heart. Arrested in 1777 at his mother-in-law's behest by a *lettre de cachet*, a warrant signed by the King, Sade was imprisoned indefinitely without trial, and without any legal recourse.

103 *It was . . . lamp*: here, as elsewhere in the text, Sade's tenses are highly erratic, switching from past to present to future from one sentence to the next. This device, known in French as the *présent historique*, was a common feature of fiction in this period, designed to convey immediacy of action.

104 *Psalms . . . enemies*: David does not in fact ask God to forgive his enemies in Psalms, but, as we have already seen (p. 8), appeals repeatedly for protection and deliverance from them: 'Strike all my enemies on the jaw; break the teeth of the wicked' (Psalm 3); 'Don't abandon me to my enemies, who attack me with lies and threats' (Psalm 27); and 'deliver me from my enemies' (Psalms 31, 59, 143).

105 *Monsieur de Nochères . . . wife*: earlier in the text (p. 65, 72) the brothers had discussed the possibility of Euphrasie inheriting from Madame rather than Monsieur de Nochères.

106 *obole*: a coin of very low value, worth only half a *denier*.

110 *Cervoiles*: Arnaud de Cervole, a mercenary and bandit, was known as the Archpriest of Vélines.

112 *sigisbée*: from the Italian *cicisbeo*, 'the name formerly given in Italy to the recognized gallant or *cavalier servente* of a married woman' (*Oxford English Dictionary*). Sade mocks the practice of *cicisbeismo* in his incomplete *Journey to Italy*.

sedan chair: the *chaise à porteurs* was an enclosed chair for conveying one person, and was carried between horizontal poles by two porters.

114 *Laura*: Sade took great pride in being the descendant of Petrarch's muse, Laure de Noves, wife of Hugues de Sade. He seems to give himself a cameo role here.

118 *a hundred louis*: Sade is referring to the gold *louis d'or* (worth ten *livres* at the time) rather than the silver *louis d'argent* (worth three *livres*); the latter was more commonly known as the *écu*.

123 *the misfortune of virtue*: the French here reads 'le malheur de la vertu', echoing the title of Sade's notorious *Justine, ou les malheurs de la vertu*.

127 *the Oyster and the Litigants*: a fable by La Fontaine, in which a quarrel between two pilgrims over an oyster is settled when the judge they appoint to adjudicate the matter swallows the oyster himself.

128 *Cadenet*: a village only a few miles away from Sade's former château in Lacoste.

philtre: a potion (often a love potion but not in this instance).

131 *She calls on the lightning . . . its final resting place*: in all three versions of the *Justine* story, the heroine is indeed killed by a lightning bolt.

135 *Cours*: later known as the Cours Mirabeau, a broad thoroughfare created in 1651 between the old town and the Mazarin quarter.

143 *on the Cours*: the Cours in Marseille (later known as the Cours Belsunce and Cours Saint-Louis) was actually built in the 1670s, a few years after these (fictionalized) events.

152 *the furies . . . Megaera's serpents*: Megaera, whose name signifies 'the jealous one', was one of the three furies, or Erinyes, who lived together in Erebus, 'a place of darkness, between Earth and Hades' (Liddell & Scott).

158 *the only child her husband had given her*: the Marquise de Ganges also had a daughter, as the *Causes célèbres* makes clear, but Sade erases her from his

version of events. At this point in the novel, he begins to draw heavily on the *Causes célèbres* once more (see Appendix).

161 *suborners*: to suborn is to induce someone to give false testimony.

167 *the solace of the holy table*: the Communion table. Perret is bringing Euphrasie the viaticum, the Eucharist administered to someone who is about to die.

171 *Candia*: the name for Crete while it was a Venetian colony. The siege of Candia (1645–69), the focal point of the war between the Ottoman Empire and the Republic of Venice, had entered its final and most bloody phase by the time the Chevalier and Marquis are said to have arrived there.

APPENDIX

Title: from an English translation of Sade's source, Gayot de Pitaval's *Causes célèbres*, entitled *A Select Collection of Singular and Interesting Histories*, vol. 1 (London: A. Millar, 1744).

173 *20,000l.*: 20,000 *livres*.

174 *Fontenelle*: an allusion to Fontenelle's *Lettres galantes du Chevalier d'Her . . .* (1685): 'The face is everything, it is through the face that one is beautiful . . . a beautiful arm is not beautiful unless it belongs to a beautiful face' (Letter 28).

175 *Maynard*: this should be Mignard. Pierre Mignard, and his brother, Nicolas, both painted portraits of the Marquise de Ganges.

176 *Vous, à qui notre foi . . . le chef d'œuvre d'un Dieu*: a slightly adapted version of a sonnet from Abbé Cottin's *Oeuvres galantes* (1663).

177 *St. Andrew*: Saint-André de Villeneuve-lès-Avignon.

timeously: in good time.

179 *prevention*: predisposition.

184 *pistoles*: the *pistole* was a Spanish coin which circulated in France as an equivalent to the *louis d'or*, a gold coin worth eleven *livres* at this time.

trepanned: ensnared.

189 *fits of the mother*: fits or suffocation of the 'mother' (where 'mother' means 'uterus') was an earlier term for hysteria, a disorder attributed to the womb moving upwards and putting pressure on other organs.

orvietan: a medical concoction that was claimed (wrongly) to work as a universal antidote against poisons.

190 *poniard*: a small, slim dagger (from the French *poignard*).

192 *Lacedemonian*: the story of the Spartan boy and the fox may be found in Plutarch's *Moralia*.

194 *May 5*: Pitaval's original text mistakenly states May, not June, an error duplicated by the translator here.

196 *signalized*: distinguished.

Melchisedech: according to Genesis, the King of Salem and priest of El Elyon, but of unknown parentage.